THE DRUID

THE DRUID

THE LAND OF BROKEN ROADS
BOOK TWO

Ryan English

Podium

To my dear sisters, Crystal and Emily.

Cover design by Tom Roberts

ISBN: 978-1-0394-8184-8

Published in 2025 by Podium Publishing
www.podiumentertainment.com

THE DRUID

CHAPTER ONE

-I think I smell humans,- said Socks. The pup's voice in Dirt's mind sounded quiet and low as he slowed his run and stopped. After glancing around, he padded silently toward a small copse of thin trees, where he sniffed the ground for a trail.

Dirt sat up in a hurry and thought, "*Share it! I want to see, too.*"

Socks obliged, and their senses of smell merged into one, shared across their mental link. Dirt's little human nose was completely ignored against the sensory overload of Socks's big wolfish one. As always, the big pup smelled more than Dirt saw, even though Dirt's human vision could see much farther. Faint game trails and their spoor, a stray feather from a hunting bird, five kinds of trees. An ants' nest.

Even the midafternoon sun seemed excited now, peeking out from one of the stray clouds to watch the big wolf pup creep along and smell everything left and right, trying to pick up another hint of something that wasn't little Dirt up there on his back. Dirt looked at the minds in the area, his natural vision fading against the colorless, directionless mind-sight. The light of Socks's mind was huge, of course, since he was right there, but other than him, he found nothing but little plant minds and a surprising number of small mammals huddled in the grass, full of fear once they heard or smelled Socks approaching.

Socks turned around and backtracked to where he'd first smelled it. He lifted his head high in the air and inhaled the gentle breeze, trying to catch a note of something unusual.

At once they said, "*-There!-*" The human scent was too faint to tell much about the owner, not even the person's sex or age, but it was a scent Socks had only ever smelled on Dirt. Socks licked his snout and let the air drift against his wet nose to help him find the direction the scent was coming from. It wasn't from that copse of trees after all—it was drifting along the breeze that rolled across the bumpy plains here in the foothills.

"Don't run too fast. Try and sneak so you don't scare them. If we see them first, maybe I'll go and you can wait," said Dirt.

-I won't scare them.-

"The first time I saw you, I was so scared I peed. And you're even bigger now. Remember that? You just walked up and sniffed me, and I just about died from terror."

-But I want to meet them too.-

"You will, but let me go first. If we find them."

-We'll find them.-

"Yeah."

Socks didn't run at full speed, but neither was he slow. Dirt supposed that was fine, although anxiety began to twist around inside his chest. He didn't want the first humans he'd ever met to run away screaming because they saw Socks first. Or do something profoundly foolish, like try to cut him with a sword. And if they were all the way out here, in these uncharted wilds, they'd have weapons.

Dirt clutched his knife in one hand and squeezed the Home-staff resting across his legs with the other. Should he leave those back with Socks, so the humans didn't think he was a threat? No, it should be fine, since he was still a child. He was only two months old, although his body was eight years old. And some of his memories were much, much older than that.

No, he had to bring the staff along so Home could see the other humans. And he had to bring his knife, just in case. Prisca had tried to kill him, before she recognized him. Then she'd tried to kill him twice as hard. She'd been undead, but nonetheless, Dirt preferred not to risk it again.

The scent of human grew stronger bit by bit, each puff carried by the wind telling them a little more. It wasn't one human; it was two men and one woman. They weren't scared, but they were wary. They were healthy and smelled like leather and fur and oil and dust and salt and grain and more, on top of their human scent.

When their minds began to glow faintly in Dirt's mind-sight, he thought, *"Okay, Socks, I think I can find them from here."*

-I don't hear them yet. We will get a little closer.-

"Okay," said Dirt. He gripped his weapons even tighter to assuage his increasing nervousness. He kept trying to force it away, but it came back each time he thought about how to make a good impression. He wanted to be cheerful, not nervous. Which made him nervous.

Finally, Socks hunkered down behind a tiny hill the size of a sand bar, and Dirt slid off him to the ground. They melded their sense of sight and hearing, and Socks closed his eyes to keep Dirt from getting dizzy. With the wolf's sense of hearing, Dirt knew exactly where the humans were. They were walking in a different direction, just a hundred or so paces ahead. Their cloth and leather swished, bits of metal plinked and clanked, their footsteps thudded. They were not very sneaky.

Dirt crept up behind them, eighty paces, fifty. He paused to look into their minds and found them all more complicated than he expected. Each human mind had several layers, and they weren't all in perfect accord with each other. *"Is my mind like that?"* asked Dirt.

-Yes. You have thoughts at speech level, faster thoughts below that, and one more layer that isn't words at all. Just watch the top layer, and you'll be fine,- replied the giant wolf pup.

Dirt looked into their minds again and realized that Mother had been right—most humans didn't have any mind-sight. Their thoughts were unstructured and undisciplined in a way that told him they never suspected anyone might look.

The second thing he noticed was that he couldn't understand them. Their minds were full of words that he didn't recognize. It had never occurred to him that this was even possible.

"Socks, something is wrong! They have . . . I don't know how to talk to them!"

-Silly Dirt, they are just speaking another language.-

"What do you mean?"

-Did you think wolves and humans just have the same words for everything? And trees?-

"You don't even use words unless you're talking to me."

-Exactly,- said Socks. The pup was amused, but that just made Dirt more aggravated.

"That doesn't make sense. Words are words!"

-They just use different ones.-

"Okay, fine, but how do I talk to them?" begged Dirt.

-I will ask Mother, but you should go ahead anyway. Just talk to them like a wolf. There is much you can say without words,- said Socks, urging Dirt onward and sending him a mental puff of courage.

Well, that was easy for him to say. He wasn't about to see the first of his own kind that he'd ever met his whole life.

Dirt scowled and started moving in their direction, down through the brush. If he hesitated too long, they'd just walk away, and he'd have to chase them farther. He thought about trying to make noise so they'd know he was here, but they'd probably just think it was an animal.

He decided to move quietly until they could see each other, and make a little noise then. Their trail wasn't a hard one, and they seemed to prefer to go around things rather than over them. Which was fine with him. Dirt followed their sound between some sticker plants and under a tree that had fallen against another one and was still propped up. From there, he went around a huge mound of vines, and then he saw them.

Two men with short dark hair and one woman with long dark hair. All of them had clothing from the neck down and satchels on their backs full of all kinds of interesting mysteries.

"Ho has sentit?" said the woman. The three of them froze and listened, and Dirt scuffed a plant, trying not to tremble in fear. This was it.

They turned and regarded him in shock. He didn't have to see their minds to know that. Their eyes went wide, and the woman even let her jaw drop.

Dirt stepped forward again and tried to smile warmly. "Hello," he said with his voice.

"D'on carai ha sortit?" said one of the men, the one with the short beard. His eyes were a fierce black that matched the cloth around his neck that draped down his shirt.

"No en tinc ni idea. Mai he sentit parlar d'una tribu que visqui tan lluny," replied the other man, the one with only stubble on his face and round cheeks.

Dirt let go of his knife, leaving it in the sheath under his armpit, and waved. "My name is Dirt. It's nice to meet you." His heart thumped against his rib cage, and his toes curled into the grass for extra support.

"*Ell és brut,*" said the woman. Her face was pinched and lined with wrinkles like the men's, but even through that he could see her disgust. Her mind carried the same idea—he was filthy. She was disgusted at how dirty he was. It had never occurred to him, not once in the two months he'd been alive, that it mattered. But he looked down at himself and saw the coating of grime from head to foot with different eyes. Dirts of different colors, the oils from Socks's fur, and his own sweat painted almost every patch of skin. Only his face was clean, probably from being licked by Socks so much.

Naked, too. The fact that he was naked way out here seemed to them to make him appear unruly and wild, partially inhuman. If he'd only been dirty, that might be one thing, but dirty and naked and wild were a combination they shied away from.

Panic set in. He should have known! He should have bathed first, somehow. Maybe made a little skirt of leaves to wear. How could he have forgotten that? A wolf didn't care, and neither did a tree. But it mattered to humans.

"I'm sorry. I can wash off!" he said, trying to mimic the action of wiping himself clean with water.

"Ens pot entendre? L'entén algun de vosaltres?" asked the bearded man, looking at the other two.

Dirt compared them to himself. They were human, wearing things they had fashioned themselves. Clothing made from plants and animal skin, cut and shaped in just the right way. Tools and weapons, supplies for the journey. And what did he have? Nothing. A knife and a stick and a coating of grime from hair to toes. What Dirt saw of himself in their minds pained him. They despised his filth and nakedness, and distrusted his presence here and what it might mean. They were looking around for others, other wild and vicious men hiding in ambush.

"I si la seva tribu és hostil? Mira, porta un ganivet," said the woman.

"Si la seva tribu és hostil, llavors estem morts," said the beardless man. His hand strayed to the sword at his waist.

Dirt saw it and held the Home-staff forward in both hands, ready to fight. Why? What was happening?

"L'hem de fer callar o ignorar-lo?" asked the woman. She got a hard glint in her eye that was in no way feminine. She was as different from gentle Home and the other dryads as it was possible to get.

Tribu. Hostil. Those words were close to ones Dirt knew, and he shouted, "Tribu not hostil! No hostil, no tribu at all, just me. It's just me." His voice was shaking, and his courage was about to fail completely. He hadn't known what to expect from them, but disgust and fear? It was unbearable. "No hostil. Not hostil."

The three of them relaxed, slightly. Not completely. The bearded one kept his hand near his sword, eyes ever vigilant. He asked, *"D'on ets, noi?"*

"I'm sorry, I can't understand you. Friend? Do you know 'friend?'" He held his hand out for one of them to hold it like the dryads did anytime they went anywhere together. What more friendly gesture could there be than that?

"Demana menjar?" asked the woman, looking at her two companions.

"Pot ser. Dóna-li una mica de pa i mira si se'n va," said the bearded man. He slid his satchel around from his back and unbuckled the flap, keeping it shut. He dug around inside for a moment and pulled out something pale-tan colored, about the size of Dirt's fist. He handed it to the woman.

"Per què jo?" she asked, annoyed.

"Tu ets la dona. Tu tractes amb els nens," he replied with a grin.

The woman took the object from his hand and stepped forward, painting a false smile on her weathered face. She held it out to Dirt, clearly intending him to take it. When he didn't immediately grab it, she shook it toward him to make sure he understood.

He took it, and as soon as he felt it in his hand, he knew what it was. Bread. Dry old bread, the first he'd ever seen. "Thanks," he said, trying to smile instead of cry. "But I don't need your food. I have my own. What I want from you is . . . I guess . . . I just wanted to see other people. I've never met other humans until now."

"Per què no se'n va?" asked the woman, glancing back.

"Tu em dius," replied the beardless man with round cheeks. He stepped sideways to look at something in the distance.

Dirt was tempted for the first time to speak directly to their minds, to push the raw ideas into their heads and make sure they understood him. His heart felt like it was ripping in half. He wanted desperately to be with them, to hear human voices, to hug them and hold their hands and learn how to be a human. The rest of him wanted to run away in shame and hide until they went away.

"Can you tell me where I can find more humans?" he asked. He felt his voice getting softer, like it was already trying to hide.

They didn't answer, instead just glancing at each other while they tried to figure out how to deal with him. They were growing more anxious the longer he stood there, as if he might present some sort of threat.

He knew he'd failed. They couldn't understand each other, and they were not here to be friendly. He started talking, hoping that somehow some of it would get through.

"My name is Dirt, and my best friend is a wolf pup. He's the strongest of the brood, and we're exploring the world together. I'm also friends with a forest of trees so big I've never been to the top, and one of them gave me this. It's a part of herself so she can always watch," he said, gesturing with the staff. They flinched back slightly, as if he might leap forward and try to whap them with it.

Dirt's heart was breaking, and this wasn't working. He continued. "I lived three thousand years ago and forgot everything. I killed an undead wizard. I fought goblins, and Socks and I faced even scarier things than that. I'm not lonely, but you're my own kind. I promise I'm valuable. You're humans. Please."

"Està balbucejant. Anem només," said the bearded man with the sharp black eyes. He waved for the others to follow him.

Dirt stepped forward and said, "Wait!"

The beardless man drew his sword and pointed it at Dirt. *"Ves-te'n, noi. No ho tornaré a preguntar,"* he said. The meaning was clear. Go away.

Dirt stared, unmoving. He couldn't believe it. They'd really kill him, just to be rid of him?

"Dirt," he said, pointing at himself. "Dirt. My name is Dirt."

The beardless man lowered his sword, slightly, pointing it at the ground instead of at Dirt's face. "Derrrt?" he said, rolling his r. "Hèctor."

He pointed at the shorter, bearded man and said, "Ignasi." Then the woman. "Marina."

Strangely, all three names sounded familiar to him. Hèctor sounded like Hectorus, Ignasi like Ignasius, and Marina was familiar as well. He might have even known people with those names, long ago.

Dirt brightened, realizing they weren't so foreign after all. "No hostil," he said, stepping slowly forward. He reached his hand out, covering Hèctor's sword with it. "Hèctor no hostil. Ignasius no hostil. Marina no hostil. Dirt no hostil."

"Hèctor si hostil," said Hèctor. He raised his sword and pointed it at Dirt's face again.

"Why?" said Dirt, eyes filling with tears. He'd tried everything. What was wrong with them?

Dirt heard the familiar sound of Socks landing gently from a jump. The pup ended up right above him, the shadow from his nose covering Dirt's face.

The humans blanched and stepped back. The scent of terror filled the air, and their minds reeled, unsure what to do. They began shouting to each other, too fast and confused for Dirt to make out any of the words.

Socks growled, teeth bared in menace. Saliva dripped from his lips and landed around Dirt.

Hèctor whimpered, face twisted. He tried to turn and run, but he couldn't move his sword. It stayed in that spot in the air like it was buried in wood. Dirt realized Socks was holding it with his mind.

"Socks, don't kill them! Please don't kill them!" said Dirt aloud, turning and waving his hands. *"Please don't!"* he sent in thought.

-I do not like them.-

"Please, I don't want the first and maybe only humans I meet to get killed right away. I don't want that to be my only memory, forever."

-I won't kill them. Instead, we will hunt them.- The big pup stepped forward, placing a clawed paw right beside Hèctor's sword. He leaned down, sniffed the man, and growled again, low and loud enough to make the ground tremble.

The others fled in total panic, and from what Dirt could gather of their minds, they were hoping that eating Hèctor would slow Socks down enough for them to get away.

Dirt grabbed Socks's foreleg. "Don't! Please, don't!" he begged aloud. Hèctor's eyes met his, pleading and terrified. "Please, Socks, let them go! They didn't know! We just can't understand each other!"

-I'm just scaring them.-

Hèctor looked up into Socks's eyes, the wolf pup more than twice his height. Then he let go of his sword, which remained stuck in midair, and fled after the others. Socks barked at him, and the man ran even faster, stumbling and losing a shoe.

-We will follow them at a distance and watch their minds and see what they are doing. I bet they lead us to the other humans. How does that sound?- asked Socks, his demeanor suddenly shifting. He wagged his tail happily and let his tongue loll out.

Dirt sighed. At least Socks's antics were keeping him from crying in bitter disappointment. He had been about to break into bitter weeping, but Socks had killed the mood, and that was probably for the best. He took a few deep breaths and decided it could have gone worse. It could certainly have gone better, but it could have gone worse. And there'd be more chances.

"What are you going to do with the sword?" asked Dirt.

-Maybe I'll give it back to him if he's nice to you. Maybe I'll keep it. I haven't decided. But watch this!- replied Socks with excitement. The sword began swiping fiercely through the air, swung only by the force of Socks's mind. It flew in wide, swift arcs, making circles around them and trimming the brush.

Dirt watched with growing envy. *"I need to learn how to do that with my knife."*

-Let's give him his shoe back,- said Socks. The pup picked up Hèctor's shoe with his mind and flung it forward with stunning force into the distance.

From down on the ground, Dirt couldn't see far enough, so he watched in Socks's mind as the shoe smacked the poor man in the back of the head, still running. The humans hadn't made it very far, it turned out, since they were probably running without magic.

-This might be too easy,- said Socks.

"Better than too hard. And more fun than waiting around for the Devourer to find you," said Dirt, doing his best to soothe his troubled heart. It would take some time, though. It still stung.

Dirt looked around for the bread, which he didn't remember dropping. When he found it, he was pleased that it hadn't been stepped on. He dusted it off and turned it over, considering it carefully. The giant pup lifted Dirt up onto the familiar spot on his back, and Dirt crossed his legs and sat down, laying the staff across them. He held the bread in both hands, trying to decide whether he wanted to eat it now, or save it for when he was hungry. Either way, Socks would probably want a taste, so they'd have to share that sense first.

-There will be other humans who like you, Dirt. You are not the runt of the litter. Mother would not have eaten you, if you were a wolf,- said Socks. He turned his head to look at Dirt with one eye. *-Next time, I'll lick you all clean first.-*

Dirt smiled, letting his friend spread a bit of warmth into his heart. *"Sounds like a plan. Let's go!"*

CHAPTER TWO

After waiting a sufficient time for the humans to think themselves safe, Socks followed silently after them. They were just far enough that Dirt had a hard time seeing any of their thoughts, but Socks still could, and he would get closer once they relaxed.

-Share your taste, and eat that human food,- said Socks.

"I'm not that hungry right now," said Dirt.

-No, you're afraid of being disappointed that you don't like it.-

Dirt scowled at the back of his friend's furry head. Socks was right, of course, and Dirt hadn't even realized he felt that way until the pup said it. He had enough of Prisca's memories to picture low tables covered in delicacies of every variety, with sliced and arranged fruit, tender meats with rich sauces, fragrant wine. But that had been an eternity ago. That was the food of the Sunset Empire, which was all ruins.

No, the more he thought about it, he was getting nervous about humanity in general. What if they all just lived in holes in the ground now instead of grand buildings? What if they were all wary and dangerous? Dirt had deliberately avoided most of Prisca's memories of people, but he still knew how they were supposed to act. Dignified. Graceful. Speaking in warm tones, telling stories or poems or discussing matters of state. What if all that was gone? Everything, not just the buildings? What if humans were little more than clever goblins now?

Dirt pulled out the ancient knife, blade still undulled and free of any blemish. He admired its perfect shine, the smooth curve of its blade, the delicate handle. Humans had made this. If this level of artistry, if painting and music and architecture and everything was gone now, he wasn't sure he could bear to live among them.

-They still have cities. The woman is thinking about one, from when she was little. I think they're looking for it. Now eat the bread. I want to taste human food and so do you,- said Socks.

Dirt braced himself internally and shared his sense of taste, then his sense of smell as well so Socks could get the full human experience. The bread was about the size of his fist, maybe a little bigger, but flat. It was thick as two fingers and rectangle-shaped, probably so the humans could stack and carry them easily. He sniffed it, but it hardly had any aroma at all. Something faint—a soft, warm smell, but hard to place.

He took a bite, or tried to. It felt like he should be able to bite right into this, that it should be soft or maybe chewy; he wasn't sure. But it was hard as a plank of wood, and he had to grind off a corner with his teeth and get it wet with saliva to eat it at all. Once he did, the flavor was fine but not memorable. It was salty, which he'd never tasted before except for sweat, and that helped bring out some of the grain and other mild flavors. But mostly it just tasted crumbly and dry and old, and he only had the patience to eat half of it. *"Do you want the rest of this?"* he asked Socks.

-No, there's not enough there to bother. Why do you think they eat food like that? They had to make it and carry it all this way. Why not catch a rabbit and eat that?- asked Socks. The big pup felt disappointed, but more for Dirt than himself.

"I don't know. Maybe they can't catch any rabbits. Maybe they're too slow and dumb," said Dirt, his mood souring.

-They were smart enough to make one of these,- said Socks, swinging his sword through a tuft of little round leaves on a bush, sending them flying.

"That's a good point," Dirt admitted.

After that they crept along for a while, following the humans. Socks said they were still being wary, so he kept a bit too far back for Dirt to get a clear image of their minds, making it hard for him to learn anything.

But since he was watching already, Dirt's mind-sight found a flock of little birds resting in the high branches of a tree nearby, happily chirping to each other and keeping an eye out for danger. The humans were slow, which meant Socks was creeping so quietly that the birds didn't notice until he and Dirt were right underneath.

"Wait!"

Socks stopped and lowered slightly. *-What is it? Oh, birds again?-*

"Yes, but this time I have an idea. I'm going to watch how they decide where to land." Dirt prepared himself, focusing on the little bird-minds as clearly as he could, then clapped to startle them. It had the desired effect and put them to flight.

Socks silently followed them to the next tree, where they landed again after deciding that the boy and wolf down below weren't much of a threat.

"One more time. Can you bark? Not loud enough the humans will hear."

The wolf pup gave one short bark, which was probably too loud, but it was fine. The birds flew from that tree to the next, which had dead branches on top for them to grab with their little feet.

-Did you see what you wanted?-

"I think so! There's just one bird in front who picks where to land, and they all watch him. So I just have to make him think . . . Okay. Next time, follow under them, okay?"

-Okay.-

"Okay, one more bark."

Socks barked again, amusement growing in his heart. The humans in the distance were interesting, but only for so long. This was starting to seem fun. Dirt patted him in agreement.

The birds flew again, and this time Socks quickly stepped out underneath them. The little flock flew over an open area, and Dirt found the mind of the lead bird quicker than he'd hoped. It saw them below and had the thought of "danger" but Dirt told it "safe" instead. "Safe, safe, safe," he repeated. The bird's mind was too simple to realize the thought wasn't its own, so it gave the faintest gesture midflight, and the whole flock descended.

All at once, twenty birds no larger than Dirt's hand landed everywhere, on his hair and shoulders, all over Socks's fur. Dirt squealed in laughter at their tiny feet tickling his skin. Socks looked up at him and wagged his tail. *-They're tickling my fur, too, and it makes me want to shake them off. But I won't.-*

"Good, don't! Not yet, anyway."

They hopped all over, bouncing with both feet instead of walking. Some of them found crumbs from the bread and ate those with eager haste, and Dirt suddenly wished he'd kept the rest instead of tossing it. He needed a bag, he decided. He was starting to have things to carry.

Dirt held out a finger to mimic a tree branch, and a bird flapped up and landed on it, letting him finally get a close look. The handsome little thing was surprisingly colorful, with a black chest and beak and a line of red on its head that went down its back. Its cheeks were stark white, as were its tailfeathers, and its wings had streaks of red, brown, and black in them. It regarded Dirt with one lively little eye, and a moment later, the whole flock took flight again and disappeared into trees farther away, across a patch of rocky grass.

-Do you want to keep chasing them?- asked Socks, wagging his tail.

"I think I have a better idea. Haven't you wondered what all those little critters are that hide in the grass and run away whenever we get close? Let's see if we can look at some of them."

Socks sniffed the wind, then licked his nose to better feel which way it was moving. He snuck silently into the wind, so nothing could smell him coming. He moved slower than usual, being what he himself considered quiet, with his exceptional hearing.

He hardly had to go far for Dirt to find some good candidates, and only a little coaxing got the owners of the tiny minds to come out into the open where he and Socks could see them. Dirt jumped down to get a better look, making way too much noise and scaring half of them away. But not all. Dirt caught them with thoughts of safety just in time, and they resumed doing whatever it was they were up to before.

A mouse was the first, a furry, curious thing smaller than Dirt's finger if he didn't count its thin tail. When Dirt lowered his hand to maybe pick it up, it jumped on him and ran up one arm, across his shoulders, and into his hair, which got another squeal of laughter. The thing was digging around in there looking for food, and before it could find any, Dirt plucked it out and held it in his hand. It peeked at him and sniffed his scent, always moving, tiny heart racing. Then it jumped off into the grass and moved on, eager to be out of open visibility.

Another mouse, and another, and soon Dirt could pick their minds out from the rest. The next was a rat, much larger than a mouse but shaped basically the same. It moved slower, and its tiny fur coat didn't look as glossy, but its mind was bigger, making it easier to understand. Once it decided Dirt and Socks weren't threats, it became relaxed, even playful and affectionate.

Plenty more mice and rats, all creeping through the grasses. Overhead, larger birds circled and looked for them, and once Dirt picked up a mouse, only to have a hawk snatch it right off his palm and carry it away to eat. It happened so fast he didn't have time to react before it was gone.

They found a little snake, a weasel, and a squirrel before Socks finally got bored and said, *-Let's go find something bigger. I want to eat meat.-*

"What about the humans?"

-You weren't paying attention to them right now anyway, and they will be easy to find.-

"Are you sure you'll be able to come right back here?"

-Of course. I can smell our trail. And even if I couldn't, I can feel where we are.-

Dirt paused and looked up, meeting Socks's eyes. The pup licked his face once, quickly, to tease.

"What do you mean you can feel where we are?"

-Look closely, and I'll try to feel it clear enough for you to see,- said Socks. The pup turned his mental gaze to a sense that was so subtle and natural that Dirt had never noticed it before. There was a slight tug, or perhaps just a corrective influence, that guided him in one particular direction. Socks knew somehow how far right or left he was, how far forward and back, in relation to it. The sense was pervasive, constant, but so quiet that Socks never consciously thought about it. Until now, apparently.

-I just realized humans don't have that. How do you get around?-

"Wait, this whole time, you could feel exactly where you were? Is that how you always know where you're going?"

-Yes. How else?-

"I guess I just go toward things I recognize. And I thought Mother told you the way, or Father, maybe. I had no idea!"

-I never thought about it with you, since we are always going the same places. But those three humans have no idea where they are. The woman is trying to recognize things and remember, but they are lost. Once I realized that, it made me wonder how that was possible.-

Dirt looked around at the wilderness surrounding them, the lumpy hills with snaggly trees and thick brush, the bare, rocky mountains beyond. In truth, he had no idea where they were in relation to the dryad forest or anything else from longer than a day or two ago. *"We used to put up signs with writing, and they'd say, 'The water is that way, the town is this way,'"* he said, remembering. *"And there were maps, pictures drawn that would tell you where to go."*

-Perhaps humans build houses because they do not often have to travel. Wolves have to look everywhere for prey, but apparently humans don't. At least not as much.-

"The grain to make bread is grown in the ground, so I bet you're right. How about I follow the humans closer for a while so I can see their minds, and you go hunt? I'll stay a little closer to them, but just enough to see clearly, and far enough not to get caught. I know you think it's boring, and I haven't had a good look in hours."

Socks looked back at him, somewhat surprised. *-You don't want to come?-*

"No, I do, but I want to do this more. Maybe if I learn to talk with them, we can figure out where the city is they're trying to find."

-Fine, but if something comes, make your skin hard like we practiced and hit it with the staff.-

"I will. And if it's something too dangerous, I'll run away." Dirt stood and stepped up toward the pup's ears, which he scratched vigorously before jumping down.

Socks leaned down and sniffed him, then said, *-They are that way.-*

"I know. I can see their footprints. Remember not to eat too many bones."

-I'll remember.-

Socks left at a run, and Dirt watched him disappear toward the mountains. Up close, Socks was cuddly and friendly, and far away, he looked normal size. But there was a middle distance, where Dirt could watch him in comparison to little trees and things as he ran by, that Dirt could really feel just how big the pup was. He must have been twelve feet at the shoulder now, and his fuzzy gray puppy fur was slowly being replaced by sleeker, darker fur on its slow journey to black, and he ran with such slick grace that he seemed more shadow than animal. With such a busy landscape, he was soon out of sight.

It had been several weeks since they'd been more than a dozen paces apart, and now it felt strange to be alone. Dirt carried the staff over both shoulders and followed the footprints. He noticed the humans tended to walk around hills instead of over them, and around thick brush instead of through it. Socks didn't much care about either of those things, and Dirt hadn't really thought about it.

Dirt inhaled a little mana and started catching up. It only took him a few minutes to get close enough to see their minds clearly, perhaps a couple hundred paces away. He avoided going anywhere he could see them with his eyes, since they'd be able to spot him if they did.

Now that he was close enough, he kept his eyes and ears open as much as his mind, listening for their sounds and avoiding stepping on anything that might make too much noise. He figured they only heard as well as he did, so if he didn't hear them, they probably didn't hear him. Which was good, because this particular spot had a bunch of larger trees that shed bark and dead branches and that left him fewer places to step than he liked.

The woman, Marina, was taking the lead. Like Socks had said, she seemed to be trying to find a place from a long time ago. She remembered leaving that place, a city, in a hurry, and watching the mountains and landscape as they traveled. She had been scared then, perhaps a child. The memories were faint and disconnected, and it seemed like she'd filled in too much with imagination and was probably doing that right now as she strained to remember more.

The men were cross with her, too. They feared how far they'd come and resented her and each other. Their imaginations were filled with bands of naked savages swooping down out of trees to feast on their flesh. Tribe—tribu. Wild tribes, that's what they meant. What they thought Dirt was.

He learned other words at a rapid pace, since the two men were having loud arguments in their minds with no one, and the woman was looking all over and thinking about the things she saw. Many words were similar enough to his language to reassure him they were indeed related—words like *lluna* for moon or *sol* for sun. Some weren't the same word but related to a similar one. Their word for grass was *herba*, and their word for clothing was *roba*. He pieced out others, such as the words for he and she, but it was tiring, and he started losing interest.

Dirt sat down to rest, even though it was just his mind that was tired. "Can I have some sap now, Home?" he asked the staff. As always, she couldn't reply, but the sap started to appear on its side anyway. Silent as the staff was, it was nice to know she was listening.

An earsplitting cry filled the air from above, making Dirt drop the staff and plug his ears. It sounded like one of the large birds that liked to circle overhead, especially near water, but the sound it made was lower in pitch and much louder. It punched right into Dirt's most basic instincts. Like when hearing Socks growl or seeing the undead move, his whole body screamed DANGER.

But he knew that sound. He looked up, seeking out the gryphon overhead. It didn't take long to find—it circled above the humans, a couple hundred paces ahead through the brush. It flew with all four legs tucked in, which made it look like a regular bird, just enormous. This gryphon was reddish-brown with tips of gold on its wings and tail.

The humans' minds filled with one word, standing out against white-hot panic: *grifó*. Well, that was another one Dirt knew, now. Gryphon was *grifó*.

Hèctor had one other word in his mind, though: *espasa*. The poor man felt helpless and naked without his sword and had no idea how he was going to defend himself. He started scanning the ground for weapons and picked up a rock.

That was the wrong thing to do. Dirt knew that from experience. Don't pick up a weapon in front of a gryphon. He ran forward at top speed, burning mana to leap over trees and crash through brush like a tumbling log. It took him only an instant to land in the middle of the surprised and terrified humans, but that was almost too late.

Dirt whapped the rock out of Hèctor's hands just as the gryphon began its dive. Dirt hadn't seen enough of the beast's thoughts to get their flavor, so he improvised "friend! safe!" as emotions, and fired that into its mind.

The gryphon reared back in midair, then landed a few paces away, confused. Dirt said, "Bon ocell!" which he hoped meant "good bird" in the humans' language. He wasn't sure if it was the right kind of good, but the gryphon didn't know either, so it didn't matter. He corrected himself. "Bon grifó!"

Dirt stepped in front of Ignasi and Marina, waving his arm for them to stay back. He put down the Home-staff and stepped forward again, sending the gryphon feelings of warmth and happiness.

The beast was too big to be stupid, nearly as big as Socks was when they first met. It was smarter than goblins were, almost smart enough to understand that the thoughts weren't its own. But not quite. Not quite. It finally accepted them and stepped forward to rub little Dirt with the top of its head.

Dirt happily patted and scratched it, which made it poof out its feathers in contentment. It kept a wary eye on the other humans, though, and Dirt finally saw enough of its thoughts to understand what made it so mad. They'd gotten too close to its nest, which was just a short distance to the side, uphill amongst an exposed slough of boulders.

Dirt turned back to the shocked humans to explain. Ignasi held two long knives and Marina a bow, but both were letting them droop toward the ground. Hèctor held the empty sheath of his sword up like he was going to fight with it.

"No allà," said Dirt, pointing toward the nest. "No allà." *No there.*

Then he pointed the other direction, away from it, downhill. "Si allà. Si. Anem." *Yes there. Yes. You go.* Or at least he hoped that's what he was saying.

He went back to scratching under the gryphon's feathers. "Bon ocell, bon grifó." As much as it enjoyed having its chest scratched, once it saw the three adults heading away, it gave Dirt a little bark and took off, returning to its nest to make sure everything was still fine there. It expected its mate soon, and the young were hungry. From how the gryphon thought of them, they must be the most adorable things in the world, and Dirt badly wanted to go get a peek.

Unfortunately, that would be profoundly foolish, so he didn't. He could probably defend himself against one, strengthening his skin against its talons and beak while he ran away at top speed, but he'd rather not find out the hard way he was wrong.

The three adults had only gone a few paces before the gryphon took off, and once it was gone, they turned again to stare at him, almost too bewildered to think in words.

Dirt picked up the staff and found that Home had made him a big lump of sap despite all the commotion, and he picked some of the grass out of it and took a bite. Then he waved goodbye and left, grinning widely as he chewed, enjoying how it stuck to his teeth. Socks would probably be back soon anyway, and there was no reason to scare them all again. Yet.

One thing was sure—they'd be nicer to him the next time they saw him. Maybe tomorrow. Or the day after that, giving him enough time to learn more of their words. Silly humans, he thought. They seemed more helpless than he was, which was a new feeling. He grinned with pride and took another bite.

CHAPTER THREE

Two days later, Socks was truly getting bored, and Dirt wasn't sure he'd keep following these slow humans for much longer. They weren't as fun as Dirt, since all they did was wander and argue. The pup even got tired of slashing that sword through the air, so he threw it back to them, and they thought it fell from the sky. That was fun.

But around midday, as Dirt was chewing up the bones of a squirrel for the marrow, Socks smelled water and left the humans' trail at a full run. Dirt nearly rolled off backward and had to drop what was left of his lunch so he could grab on.

The pup ran toward the mountains, following the breeze blowing down from the heights. He leaped over clumps of trees and shrubs and ran straight over the bushes with his long legs until they found it—a quick-moving stream, ten paces across at its widest and mostly shallow. The water rushed loudly down toward the valley below, splashing over boulders as it went.

Socks stepped into it and made his way upward. *-Let's go see where this comes from.-*

Dirt perked up at that. It had never occurred to him that a stream had a source. *"Where do streams come from?"*

-I don't know.-

The pup splashed loudly as he ran up the stream, making as much noise as possible and enjoying how the water flew everywhere. Even Socks's sure steps slipped on the wet rocks every now and then, leaving

Dirt to hang on for dear life or get tossed in. If the water splashing up hadn't been so cold, it would have been a lot more fun.

It turned out the stream was far longer than anticipated. Socks and Dirt hadn't spent much time in the mountains, since getting around up there was harder and there was plenty to see down below. But the canyon just kept going and going and going, and eventually Socks got tired of all the splashing and extra work and decided to walk beside the stream instead.

Game trails wove all throughout the brush and trees alongside the water, breaking away to head up the mountainside or around a cliff or into a side canyon. In narrower parts of the canyon, Socks had to leap from rock to rock, or creep precariously along an incline without sliding down, or some such thing.

And there was certainly plenty to look at. The plants down by the stream were soft and full, brighter green than grew anywhere else. Tall, thin trees with yellowing leaves sagged under the weight of moss. Vines crept into the edge of the water, where their leaves were too torn up to grow any farther.

In some places, the canyon floor widened, and the stream slowed and spread, and in one spot a bunch of fallen trees and branches dammed the flow, creating a big pond. Dirt's mind-sight told him there was some sort of critter hiding in the dam, where it seemed to live. Two of them, in fact.

Socks stopped at the little pond, finally resting after a long, tiring run. He lapped up some water to rejuvenate, and Dirt slid off his back. But when Dirt leaned down for a drink, Socks gracefully put his big nose under Dirt's backside and tossed him halfway across the pond.

Dirt screamed until he hit the water, face-first. Socks waded out, pleased with himself. The water only came halfway up his torso, but that was plenty deep for Dirt to swim. After the initial surprise dunk, the water warmed up a bit, and things got a lot more fun.

Socks pulled fish out of the water with his mind and looked at them, curious about their different colors. He ate a couple of the big ones, but there weren't enough of them for a proper meal, so he let most of them be.

Dirt swam in circles, trying out different ways of pulling himself through the water. He used only his arms, or only his legs, or turned over and over like a rolling snake. He turned sideways and flipped his feet like a fish, and all sorts of other methods. He even climbed up and jumped off Socks's nose a few times, but the water wasn't deep enough to get thrown very high.

After he tired out, he had Socks pull a fish out for him, and they shared their sense of taste. Dirt took a bite and immediately decided he didn't like the scales, since they stuck all over his mouth and in his teeth. But the meat was nice, so soft it came apart just by pushing it with his tongue.

-I wonder if there are any fish big enough for me to eat,- said Socks.

"Probably somewhere. I bet we find some eventually. Maybe somewhere with a lot more water," said Dirt. He ate the whole thing, since he found he could chew the bones enough to swallow. The eyes popped when he bit them, which was a surprise. He'd always thought eyes were solid, but they were full of fluid that had a lot of flavor. He'd never eaten one before, since animal faces didn't have enough meat to bother.

Socks climbed out, shook the water off, and lay down to rest in the sun and dry out all the way. Dirt followed him but stopped at the edge of the water and did his best to scrub himself clean instead. He did a thorough job, even between his toes. Socks had to lick his back clean where he couldn't reach.

Dirt was only satisfied after he got a good look at himself through Socks's eyes, turning in a slow circle to make sure he was all clean.

-Now you look like a proper human,- said Socks, probably teasing.

"Well, I hope so. I'll have to let the humans see me before I get dirty again."

-What are you going to do about clothing?-

"I don't know. Do you think they'll care as long as I'm clean?"

Socks huffed in amusement. *-Now they can't smell everywhere you've been. It makes you more of a stranger than before. Humans are silly.-*

"I did save them from that gryphon, so they should be nice to me next time."

-How much of you has to be covered to be considered clothed? Could you just tie some vines together?-

Dirt sat down and leaned into Socks's fur while he thought about that. Prisca had worn a dress of gold, as had the dead human named Callius. And Prisca's memories did include views of the grand cities, with people filling the streets, but they wore such a wild variety of things there was no way for the eye to take it all in. Not only that, but her memory was ancient, and she hadn't been looking all that carefully in the first place. Nothing he'd taken from her told him clearly what a human was supposed to wear, especially a young boy. However, it didn't seem like what the humans had on—thick pants and shirts of heavy cloth and leather—matched anything Prisca remembered, or that all those buried skeletons had been wearing.

-These humans don't speak the same language, so I bet they don't have the same ideas about clothing anyway. Those memories won't do you any good,- said Socks. *-Maybe you should ask these humans, and then forget about them, and then you'll know for the next group you meet. I am not sure if these ones will forgive you.-*

"Yeah. But after watching their thoughts for a couple days, I almost feel like we're friends already. I feel like I know them."

-They don't know you, though.-

"I know. I wonder if I should keep it a secret that I can see their minds. Didn't Mother say most humans can't do that?"

-Maybe you can ask these ones about that, too. That and clothing. And then if it goes poorly, it will be okay because you'll know for the next ones.-

"I guess that works. Then maybe I can wood-shape some clothing. Actually, I think I'll try that now just to see."

-Give it a try. I want to sit here for a while anyway, until I am dry.-

Dirt picked up the Home-staff and inhaled a bit of mana, then tried shaping a thin sheet of material out of it. It worked, but not very well. The material he got wasn't flexible enough, and after creating a section a few hand-spans in length, he broke it off and poked at it, turning and flexing it to see if it would work. The more he played with it, the more it cracked and creased and came apart.

He tossed that aside. It needed to be more flexible. With that in mind, he shaped another length, a big, flat square that was thinner, lighter, and greener. It was flexible like he wanted, but when he pressed it over his knee to see how it'd behave, it split apart.

Well, that wouldn't work. He made some viny threads next, thinner than his pinky fingernail, and tried to weave them together. The first attempt resulted in a huge clumpy knot, and the second attempt just kept coming apart. There must be some trick to it, but he couldn't figure it out. Not on the first couple tries.

-Little Dirt, look at the minds. There are a bunch of things sleeping somewhere nearby,- said Socks, perking up.

Dirt opened his mind to Socks, preparing for a full mind meld. Realizing what Dirt had in mind, Socks opened his as well, and their thoughts slid together and became one.

Socks and Dirt said, "*-Okay, let's see what Socks was looking at and where they are.-*"

"*-Yes, let's.-*"

Dirt's body stood up and moved a few steps away, and they opened their mind-sights to see what was around. Dozens of lights appeared in a clump, all bigger and more complicated than typical beasts. But they were all sleeping, which made it hard to judge what they were.

With two mental perspectives instead of one, Socks and Dirt could easily point out the direction, and it turned out these were all underground. Not under the pond, but off inside the mountain to the right.

Dirt's body climbed back onto Sock's body's back, and they padded uphill to see if there was a big cave, or maybe a deep hollow. There wasn't. Just rocks. Socks's nose couldn't find any unusual scent trails, or even any air that smelled like it was blowing up from underground.

"*-They look too bright to be regular beasts. Even asleep, we can tell that much.-*"

Socks and Dirt made their way over the peak, which was farther up than it looked, and down the other side. Only then did Socks's nose pick up a new scent—the wind blew it down the mountain, away from where they'd been, but it was a human-like scent. Not human, though. Not goblin, either, but something similar.

They followed the scent carefully down a rockslide and into some dry brush, which Socks gracefully stepped through. A trail came into view, much like a game trail except a little wider. The scent was much stronger on it, and Socks picked up notes of hunger, eagerness, weariness, and many more such things. It wasn't just a few creatures here—there were too many to tell the individual scents apart.

Socks and Dirt looked at the minds again, and many more came into view. Perhaps hundreds of them, down inside the mountain, mostly clumped together. Most of them were sleeping, but not all. Some restless infants stirred, and tired mothers fed them, but all were so weary and inattentive that Dirt and Socks still couldn't tell what they were.

The trail led them to an opening, a dark entry into the mountain dug right next to a boulder bigger than Socks. A warm wind blew out from inside, rich with a thousand new scents.

"-Socks is too big to fit in there. Should we send Dirt in?-"

"-Dirt might be too weak. Look along the entryway—those look like claw marks. It looks like they can dig right through stone when they want to.-"

"-Perhaps, but they are asleep. He should be fine if he hurries. He is not completely helpless. Let him bring the Home-staff and his knife, and fill up with mana.-"

"-Dirt cannot see in the dark without making a light.-"

"-Then let us make a light. They are asleep.-"

"-We will make a light and go in, then. We do want to see what they are.-"

Keeping the mind meld strong, Dirt's hand raised and snapped his fingers. A small ball of flame appeared over his head, almost invisible in the bright midday sun. He stepped up to the entrance and they shifted their focus from primarily centered in Socks to being primarily centered in Dirt.

Dirt held the Home-staff in front of himself as he walked in. They were sure not to move him too quickly, lest Dirt's eyes be too slow to adjust and he step on something noisy. Each step took them farther into darkness, and after twenty paces, Socks's body closed his eyes, since there would be nothing to watch from that point.

Socks and Dirt sniffed the air, wishing human noses were more effective, but there was no thick water in the air, or anything to smell other than the rank body odor. It was making Dirt's eyes water, so they wiped them and plugged his nose with their fingers. The firelight bobbled behind, just overhead, and when Dirt finally descended into true darkness, it lit up the interior of the cave bright as a torch.

The cave was mostly natural, with an uneven ceiling and walls. But anywhere it grew too constrained for something the size of an adult human to walk through unhindered, it had been clawed away to make room. There was no dirt down here, either—all the digging happened through solid stone. Dirt and Socks wondered if they could find a claw to keep, since they must be impressive.

"-Something occurs to us. Are the creatures digging, or do they herd some sort of beast that does it?-"

Dirt stopped walking forward, and they took another look at the minds around them. Down much deeper, they found smaller minds, but those were awake, and it didn't take long to figure out they were something else. Those were probably being herded. Those didn't seem to have eyes at all, sensing the world with sound and smell instead. Their minds seemed more insect than animal.

"-Those must be herds kept for food.-"

Dirt crept carefully down the tunnel as Dirt and Socks kept watch with mind-sight. Nothing stirred or registered their intrusion. They knew they were getting closer to the first clump of the mysterious creatures, and when Dirt's body got within a stone's throw, the tunnel opened into a cavern of decent size. Smaller than the interior of Prisca's schola, but big enough not to feel cramped. No part of it was flat, with the floor curving up or downhill with the natural flow of the rock, but every inch of ground was occupied. Mats of woven grass, small baskets and pottery, trinkets of every shape and variety.

Lumps of furry, sleeping bodies. They looked like nothing Dirt and Socks had ever seen, with long, muscular arms and ugly faces. Each was bigger than an adult human, both in height and thickness. They wore clothing of a sort—simple loincloths of tightly woven plant fibers, held in place by thin belts of some sort of twined rope.

Between the dim light and the fur hiding much of their appearance, Dirt's human eyes had a hard time gathering enough detail to get a thorough picture of them. They had him creep closer, slow and silent, until he was only three paces away from one.

Dirt and Socks couldn't even tell what sex it was because of the loincloth. It had nipples that might have been long enough for suckling, but if they were female breasts, they weren't pronounced enough to have any milk. It had a wide mouth, open and dripping drool. Its deep-set eyes twitched with dreams, and its round, narrow head made it look both dangerous and stupid. The creature's heavy breathing had a rasp in it, one that Dirt and Socks were sure would cause it to cough and wake at any moment.

There were more. Dozens more, just in this clump, all distributed haphazardly throughout the cavern. Some were noticeably smaller than others, but this group had none of the waking infants that Dirt and Socks had spotted elsewhere.

The sheer stench of them was enough to get Dirt and Socks to think it was time to leave, but before they did, they had Dirt check some of the baskets for cloth, which they hoped to steal. Having a sample would make it much, much easier for Dirt to figure out later, and that would solve the clothing problem. And perhaps some food, if they had any, just to see what it was.

Dirt and Socks kept an eye on them the whole time, carefully stepping on the quietest things they could find. The first basket was full of shells, which was curious. Where had those come from? Another basket had long, thin bones, all the same size, and likely useful for something they couldn't guess. The next had a few dried fruits in the bottom, but they didn't look appealing enough to steal. Finally, Dirt's gaze fell on a knee-high pile of their rough cloth. On a sudden whim, they had Dirt pick the whole thing up and turn to leave, hurrying this time.

The boy's body danced back across the cavern floor like a spider, trying not to drop anything. The staff was awkward, and the cloth kept wanting to sag or dip everywhere as different places came out of order.

It turned out not to be enough. He let the barest end of the cloth drag across the face of the first creature he'd examined, the one closest to the door. It snorted and stirred, and Dirt gave up sneaking to race back up the tunnel as fast as he could go. His bare feet slapped the stone far too often, letting the sound echo in both directions. The cloth unraveled more as he ran, tangling his feet and nearly tripping him.

Their mind meld slid apart, and half of Dirt's world disappeared. The overwhelming scent of creature instantly became a wretched stench, so thick on the air he was sure he felt it burning his lungs.

-They're waking up. Hurry, little Dirt.-

"I'm hurrying!" He reached a spot that had been much easier to slide down than it was to climb up, especially holding a staff and a bunch of loose cloth. He inhaled mana and jumped, but in his haste, he went too far and cracked his skull on the stone ceiling above where he wanted to

land. The surprise pain made him drop the staff, which clattered all the way down and out of sight.

Dirt dropped the cloth and ran down after it. It didn't tumble all the way back into the cavern, thank Grace, but it still cost him precious time. He spared a glance at the minds, and at least two were now awake, hearing him in the tunnel and getting angry about it. Very angry. Dirt was an intruder. They could smell him, and he was not making their sounds.

With the staff in hand, he ran using mana and went so fast his eyes had trouble following the turns of the tunnel. He picked up the cloth as he went, but let it drag in a long trail behind him instead of trying to keep it bundled up.

The sunlight was blinding when he burst out of the cave, and Socks had to pick Dirt up with his mind and put him on his back. The pup stepped back from the entrance but didn't run.

"-They're mad, Socks. Like wasps, and I went in their nest.-"

-I know. I want to see them. Maybe they will want to fight and it will be fun.-

"I don't know. There might be a lot of them coming out of there," said Dirt, nervously trying to roll up the cloth to make it easier to carry.

-If too many come, then we will just run away. But I want to see them in the light. And they are big to you but small to me.-

Dirt sighed and braced himself, filling with mana just in case.

The screams came out of the entrance before the creatures did, shrill and long and piercing. Socks's hackles rose underneath Dirt, which just made him more nervous. At least Socks was preparing to take it seriously.

Socks grabbed the first creature that came out of the tunnel with his mind, pulled it into the air, twisted it in half, then threw it back down the tunnel. Its halves didn't go far, slamming into the tunnel wall with two heavy thuds and splashes of blood and viscera. The second one came out bruised and enraged, screaming with a high-pitched voice that didn't match its furry, bulky body.

The pup lifted that one in the air and brought it closer to examine. He rotated it in every direction like Mother had done with Dirt, and it screamed the whole time. The thing's arms reached down past its knees, in part because the legs were short. Instead of hands, it had long, thick claws that didn't look like they could move independently. There was nothing to see in its mind but white fury and an underlying vicious cunning as it tried to think of a way to get to Socks's eyes and rip them out with its claws.

In the few heartbeats it took for Socks to look the creature over once or twice, four more came out, then six. Socks created a web of sparks between himself and the beasts, which erupted into a wall of flame. He pushed the flame over them, igniting their fur and searing their tiny eyes and lungs. Their screams of anger turned into helpless agony.

Socks twisted the head off the one he was holding up and threw the parts away. He called up another wave of sparks and sent them into the tunnel. When he ignited them, the flames caused a deafening explosion, and flame shot thirty paces out from the tunnel. The exit was angled up and away, which was good, because he and Dirt would never have dodged in time.

-I didn't know it would do that! Plug your ears. I'm going to do it again.-

Dirt had to hold the staff in the crook of a knee, but once his ears were plugged, Socks created another explosion inside the tunnel. It was loud, even with ears plugged, and Dirt felt it slap his insides. It made him nauseous.

"-Okay, no more of that, please," said Dirt.

-Fine. I think they stopped coming out.-

The pup was right. The area was quiet again, and all screaming had ceased. Dirt breathed a sigh of relief and settled in a bit more comfortably.

-Wait. I think I woke the rest up.-

Dirt looked with his mind, and although he couldn't tell direction by himself, he could still see hundreds of them waking. Some were confused, but most were simply angry. They didn't seem to have any fear at all. None.

Socks turned and started back up over the peak, toward the little pond from before. Behind him, a crowd of the beasts rushed out of the tunnel, so quickly Dirt thought they must be organized. Up ahead, the ground burst open, and more sprang up into the sunlight, dark fur glistening. Then from somewhere else, another erupting shower of earth and rock and a new tunnel spat out twenty more.

Now there were fifty, all racing forward on their stumpy legs and strong, vicious arms, screaming with high-pitched voices. More minds came into view, and new tunnels burst open all over the mountainside, and then there were a hundred. Two hundred. Five hundred.

Socks and Dirt were surrounded.

CHAPTER FOUR

Socks sniffed the air, nervously flitting his tail.

"Are we going to run?" asked Dirt. *"Should I lie down? Or are we going to fight?"*

The closest group of beasts rushed on all fours, their mighty front claws tearing up the ground and spraying gravel and splintered stone behind them.

Socks barked at them, as loud as he could. Waves of air pressure flew down the mountainside, ripping everything they passed. The creatures were shaken but not deterred. With so many minds, Dirt couldn't tell them apart, but he was shocked the things still weren't afraid.

The group resumed its charge, and Socks summoned sparks into their path, which he ignited once they were too close to stop. He fed mana into the flames, causing them to roar up higher, higher even than the tips of his ears. Even so, six made it through, as good as dead but still moving. Socks killed them one by one with his mind, but the last one got close enough the pup had to pin it with his claws and tear it in half with his teeth.

Dirt thrust fear into as many of the nearby minds as he could—a desperate, urgent terror that wasn't completely separate from how he was starting to feel. The emotion simply slid right out of their minds, leaving only momentary confusion if it left anything behind at all. It mostly didn't.

"I don't think they can feel fear."

-Mother never told me about these,- said Socks. The pup was starting to get nervous, which didn't help Dirt keep his calm. More of them kept popping out from underground, and those ones hung back and watched, eager for Socks to try to flee in their direction.

"Can you run through them?"

-I'm worried about their claws. Even I can't dig stone that easily. I don't want to run through, or they will catch my legs.-

"What about jumping?"

-Where will I land that they can't come get me?-

Socks surrounded himself and Dirt with a wide circle of sparks, which erupted into a wall of flame. He kept the flames burning to buy time as they discussed.

"We just have to get far enough away to run. We don't have to fight them all," said Dirt. He pulled his knife from its sheath and tossed it into the air for Socks, who caught it with his mind. *"How's your mental stamina?"*

-I have more than you,- said Socks with a mental snort.

Dirt grinned, not wanting to argue. Socks *probably* still did have more. Probably. *"Then let's fight seriously. This will be good practice."*

A beast ran through the fire, waving its thick claws as if to cut the flames. It didn't work, and by the time it got close all its fur was burned off, leaving hideously miscolored patches of skin that ranged from its natural black to a raw pink. The flames had blinded it, but it stumbled forward anyway, hoping to get a lucky swing. Socks buried the dagger in the top of its skull, then withdrew it and let the thing drop.

-I am tired of getting my belly cut open,- said Socks, letting a little childish self-pity come through with the thought.

"We won't let it."

Dirt stood and ran forward, holding the Home-staff in both hands. He leaped off Sock's nose, and the pup flung him high into the air.

Socks and Dirt slid into the mind meld. It stung their brains slightly to do it again so soon, but they ignored it and pressed on.

They threw the boy down into the nearest crowd, where he spun the Home-staff with mana-strengthened arms. Even though the beasts were nearly twice his height and weighed five times as much, the staff was unstoppable. It struck with greater force than its density could explain.

Quick swipes shattered several knees and one skull before the wolf's eyes saw an attack coming that the boy's body couldn't slide away from. They pulled him up into the air and flung the dagger in, swinging it in a slashing arc. It sliced with pleasing effect, its force braced against Socks's huge body. Three more went down.

But injured and dying beasts are still dangerous, and these ones died slow. From above, Dirt's eyes saw one jump out from under a tumble of wounded bodies, bleeding heavily from a gash straight across its chest that had missed its heart. Both lungs sliced into, it coughed blood as it made one final attempt to get its claws into Socks's front leg. Socks and Dirt threw the boy down from the air to crush it with the Home-staff. It didn't get back up.

"-We should focus on clearing a path.-"

Dirt and Socks threw the boy forward into a less-crowded spot. Two sets of eyes guided every swing into a joint, crushing the knees of four more in an instant. Screams of rage became screams of pain. The wolf landed close to the boy, one paw pushing down a beast as it tried to get back up. Dirt and Socks surrounded themselves with sparks and ignited a ring of flame to guard them while they judged the next spot.

The mountaintop was getting crowded. Even from up in the air, the boy's eyes found fewer and fewer spots empty enough for the wolf to land without being at risk.

"-We need to kill instead of injuring.-"

They threw the boy forward to the next spot and held him in the air just above the beasts. The boy spun in midair, swung down, and got a solid crack on the closest head, shattering it and sending red and pink matter out the back of its skull. Then they pulled him sideways, out of the way of the sudden attack from its neighbor. The boy swung again, catching this one where its ear might be, if it had any. It collapsed.

The wolf ripped the arm off a beast with his teeth and kicked another one away with his back leg, then jumped to land in the opening the boy had created.

They leaped again, throwing the boy ahead to clear a space. The beasts clumped to try to grab him from the air, but the boy spun like a descending leaf, cracking three more skulls in a motion that even the wolf's quick eyes saw as one smooth arc. The wolf spun as well, lashing out with claws and teeth as several of them got too close. The boy's eyes helped guide his strikes, and four of them lost their viscera before the first one fell.

"-This is a lot easier when one body doesn't have to try and watch everything himself.-"

"-We did not think the boy's body would be this useful, but this is effective.-"

Two together minds could process much faster than two apart, but the cost of such mental strain was increasing each moment. That was a concern for later, though. Having spared a moment to catch a breath, they nodded to themselves, beginning to think they might actually get out of this unscathed.

From above, closer to the peak, the beasts pushed a round boulder out one of their holes. It rolled with unstoppable force, crushing everything on its bouncing path down the mountainside. But Socks and Dirt were far too nimble, even if the beasts had aimed right. It rolled harmlessly past them without even having to dodge.

Socks and Dirt breathed a sigh of relief, but a slow rumble turned their eyes back toward the mountain top. Four more boulders came rolling, then ten more, then another ten. From one instant to the next, the mountainside was all but filled with them.

Their bodies froze in sudden panic, even the wolf's. There was no time to think, even with two brains for the task. The boy flew upward out of reach, and judged the boulders' paths as closely as he could.

All around them, the beasts hunkered down, some digging in. Socks and Dirt wished they could do the same with the wolf, but he was too big.

The wolf dodged left, then ducked under a heavy one that had started bouncing. It was close and stroked the fur of his tail as it passed. The next two, he jumped over in one bound, then left again. Then another jump.

And then no more came. The ones below kept rolling and sent up loud cracks and thumps that the wolf felt in his paws, but no new ones got pushed out. For a brief moment, the creatures stayed down, unsure if more were coming.

"-Should we head into the valley instead of back up into the mountains?-"

"-Why?-"

"-Because they live in the mountains.-"

"-Isn't that the wrong way? What about the humans? Do we still want to follow them?-"

"-We can always circle around. Dirt can probably talk with them now, and there is more he wishes to learn.-"

"-Socks is getting bored.-"

"-Not after this.-"

"-That is true.-"

They sent the boy rushing down the open trail left by the tumbling boulders, the wolf following a few steps behind. The boy swung the Home-staff wildly to fend off any rising beasts, and the wolf flung any away who got too close.

A larger boulder took a turn toward a group of five or six, slow to rise. It bounced right over them, leaving them perfectly unharmed.

Dirt and Socks carpeted the ground with fire and leaped over it, passing over before the beasts even started screaming.

From there, it wasn't too far until they had escaped enough of the gathering horde to dodge the rest. Socks and Dirt put the boy on the wolf's back and finally let their minds slide apart.

A wave of nausea and dizziness hit them both so bad that Socks stumbled and rolled, nearly crushing Dirt, who barely managed to hang on.

Even with dozens of beasts still running toward them, it took the poor wolf three tries to get up and get moving again, and after a moment, he had to stop and vomit. Hearing it made Dirt sicker, and he barely slid down in time to add his own lunch to the disgusting mess.

Through a pounding headache, Dirt said, *"Are you okay, Socks? Do you want me to just run alongside for a bit?"*

-Yes. I'm worried I'll fall again.-

"It looks like we need more practice."

-Can you run? Will you be okay?-

"I'd rather run than get caught. They're getting close."

Dirt forced himself to get moving, ignoring the full-body churn that only slowly faded as he ran. Thank Grace he had mana to rely on and no difficulty keeping it flowing, despite his other problems.

The two of them descended the rest of the way into the little mountain valley, which wasn't particularly large. It was flat and mostly empty, with a crease down the middle that he hoped was a stream. Brush and trees grew on the west side, toward the sunset, but the mountains to the east were much barer and rockier.

-Let's cross and go up those mountains and rest there. That should be far enough away that they leave us alone.-

Dirt followed the pup across the valley, speeding through the tall grasses and bare patches, over rocks and around bent and stunted trees. They crossed the crease in the valley, which was a stream with so little water in it they only stopped long enough to wash the vomit out of their mouths.

Running was never restful, since Dirt always had to watch where he was going and turn this way or that, but it was restful enough. His headache faded, as did his nausea. By the time they reached the opposite end of the valley and headed up the smaller, bare mountains, the beasts chasing them were too distant to spot, or had returned to their holes.

Finally, a knot of fear that Dirt hadn't quite realized was there untied itself and went away. They were fine. Gods in Glory, what a mess that had almost turned into.

-Let's rest at the top. I want to see what's on the other side first,- said Socks.

Dirt sighed inwardly and made himself keep going, but the worst was already over. This row of mountains was smaller, too, more like oversized hills than anything. Once they reached the flattish, rounded top and looked down the other side, a much larger valley opened before them, with another range of mountains far across to the east. The valley floor was wet, with countless little streams and small lakes everywhere. Patches of lush green contrasted with bare patches of dry yellow, fading into gray, dusty distance.

A fair distance to the north, a pale tower looked out over the plains, not very impressive from so far away. Still, it captured the eye, and Dirt wondered how old it was, and how long it had been there. The landscape was broken up by straight lines, which Dirt thought might be fences or short walls. Or perhaps roads; it was hard to tell from up here. Some of those spots inside might be little buildings. Houses, maybe.

Whether or not Socks noticed the tower, it wasn't the most interesting thing to him. He said, *-I think I can carry you now. Let's go a little farther. I want some of that water.-*

"No, it's fine. I'll just run."

The descent from the hilltop was easy, with a long gentle slope covered by grass, and down in the valley, the air was warmer and humid. Much of the ground was muddy, which resulted in Dirt completely losing the benefit of his earlier bath, since Socks kept splashing him. The water was mostly shallow, everywhere they found it. They checked four different spots before Socks found what he wanted, which was water deep enough for him to dunk his head and feet and wash away the vomit smell.

Dirt scrubbed the fresh coat of mud off, then unwound the cloth from around his chest and washed it out as well. It left a surprising amount of dirt behind in the water and came out a different color, more of an off-white color than the pale brown it had been before.

They rested on the banks, feeling more rejuvenated by the minute. Dirt asked the Home-staff for sap, and Home made enough for both of them to fill their bellies. They had no trouble keeping it down.

-Did you see that tower? Do you want to go look at it?-

"Yes, of course. It doesn't look like anything I remember, so I wonder if it's newer. But, wait! I just thought of something. Socks, guess what!"

-What?-

Dirt sent the pup a mental image from the woman, something she barely remembered but which they were looking for. It was small village, full of humans, with a huge stone tower in the middle. In her memory, it was gray and square, not white and round, but nonetheless, he had to wonder.

"Do you think it could be the same one, and her memory just got messed up because it was so long ago?"

-Maybe. If so, they are looking in the wrong place.-

"Well, no wonder the men are so mad at her, then."

-We can go look at it up close, and then we can ask them.-

"Yeah. Let's do that."

The two of them looked back toward the hills, thinking of the small valley and long mountain canyon beyond, and the humans far on the other side wandering through brush and rocks looking for something they would never find.

"I'm adding something to the plan. Let's go look at it first, and then I'll figure out how to make clothes. Then we'll go find the humans," said Dirt.

-Fine. But if this is the right place, how will we get them over here? I don't want to go back where those creatures were.-

"We'll figure it out. And when they see we took them where they wanted to go, they'll HAVE to like me. Both of us."

CHAPTER FIVE

The lines in the area around the tower turned out to be fencing made of old, crumbling wood—logs laid through x-shaped posts that had mostly collapsed. They cordoned off respectably large areas of irregular shape, now overgrown and lacking any obvious purpose.

Socks padded through at a slower pace, content to look at everything and take it easy, and that was fine with Dirt. It was an afternoon for relaxing, after the day they'd had so far.

Prisca had a clear memory from her youth of riding a horse through farmland, and it had looked something like this, even though it had been elsewhere. In contrast, though, the empire's fields were never so disorderly as this. The fields of the empire were all straight lines and deliberate curves, each field containing the same amount of ground. Nothing like here.

The farmland in her memory had been full of tall yellow grass that Dirt knew to be grain, even if he wasn't sure what it was good for. There was plenty of grass without having to mark off sections of ground and grow it on purpose. It wasn't good for eating; of that, he was sure. He'd tried.

Prisca had been feeling wealthy and joyous in that moment, but that just made all this dead land look more desolate in comparison. She had been feeling rich and journeying through healthy and well-maintained lands, and this was not that.

What might have once been ditches for irrigation were now shallow dips. Small houses—huts really—stood forlorn, half of them toppled to the ground, and the rest still coming apart. The tight thatch of their roofs was little more than rotted clumps of grass, where anything was left of it at all. The mud-and-wood walls fared a little better, but the rain would wash them away eventually. The wooden fences would rot, the uneven lines carving up the landscape would fade, and nothing would be left at all to say anyone had been here.

Except the tower. That still stood, sturdy as ever. The main door was missing and all the openings for windows were empty now, but the roof was intact, and its pale stones weren't going anywhere. It was a respectable size, though not as tall as Mother. As Socks took them closer, the number of fields decreased, and the houses multiplied. Some had sturdier walls and roofs of clay, and enough of them remained to tell that a fire had destroyed parts of the town.

Socks sniffed around at everything he found interesting, which was a growing number the farther they got, and Dirt was content to let him take his time, since he wanted to see everything too. Some of the decaying houses still had stuff in them—burned furniture, ancient piles of rags in places where water was less frequent. Rusted metal tools.

-This happened after Marina was here. How long ago do you think that was?-

"I don't know, but probably a long time. Her memory of it isn't very clear."

-I wonder how long it takes for things to rot this much. Is it a long time, or a short time?-

"Neither of us have been alive long enough to guess. But can you still smell the fire? What does it all smell like?"

Socks sniffed around again, poking his big nose through the window of a nearby house, then pulling it out and looking inside. *-Well, for one, I don't smell human anymore. Not anywhere, even the bones. Do you want to go in any of these houses?-*

Dirt leaned over, considering. *"I guess so. This place isn't from my humans, when I was alive last time. We never made stuff that looked like this. But I should still go see what there is to find."*

-If you are lucky, perhaps you will find some human clothes, and then you won't have to make them.-

"Really? Do you think so?"

-Not all of this is burned or rotted. I think whatever happened here was fast, and any who escaped didn't come back. Maybe they're all dead.-

"Well, if they stirred up all those digger creatures, then I wouldn't be surprised."

-You go in the houses, and I'll go look elsewhere. Don't get sad again and cry.-

"I won't," said Dirt, but Socks leaned down and licked his face anyway. Dirt patted him on the nose, then looked around for a likely house. The closest one had a mostly intact roof of clay tiles, making it as fine a choice as any.

Dirt stepped in through the doorway and found the door lying flat on the old wooden floor, a few steps inside. It had been smashed open, it seemed. Cracked and beaten before finally being knocked over.

The walls were white plaster, once, until the fires. And before the fires, something had marred them. Perhaps blood, perhaps something else. Dirt wondered if there had been a fight in here, or even just a slaughter. All the furniture was smashed, as if done on purpose, but most had survived the flames. Only the left side of the house had burned, leaving the rest of the house intact.

Dirt stepped out of the first room into the next one. It was smaller and full of shelves, all full of pottery and glass jars, none of them shattered. The ones he could identify were full of old dried fruit and vegetables, all gray with mold and decaying to dust. Still, some of the color remained on a few bits of old fruit, making Dirt wonder if it was still edible. He decided not to risk it. Socks had warned him about eating like a scavenger.

Other than that, the room was unremarkable except for two human skeletons, one adult and one child. Judging from the state of their bones, something violent had happened to them, but it was so long ago that Dirt almost didn't notice them lying there in the midst of all the other decaying garbage.

The next house was much like the previous one, and the one after that. Dirt found plenty of things that might have been useful if he were planning on staying or had some way of carrying everything. Hammers, awls, chisels, and larger tools he wasn't familiar with, some of them with little or no rust. Knives, but none of them as clean and perfect as the one he already had. Oil and lamps to burn it in. Candles. Flint and rusty iron that could still spark if Dirt scraped it enough.

Clothing, too. Every house had a spare set or two. Shoes and pants and shirts and plenty more uncut cloth besides, most of it damp and rotting with mold inside when he unfolded it. Well, if he didn't find any that were in good shape, one of those might do.

Most houses didn't have any dead in them, and never more than one or two. And most of the corpses Dirt found were skeletons, except a few who'd landed in dry spots and mummified instead. The clothing the dry ones had on was in even worse shape than the stuff on the shelves or in boxes. One particularly disappointing shirt was on a boy just his size, face dried and shriveled, eyes empty and teeth bare. It was all clean on the front, but when Dirt turned the corpse, it had rotted away completely underneath. Half a shirt.

Dirt decided the only truly interesting thing he would find here was clothing, and only if he was lucky, so he began tearing from house to house, looking for dry places and things unburned. He upended baskets and wicker chests, lifted fallen furniture, kicked through ashes.

Finally, *finally*, he found a single pair of pants that were small enough for him to put on. They were dusty with ash and had been partially buried under an old bed that had fallen in, covering it with straw. But when Dirt shook them out, their dark green color returned and revealed a decorative stripe of interlaced red boxes down the side of each leg. The rope belt sewn into the waist even had the knot still in it, and after picking at it a bit, Dirt learned the how to re-tie it.

He pulled them on, and his first thought was that the cloth was softer than ferns, but not as soft as puppy fur. He wouldn't wear them all the time. Only when other humans were around. He decided that immediately. They were also too long for him, and so baggy they'd never stay up if he didn't tie them tightly. Dirt took his knife and thought about cutting off the bottoms, but he'd regret losing that nice hem with its charming coloring. After a moment of thought, he rolled them up instead.

He finally had clothing, and it was in good repair. It wasn't even that old, really, not on the scale of things he was used to.

-Congratulations, little Dirt. Now you can toss that other cloth away because it still smells like those digger things. Get rid of it, and then come to the tower. I found out what happened to this place.-

Dirt obliged and untied the creature's rough cloth from around his torso, then tossed it with deliberate disdain into a moldy pile of old bedding. Then he grinned and ran, feeling how the cloth pants tugged his legs as he went. What a strange thing to do. Pants, of all things. Humans were silly.

The roads were only identifiable because they had nothing in them but grass, but that made easy running. Dirt reached the tower in an instant and went in through the large empty doorway to find Socks wagging his tail next to a pile of skulls.

-Goblins got them. Many goblins, I am sure. They brought all the heads and left them here.-

Dirt stepped over to the skull pile, which was almost as tall as he was. Hundreds. He almost wanted to count them to find out just how many people lived in a place like that, but decided against it. He wanted his new pants to stay clean for as long as possible.

"How do you know it was goblins?"

-Because of the dead goblins. Look, here and here.-

The goblin skeletons lying on the old, marred wood of the tower floor were impossible to mistake for human. For one, they were wider and thicker, and for two, the fangs gave it away.

"If this is all the heads, where are the rest of the bodies? And I found a bunch of skeletons with heads still on them."

-I don't know. Do you have another explanation?-

Dirt thought about it for a moment. *"I guess they took the rest of the bodies home to eat."*

-Oh. I bet you are right. So do you like your pants?-

He danced a bit to show them off, then said, *"They're okay. I just hope Marina and Hèctor and Ignasi like them."*

-They look looser and baggier than what those humans had on.-

"Yep. But I'll grow into them."

Other than the giant pile of skulls, the ground floor of the tower was a respectable chamber, or at least, it had been. Now it was largely empty, with a roof a couple feet above Socks's ears and three large fireplaces along the wall. Whatever furniture had been in here once was long since burned, along with the stairs to the next floor. The next floor itself, however, was still fine. They'd only succeeded in burning the stairs. It was possible the stairs had been torn down first, and burned second.

The wood floor was stained nearly black, and the more Dirt looked at it, the more he thought it was dried blood. So much of it that almost none of the floor was untouched. So much it must have been a pool deep enough to splash in. The majority of humans had probably been killed in here. They'd run in and hid, but the goblins had taken down the huge doors.

Dirt looked at the stairs again, wondering why everyone got killed here instead of up higher. Then he remembered something he'd hardly taken note of and ran back outside. Sure enough, the windows all had awnings to keep the rain out, and long streaks of black under each one told him the goblins had built fires on the outside. The smoke must have gone up into the windows and made it impossible to breathe, so the humans inside had to come down. That was his best guess, anyway.

Dirt went to the opening, stumbling through the half-burned chunks of wood in the pile, and jumped with mana. He shot up through the gap and landed on the bare edge, waving his arms to keep from falling back out. But Socks gave him a little push with his mind, and Dirt was safe.

The second floor was curiously untouched, compared to the lower floor. A stain of smoke and a layer of ash over everything hid the room's color beneath a coating of gray, but none of the furniture was smashed. Long streaks of black along the wood floor told him that a few stragglers might have been killed up here and then dragged down the stairs. If so, that confused the story he was trying to put together about what happened, but the room was otherwise tidy.

Desks and shelves filled the space, full of paper. Paper everywhere, all kinds of it. Dirt stepped over to a desk and picked some up and found it full of letters he couldn't read. He only recognized half of them, and nothing made sense, even when he tried comparing it to the new human language he'd been learning.

Each of the flat walls had a window in the center, which was the only light in the room. Sunrays shone in through the dusty air, illuminating the spots close enough to be damaged by years of wind and rain despite the stone awning. Most of the room was untouched, and for the first time in his life, Dirt truly felt like he was in a real human place. Not an old, lost place, preserved only in stone and memory, but an actual human place, separated from life and vibrancy by only a few short years.

Dirt walked over and sat in a chair, just tall enough for his toes to dangle. He leaned forward and rested his elbows on the table and wondered what a person who sat here might do all day. The wind didn't seem to touch this spot when it blew through the room, and the papers were stacked right where the last person had left them.

-You are looking at things up there, aren't you? Share your sight with me.-

Dirt quickly complied and went around looking at everything again, especially the papers. Socks was curious about all the little scribbles on them, and the furniture. Armrests on chairs, of all things, merited a great deal of his attention. Dirt found it all amusing and marched around examining things until they got bored. The stairs up to the third floor were intact, but creaked when Dirt went up them.

-The stairs farted,- said Socks, which got an out-loud bellow of laughter from Dirt.

"I guess you have one thing in common with stairs, then. You both fart when I get on you."

Then he had to make the stair squeak over and over again and laugh, accompanied by waves of deep amusement from the pup.

The third floor wasn't open like the lower two—the stairs ended at a door, which opened easily when Dirt turned the latch. It opened inward, not toward the stairs, and a sturdy wooden post leaned on the wall beside the doorframe. Dirt stepped inside and shut the door to get a closer look. Iron hooks in the doorframe made a place to put the post and hold the door shut. He even lifted it, heavy enough he needed to use mana, and dropped it in place. The door wasn't opening with that there. So had the people up here been smoked out? Or had there been some who waited out the attack and left afterward?

Beyond the door was a hallway with a lower ceiling than the floors below. Six doors lined the hallway, three on each side. Four of them opened to bedrooms, perfectly untouched. The doors had been shut during the fire and stayed that way ever since. The two bedrooms with windows were musty but still livable, and the two without windows were fresh as the night of the massacre.

With shaking hands, Dirt removed his pants, pulled away the blanket from a bed, and prepared to climb in. For reasons he couldn't explain, it made him incredibly nervous. Like he wasn't supposed to be there.

Not allowed. Not his place. Dirt was a wild creature and belonged huddled on the ground, not resting on clean sheets and a comfortable mattress in a safe room atop a stone tower.

Dirt opened a bit more of his mind and shared his sense of touch, along with his sight. That was somewhat more involved and would result in a headache again if they kept it up, but for just a moment, Socks got to find out what it was like to be a human going to bed.

He climbed into bed slowly, sliding his bare skin across the gentle cloth. The soft sheets smelled like linen and dust, a strong, clean, welcoming scent that tickled his nose. He laid his head on the pillow and pulled the blanket up to his chin and immediately warmed right up. The heavy blanket pressed down on every inch of him, holding him tight.

-Are we going to take a nap? Because I'm still down here with nothing but a pile of skulls,- said Socks, trying to hide his envy.

"No, I just wanted to see what it was like."

-It always feels weird that you have no fur.-

"If I had fur, I wouldn't be able to feel the cloth."

-Well, that does seem comfortable. Not all human things are silly, I suppose. Beds are not silly.-

"Someday, I'll have humans make you one. A great big one, just for you."

-Come down, if you are going to. I think I do want to take a nap.-

Dirt ended the sharing of his senses and slid back out of bed. He carefully spread the blanket back how he found it, even and free of any wrinkles. He tossed his pants over his shoulder instead of putting them back on and made his way down to Socks without checking the other rooms. There might be more things here he'd want to see, and maybe they could even stay for a few days until the Devourer got close to finding Socks again.

But for now, he had more important things to do. He and Socks left the tower to find a shady spot in an overgrown field just outside of town where they settled in for a nap. The nap was a long one, and when Socks woke first and licked Dirt awake, the sun was slipping toward the western mountains.

-Are we going to try and find the humans now? Or wait until morning?-

"Well, after that nap, we won't be sleeping anytime soon. Let's go find them. You'll be fine seeing if it gets dark, right?"

Socks huffed in feigned indignation and tossed Dirt up onto his back, staff, pants, and all. Then he took off at a run, excited about the coming dusk and cooling air. They raced across the valley at high speed, too fast to examine anything they passed.

Their path went around the mountain peak claimed by the digger-beasts and missed the canyon with the stream entirely. Socks had great fun leaping downhill at top speed, so happy in midair with the wind in his face he may as well have been born a bird. Dirt enjoyed it slightly less, since it always seemed like he was about to drop something, but he still whooped in excitement at the incredible distances the pup could cover with a single downhill jump.

The path through the mountains to the previous valley was long enough that night fell before they reached it, and Dirt declined sharing their sight. He was content to watch the stars above come out as the cloudless sky moved from blue to purple to black. The Home-staff gave him a dinner of sap, which he chewed thoughtfully as he stared upward.

In the daytime, the sky seemed an empty void that could yank him up to hurtle forever into emptiness, but at night, the stars made the sky feel closer. The lights were still impossibly distant, but there was a limit to them. If something flung him upward at night, he wouldn't fall forever. He would land on whatever was holding them up.

Down here on the ground, there was very little for Dirt to see, but Socks had no trouble and hardly slowed down. The starlight was enough for him, coupled with his senses of smell and hearing. Dirt watched the pup's mind from time to time, always enjoying how vivid it was, with so much more sensory information than Dirt took in. And underneath it all, that tug northward that he hadn't known about before, directing Socks anywhere he wanted to go.

The pup smelled the humans fairly close to the stream and followed their trail from there to a little campsite they set up. He approached close enough for Dirt to smell the smoke from their campfire and hear them arguing.

"Fa setmanes que no he vist ni una pista de cérvol. Què menjarem quan ens quedi sense pa?" Hèctor was saying, his voice raised. Something about not seeing tracks for a while, and *What are we going to eat when the bread is gone?*

Marina shot back, "No ho sé, Hèctor. Troba una altra cosa. Sé que estem a prop de la torre. Hem de ser. Reconec aquestes muntanyes. Conec aquestes plantes. És només una mica més lluny." *I don't know. Find something else. We are close to the tower, something about mountains and plants. Something farther.*

Socks said, *-Wait, Dirt. Let's get them some birds to eat. If you want someone to like you, you should give them food.-*

"Oh, that's a good idea. Can you smell any? And by the way, I'll give you more sap for dinner when you're ready."

The pup crept silently away from the camp, leaving them to argue. He sniffed all around until he found a scent he'd passed up earlier—birds big enough to bother with, the size of Dirt's forearm. He crept up to the nest, which was tucked away in some bushes where Dirt would have trouble climbing in. The pup's long legs simply took them over the worst of the tangle.

-Here.-

Dirt slid down, landing loudly and shaking a bunch of leaves. The birds immediately flapped their wings to escape, but Socks hit them with a wave of mental force and knocked them from the air. Even though they were white, Dirt had to feel around until he found them, and he decided four was enough since he didn't need any.

He pulled his pants on, tied the rope belt, then jumped back up.

Socks carried him back to the camp, and Dirt slid off his back, all four dead birds tucked under one arm and the Home-staff in the other. He braced himself, taking a deep breath.

The humans fell silent all at once. Dirt almost panicked, thinking they'd spotted him before he was ready. He hadn't even thought of what to say yet.

But it wasn't him they'd seen. Socks could smell their fresh terror, and in their minds, Dirt found two huge glowing eyes staring down from the darkness. Oh, they'd just seen Socks's eyes reflecting the firelight. Thank Grace!

Dirt walked toward the camp, only a couple dozen paces. He strode with forced calm and fearlessness until he was well within the firelight.

The three humans were too terrified to move. They were like prey that hoped the predator would move on if they played dead.

He took another step closer, close enough to start feeling the heat from the little fire. "Hola. Crec que estàs perdut," he said. "Tens gana?" *Hello, I think you are lost. Are you hungry?*

He smiled warmly, held the birds toward them, and waited for their reply.

CHAPTER SIX

The three humans stared dumbfounded until Dirt got uncomfortable just standing there. But he wasn't going to give up already, so he stepped close and sat down by the fire, keeping a nervous eye on it to make sure it stayed inside the ring of stones.

Marina was the closest, and she shied away from him, scooting backward while trying not to make it obvious.

"No tinc por," said Dirt. *I'm not scary.* At least, that's what he hoped he said. It was a little ambiguous. But he smiled and twisted the head off one of the birds, since there was nothing edible on them, and tore the skin off it with his teeth and fingers. Then he held it out to Marina, licking the blood off his teeth. She kept her hands down and didn't take it from him.

Socks stepped fully into the light and sniffed the three humans, but not right up close, since they wouldn't appreciate that. *-They smell hungry.-*

"En Socks no fa por," said Dirt. *Socks isn't scary either.* Probably what he said. "I tampoc os vol menjar." *Or want to eat you.*

Ignasi absentmindedly tugged his short, dark beard and said, "Pren-ho, Marina. No els volem ofendre." *We don't want . . . something.*

"Què se suposa que n'he de fer amb aixo?" she replied, somewhere between horror and disgust. *What am I supposed to do with it?*

"Es menjar!" said Dirt, gentle laughter in his voice. Gods in Glory, what was wrong with these people? He held the skinless bird in his teeth and tossed the other three to the humans, one each. They caught them, thankfully. Then he took his bird, gripped it in both hands, and bit deep into the guts, sucking them out and swallowing them whole. "Menja-t'ho!" *Eat it!*

Socks leaned down and licked the blood from Dirt's face and said, *-Be careful. You are getting dirty.-*

"Oops, I forgot. Thanks! Are you going to talk to them, too?"

-No. I want them to talk to you instead.-

"Dirt," said Hèctor, almost correctly.

"Si! Dirt," said Dirt, pointing at himself. "Ets Hèctor, Ignasi, Marina." Then he pointed up at Socks and said, "Socks. És amic meu." *He's my friend.*

"Dirt, on són els teus pares?" *Where are your something?*

"Pares?" said Dirt, unsure what that word meant.

Marina saw his confusion and said, "Pares. Mare. Pare."

"Oh!" He knew what they were asking. Where were his parents? "No tinc pares. Tinc arbres i llops." *I don't have parents. I have trees and wolves.*

Hèctor asked, "Estàs sol aquí fora? On és la teva tribu?" *Are you alone . . . Where is your tribe?*

"No tinc una tribu. Però no estic sol. Tinc a Socks. I tinc a Home," he said, pointing at Socks and the Home-staff lying on the ground beside him. *I have no tribe. But I'm not alone. I have Socks and Home.* He took another bite from the breast-meat and chewed it slowly, pushing it around with his tongue and enjoying the flavor.

"Home?" asked Marina.

Dirt lifted the staff with one hand to give her a better look. "Forma part de Home. Ella és un arbre. També amiga meva." *This is part of Home, who is a tree and my friend.*

Marina said, "El teu amic . . . és un pal?" *Your friend is a stick?*

Socks huffed in deep amusement and wagged his tail, which got a grin out of Dirt as well. But for Marina, he didn't need to look at her mind to see her pity growing. It was clear on her face, and seeing it made him unable to laugh.

"No, Home és un arbre gran, gran, gran. Més gran que . . . aquella muntanya," he said, pointing at the mountain. *Home is a big, big, big tree. Bigger than the mountain.*

The humans didn't seem to believe him, and Dirt didn't trust his language skills to explain more fully. So he resorted to taking another bite and chewing thoughtfully. He wasn't even hungry, and the more he ate the less he wanted to continue, but he wasn't sure what else to do.

Finally, Ignasi took out a smaller knife he had tucked in his belt and began preparing his own bird, and soon after, Marina and Hèctor followed suit.

Socks said, -*They haven't said anything about your pants.*- He huffed again and gave a tiny growl, not menacing at all. He still found the whole situation hilarious, but the humans didn't know him. They froze, suddenly full of fear again. No, they'd been full of fear the whole time; it was just that they'd been able to ignore it and start calming down.

Dirt hurriedly reached back and patted Socks on the side of his nose and smiled. "Socks vol . . . saber si . . . t'agraden . . . els meus pantalons." *Socks wants to know if you like my pants.*

"Si," said Marina. "Molt bonics."

"Aquesta és . . . la meva primera roba," said Dirt. *This is my first clothes.*

The humans weren't sure what to make of that, but they did seem relieved that Socks wasn't mad at them.

Dirt watched with curiosity as they discarded the guts into the fire, which he didn't mind, since it wasn't the best part anyway. But then, instead of just eating like normal, they broke sticks off a nearby bush, sharpened them, and skewered their dinner. Then they held the bird over the fire. Dirt almost jumped forward to stop them, suddenly angry they'd go through so much trouble just to spite a gift from him and Socks, but they didn't toss the birds *into* the fire. Just over it.

He looked back at Socks, and the pup said, -*I have no idea what they are doing. But if they burn those birds, I am not getting them any new ones.*-

Dirt stared as they watched for something about the meat to change, but it wasn't clear what. Aside from paying attention to the food, the rest of their minds were full of spinning ideas and words that Dirt could hardly follow. Still afraid, though. They were still terrified. He couldn't blame them, since the first time he saw Socks he'd been so scared he peed, but he also didn't know if there was anything he could do to help them relax. They'd just have to get used to having him and the big pup around.

He still had half of his bird left, so he went to take another bite. But Ignasi stopped him, reaching for it and saying, "Aquí, deixa que jo també cuini el teu." *Here, let me something yours.*

Dirt hesitantly handed it over, and the bearded man stuck it on the end of the same stick he was already using. Then he held both birds over the fire while Dirt watched with growing anxiety that it would taste like ashes now.

After a moment, Socks stood and sniffed close to the fire. *-You can smell that too, right? They're burning it, but in a different way.-*

Dirt lifted his nose and sniffed around as well, and now that the pup pointed it out, a new scent rested on the air. It reminded him of something burned alive by Socks's flames, but without all the sickly sharpness. There was no burning hair, for one, and that made a huge difference.

The moon peeked out over the mountains to the east, smaller than it had been last night. Socks noticed it and stood. He filled his cavernous lungs and gave a long, mournful howl, which rose to the sky and filled the whole valley. Everyone paused and listened for a reply, but none came. Socks howled again, just as sincerely. No answer.

"I didn't hear anyone. Did you?" asked Dirt.

-No. It is strange to be away from wolves for so long.-

"Do you feel lonely?"

-Not yet. And in another month or two it will be time to return. Once each season.-

"Yep. Are we going to let Home bring us with root travel, or do you think you'll want to run?"

-I don't know. It will depend on whether we see the Devourer or not. If he's close, then I will not dare run.-

Everyone fell into a reverent silence after that, the humans watching the fire and Socks gazing up at the moon and stars, even though he couldn't see the details on something that far away. He just enjoyed the light.

Dirt found himself shying away from looking at the humans' minds too much, because now that he was so close and could see it all so clearly, all three of them were beset with deeply personal worries. It felt like an invasion of their privacy. Hèctor still had a mate at home, a *dona*, and he was remembering a hundred things about her. Her voice, her hair, their arguments, mating with her. They seemed to have a bad relationship, but not always. Ignasi had no one waiting for him, but thought about his animals and wondered if they were being fed. He thought about a woman and wished he had taken her as his mate. His *dona.*

Marina had no thoughts of home, but sent her mind back over and over into her childhood, people she hadn't seen in many years.

Dirt quit looking. Until just now, he'd forgotten about privacy entirely. He had no need for it so far, except a few rare times when he wanted to be alone out of sheer weariness. What was the point of privacy around Socks, or Callius or Home? Or Mother? Imagine even *trying* to hide something from Mother.

But there were things he didn't want the humans to know yet, like that he had mana, or that he could see their thoughts. Influence them, too, if he tried. Probably. Maybe someday he'd want to, like if someone was trying to hurt him, but right now, he wanted to prove that he could live among humans as a human.

Ignasi pulled his birds from over the fire and looked at them, poking the roasting flesh here and there. He didn't see what he was looking for and put them back to keep going.

Dirt asked, "Una pregunta. Per què esteu aquí?" *I want to ask, why are you here?*

Marina was the one who answered. "Estem buscant alguna cosa. Hi havia un poble on vaig viure quan era petita i està molt lluny. El lloc on vivim ara s'està tornant insegur i potser necessitem una nova llar. Potser si el meu vell poble i el meu nou s'ajunten, podrem sobreviure una estona més."

She talked fast enough that Dirt couldn't quite follow everything, but he already knew what they were looking for, so it didn't matter. They were looking for something, a town she lived in as a child. Something about unsafe, and if they find it, perhaps they will survive longer. Something like that.

Dirt said, "No conec cap . . . poble, però sé on hi ha . . . una torre blanca. És sobre aquestes muntanyes." *I don't know any towns, but I know of a white tower. It's over those mountains.*

The three humans' eyes shot to his face, expressions suddenly focused. "Torre blanca?" asked Marina, trying to sound gentler than she probably felt.

"Si, torre blanca. Podem anar, però tu has de caminar. Socks no et portarà." *Yes, a white tower. We can go there but you will have to walk.*

Socks won't carry you. "És la torre el que esteu buscant?" *Is the tower what you are looking for?* Dirt asked hesitantly, not sure how to tell them everyone was dead.

"No, està en camí. Però si trobem la torre, no estem perduts. Des d'allà el puc trobar," said Marina in a rush, her hands shaking and making the bird tap against the burning wood. *No, but it's on the way. If we find the tower we are not lost. From there we can find . . . him? It?*

Dirt smiled, eager. They finally saw him as useful, so that was a good first step. Now, they could all go together to the final destination, and they'd introduce Dirt to everyone, and he would be friends with a hundred humans all at once. He said, "Tothom a la torre . . . està mort. Però trobarem el teu poble . . . i allí seran . . . vius." *Everyone at the tower is dead, but we will find your town, where they are alive.*

That was the wrong thing to say, though. Marina gasped, and both of the men tightened their grips on their sticks and got a hard look in their eyes.

Ignasi asked, "Mort? Tothom?"

Dirt looked down, already feeling his plans dripping away. He hoped he hadn't completely ruined it. "Sí, tothom. Ho sento." *Yes, everyone. Sorry.*

From nearby, an owl hooted loudly, and everyone turned to try to find it in the darkness. Except Socks, who could hear exactly where it was and didn't need to.

Marina asked, "És per això que estàs sol?" *Is that why you are alone?*

"No."

Dirt looked at each of their faces in turn and already second-guessed his decision not to look at their minds. He could tell just by looking at them that they were deep in thought, their hearts filling with a dozen new concerns. And he could guess what ones: How did they all die? Is anything left? When did it happen? What about the town?

But rather than peek and know for certain, he decided to wait and see what thoughts they voiced. Until then, he could be patient.

They didn't ask him anything else, though, which surprised him. Instead, they waited until their birds were burned up enough, and once satisfied, Ignasi held the stick toward Dirt, then thought better of it and pulled it back again. He found a second stick, a smaller one, and stuck Dirt's bird on *that,* and handed it over.

Dirt took the stick and held the meat to his nose and gave it a good long sniff, filling his nostrils with a delightful scent. The heat radiating off the cooked meat and bones warmed his face in a pleasant way, and he decided he was hungry after all.

Before he took a bite, though, he held it over for Socks to smell. The pup gave it several long sniffs, then raised his head and let his tongue loll out. *-Share your taste.-*

"Of course!" Dirt obliged and that part of their minds slid together. He gingerly took a bite of roasted flesh, a small one so he wouldn't burn his tongue. Then another, bigger bite, and another, until his cheeks were stuffed. *"It tastes different, but there's a lot more flavor now. I think I like it. What about you, Socks?"*

-I think I want enough for me to taste by myself. I might come back with twenty birds,- replied the pup, joking. Mostly.

Dirt laughed, which got surprised looks from the humans. He hurried to explain, "Socks vol provar-ne. Va dir que . . . tornarà amb molts ocells. Però era una broma." *Socks wants to try some, and he said he will come back with many birds. But it was a joke.*

Hèctor carefully asked, "Com saps el que ha dit?" *How do you know what he said?*

Dirt should've seen this coming and had an answer ready. Should he just tell them now that he could see minds, and that's how he and Socks talked? No. He didn't know what they'd think about that. Until he knew, he wouldn't say. He blurted out the first thing that came to his mind. "Puc parlar amb animals." *I can talk to animals.*

The humans nodded and went back to eating, and Dirt breathed a sigh of relief. They kept an eye on him, though, glancing up every now and then at him and Socks, still unsure quite what to make of them. Well, that was fine. They'd get to know him better over time. They would be a lot easier to get to know than the dryads had been.

Dirt was pleased that he was communicating so well, though. He felt like he learned a new word every single sentence. He'd been expecting it to be harder. A few more days, and it might be as natural as his real language.

After everyone was finished with their dinner, they unrolled blankets from their packs and tucked themselves in, fully clothed. Marina slept on the end, and Ignasi was in the middle.

Socks lay down, and Dirt took his accustomed place nestled in against the pup's neck. As they drifted off to sleep, Socks said, *-I want humans to put a whole bull on a fire for me.-*

Dirt smiled and patted his fur. *"The first one we see, I'll make them do it."*

The next morning, Socks and Dirt woke much later than the humans and found them quietly waiting, all packed up and ready to go. The sun wasn't quite up over the mountains yet, but the dawn was bright and probably had been for a while.

Marina smiled and brushed some brown hair out of her eyes. "Are you ready to go?" she asked, in their language.

"Not yet. I want to eat first," replied Dirt, pleased that it was becoming ever more natural to him. It seemed that conversing last night had caused a hundred little pieces to all slide together while he was dreaming, leaving him with a more complete picture of their language than when he went to sleep.

He crawled out from his little nest in Socks's neck fur and stretched. He stepped a few paces away so it wouldn't splash on anything and peed, then came back to the empty ash pit and sat down. The three humans were hiding half-smiles, amused at something he couldn't guess. But they didn't choose to share so he didn't peek at their minds. In fact, he would have to be careful not to admit knowing things he could only learn that way, or they'd figure it out.

In his language, Dirt told the staff, "Good morning, Home. I hope you slept well. Are you awake yet? Can I have some sap?" He hugged it, and while it wasn't the same as her dryad, it would have to do. And sure enough, soon after, she made a big glob of sap for him, which he pulled off and started chewing. "Can you please make some for Socks, too? I'll wake him up in a minute."

The sap for Socks had to be made in sections, since it got too big and bulky to carry. Once the first bit was done, a round ball bigger than Dirt's torso too heavy to lift without mana, Dirt gave the pup's mind a gentle push to wake him up. Without even opening his eyes, Socks opened his mouth, and Dirt threw the sap in. Then he sat back down and waited for the next glob.

The humans were very curious about all this, watching without trying to hide their amazement. Maybe they just didn't know anything about trees, though, because sap wasn't a strange thing at all. They did let Home fill up their waterskins, though, once they saw that she could make water as well.

After breakfast, Dirt decided to walk instead of ride, since he'd do a better job keeping pace for the humans than Socks would. Dirt led the group, and Socks walked behind, content to smell them and anything else interesting while he kept watch.

There was very little chatter because it turned out that walking straight up a mountainside was tiring for normal humans, who had no mana to burn to make it easy. Dirt could sympathize, too, since it hadn't been that long since Home made him run up all those stairs. But they didn't complain and followed Dirt right up into a canyon between two flat peaks and into the mountains proper.

Dirt wasn't used to traveling so slowly. He'd run everywhere even before he got mana, but the adults would never stand a chance keeping up if he did that. They had those heavy packs to carry, after all, and he just had pants, a knife, and a staff. And a colorful rock when he saw one, and a shiny green beetle, until it flew away.

When Dirt found a second colorful rock, this one pure white and round, unlike anything else nearby, Marina must have seen him trying to decide whether to keep it or not. She said, "Why don't you put it in your *butxaca*?"

"My what?" he asked.

She took the white rock from his hand and found a fold of cloth on the side of his pants, up near the top, and pulled it open. She dropped it in and patted it. "Butxaca."

Dirt looked down and patted it himself, amazed. He'd had no idea! Pockets. These pants had pockets, and he hadn't noticed.

Socks walked up and leaned directly over Marina to get a look, which made her freeze and try to hide her sudden terror.

-Now I wish I had some of those.-

"You would look silly in pants," said Dirt.

Socks huffed in amusement. *-That isn't stopping you. And I could wear two pairs.-*

Dirt laughed as they shared that mental image back and forth. "He says he wants pants now, too, so he can have pockets," said Dirt in their language, but from their expressions, that didn't clear anything up.

He shrugged, and they kept going.

Socks and Dirt took a nap in the middle of the day like they always did and had a lunch of sap. The adults munched on some more of their dwindling supply of bread, and Dirt resolved to help find something to cook for dinner that night.

Traveling in the mountains was slow. Even when they could follow a game trail, just the fact of going uphill made Dirt's feet drag and shortened his steps, and it was worse for the adults, who had no mana to burn. Dirt wondered if he could teach them to use it somehow, but then he remembered what it had taken for *him* to learn and decided against even mentioning it.

That evening Socks killed a hunting cat and brought it to cook. Dirt made sure they gave Socks all the guts to eat, and then cooked the rest. The four humans only ate about a third of the roasted meat, and Socks got the rest. He was about to swallow the whole thing in one bite, but then he paused and looked up into the distance. A moment later, he wagged his tail happily and looked more relaxed.

-Mother says not to eat the bones. Cooked bones will hurt my stomach until I am older.-

"She's watching still?"

-Yes.-

"I'm glad. I guess they're not so far away after all, sort of like Home."

Dirt took out his knife and started carving the meat from the bones, explaining that cooked bones weren't good for Socks. Ignasi started helping with his knife, and Dirt couldn't help but compare the two. Dirt's was far, far nicer, flawless and sharp with a gently curving blade. Ignasi's was smaller, less gracefully designed, and losing its edge.

The next day proceeded much the same, trudging up and down mountains, following canyons in and out, clambering over boulders and around bushes and trees. One place was nicer than the rest, with a soft floor and pines tall enough for Socks to walk through underneath and enjoy the shade.

Late in the afternoon, Socks suddenly barked, loud enough for it to echo off the peaks and come back down into the dry canyon they were in.

-I smelled goblins. I think there are some around.-

Dirt opened his mind-sight and kept walking, looking for anything around that could be dangerous. Sure enough, after another couple thousand steps, he found a sizable group of them gathered somewhere nearby, eager and waiting. Their minds were full of anticipation and hunger and from what they were looking at, they seemed to have set up a hasty ambush not much farther up the canyon. He wondered if they'd been there all day, waiting for a deer or something, or if they'd known Dirt and his little group were coming.

"They're up there, I think, just over those rocks."

-I know. I can hear them already.-

"What are we going to do about it?"

-I'll take care of these ones. You just wait here. It'll be fun.-

"Okay."

The pup leaped over Dirt and the humans and raced at full speed up the canyon. After walking so slowly for this long, Socks seemed shockingly fast, and Dirt felt a pang of envy that he had to wait here. A moment later, countless screams rose on the air, high-pitched and full of fury.

"Socks found some . . . they are green, and this tall, and shaped like humans," said Dirt, halfway into the sentence before he realized he didn't know the word.

"Goblins," said Hèctor.

"Goblins," said Marina, quieter.

"Si, goblins!" said Dirt, happily. "But Socks will take care of them. He is ready to have fun."

The four humans watched up the canyon and listened as the high-pitched screams of anger became fear and pain and were silenced one by one.

CHAPTER SEVEN

Dirt tried counting the goblin minds, but Socks killed them too fast. It seemed every time Dirt made a couple groups of five, Socks killed three or four, and Dirt had to start over. The pup was having a great time, jumping from spot to spot and landing claws first. He didn't even use his mind to rip them apart, preferring to do it directly.

Some he gripped in his teeth and threw high enough that they screamed, inhaled, and screamed again before they landed. Dirt felt the thud in his chest when they hit the ground. Others, he gripped and shook violently until they quit moving. His front and back claws were longer and thicker than Dirt's forearm, and that was plenty to dispatch a goblin.

By the time he was done, his front was bloody from paws to ears, and his hind legs all the way up to his torso. Indeed, there was very little of his gray fur that didn't sparkle red in the sunlight as he happily trotted back.

Dirt grinned and told him, *"Now who's the dirty one! Where are you even going to clean off?"*

Socks looked pleased as ever, tongue lolling out and panting from the exercise. He picked up Dirt with his mind and licked him from stomach to eyebrows, leaving him pink with bloody froth. Dirt laughed and twisted in the air, trying uselessly to get away.

-Uh oh. You got messy again. I'll have to lick you clean,- said Socks.

Dirt squealed as Socks licked him thoroughly, since something about it made Dirt feel more ticklish than normal. *"Don't lick my pants! I just got them!"*

-I'm not.-

Dirt kept squirming and trying to shuffle off Socks's mental grasp, to no avail.

-It's more fun when you hate it.-

"I don't hate it! I love it! Keep going! No, stop!" He laughed so hard he started coughing, and only then did Socks finally set him down.

The humans were too stunned to speak. They looked scared, too, which Dirt found surprising. They were trying to hide it, but Dirt could still tell. But why? What was there to be scared of?

Socks had killed goblins. That was a good thing. And then he'd proven he was friendly by licking Dirt all over. What more could they want? He was tempted to look at their minds again but resolved to figure it out without looking. He almost did—he still had words to learn, after all, but decided not to. Better to see what they did first.

Dirt turned and patted Socks's nose, never mind the blood. "Don't fear him. He is my friend. Isn't he . . . *bonic?"* He wanted to say "cute" but the only word he knew that was close was "beautiful."

Hèctor swallowed with a dry throat and said, "Very beautiful. Dirt, pots volar?"

Dirt tilted his head. *"Volar?"*

"Si, volar. Pots volar?" Hèctor flapped his hands like a bird.

"Volar?" said Dirt, mimicking the motion. "No. I can't fly. Socks lifted me up. Oh, is that why you are . . ." He couldn't think of a fitting word so he stood rigid, eyes wide, trying to look stunned.

He must have looked silly because Ignasi laughed, a throaty, rasping sound that added to his rough charm. "Boys do not fly, in our experience. And wolves are not so big. Però ens hi acostumarem."

Dirt didn't catch that last bit, *we will something.* It was too late to look at his mind and figure out what he meant. But Socks never stopped reading them, apparently, and said, *-It means "get used to it."-*

"Ah!" said Dirt aloud, nodding. "Si, us acostumareu. Però no puc volar." *Yep, you'll get used to it. But I can't fly.*

Dirt looked at them, trying to decide if he'd already made a huge mistake. How was he supposed to know what was normal? Did they not have anything where they lived that could lift something with its mind?

After an awkward moment of the humans standing there blankly looking at each other unsure how to proceed, Ignasi patted his companions on the back and said, "Come, Marina, Hèctor. Let's keep going." The man seemed full of an odd sort of good humor that resonated with Dirt. It felt like the amusement of giving up and letting fate win.

"Through that?" said Marina, pointing at the carnage-filled area just up the canyon.

Ignasi didn't reply, since the answer was obvious. Instead, he gestured to Dirt, urging him forward with a wry, toothy grin behind his beard.

Dirt nodded, readjusting the strap holding the knife sheath under his armpit. He pulled his pants up a little and redid the knot, which was coming loose after being tossed around by Socks.

Then they were off, making their way up the canyon. The fight had taken place in a small, round cavity, a little meadow that looked like part of the mountain had been scooped out to leave a hollow. Socks had made a tremendous mess, one which filled Dirt with admiration. Dozens of goblins had been waiting, and now it looked like the area had been painted with them. Bits of innards hung from trees with split corpses underneath. Not a single one remained intact. Many were torn in half at the stomach, connected at surprising distances by thin ropes of entrails. Others were simply dismembered, losing arms, legs, or heads in the process. He'd even gone back for the ones he'd thrown into the air, grinding them apart against the ground.

Anything Socks had picked up, he'd shaken violently, flinging blood into even the most surprising places. Under leaves, on the *backs* of trees somehow. The ground was muddy in places and sticky in others and finding places to step where Dirt wouldn't get his pants messy was no easy task. The stench of the place was so strong that even Dirt felt the heady rush of too many scents at once. Innards, blood, sweat, feces, rot, fear, and pain, which he was sure he could smell himself.

He grinned widely and told Socks, *"It looks like you had fun."*

-I did.-

Marina gagged loudly behind him, trying not to vomit. Dirt turned, confused, to find her and Hèctor looking visibly ill. He glanced at their minds, and a wave of nausea hit him. They were so filled with horror and disgust they could hardly walk. Except Ignasi, who was still riding on a rapidly fading wave of good humor. He'd noticed how amused Dirt was, and it made him as uncomfortable as the indistinguishable bits of goblin dripping from the trees did.

Dirt was more confused than anything. "Why are you . . . like that? It is just goblins," he asked. "Are you not happy they are dead?"

Marina coughed and dry heaved, then closed her eyes and leaned on Hèctor, who fared just as poorly. Ignasi looked pale but collected and said, "This is not an easy sight. I have never seen so much blood."

Hèctor said, "It's the smell. The smell is too much." Talking proved to have been a bad idea, and the man gagged and spat out a mouthful of vomit.

Dirt had made another mistake. He should've asked if they wanted to go around, and now it was too late. They were in the middle of it, and the only way out was forward. But again, how was he supposed to know? It was just blood. They were just goblins.

"Does this help?" asked Dirt. He inhaled a large amount of mana and called up some wind like the dryads had taught him. He waved the staff and made it blow down from higher up the mountain, carrying the scent out of the little divot-meadow and away. "Let's hurry, and then you won't smell it anymore at all."

Dirt danced through the carnage to keep his pants clean and led the humans forward while the ever-amused Socks followed behind. He didn't understand what the problem was any more than Dirt did, but he thought it was funny to find yet another way in which humans were fragile.

The wind helped, and Dirt didn't feel bad in the slightest looking at their minds to know for sure. All three of them were wondering if he'd made the wind, directed it, or simply detected it was about to start blowing. Despite Socks saving them from having to kill the goblins themselves, the humans were less confident about Dirt than before.

The terrain got rougher after that as they exited the top of the canyon and had to trudge up a steep incline toward the top of the mountain. Dirt decided not to fill his legs with mana and make it easy, out of sympathy for the other humans who didn't know how. He didn't want to get too far ahead of them or make another mistake.

Walking straight uphill was not easy, though, and his legs burned. Sweat poured down his face and torso and quickly evaporated in the brightening morning sunlight. Looking back, the humans were having no easier time. Hèctor seemed to be the strongest of them, and periodically he helped Marina cross unsure ground or gave Ignasi a hand to pull him up a rock. Dirt hoped they noticed he was tired, too, just like them.

When they finally reached the crest of the mountains, finally able to enjoy the flat terrain between the two closest peaks, everyone but Socks was ready for a break. Dirt wiped sweat from his forehead and chest and licked it, enjoying the salty flavor.

Socks helped him with that by licking him front and back. The big pup liked the salt as well, and that was the only place to get any. Then, fortunately for the others, he smelled water and left with a tremendous sudden leap to go find it and wash off. The blood would have worked its way out of his fur over a couple days, and in the meantime, Socks enjoyed being smelly. That meant that going to wash it off was an act of consideration, and Dirt resolved to thank him later.

The humans were visibly relieved to have Socks gone, which made Dirt feel slightly affronted. Or maybe just disappointed. But he said nothing. Instead, he smiled and said, "That was hard!"

"We usually like to go around instead of over," said Ignasi, still breathing heavy.

Marina dropped her pack and sat on it with her head in her hands. Looking at her mind, Dirt saw she still felt sick and couldn't stop thinking about the gore. He considered trying to nudge her thoughts elsewhere but decided against it. She might notice.

Ignasi and Hèctor sat on either side of her, resting on their own packs, and Dirt found a patch of dry straw to sit on. The three humans drank sips of water from their pouches and breathed deeply. Looking at their minds, they were trying to wash away the memory and quell their own nausea. Marina had it the worst, since the men enjoyed the scenery here more than she did. Up here between the peaks, with the distant mountain ranges and long canyons, the slopes carpeted in pines, the grand distances stretching into eternity in every direction, every sight was wondrous. It invigorated them and filled their hearts with beauty. But not Marina. She didn't appreciate it in the same way.

"Home," he asked the staff in his language, "can you make some sap for Marina? She's not feeling well."

But instead of producing it like he expected, the staff made some tiny white threads like the dryads had used to explore his anatomy. The threads pointed toward Marina, pulsing at her. "Oh, you want to take a look at her insides?" he asked, still in his language. Maybe it was a good thing they couldn't understand it.

The threads pulsed again, almost eagerly. "Okay. But you have to promise not to hurt her or make her feel worse. And don't snatch her with root travel. The men would be scared, and so would she."

Dirt stood and stepped politely over to Marina. In their language, he said, "Marina, this wood is part of a big tree. Remember I told you the tree is my friend? The tree wants you to hold this. Will you hold this? Don't be scared. Nothing bad will happen. I think she wants to help you. She is nice." He struggled to put so many sentences together, but keeping them all simple helped. He held the staff out for Marina to take.

The poor woman looked up and gave him a withering look of exasperation.

"I am sorry. I know you feel bad inside," said Dirt. "It makes me sad. I am trying to make you happy."

"Just hold it, Marina," said Hèctor, eyes showing more caution than his voice. "Who knows what other surprises he has for us." He said *sorpreses*, but Dirt was sure it meant surprises.

"I can't handle any more surprises," she muttered. But she took the staff and sat back, holding it across her lap.

"Hands . . . tight," said Dirt, indicating how he wanted her to grip it. "Good. Yes."

Dirt watched her mind to try to see what Home was doing, hoping it wouldn't cause any pain. Marina noticed the pinpricks, but they were so minor she thought her hands were just sore.

Now that he was learning the words so fast, the stream of her thoughts was easier to read than it had been a few days ago. They flew by in a long, endless thread, accompanied by other parts of her mind that gave the words meaning and context.

She wasn't happy about the boy bothering her right now. She hated the memory of all that gore and couldn't get rid of it. She couldn't imagine how *anything* could cause that much carnage, or how twisted that the boy was not bothered. She wondered if it was truly the same tower he was leading them to, if that's really what he was doing, because she was sure she'd have remembered crossing mountains like these and didn't. How long was she supposed to hold this staff? Her fingers were already getting sore, and she was getting sicker. She wanted to lie down. And on and on and on. Humans sure had a lot of thoughts.

A tiny puff of dust spurted out of the staff, right toward Marina's face. Dirt saw it because he was watching, but no one else noticed. Just a puff of pale dust that swirled in the wind and vanished a heartbeat later, but Marina smelled it first. Then Dirt, then the men. A sharp scent, but pleasant.

Her eyes widened. "I feel better all of a sudden," she said. "What is that? What just happened?"

Dirt sighed with relief that Home hadn't done something weird. "My friend the tree made you get better."

"A tree? This bastó?" she asked, still not quite getting it. *Staff.* That word must mean staff.

"This staff is part of a big tree. She watches everything. She sees the world with me."

"This is alive?"

"Yes. Sort of. This is part of a tree that is alive. A very old, very big tree."

The humans thought that over, and the idea didn't really fit quite right with them. They knew perfectly well what a staff was, and it wasn't alive, or still part of anything.

Ignasi idly scratched his beard and asked, "How old is the tree?" Dirt looked at his mind and saw that the man was trying to get him to admit to being a fae or a spirit, which made him grin. He quit looking at their minds, sensing he was about to give it away.

"She is ten . . . ten ten?" Dirt asked.

"*Cent*?" said Ignasi.

Dirt counted with his fingers. "Ten, ten, ten, ten, ten . . . ten ten ten ten *cent*?"

"Si, Cent." *Hundred.*

"Cent cent cent cent . . ." and then Dirt pointed at his pinky finger, the last one.

"Mil." *Thousand.*

"She is mil, mil, mil. Tres mil."

Ignasi nodded sagely. He said, "How old is the wolf?"

Dirt grinned and said, "A hundred days or so. He is still little."

Ignasi's eyebrows went up. "Un cadell?" He gestured with his palm low to the ground, indicating something small.

"Si, un cadell. Un cadell petit i bonic," said Dirt. *Yes, a puppy. A cute little puppy.*

All three humans jerked at that and looked at him. He didn't need to read their minds to guess what they were thinking.

Dirt said, "He is a little puppy. He will get much bigger. Much, much bigger." He smiled inwardly, imagining what they'd think if Father suddenly appeared. They'd probably fall over dead from surprise.

Ignasi nodded, trying to hide his disquiet. He asked, "How old are you?"

Dirt said, "I am only . . . one, two, three . . ." He counted on his fingers, not knowing all the numbers.

"Eight," said Ignasi.

"Yes, eight. But I have only been awake for half of a hundred days. I can't remember anything before that. I have never met a human before you."

From their body language, Dirt wasn't sure any of the three believed him. They tilted their heads back slightly, almost peering at him out of the corner of their eyes. It was subtle, but it was there. Dirt suspected that he could tell because he'd been practicing watching Socks, whose emotional cues were even more subtle.

He tried not to show that their disbelief hurt him, but that little clump of sad regret was growing, becoming truer by the hour, even though he knew in his mind that these things might take time.

He asked Home for sap again, and this time she produced it. The humans turned it down for reasons they didn't feel like giving, and which Dirt understood without being able to explain.

But despite having so much happen already, it was still morning, and there was plenty more walking to go. Looking down the other side of the mountain they were on, they would have to cross deep down into a gulch and then right back up another mountain just as big. How many more after that, he couldn't tell. Socks's swift legs could swallow such a journey in a matter of minutes, but it'd take half the day on human feet.

He stretched and said, "Water?" He held the staff forward, and the humans let Home refill their waterskins. Hèctor even said "thank you" to Home and did a fair job of not looking like he felt silly doing it. Dirt hoped that was a good sign.

Halfway down the mountain, Dirt got tired of going around the brush and started making it move instead, bending it all out of the way like he did with the ferns. He didn't have a lot of practice with things like bushes, and the ideas were different for parts of the plant that weren't normally flexible, like the solid branches. But it was close enough. The minds of the plants were honest and clear, and Dirt figured it out.

The humans discerned what was going on fairly quickly and whispered furiously amongst themselves. Dirt couldn't resist peeking at their minds for just a tiny second and saw that they were wondering if they needed to run away because they still didn't know what he was. Ignasi wanted to stay, but Marina and Hèctor were ready to make escape plans. Dirt almost turned around right then and yelled at them, *I am a human! Just a human boy!* But that would have given away that he could read their thoughts or hear like a wolf, and neither of those things would have helped.

His indignation didn't last long either, because it slid out of him like water off leaves, leaving only that growing sense of regret. He was too different from them. They could hardly understand each other. Dirt didn't even know what they considered normal, and the only way to learn was to mess up and get it wrong.

An idea struck him, and he turned. "Do you know any . . ." *songs,* he wanted to ask, but he didn't know the word. He hummed a tuneless melody and waved his hands like a little dance until they got the idea.

"Cançons. Música," said Marina.

"Yes! Music. Do you know any?"

The three of them regarded him nervously, wondering if this was some new trick.

"Please?" he begged. "I have never heard any music. Not even one . . . cançon."

"Cançó," corrected Marina. She had a hint of pity in her face.

"Not even one cançó. Please?" Dirt leaned slightly toward her, pleading. He gripped Home and held her close to his chest. "Please? I am trying to be . . . a normal boy. But my friend is a wolf. I eat bugs. I catch birds and eat with my teeth. I live everywhere." He gestured all around. "No people. No music. I am the only one. Just me. Please?"

Ignasi grinned slyly behind his beard and whispered, "Maybe we can *embruixar* him instead."

Marina almost chuckled, but swallowed it. He could see he was winning her over, and his heart leaped within him.

"Please?" Dirt begged again.

The other two looked at Hèctor, and the man shrugged and cleared his throat.

CHAPTER EIGHT

The song Hèctor sang opened a window in Dirt's mind that he hadn't known was closed. That's what it felt like. Like light shining into one of those rooms in that old tower after throwing open the curtains. It was just a simple melody, one long, flowing line without much ornamentation, but it made Dirt breathless. His jaw hung open.

It was so novel and exciting that Dirt hardly even heard the words, which were about a kingdom lost to time. The melody repeated itself as the song progressed, and by the end, Dirt found himself humming along, his brain trying to inhale the tune like it was air and he was drowning.

"That was amazing!" he shouted, once it was over. Hèctor just gave him a slightly embarrassed look and took a step backward. Dirt realized he'd stepped right up to the man, close enough to touch him. "I had no idea. Are there more songs?"

Hèctor's black eyes sparkled, even if the rest of his face remained stoic. "I know a few more."

"Please?" Dirt begged, clasping his hands together to keep from jumping forward to hug him.

"What do you think, Marina?" asked Ignasi.

"I think you should teach him a dance. How about a light-step?" she said, folding her arms.

Dirt sensed there was something going on that he was missing, but he was too excited to care, or even consider looking at their minds to figure out what it was.

"I think we can do that. Give me your hand, Dirt," said Ignasi. He stood back a bit from the others to make room and held his hand out.

Dirt jumped over and grabbed it enthusiastically. He detected a slight raise of the man's eyebrow, right before his face softened into a warm half-smile.

"No, with your other hand. Stand there, beside me," said Ignasi.

Dirt complied and lined up next to him. Ignasi lifted their interlocked hands into the air, then held his other hand out, palm up.

"Like this," he said, and Dirt mirrored it. "Now, watch." Ignasi performed a series of steps, forward a few, then back a few, then side to side and back again. Long short short, long short short. Dirt followed along, stumbling as he tried to memorize it.

"Lift your knees more. This is a dance. Good. Now, this part is a hop. Once more. Good. That will do. Marina, will you clap for us? Whenever you're ready, Hèctor."

Dirt was so nervous when the song began that he almost fell over, but Ignasi held him up and got him moving again. Marina clapped a beat for them, and each clap was a step. It took Dirt no time at all to get the hang of it, and soon he was stepping as lightly as Ignasi, hardly touching the ground as they danced.

Hèctor's song was simple again, and much more repetitive. It only had two lines. The first one changed every time and told a story of a woman dancing with different men, and the second line was always the same. Dirt wasn't sure if the second line was half nonsense words or just ones he didn't know yet, but he suspected it was just sounds. Fake words.

His pants started slipping, and he panicked. Both hands were occupied, so he tried stepping really high with his knees to push them back up again. It worked for a time, but after a series of hops that Ignasi improvised and Dirt was able to follow, the waist slid down to his knees, and Dirt lost his footing and nearly fell.

Marina laughed so hard she stopped clapping, Hèctor lost the melody, and while he didn't quite laugh, he did give up singing and grinned. Dirt let go of his panic and laughed along, his whole body dangling, and contorted as he tried to pull his pants up with one hand while Ignasi kept going.

Ignasi noticed last and just looked warmly amused. He released Dirt's hand, since a person needed both to pull his pants up.

Hèctor gave Marina a knowing look and muttered, "If so, he would be a better dancer." She snorted and wiped a tear from her eye, chest still shaking with quiet laughter.

"Can we keep going?" asked Dirt, fumbling with the knot. It hadn't come untied—it simply started out too loose to begin with, which meant he had to undo the knot and re-tie it.

Ignasi pulled a small metal cup from his pack and poured a bit of water in. "Here, have a sip. Dancing makes you thirsty."

The knot wasn't coming together very quickly, and Dirt was now growing embarrassed. "Thanks, but I just had some a little while ago. And I filled that up, anyway."

"Please, I insist. Just a little drink. Hold it in both hands, and I'll tie that for you," said Ignasi. He still had on a friendly smile, but there was something in his eye that made Dirt want to look at his mind. He resisted, though. Whatever he saw there might give him away when he reacted to it.

Dirt hesitantly took the cup in both hands like the man said and drank it. It was only a swallow or two. Then he held it, feeling awkward, as Ignasi tied the knot nice and tight.

"There," said Ignasi, standing again and patting Dirt's shoulder. He took the cup and tapped him on the head with it a couple times. To the others he said, "Does that answer it, then?" He plinked the cup with his fingernail.

Hèctor shrugged and said, "He is not a *fada*."

Dirt wasted no time. "Can we dance again? Or just listen? Do you know any other songs? How many are there?"

Marina tossed aside some of her long, dark hair, which had gotten into her face. "We can sing while we walk. There is plenty of daylight left."

Hèctor said, "Just not straight up again. No one can sing while working that hard."

Marina chuckled, still in good spirits. "Agreed. Dirt, lead us on easy paths from now on. Do we need to wait for your wolf? What was his name? Socks?"

Dirt smiled, almost reaching to hold her hand before he started walking. It was still a habit after spending so much time with the dryads, especially Callius. "Socks. And we don't need to worry. He will find us when he wants to."

But just in case, Dirt sent out the thought, *"Socks, are you having fun? I just heard music! They'll sing some for us while we walk, and maybe more later."*

-I am having fun. I found cattle. Now they are mad at me.-

"Don't let them poke you with their horns," replied Dirt, following it with a puff of affection.

-They are too slow.-

"What does this mean, *Socks?*" asked Hèctor. "Does his name have a meaning?"

Dirt blinked twice before he remembered they weren't part of the conversation. "It means . . ." Dirt squatted down and pulled up Hèctor's pant leg, just far enough to expose his worn leather shoes. "It means this," said Dirt, tugging at the sock inside it. "Because his front paws are white."

"*Mitjons?* Him? That terrifying beast? Who could ever dare name him *mitjons*?" asked Hèctor, in total disbelief. The man's hard face almost looked pale.

"*Mitjons* in my language is socks, and that's his name. I named him. And besides, he named me . . . my name means . . . this stuff." Dirt bent down and tried to grab a handful of dirt, but the ground was too hard, and he only got a pinch.

"*Brutícia*?" asked Marina, horrified. "Your name is *la brutícia*?"

"Yep! And I like it. It's a good name."

"*La brutícia*," muttered Ignasi.

"Why *brutícia*?" asked Marina. She seemed almost hurt.

"Because I was covered in dirt when we met," said Dirt. "The dirt there is black and thick, and it gets all over me."

"Is that all?" asked Ignasi. "Just Dirt?"

"I have another name, but I like Dirt, so call me that. My best friend gave it to me. My other name is Avitus."

Ignasi laughed at this, a short guffaw that the others didn't emulate. Then he paused. "Wait, Avitus? Is your other name really Avitus, or was that a joke?"

Marina said, "He sure doesn't look like an avitus."

"Wait, what's an avitus?" Dirt asked. They were saying the word in a way that didn't sound like a name.

Hèctor's brusque demeanor had been softening, slowly, but now the man had his walls back up. "Why is your name Avitus? Tell us now."

"Hèctor, come, there is no way," said Marina.

"The stories come from somewhere! Now tell us, why are you Avitus?"

Dirt stammered. "It's just my name? What's wrong with Avitus in your language? In mine it just means . . . like an old man. Sort of."

Marina huffed and said, "An avitus is a monster. He is shaped like a man in a cloak, but his skin is purple. He walks into a town telling everyone what to do, and if they don't, maleeix el poble i després marxa." *He somethings the town and leaves.*

Hèctor continued. "The town will be destroyed soon after. Monsters will come, or a fire, or a terratrèmol. Everyone will die. So tell me, why are you named Avitus?"

Dirt froze. Somehow, they remembered. Part of his story remained. The echo of his breaking the world still sounded in the ears of the living, three thousand years later. It wasn't complete, not the real story, but it wasn't too far off, and not even *he* knew what the real story was. Prisca hadn't, even though she blamed him. She'd seen before and after. She'd watched everything decay and fall apart. Rampant destruction, sparing only a few buildings like her schola. No one to clean the corpses from the streets, no one to bring fresh food. She had become that abomination only a few years later, watching from her windows as the weeds grew, as gardens burst out of their fences, as the last few buildings tumbled into bricks when vines pulled them down. And then, finally, the trees, imprisoning her.

"Stop it, Hèctor, you're going to make him cry!" said Marina. "Come on, Dirt. No one thinks you are really an avitus. There are no such things."

"I just want to hear what he says, Marina. It is a simple question," said Hèctor.

Dirt almost lied then. He felt the falsehood on his tongue and clicked his teeth shut to keep it in. Lying would damage him. He knew it instinctively. Too much of what he was depended on truth for him to risk putting a lie into the world.

"I don't remember my parents, or why they named me Avitus. No one even calls me that. I am only Dirt now," he finally said.

"Hèctor," said Ignasi. "You know what the wilds are like. There is a reason everyone is dying, and it is not him. He is not a *fada*, and he is not an avitus. That gryphon would have killed us, and if not, then the wolf, surely. Let us be glad he is helping."

The beardless man scowled back, his black eyes smoldering as he thought it over.

"He is a boy, Hèctor," said Marina. She sounded stern, but still somehow pleading. "A human boy. After all, we have seen his *polla*."

Hèctor snorted and grinned, then turned away to look into the distance.

"Marina!" said Ignasi, in exaggerated fashion. "We must not teach the boy bad words!"

Dirt timidly asked, "What's a *polla*?"

"See what you have done? You and Hèctor are going to ruin him," said Ignasi. He scratched his beard, then made a forward flicking motion. "Go, boy. Start walking before they teach you something else, like *tifarada* or *sucar*."

"Wait, what are those?" Dirt asked. He suddenly wished he'd been watching their minds after all.

That got a guffaw out of Hèctor, the most emotion Dirt had seen out of him so far, and Dirt determined he wasn't going to get an answer. Oh well. The words would come up again eventually, he was sure.

Dirt turned and resumed walking downhill, taking an easier route this time so he didn't have to bend any bushes out of the way. That whole conversation could have gone worse, he knew. He might be close to winning them over, and that lifted his spirits. He didn't get far before he started singing the first song to himself. Just the music, since he couldn't remember the words, but he sang the melody.

At the bottom of the incline, in the small, high valley between the two mountains, Marina cut in with a different tune. She stepped up to walk alongside him instead of behind and smiled down every so often when she could spare a glance away from the path. She didn't sing loudly, or even clearly. Dirt could hear that she was a little under or over the note sometimes, but he didn't care. She sang one song after another, too many for Dirt to remember, as she helped him pick an easier path. It turned out that meant going sideways up the hill at an angle instead of straight over, which Dirt had never considered.

Near the top of the next hill, Socks snuck up from behind, perfectly silently. He crept behind them, far enough back to make sure they never saw his shadow. Dirt didn't look back, so as to avoid giving him away.

-Is that music? Is she singing?-

"Yep! I finally get to hear music."

-It doesn't sound like much. It's just like talking, but longer.-

Dirt sent a puff of amusement. *"Well, I still like it. I bet you'll like dancing. We'll do that later. Did you bring any cattle?"*

-No, they are too heavy.-

"Really?"

-They're too big to carry in my teeth like Father, and when I carry them with my mind it makes my feet sore.-

"Oh. Well, maybe next time you can just bring a part, and I'll have them put it on the fire just for you."

-I should have thought of that,- said Socks. *-In fact, I'll be back in a bit.-*

The landscape turned from mountains into all hills, with lots of big dips, curved valleys filled with pale blue and gray brush and yellow grass. Dirt wondered why no trees grew in this area, but he wasn't good enough with their thoughts to ask any, and Home was too far away. The hills weren't as tiring as the mountainside had been, and Marina kept a steady pace, never slowing down.

Socks rejoined them a while later, after they'd crossed through the hilly spot and gotten to a rocky area with tall pines that kept everything in shadow. The trees were all way too short, but it still felt like the real forest, which Dirt appreciated.

The pup crept up silently behind Hèctor, who was walking last, and huffed in his hair. The man glanced backward and screamed, almost falling forward. Dirt couldn't help but laugh, even though none of the others thought it was as funny. Socks dropped the rear legs of a bull he was carrying with a heavy thud and stood there looking pleased with himself. He leaned down and sniffed poor Hèctor. The wolf had indeed bathed somewhere, and only had blood around his muzzle from, presumably, killing cattle.

"Socks! Don't tease them!" said Dirt aloud, in their language, laughter in his voice. He ran back to say hello.

"*Mitjons*," muttered Hèctor, shaking his head in disbelief. "*Mitjons*."

"Not *mitjons*, Hèctor. Socks," said Ignasi, teasing.

Socks lifted Dirt, gave him a good lick, and set him down again. Then he dipped his snout so Dirt could hug him, just above the nose. Ignasi stepped over and said, "Can I pet him?"

"Don't ask me," said Dirt.

"Lord Socks, the great and powerful, may I scratch your neck?" said Ignasi, in high spirits. Dirt glanced at the man's mind, unable to resist anymore, and found that it was sincere. He'd gone too far beyond fear to turn back now, because what would be the point?

-How come you don't call me that?- said Socks.

"*Because I've met your parents*," replied Dirt.

The pup huffed in amusement and laid his head down. *-Tell this human he is allowed to scratch my neck because he has good manners.-*

Dirt chuckled and said, "Okay, Ignasi, go ahead."

To the surprise of both Socks and Dirt, the man didn't ease into it. Instead, he jumped in, rubbing his face in the fur and scratching deep with both arms.

Marina was next, and rather than ask, she tepidly reached forward with one arm, only really giving some good scratches after she wasn't bitten. Hèctor didn't follow the others, choosing instead to stand apart and look like he was being wary of possible encroaching dangers. Dirt wasn't sure he believed it.

Socks closed his eyes and enjoyed the fine treatment. Dirt directed them to all the pup's favorite spots, then said, "Just stop whenever you're done. If you wait until he stops you, you'll scratch until your arms fall off."

-You didn't have to tell them that.-

"Yes I did."

Clouds rolled in that evening, covering the darkening sky with a blanket of deep gray that hid the stars. They stopped for the night earlier than they wanted, but there was no way to keep going unless they held hands and followed Socks, who could still see just fine. Dirt considered making a light but decided against it, since Hèctor was still unsure Dirt was human, and there was no reason to tip the scales in the wrong direction.

The men carved up the rear legs of the bull with their knives, explaining that it would take too long to cook otherwise. Even so, they had to build a wide fire and make stands from branches to put the meat on while it cooked. Hèctor cleverly cut the meat into big flaps, which were big enough for Socks to feel like he was getting more than a tiny snack with each piece.

While the meat was cooking, the three adults took turns singing songs. It was too dark to do any dancing, but in the orange glow they could still clap along and spend the evening in good spirits.

Neither Socks nor Dirt were sure if they liked the meat better cooked than raw, but it was still delicious, and a nice break from so much sap. Tomorrow, they'd finally see the tower. Dirt drifted off, hoping they wouldn't decide he was an avitus after all once they did.

CHAPTER NINE

Although Socks had chosen a tougher path through the mountains than the canyon stream would have been, when Dirt finally crested the final hill and saw the flat, river-strewn valley below, they were much closer to the ruins than the first time. Solitary and bleak, the off-white tower stood like a skeleton above the dead and silent town in the middle of the valley. All around it, damp greens and muddy browns swirled across the landscape between numerous winding streams and ponds.

"There it is!" said Dirt, pointing with a proud smile. "See, I told you Socks and I knew where it was."

But despite Dirt's encouragement, the humans felt no enthusiasm. Their steps slowed and stopped, their feet unwilling to carry them any farther. He didn't have to look into their minds to guess their thoughts.

Socks stepped up and sniffed the two men, which made them less scared each time, then huffed. They glanced back, hiding their nervousness.

"It's not completely ruined. There's still plenty of stuff there, just no people," said Dirt. "If we hurry, we can sleep in . . . Um, they're like this, with soft . . ." He tried to gesture with his hands.

"*Llits.* You mean a *llit?"* asked Marina. Dirt glanced momentarily at her mind to see what she was picturing, and it was indeed a bed.

"Yes, a bed," he said. "Lots of houses are still fine. There are just no people."

"I'm more concerned about the people, Dirt," said Marina.

Dirt shut his mouth to keep from saying anything that would bother her. He guessed she wasn't really upset about the people, because it's not like she'd lived there or known anybody. It was just a place she passed through once, twenty years ago or more. She was probably upset about whatever had killed them all.

But looking out across the valley, no goblin armies were in evidence. Some birds floated on the water or flew over the fields, but nothing else moved. If there was any game down there, it was hiding until nightfall. He couldn't think of anything appropriate to say, so he just started walking again, and fortunately, they followed.

He'd gone about six steps before Socks lifted him up and tossed him onto his perch on the pup's back. *-I smell cattle down there. Let's go find them.-*

Dirt hardly had time to shout, "We'll meet you there!" before the pup took off at a run.

After several days on his feet, it felt nice to be riding again. Socks was of the same mind and went ever faster, so fast Dirt had to lie down and hang on before they'd even reached the valley floor. He sent a puff of affection and happiness to the pup, and that was easier than talking could ever be.

A sudden leap got a squeal out of him, followed by manic laughter when he lost his grip with his toes and was only able to hang on with one hand until the pup landed again.

The second jump was less of a surprise, but Socks landed in a pond, right in the center of a flock of ducks. The poor birds honked and flapped their hardest to flee while Socks gnashed his teeth at them, but it was just for fun, so he let them get away.

The water was shallow enough for Socks to run through, so he did, splashing the whole way with infectious enthusiasm. From there it was up the muddy bank and into the tall grass, which his long legs had no problem with, and off toward the far end of the valley.

"Was there really any cattle?" Dirt asked. *"Or did you just want to play?"*

Socks just sent back a puff of amusement.

"Well, either way, I was ready to play. Should I sing a song?"

-Of all the things the humans could teach you, why did they pick how to be noisier?-

Dirt chuckled. *"Just think of it as a human howl."*

-Well, it is good at warning everyone to go away.-

Socks carried him over a broad patch of flat, swampy ground, probably half the size of that town, where the water was only a fingernail's breadth thick and the mud a foot deep. Clouds of insects swarmed everywhere, but the happy wolf scattered them just with the wind of his passing. Larger bugs hunted down the little ones, and birds darted back and forth trying to catch those. Dirt was sure there would be snakes around somewhere hoping to catch a bird, and something else that ate snakes.

Nothing around that ate wolves, though, even little puppy ones. Actually, now that he thought about it . . . *"Socks, how far away do you have to go every couple weeks to keep the Devourer from finding you? Is it bad that we came back here after a few days?"*

The pup slowed slightly and started taking an easier path, which Dirt knew meant he was focusing on something else. Probably asking Mother, in fact. And sure enough, a moment later, the pup said, *-I'll be fine for another few days, but we should move on after that. And we'll need to go pretty far. A couple days run, and then we can relax again.-*

"Oh, okay. Good. I hope I never find out what the Devourer is."

-Me, too. If he appears, then both of us will regret it.-

"Do you think I can learn how to lick wounds?"

-Not until you get better at magic. It's not something natural for you, so you'd have to figure it out the complicated way.-

"I wonder if the dryads can teach me. They can put wounds back together."

-Do you really want to find out what method they'd use to teach you?-

Dirt grinned at that. *"I'd get to find out what color all my guts are, I bet."*

-And how much blood you can lose before you pass out. And what it's like to be dead.-

Sure enough, a while later they reached the far end of the valley where a big herd of red-furred cattle were grazing. They weren't happy about Socks's arrival, and the big males stamped their hooves and snorted at him, even though they were half his size. The others raced to get into a circle, thinking to protect their young inside it.

For a smaller predator, that might have worked. Had Dirt been on foot, a stamping bull would have terrified him. The entire thing was pure muscle, hoof, and horn. For all he knew, it could outrace him even if he used mana.

But Socks had little trouble with them and made it a game. Each time one charged with sharp horns lowered, he deftly stepped out of the way, or jumped over it, or some such thing. The pup was having so much fun playing with the bulls that Dirt found himself laughing uproariously each time one missed. The bulls themselves just got angrier and angrier, and the cows huddled ever close together around their calves.

After a while, they stopped charging, although they kept trying to threaten him with snorts and waves of their horns. Once the game was over, Socks leaped on one and sank his teeth into the back of its shoulders, then pulled it to the ground. Then, in a flash, he ripped its throat out and jumped back to avoid the spurting blood.

The animal heroically regained its feet and tried to charge, but it was done for and only made it a few steps before it stumbled and fell. It wasn't long before it quit breathing.

Two other bulls tried to keep Socks away from their fallen friend, but a couple threatening barks made them keep their distance. He ripped the stomach open and lifted the rest of the carcass with his teeth to let all the guts fall out, then set it aside while he dug around for the good bits. He always ate the hearts, even though Dirt thought the meat was too tough to be enjoyable, and some bits of the lungs and liver.

-Do you not want any?-

"Not right now. I don't want to get my pants bloody. I need to ask the humans if clothes can be washed, and how, and maybe get a backpack. I also need to tie the staff on something so I don't have to hold it all the time."

-I want a backpack too, so I can carry things.-

"Like what?"

-I'll know them when I see them.-

After Socks ate all the innards he liked, he got started on the meat. The smell of blood and flesh made Dirt's mouth water, but the ground was an absolute mess. Dirt didn't even dare get down and try to cut a piece off with his knife, so he asked Home for some sap and ate that instead.

The remaining cattle found that Socks wasn't a threat to the rest of them, at least not immediately, and stopped trying to scare him off. Instead, they decided this wasn't a good place to be, and the whole herd shuffled off somewhere else. The ground was so flat there was nowhere to hide, but Dirt figured they were stupid so he shouldn't expect too much.

After a hot, sweaty nap in the bright sunshine, they took a pleasant dip in a nearby pond. Dirt had to summon more wind to keep the bugs away, and when he pulled his pants back on afterward, they got all wet, which made them cling uncomfortably to his skin, but it did keep him cool for a while as they dried.

Socks didn't run back, preferring a light trot. *-Do you mind if we take our time going back?-*

"Not at all. You want to spend time with just me, huh? I like them, but I like this more, if I have to choose."

-Yes. The humans are tiring.-

"What do you mean?"

The pup looked back to glance at Dirt with one eye, which he rarely did, since what was the point if they could read each other's minds? Dirt sent him a puff of affection and said, *"You can tell me. I won't be upset at all."*

Socks resumed looking forward and took a little hop over another muddy patch in between tangled grasses. *-They smell like fear too much. It makes me want to find out what they taste like.-*

"Oh," said Dirt, but it took a moment for that to sink in.

-I didn't eat them for your sake, but for the first couple days, it was hard. That's one reason I ran off to find some cattle. And it was nice to kill all those goblins. When something around me acts like prey, I want to bite it. I look at them, and they shy away, and it makes me want to chase them. I sniff them, and they freeze, and it makes me want to growl and watch them run.-

"I had no idea. I'm sorry, Socks. We didn't have to hang around them if it was hard for you."

-No. You must be the best human, and I will be the best wolf. Where else will you learn, if not from humans? And besides, I could see how much you wanted them to like you.-

"I guess I could have told them not to be scared."

-You did, several times.-

"I could have told them not to be scared, or you might eat them."

That got a huge burst of amusement from Socks, so much he might have guffawed if he was human. Instead he just ran a little faster, his mind sparking with good humor. *-That seems unlikely to work.-*

"You never know until you try!"

-Don't. I was more relieved than they were when they finally dared scratch my fur.-

"Well, thanks again for being so patient. You were right. I really want them to like me, because if I can be their friend, then maybe I can be friends with any other humans, too. And if I can't, then I don't know what to think."

-I am older than you. It is important to be patient with the young.-

"I'm thousands of years old, and you're still a baby!"

-Oh? Were you one day old when I found you, or two?-

The run back was full of banter and joking, and it seemed like all the funny things they'd wanted to say over the last several days were now coming out. The sun edged down toward the horizon, casting the valley into the gold of early twilight. Birds flew everywhere, white cranes and black ducks, sparrows and songbirds of every variety. Skinny little ones with long legs that liked the water and bright red ones with black heads that liked the grasses. Dirt had never seen so many in one place.

Other things crept out of their holes as well, tiny fearful beasts that snuck through the grass or crept up to the water for a sip. When Socks and Dirt realized they weren't going to make it to the tower before nightfall at this pace, Socks used ghost sight to find the humans. His mind filled with the lightless grays and blacks of the spirit world, as he perceived it, and searched high and low for their echoes.

As always, Dirt had to quickly close himself off because there was simply too much for him to process. Socks could view almost the whole valley at once, but that meant looking at every part of it all at the same time, and Dirt's little human brain simply couldn't handle it. Mother and Father could look even farther than that, although Socks wasn't quite clear on how they did it or if they used something else.

But Socks found them, and the way he showed it was sprinting forward as hard as he could, running so fast Dirt didn't dare lift his head lest the wind yank him away.

"What's going on?"

-There are some goblins hunting them. I don't think they realize yet.-

"Really? Where did they come from? I didn't see a single thing!"

-The goblins must have been in the mountains. I smelled some around, but I thought they were far away. The humans haven't made it very far yet. They aren't even halfway to the tower.-

Socks ran faster than Dirt ever remembered him going, so fast he had to use his claws to dig in the dirt to propel himself forward. It wasn't even a run anymore—each time a paw hit the ground, it may as well have been another leap.

Even at such a pace, it still felt slow.

-They are fighting now.-

Socks couldn't go any faster, and despite the speed it felt like an eternity. Dirt counted every breath, every heartbeat. Ten. Fifty. A hundred. Two hundred. Were they even still alive?

Another fifty breaths. Dirt was sure they were dead, and Socks was watching the path too closely to want to talk.

Ten more. Eleven.

And then they were there. Socks skidded to a stop with a goblin in his teeth and tossed Dirt next to another one with his mind.

"Boy?" said a goblin.

Dirt crushed its skull with the staff, even though it blocked with both arms. Home simply broke those too.

There was only one more, and Hèctor was the one who killed it with a deep gash to its neck. "Boy, boy, boy, wah-mee!" he shouted at its dying corpse. Then, in his language, "Die and go to *infern*!"

"Are you okay?!" Dirt shouted.

Hèctor said, "Ignasi took a bite on the arm, and Marina on the stomach. The rest is bruises."

"Oh, thank *Grace*!" said Dirt, not knowing their word for Grace. Or his, for that matter. What did that mean, and why did he keep saying it?

But the three of them didn't share his relief. Ignasi looked worried, and he yanked a cloth from his backpack to try to stanch the bleeding on his forearm. Marina looked pale, her eyes bleary, her lips taut. Her hands trembled. She looked down at her stomach, and Dirt saw a tear drip and fall.

All three humans had the same thought, when he looked at their minds for clarification: *She is going to die. Ignasi will lose his arm.*

The humans had killed at least five other goblins, judging from the corpses. It wasn't even a big group, and if Ignasi and Marina just got bit a little, they were both fine.

"Looks like you would have been fine without us," said Dirt, trying to find something conciliatory. Why did they think she was going to die? She wasn't even bleeding that much. Dirt had had worse.

"Barely," spat Hèctor. "I wish you had not ruined my sword."

He discarded it, tossing it on the ground. The blade was broken, about a handspan up from the hilt.

Dirt said, "We didn't break it. Socks threw it to you in one piece."

Hèctor glanced at Socks, clearly trying to decide how much he dared say. "I can't imagine what you did with it. I have never seen a sword so abused. We can discuss it later, if you wish. If it even matters."

He pulled a length of cloth from Marina's pack and gestured to her to lift her shirt, which she did, just under her breasts. The bite on her side was bad, but the goblin hadn't taken a chunk out. It got its teeth in, was all.

"How bad is it?" she asked, her heart breaking. Dirt saw even her desperation slipping away into black despair, and quit viewing her thoughts.

Hèctor stuck a finger into one of the tooth marks, all the way up to the first knuckle. "They got all the way in. I'm sorry, Marina."

She looked away. Her chest shook with sobs she repressed.

"I'm confused," said Dirt. "It's not that bad."

Hèctor scowled. "Goblin bites always fester. Soon those tooth cuts will turn red. Then they will fill with pus. Then they will turn green. Then her insides will rot, and she will die in horrible pain. We will wait with her until the pain is too much, and then end it for pity's sake. If we are lucky, we can make it to the tower, and she can die in a bed. Ignasi will survive, but we will have to take his arm off. It is that bad."

The Home-staff twitched toward Marina, and Dirt looked carefully at it to see the white threads pointing at her again. "Oh, you want to touch her again?" he asked, in his language. The staff twitched again.

Dirt looked up. "I think you'll both be fine," he said. Ignasi gave him a half-hearted smile, and Marina tried to do the same and failed.

"Ignasi, ask Socks nicely if he'll lick your arm. He's friendly. I promise. You'll get better if he does," said Dirt.

"And Marina . . ." Dirt looked at the staff again. The white threads were all gathered toward the top of the staff, bunches of them. "Can you lie down?"

Hèctor said, "Dirt, this had better not be a game or a trick."

Socks huffed and gave just the barest hint of a growl. *-The stupid human should shut up if he wants our help.-*

Dirt grinned and said, "Socks says, 'Shut up, stupid human.'"

"Boy—"

"Hèctor, are you a slow learner? Marina, will you please lie down? And Ignasi, better ask him fast while he's in a good mood," said Dirt. He gestured at the ground, inviting Marina to hurry up and place herself upon it.

Marina put her hand on Hèctor's arm to calm him down, then lay down without a word where Dirt had indicated. She cleared her clothing out of the way of her wound, which dripped lines of blood that gathered under her side and started to pool together. She closed her eyes.

"Okay. Don't move. It usually doesn't hurt, but it does feel weird," said Dirt. Then he knelt beside her and laid the staff against the wound. She hissed faintly, but he was being gentle, so it was probably in surprise.

The threads plunged into her skin and disappeared. They pulled the staff tighter against her, and that did look like it stung. She gritted her teeth and didn't say anything, though.

Dirt carefully let go of the staff, letting the other end rest on the ground while it did its work. He stood and gave a scolding look at Ignasi and pointed at Socks.

But Marina gasped, and Dirt looked down again to see the Homestaff changing shape, twisting and spreading out on the ground searching for something. One of the rootlike vines found a clump of grass, and a moment later, Marina vanished completely. The staff turned straight again and clattered to the ground.

"Oh," said Dirt.

CHAPTER TEN

The men were too stunned to speak. Ignasi even dropped the cloth he was holding over the bite. Socks snuck in and started licking the wound, and it took three licks for Ignasi to notice and react. "Thank you, friend," he said, patting the big pup's nose. But his eyes were still on the empty space on the ground where Marina had been lying, and so was his mind.

Hèctor stepped onto the vacant spot, but gently, as if he thought she might be invisible. She wasn't, though. She was truly gone. He turned with a look of horror to Dirt and asked, "What have you done with her?"

Dirt picked up the staff. "I . . . well, it's hard to explain. But she'll be fine!" he said. Then, quietly, to himself, he added, "Probably."

Hèctor's eyes burned with unhealthy intensity. "Please try."

"Okay, do you remember when I said this was part of a big tree? And she was my friend? Well, one thing the trees can do, is make you travel through the, uh . . ." Dirt didn't know the word for roots, so he pulled up a tuft of grass and pointed. "These."

"Arrels?" said Hèctor.

Dirt peeked at his mind just to make sure and said, "Yes, *arrels*. They all touch each other underground, and that's how they talk."

Ignasi said, "Trees do not talk, little Dirt." He got one last lick from Socks and looked down at his forearm in confusion.

"They do. Everything with a mind can talk, somehow," said Dirt.

"Trees do not have a mind. They cannot think. They are just trees," said Ignasi. He held his arm up and looked at it, finally losing that glazed look in his eyes. His poor mind steadied itself. He realized he wasn't bleeding anymore.

"Shows what you know. Is your arm better?"

"Hèctor!" said Ignasi, holding his arm out.

"What?"

"Look at my arm!"

"In a moment. Dirt, where is Marina? Where is she?"

"She's . . . she's in the forest. Far, far away. But they'll give her back soon. Maybe in just a day or two, once they . . ." Dirt paused. He'd almost said "learn everything they wanted to from her." Instead he said, "Once they are sure she will be fine." Which was probably *also* true.

"Hèctor, look at my arm. The bleeding stopped. I hardly even feel the pain now," said Ignasi, trying to sound calm, but with so many mental shocks one after the other, he was close to manic.

"Dirt, you must give her back," said Hèctor. Dirt looked at his mind again, and it turned out the man's primary concern was that she was the one who knew where they were going, and without her, all of this was pointless. There was more to it, but the man's mind was in such a chaotic state that Dirt doubted Hèctor understood better than he did.

"Okay! I'll give her back. Let's go to the tower first, okay? Can you walk?"

Hèctor started to say something angry, even raising his fist, but a quick huff from Socks changed his mind. He glanced nervously at the big pup and lowered his fist again. At that moment, he seemed to regain control of his wits. The wildness in his eyes faded and left only pain behind. His hands shook from overstress, but he stood straighter and took a deep breath. Then another. He relaxed, slightly.

"It's okay, Hèctor. I know how scary goblins can be. One time, I got punched by a goblin so hard it cracked the bones in my face. Right here," said Dirt, pointing at the area around his eye. "It hurt every night until Socks's mother fixed it. Look."

Hèctor looked unconvinced, so Dirt pulled his cheek back with one finger to show the three missing teeth on that side. "See? It knocked some of my teeth out."

The man leaned down for a closer look, lifting Dirt's chin. He scowled and sighed, but didn't say anything. Then he finally went over to look at Ignasi's arm. He pulled at the toothmarks, looking in to see how deep they still were.

"Socks licked it, so it'll get better by tomorrow. He does that to me all the time. I get cut a lot," said Dirt.

Ignasi smiled, but it was a bit forced. The man still had too much fire and sparks in his blood to fully relax, but at least he was in control of himself.

Hèctor exhaled loudly, still trying to relax the rest of the way. It wasn't easy so far. "I think I could use a drink."

"Oh, are you out of water?" asked Dirt.

"No. I want *vi*."

"*Vi? Vi* . . . Oh, vinum! Wine." The word was close to Dirt's language, and Hèctor's eyes lit up, telling him he'd guessed correctly.

"Can your staff make wine?" asked Hèctor.

"No, but I bet I know where you can find some."

"Where?"

Dirt pointed toward the tower. "They killed all the people, but they only burned some of the houses. There's lots of stuff there still. I found these pants, so I bet someone had wine."

Ignasi asked, "Did you find some? Did you already drink it?"

"No, I didn't look. I forgot it existed until now," said Dirt. And rather than explain, he turned and started toward the tower. The men fell in line behind him.

They'd picked a terrible spot to try to cross, it turned out. Maybe it looked straight, or maybe they were being chased by goblins and not paying attention. Whatever the reason, they had to contend with tangled shrubs, then a wide, waist-deep lake with thick mud underneath. On the other side of the lake was a sort of grass with thick stalks and tufts of fur at the top, which were taller than Dirt was. Taller than Ignasi and Hèctor, too, it turned out.

However, Dirt discovered that he could run and jump against the tall grass and it would break his fall and flatten, without even having to use mana. Then Socks had to try and leaped right over the three humans to land with a heavy thump. He rolled over and got up, having flattened a sizable area. Then he leaned over and fell to his side, flattening even more.

Dirt cheered, then ran and jumped again, flattening more. Between him and Socks, Hèctor and Ignasi didn't even have to push any out of the way. It wasn't as fast, but it was a lot more fun. The two men were even smiling by the end.

After exiting the tall grass, they had to deal with mud again, or short grass that grew in mud, or small, scarcely moving streams. One thing after another and none of it easy to cross.

Dirt kept picking up the pace to make sure they made it to the town before nightfall, but even after pushing as fast as they could go, they didn't. Once it got too dark for human eyes, Socks moved to the front and led the way himself, since he could still see just fine. The next hour was spent wide-eyed for the rest of them, walking with a shuffle-step to keep from tripping.

The last bit of the journey happened under a bright moon, though, once it finally came up. The moonlight almost ignited the pale tower, causing it to shine brightly against the surrounding dark blues and grays and beckon them onward.

The town was just as Dirt and Socks had left it a couple days ago—silent and still except for crickets and birds. Rather than cheer for joy, which Dirt had almost expected, the men slowed and grew somber as they walked past house after quiet house.

"This is not a good place," said Hèctor. "It is a place for the dead."

"What do you mean?" asked Dirt.

"I mean that it is a place of *fantasmes*," he said.

"What's that? What's a *fantasma*?"

Ignasi answered, wearing a brave but insincere half-smile. "It means someone who has died. Their body is dead, but their *fantasma* still walks."

Dirt swallowed the rush of fear that filled him. The word must mean skeletons. The dark wasn't so scary, not with Socks around anyway, but all the same, the shadows under the moonlight suddenly took on a much more sinister hue. He said, "Does that happen a lot with dead humans? Do they get up and walk around?"

Hèctor's black eyes were deeper-set than Ignasi's, which made them disappear into shadow to leave him looking like a skull. He glanced around and unconvincingly said, "Of course not. Just their *fantasmes*, if their bodies are not buried."

"A *fantasma* is inside you, right?" asked Dirt, pointing at his chest. Not that it would do any good in terms of clarifying.

"Yes," said Hèctor.

"Okay, then I've seen at least one walking around."

The man spun to face him. "Here?"

"No, in the forest."

"The forest where Marina is?"

"Oh, well, it's a big forest, and that one's dead for good," said Dirt. "Socks, do you hear anything moving? Any underground scratches?"

Socks raised his head and turned it this way and that. He tilted his ears toward the ground. *-No. Just bugs and critters.-*

"*Okay, will you tell me if—*"

-Of course I will tell you, silly Dirt.-

"Nope, he doesn't hear anything."

"You cannot hear them until it's too late," said Ignasi.

"No, Socks will hear for sure. They're not *that* quiet," said Dirt, trying to remember whether he'd seen Prisca hovering at one point. He didn't think so.

The men chose not to argue, and ultimately neither they nor Dirt were much comforted. The town might be safe, or it might not. He had to admit that he had a habit of waking up sleeping dangers everywhere he went.

Hèctor asked, "Dirt, you said goblins killed everyone, right? How do you know?"

"From the dead goblins we saw."

"How do you know they killed *everyone,* I mean?"

"I guess I don't know. But there were a lot of skulls in the pile."

"Can you show me?"

"Sure, it's just in the tower. You can just walk right in and look."

Ignasi butted in and said, "I think I don't want to see that right before I go to bed. We should find a spot to sleep, and deal with the dead in the morning. And if a *fantasma* comes to snatch us in the night, so be it."

Dirt helpfully said, "Just so you know, some of the houses have bodies in them. Not everybody got killed in the tower."

Ignasi shuddered. "Let's find a *graner*, then."

"What's that?"

"Where animals sleep."

Dirt didn't know what that meant, since animals sleep in all kinds of places, but the men searched nearby until they found one. A barn, it turned out. *Graner* meant barn. And it wasn't much of one, just three walls and a roof of wooden shingles.

But the ground was flat, and the grass growing under it was sparse enough not to be uncomfortable. The two men settled in and made a small fire, which served to chase the shadows away and soothe their dread. Dirt gave them both some sap for dinner so they wouldn't have to eat that terrible bread.

Ignasi stretched and lay down first under his thin blanket. Hèctor followed shortly after, and the two men lay wide awake, listening for the sounds of an approaching *fantasma* and hoping none showed up.

Socks simply put both of them to sleep with a mental shove, then said, "Let's go look around."

Dirt grinned and stood back up. *"You've been wanting to stay up a lot lately."*

-Wolves are supposed to hunt at night, so that's when the Devourer prowls to find us. That's why Mother always made us sleep at night and go out during the day. But I'm sure we're fine for a bit.-

"Are you sure it's safe, then? What do you want to go do?"

-Just come with me for a moment.-

"Of course. Let's go. Do you want me to ride?"

Socks picked Dirt up and tossed him on his back, then crept away in silence. Everywhere else was silver and black from moonshadow, but the old barn had a warm yellow glow from the dwindling fire that made it seem a welcoming place.

-Fantasma doesn't mean skeleton. I think it means ghost.-

"Why do you think that?"

-Because, look.- Socks opened his mind for a connection, and Dirt received it. The pup shared only one sense, though—a magical one. Ghost sight.

The town lit up into perfect clarity, just as it appeared during the daytime, except only blacks and grays. Socks was careful to keep it constrained to within a couple dozen paces to keep from injuring Dirt's brain, but that was enough for him to get the idea.

In every window and doorway, under every shadow and beside every gate or corner, was a human face. Some had full outlines, and others were just shapes, but they were everywhere, in every direction. They waited silently as corpses, perfectly unmoving, watching with unblinking eyes.

A bone-deep chill passed through him that had nothing to do with the temperature. His human eyes sought out the same doorways and windows and found nothing but blackest emptiness. Or did he? Did something move?

-I didn't use ghost sight here last time, but this time I wanted to look for goblins, so I did. And I found them like this, just watching. I asked Mother, and she said they're the spirits of dead humans.-

A sense of menace gripped him, but Dirt wasn't sure if it was real or imagined. *"Can they do anything? Can they touch us?"*

-Usually not. That's what Mother said.-

"So sometimes they can?"

-Maybe.-

Dirt tried to calm himself as he watched the crowd of the dead through Socks's senses. Men, women, and children, their faces everywhere. If Socks looked too hard at one directly, it seemed to lose its distinctiveness and fade, only to reappear elsewhere.

"What would make them dangerous?"

-I don't know. I think all they can do is scare you, maybe, since they're dead. They're just spirits now.-

Socks made his way farther into town, watching with ghost sight the whole way. He kept it limited to close by, though, so Dirt could share it. Dirt's human eyes saw farther in the moonlight, and it was disconcerting to see how each empty shadow filled with specters when the two of them got close.

Nothing moved, though. Not even the wind. The air was heavy and cold, almost as thick with humidity as the forest, but it didn't smell right. Too much swampy ground nearby gave it a scent like rotting plants.

There was a faint pop from inside one of the houses, and both Socks and Dirt swiveled their heads to look and listen closer. But it didn't repeat. Instead, only silence.

Until a bird hooted, probably an owl. It glided over them, flying without a sound, and disappeared over a roof. Dirt was surprised he couldn't hear its wings flapping.

-I heard its wings, but they're very quiet. It's a quiet bird. It must be a hunter.-

No further hoots came, which only drew out the silence. They crept along, watched by the dead, until they got close enough to the tower for Socks to see it with his ghost sight. Strangely, the closer they got, the dimmer the view in ghost sight became. Socks slowed a bit, confused.

As soon as they were close enough, the tower burst into view like a roaring inferno, engulfed in black flame that swallowed light and distorted everything around it. Tongues of black fire leaped from windows and climbed up the outside of the tower. Inside the flames, the spirits manifested fully, every detail clear as reality. They twisted, mouths open, suffering and screaming as the flames consumed them. Their flesh melted and cracked. Their eyes burst and ran down their splitting cheeks.

Dirt slammed the connection shut, and the tower became just a tower. Empty and white, standing silently in the moonlight.

-I'm sorry, little Dirt. I wasn't expecting that.- The pup followed the thought with a burst of emotion, mostly sympathy for his little pet. Dirt's heart pounded, and nausea swirled as terror twisted up his guts, but he let himself be soothed, even as his soul trembled from knowing what was happening unseen, so close by.

Dirt didn't reply, choosing instead to bury his face in the pup's soft fur and breathe deep, filling his nose and chest with wolf-scent. He was safe. The ghosts couldn't hurt him. He tried to stop being afraid, but he couldn't because he knew they were still there. He knew.

-I wonder why the tower is burning like that. That didn't happen in real life. Oh, never mind. It stopped. What are they doing now?-

"What? What happened?" asked Dirt, but he could tell without Socks even saying anything. There was something sickly and malicious in the air, something he could feel in his deepest parts.

A thump landed nearby, so out of place and startling that even Socks jumped and yelped in surprise. They looked at the source and saw a severed human head, someone they didn't recognize, with eyes staring lifelessly and fresh blood oozing out the neck. Dirt blinked, and it was gone without leaving even a mark on the grass.

They heard a muffled voice from the other direction and spun, only to see nothing at all. But they heard it again, faintly. A woman moaning in pain.

More sounds came—the wretched thunk of a blade hacking into flesh, screams of suffering far away. Footsteps. Quiet laughter.

Dirt felt a tug on the Home-staff, a jolt like they were trying to take it away from him. Then another on the strap holding the knife sheath. He screamed.

-Hold on. We are leaving.-

Socks turned and jumped forward, but Dirt was yanked backward by his hair, right off the wolf. He felt the ghostly fingers as they pressed his scalp, each one distinctly.

Dirt forgot to protect himself with mana and hit the ground hard, knocking the wind out of him and stunning his diaphragm so he couldn't breathe.

He tried to get up, tried desperately to inhale and resolve the burning in his chest from lack of air, but he couldn't. Just short, useless gasps.

The ghosts fought to hold him down, hands pressing on him briefly and disappearing. A cold feeling encircled his neck, like a blade of iron eager to cut.

He screamed, just one short burst, and regretted it since that was the last of his air. He managed to gasp a partial lungful, then another, and avoided passing out. He still couldn't get up. Something kept pushing him back down, dragging him backward.

Socks's mind clamped on him heavy as a tree trunk and pulled him the other direction, his entire body at once. Ghostly fingers slipped off him, some pinching or scratching or pulling his hair. But he came free, flying upward out of their grasp.

From above, Dirt could finally see them with his naked eyes. In every window and doorway, under every shadow and lurking in every corner, were the spirits of the dead.

CHAPTER ELEVEN

It didn't matter where Socks put Dirt. On his back, under his belly, or even floating in the air, the ghosts found him immediately. Their fingertips brushed his skin or pinched him. They tugged his hair or the hem of his pants. Whispers from empty air wormed into his ears, rarely distinct. When Dirt could make out what they were saying, it was in Hèctor's language and didn't make sense, things like, "Is this the one?" or "They're coming."

Socks snarled at the empty air and clawed at shadows, to no avail.

"Let's just go! Let's get out!"

-Where?-

"Just anywhere! Out of town!"

Socks dug his claws into the overgrown dirt road and lunged forward at full speed, leaving the two men behind, hopefully unnoticed by the unquiet dead. The ghostly whispers faded against the sound of rushing wind, and the town was small enough it took no time at all. The pup didn't go too much farther, though, and once they were truly out into the brush, Socks turned and looked back again. Dirt felt deeply unwell, crazed with fear or some similar but deeper thing. He couldn't make himself calm down, even though they were safe now, so he just clung to Socks's soft gray fur and waited.

"What about Hèctor and Ignasi?" he said, poking his head up. He couldn't bring himself to look at the town, though.

-They look fine so far. Do you want to go back?-

"I guess not."

-I wonder why the dead humans are only bothering you and not me. Maybe this is why Mother never warned me about them. Do humans just stay where they died forever?-

"I don't know, but that doesn't sound right. The gods . . . the gods should . . ." Dirt puzzled over that. Anything to distract him from the other things in his mind right now. *"Socks, did Mother or Father ever tell you about gods? What they are?"*

-I asked after you saw that statue down there, but Father just said not to worry about it because they don't matter anymore.-

"Did you get the milk?" asked a man standing nearby, fully formed. The moonlight made his pale shirt and hat glow, but he cast no shadow. He vanished a moment later.

Dirt shrieked and buried his face.

"Wake up, Galla. We have to go," whispered a woman's voice nearby.

"Go! They found us again!"

-I know.-

Socks dug in and ran again, circling the town this time instead of just running straight away from it. He stopped on the opposite side, and back a bit farther.

They paused, the pup watching with ghost sight and Dirt straining his ears to listen, hoping he heard nothing. Just crickets and some far-off chirping, and both of their heartbeats. Dirt was so scared that his was faster right now, which almost never happened.

-I never see them moving,- said Socks. *-I wonder how they go from place to place.-*

Dirt didn't care enough to answer and didn't want to know. He never wanted to see another one as long as he lived. He felt like he was suffocating under crushing dread. All he could do was bury his face in the pup's fur and try to think of something else.

-I don't see as many on this side. I think this was the right place to go. There are some by the two men, but I don't think they're waking them up. Probably giving them nightmares.-

Socks padded around quietly, looking into town from different angles. No ghosts appeared, and no whispers floated on the still air.

"I hate this. I wish I could at least know when they were coming. How do people deal with them? Are there just lots of them around, and humans all live like this?"

-That sounds unlikely. What do you want to do now?-

"I don't know. You?"

-I think I am figuring something out. Just relax for a bit.-

"About what?"

-About ghost sight.-

"What about it?"

-How it works.-

"What do you mean?"

Socks didn't answer right away, and Dirt realized the pup had not an ounce of fear in him. Probably since they were leaving *him* alone. He was concerned and pitied his little human, but he wasn't scared. That was comforting. Slightly.

-I want to know why I can't see them move.-

"Maybe ghost sight isn't actually the spirit world," said Dirt, not really giving it much thought.

Socks lifted his head up backward and looked at Dirt with one eye. *-Why do you say that?-*

Now that he was on the spot, he had to hurry and come up with something, so he said, *"Well, I'm pretty sure they're moving, and since you can't see them doing it, what you see isn't where they really are."*

-That's what I was thinking. Why don't I see spirits all over the place, all the time? I never really thought about what it was I am looking at, but now I wonder.-

"Is a ghost different from a spirit? I know it's just words from my language, but maybe that's a clue?"

"They're gonna kill you!" said a man nearby, his voice quiet even though it sounded like a yell.

Dirt whimpered and tried to be strong, but knowing another dead person was right over there was too much.

-All right, I am getting annoyed with this. Hang on, little Dirt.-

Dirt buried his head, relieved to be finally leaving the town behind. He promised himself they'd come back for Hèctor and Ignasi, if for no other reason than to make sure they got Marina back, or what was left of her. Hopefully all of her, happy and healthy as ever. He kept his eyes closed, and as Socks ran, the moving air created a chill that felt somewhat soothing.

It was a short run, though. Much shorter than Dirt expected.

-All right, you humans. Wake up and tell Dirt how to take care of ghosts,- said Socks in the new language. Loudly. Not just for Dirt to hear.

Dirt shot up and found himself in that barn where Hèctor and Ignasi were sleeping. The men were shocked awake, gasping and reaching for their weapons.

-Do not grab those. Tell Dirt how to take care of ghosts. They are bothering him.-

"He speaks!" said Ignasi, stunned, jaw hanging open. His beard had gotten all disheveled, and he pushed some of the stray hairs out of his mouth with his tongue.

"No, he does not speak. That was something else," said Hèctor, wary.

Dirt slid off Socks's back and immediately regretted it, because the whispers started up again.

"Of course he speaks," said Dirt, anxiety redoubling. "I told you I can talk to him. Now, listen. Do you hear that?"

The men paused, never taking their eyes off Socks, who only barely fit under the roof. "You can't bring it," said a little girl, plain as day. She sounded younger than the dryads.

Hèctor's eyes hardened, and Ignasi went pale.

-Well? Do you know or not?-

"My apologies, friend Socks. I am slow to wake up. What is going on?" said Ignasi, running his hand down his face and tugging his beard to help wake up.

-It is dead humans. They will not leave Dirt alone.-

"How is he doing that?" asked Hèctor, looking around. He poked a finger in one ear and twisted as if cleaning it out. He inhaled sharply and spun, looking behind himself. "Something touched my shoulder!"

They were starting to become visible again. Vague shapes in shadow, hints of movement in the corners of his vision.

"Please," begged Dirt. "Please hurry and tell me what to do."

Hèctor said, "The dead are upon us. It is too late."

-There has to be something. There are more dead than living, so if they could kill you, there wouldn't be any of you left.-

Dirt asked, "Isn't there anything? Will they at least go away in the morning?"

Ignasi said, "If we let them be, we will not be here to see the morning."

"So what do we do?!" yelled Dirt, trying his best to keep from growing frantic and screaming.

"Fire. The light might preserve us for a time," said Hèctor, turning to look for wood.

Socks yanked the frame right out of a nearby wall with his mind and split it in midair. He dumped the pile of shattered wood fragments right next to Hèctor. *-What else?-*

Hèctor wasted no time and took an armful of firewood and stepped to the coals of the small fire from earlier. He set the wood in a triangle shape and leaned in to blow the embers. As he worked, invisible hands pulled his arms back, and he fought against them with decisive forcefulness.

-Get back. I will light it,- said Socks to everyone.

Hèctor looked up, worried, but he backed away without arguing. Socks made a few sparks in the triangle and ignited them, and a moment later, the flames were waist-high and hot.

-Now what?-

Ignasi said, "Now we wait. If they are strong enough to put the fire out, our souls will join theirs."

"That's it?" Dirt asked.

Hèctor said, "If it were our town, we would all gather together and hold a festival, with songs and bright fires to drive them out. We would put up signs to keep them away, and shout until they leave. Then we'd all get drunk. But this is not our town. There are some places that should never be touched. I should have known. I felt it when we walked in here. I should have paid attention."

"That can't be all! How do you keep them away the rest of the time? Does this happen every night in a human town?" said Dirt. A fingertip traced his spine from his neck to his pants and gave them a gentle tug backward. He ignored it, but couldn't keep from shuddering so hard his teeth clacked.

Ignasi said, "This is their place. Hèctor is right. Our best chance was not to disturb them."

A burning man, arms waving wildly, ran into the barn from outside and crashed into the fire. The area smelled like burning hair and roasted flesh and a scream of pain split their ears. And then stopped. The scent vanished. The man vanished. Socks picked up the scattered fire logs with his mind and put them back.

-Why weren't they here in the daytime?- said Socks, loudly enough to get through to the minds of the three stunned humans.

"They cannot abide the light," whispered Hèctor. "Their place is dark and cold. Empty."

A boy screamed, shrill and desperate. Goblins laughed, and a series of sickening thuds filled their ears. When they looked for the source, there was nothing there.

Dirt slapped a hand to his neck, feeling a deep scratch. When he pulled his palm away, he saw blood.

-Dark and cold and empty? Then make more light. Dirt, make a light.-

Dirt couldn't move. He stared at the blood in horror. The ghosts could hurt him for real. They were going to kill him. He was going to die here and become one of them.

-Dirt. DIRT.-

"What?" he whispered, unable to tear his eyes away from his palm.

Socks howled, so loud the humans had to plug their ears with both hands. His enormous lungs kept the note going, going, going.

Then he inhaled again and howled once more. *-MINE,-* yelled the wolf in their minds.

In the silence following, there were no whispers, no ghostly voices. No fingers traced Dirt's flesh or tugged his hair.

-Now, my dear little Dirt, make a light,- said Socks, tenderly, desperately.

Dirt complied before he'd fully regained his wits. He snapped his fingers, and the little ball of candlelight appeared above his head. In the light of the flames from the fire, it had hardly any effect.

-Make it bigger. Brighter.-

"I can do that," said Dirt. He inhaled mana and fed it in, and when the ball of flame started to get bigger, Dirt compressed it instead. He pictured the sun in his mind, just a little thing the size of his pinky fingernail in the sky, but with tremendous, unwavering power.

The flame gleamed hotter as it compressed. Its color brightened from orange to yellow to white until it shone more brilliantly than even the waist-high flames.

Then Dirt made a second one, only possible after watching Socks make fields of sparks so many times. Then another. He held his palm out and gathered them to it, having them slowly rotate around each other in the air.

-Good. That is very bright. They do not like it. I think I know what ghost sight is,- said the pup, just to him.

"What?"

-It's the border. The skin where the spirit touches the physical, or maybe the world of magic. I'm not sure, but that's what I see. It's not either place, just between. Too much happening on this side pushes them back out. Noise and commotion and light. You are good at those things, so make them.-

Dirt pretended his fear was anger and turned and strode out into the night. He made the lights leave his hand and circle above his head like gems in a crown of glory.

"Come get me now, you dead ghosts! Come get me now!" he shouted. He stomped as he walked and swung the staff in front of him like he was swatting away goblins.

Ignasi and Hèctor rushed out after him, followed by Socks. The pup sent him a puff of affection tinged with pride and relief, and Dirt sent it back. His mind felt clear now. It was bright as sunlight out here, and nothing could harm him.

"Where are you going?" asked Ignasi. He seemed calm, like he was starting to get used to this.

"I'm going where the stupid ghosts came from. That's what they get for messing with Dirt!"

The swirling lights above his head made shadows dance everywhere, as if trying to escape the burning gaze of one that could eat them. Some whispers still reached him as he got closer to the tower, but not many.

Each footstep was heavy, resolute, and unwavering. Dirt felt like something long forgotten had awoken in him, a portion of the man he might once have been. His mind was clearer than ever as the focus required to keep the lights burning pushed away all unrelated and useless thoughts. Mana cycled naturally within him, guided by a will sharpened to razor's accuracy.

Dirt stopped before the tower, burning white light piercing every window. Inside the main door, however, on the ground floor, the interior was shadowy and dark. Black fog swirled as a sense of menace and hatred assaulted his spirit.

"Be gone!" he screamed, his voice high-pitched, like a woman's. It had been a long while since any part of him had seemed wrong, but it wasn't the voice he expected. He gestured with the staff and screamed again, so fiercely his whole body tightened up. With full discipline and sincerity he commanded, "Be gone!"

The blackness swirled. He'd been wrong. It wasn't fog. Something in there was eating the light itself.

Dirt waved the staff and summoned a strong gust of wind to blow right into the doorway. He heard it knocking the dry bones around, crushing the skulls in that pile against the walls. He stepped forward. And again.

"Try and eat this, you old ghosts! Come eat this light!" He made a fourth light. A fifth. The gleam from the pale tower stone was so bright it hurt his eyes, and everything else was black from losing his night vision.

He stepped forward again. And again. Right up to the doorway. The wall of quivering blackness was an arm's reach away, retreating by inches under the assault of the wind and lights.

-Don't go into that.- said Socks, just to him again.

Dirt blinked, having almost forgotten anyone else was around. It felt wonderful, reliving his old self. *"I won't."* He waved a hand and fired a light into the midst of the blackness. It shook and struggled as if poisoned from inside.

He stepped forward again and the black retreated. "Be gone, dead ones. Harm the living no longer!" Dirt waved a finger and stuck a light to the interior wall, right above the doorway. He created another one, as bright as the rest. He stuck it to the wall a few feet to the side. Then again, and again.

And then it was over. The blackness succumbed and split apart, leaving nothing but a messy, well-lit room, dominated by a pile of skulls.

Socks poked his nose in the doorway and gathered the skulls together with his mind. Then, with one solid swat, he crushed the entire pile into dust, which the wind carried out a far window and into the night, where it spread into a cloud and slowly dissipated.

Dirt let all the lights wink out except one, finally relaxing. He exhaled and leaned on the staff.

All was silent again. Not even crickets or birds this time, after all that ruckus. No shapes hiding in shadow, not gentle tugs or menacing whispers.

-They're gone. That seems like too much work for just a bunch of dead humans,- said Socks, to everyone again.

Ignasi laughed.

CHAPTER TWELVE

Dirt looked up into the broken stairway that led to the second floor and thought about that bedroom. It didn't seem quite so tempting to sleep in anymore.

"This place feels different now," said Hèctor.

"Different how?" asked Ignasi.

"Just different," said Hèctor. He peered around as if looking for something, but his eyes seemed vacant.

Socks poked his head in the doorway and said, *-I told you they are gone. Come out of there.-*

It really *did* feel different now, although Dirt wasn't sure if he was imagining it or if that tremendous sense of relief was just from him. He still had liquid fear in his veins making his fingers tingle and his head feel swimmy, but only a little, and it was fading fast. Socks would probably be smelling it on him the rest of the night, though, because it had been a *lot.*

No sooner had Dirt walked out than Socks leaned down and licked him a bunch of times. Dirt started giggling and backed away and thought about running, but it was too dark to play chase right now. "Okay, lean down here!" he commanded.

Socks lowered his nose, and Dirt hugged the pup's face with enthusiasm, squeezing as hard as he could. At times like this, it was hard to deny just how fast Socks was growing. Dirt couldn't reach around as far anymore. They could still nuzzle their heads together, though. Sort of.

Mostly Dirt did the nuzzling because if Socks pushed back, Dirt would fall over.

The two men followed close behind. Ignasi scratched Socks's skull around his ears. Hèctor looked like he wanted to, but didn't.

Dirt let the lights wink out, sighing quietly as the mana stopped channeling through him. The darkness was complete, but he didn't mind looking down the road while his eyes readjusted. It might be dark, but there was nothing there anymore.

The men slept in the same barn, but this time Socks lay right outside, and Dirt could tell how it put them at ease without even looking at their thoughts. They smiled and moved with grace instead of caution, chatting quietly. Dirt snuggled into his usual spot in Socks's fur and nodded off sending puffs of affection back and forth.

Morning came late, with the sun well into the sky before Dirt finally stretched and yawned himself awake. Socks was nowhere to be seen, and neither were the men. Dirt smiled to himself as he imagined Socks following them around, sniffing at everything and asking what they were doing.

Besides, that was Dirt's job. He got up and stepped out from under the roof, then used a little mana to jump on top of it. Sure enough, Socks wasn't too far away, peering into a house window and wagging his tail.

Dirt hid his thoughts and crept as quietly as he could, stepping slowly to keep even two pebbles from rubbing against each other. Where he had to step through grass, he drifted his fingertips across it and asked it to bend out of the way. He even slowed his breathing to keep it from making the slightest sound.

Inch by inch he crept forward, slow as a hunter, silent as death. Closer. Closer.

"WAAAAAGH!" he shouted at the top of his lungs, right next to Socks. The pup squeaked and jumped three times his height in the air, body twisting as he tried to right himself and face the threat. He landed awkwardly on the house next door, and his front paws went right through the rotting roof, where they got stuck.

Dirt laughed so hard he almost cried, and watching Socks trying to extricate himself without pulling the house down made it even better. All this time, and he'd never gotten that close without getting caught.

Socks could hear his heartbeat. He could smell what Dirt stepped in two days ago. Sneaking up on him was impossible unless he was thoroughly distracted.

Socks finally managed to get his paws out while leaving the house's walls intact, although it didn't really matter because no one was ever going to live there. Dirt ran over and said, *"Good morning! I'd say I'm sorry for scaring you but that would be a lie."*

-I am going to summon a ghost if you do that again,- replied Socks.

"You are going to BE a ghost if I keep doing that, since I scared you to death. Be careful, little pup, for I am now a fearsome predator. You'll never see me coming."

That got a puff of amusement from Socks, who replied, *-You are the Devourer. Of sap and squirrels and birds. Now, come and see what the humans are doing. It is interesting. And watch your back, because I'll get my revenge.-*

Hèctor and Ignasi had come out to see what was going on, and as they watched Socks shake the roof tiles out of his fur, they just looked at each other and kept their opinions to themselves.

They waved for Dirt to follow and went back inside. The house was untouched by the weather, with tight shutters over the windows that had stayed closed all these years and thick wooden tiles on the roof to keep the rain out. It smelled like dust and mysteries, faint and curious. It made the house seem older than it was, which was fun because Dirt knew what old looked like, and this wasn't it.

"They locked this house up like they were going to come back someday," said Ignasi, with warm and eager eyes, "which is perfect for us, who want to steal all their stuff."

Hèctor snorted and knelt by a plain wooden chest and resumed throwing out all the clothing piece by piece.

"Do you want a new shirt?" asked Dirt, since those looked like shirts.

"No, I'm looking for a certain kind of cloth. They might have something worth carrying," he explained.

"Like what?"

Ignasi said, "Silk, dear Dirt. Hèctor thinks he's about to find silk. I think he'll only find other things a woman likes to keep hidden."

"Like what?"

"Never mind that. Do you know what silk is?"

"No."

"Do you know what grain is?"

"Yes."

"Good," said Ignasi. He handed him a small wooden barrel, a heavy one. The lid was popped open, and it was full of pale-brown seeds. "Take those idle hands of yours and pull all the bugs out, and I'll tell you what silk is."

"Why am I pulling the bugs out?"

"So we don't have to eat them, boy," said Hèctor. "We're using that grain."

"No, I mean, what's wrong with eating bugs? I eat bugs all the time. Or I used to. It's hard to find big juicy ones anymore," said Dirt. He looked closer at the grain, which turned out to contain more bugs than he noticed at first. Little ones, small as the grains or smaller, and dark in color. He picked one out and found it old and hard, not worth eating. He tossed it aside. "They're good. I like grubs the best because they're chewy on the outside and liquid inside. They're fun to eat."

Ignasi swallowed and looked nauseous. "Dirt, never tell anyone about eating juicy bugs ever again. Especially not me. I think I believe you actually eat them."

"Well, of course I do. Or I did, before the trees started giving me sap. What else was I supposed to eat?"

Hèctor suppressed a grin and said, "Yes, Ignasi, what else was the boy supposed to eat? Dirt, if you ever spot a big juicy one, let us know so we can share with him. He was telling me the other day how much he wants one."

Dirt caught on, so he played along. "I will. The best grubs are as long as my finger, like this, and when you're chewing on one, you can play with the others. They're really wiggly, and all their little feet tickle your tongue until you bite them a few times. Sometimes I'll bite one in half and leave the other part moving while I chew."

He picked out another little dark bug from the grain and popped it in his mouth. "Hmm. Crunchy. Not very good, though."

"I won't be able to tell you about silk if I'm busy vomiting," said Ignasi. He really did look sick, which made Dirt and Hèctor give each other conspiratorial grins. Dirt realized then that their relationship had changed, and it warmed him up inside.

Ignasi held his hand up for Dirt to stop talking and took a sip from his waterskin. He swished, swallowed, and took another sip. "No, it's too late," he declared. "I think I'm going to die."

Hèctor snorted. "We can only hope. But please, do it outside."

-Stop talking about bugs, and tell us about silk,- Socks told everyone. His big yellow eye took up the whole window, making him seem monstrous.

"Silk is cloth, finer and lighter than anything else," said Hèctor.

"That's it?" said Ignasi. "Hèctor, you are terrible at this."

"What?"

"Hèctor, this is a boy, and that is a puppy," said Ignasi, pointing. He tugged at his beard and said, "You must tell them stories."

"Then be my guest."

"I can't be your guest because this isn't your house."

"Then keep your mouth shut."

"How about I tell a story instead? Dirt, you know nothing of the kingdoms of men. Is that right?"

Dirt took a second to realize he was meant to answer. "Mostly. I know about some things from a long time ago but nothing recent."

"How long ago?"

"Three thousand years."

Hèctor looked up, his black eyes piercing again. "Where did you learn about anything from three thousand years ago?"

Dirt considered carefully how he wanted to answer, but Socks answered for him first. *-If your story is any good, then maybe we'll tell you.-*

Ignasi said, "If it's Hèctor's story, it won't be any good, so I'll tell it instead. My grandfather was a man named Tomàs, and when he was a boy, his grandfather told him what he was taught by even older ancestors. And that is this: in the days before the Three Kingdoms of Camayans, they were all one kingdom, which stood for hundreds of years. In those days, men made mighty ships to sail the oceans and look for lands more welcoming. They were shaped like a seed, with a point at the front and flat at the back, and they floated high on the water, taller than buildings. No expense was spared, with decorations from front to back. Carved wood and inlaid bone and brass. Such a ship might hold a thousand men or more, with room inside for their horses and provisions for months of travel.

"Some ships departed and never returned, lost without explanation. Others found fertile land with water and safety and claimed it. Some grew prosperous, while others failed and were lost. But many more ships found new kingdoms of men. Kingdoms of mountains, of plains, and of water. Men of all kinds. The ships returned with goods: gold and silver, crops that we still grow to this day. Tools and writings useful for knowledge. In those days, every man had enough food, and the king's men fought back the beasts that hunted us.

"Of all the goods from those marvelous places across the water, the finest is silk. Silk is like a dream made of feathers, so gentle you believe it will fly apart if you blow on it, but sturdy enough to wear. My grandfather never learned where it came from, and none has been made since the ships were lost. Dirt, please stop eating those," said Ignasi.

Dirt put down the grain-bug he'd been about to pop in his mouth without realizing, and chewed on a piece of grain instead. "Sorry. I'm listening. Was that all?"

"No, it was not all. Those days, the days of that One Kingdom, have been gone for over two hundred years. Long enough to be forgotten by most. And some even say the One Kingdom was not the first—that other kingdoms came before it. That men were once so prosperous that we fought against each other instead of the wilds.

"But those days are long, long past. The One Kingdom fell for the same reasons so many towns do. Do you know what those reasons are?"

Dirt said, "Well, you're the first humans I ever met, so, no. I have no idea. Why is that?"

"The wilds, little Dirt. It is always the wilds. This is something so basic that it almost didn't occur to me to ask. Goblins, for example. Is one goblin a problem? Are ten? If there are ten goblins, then twenty men will kill them. But those ten goblins are only discovered after they kill a cow or a child or a family. Then the whole village is poorer—one less cow, one less child, one less family. Bit by bit, over many years, the towns and villages shrink. The land they can safely farm decreases; the risks they are willing to take while hunting grow fewer.

"Perhaps a great hunter comes who kills many goblins. Maybe even kills them all. And then for a generation or two, the people prosper and regrow. But only for so long. The wilds always creep back in.

"And that is not all. Goblins are not the only cause. Some fields become tangled with new plants that resist the plow, forcing us to ignore them until they grow thick enough to burn. But that means that for a year or two, an entire field grew no crops and someone went hungry. If this happens in a poor year, maybe a child starves who might otherwise have lived.

"Those are just the slow things," said Hèctor, sighing in disappointment after getting to the bottom of the box and not finding any silk. He tossed everything back in and started looking into other containers spread throughout the room. "Not everything is slow."

Ignasi nodded and said, "Indeed. Not everything is slow. Sometimes there is a calamity, and a whole rich town will be wiped out in a night. From one day to the next, everyone is dead, without even time to gather their goods and flee. An army of goblins who grew clever, for example, as seems to have happened here. Or causes we never learn. Perhaps someone offended one of Socks's siblings."

"Or an avitus showed up," said Hèctor with a scowl directed at a small vial he was sniffing. "Do you see this? Smell it."

Dirt peeked in and saw a thick, dark liquid inside. He sniffed it and was repulsed. It smelled like rot, so bad it hurt his nostrils.

Hèctor held the little pot to the window for Socks, who sniffed it as well, so much it made a rushing air sound. "What does that smell like to you, Socks?"

-It smells like lots of plants. Plant oil that went bad and rotten, but with flower scents and something sharp I've never encountered before,- replied the pup. *-What is it?-*

"It's scented oil to make a woman smell nice. But it has a hint of cinnamon in it, which is something we haven't been able to get since before I was born. My father had some, powdered in a glass jar. The woman of the house probably got this from her grandmother. If she'd left it closed, it might still be good. Hard to say. But she left the lid off, and now it's garbage," said Hèctor. He set it down and put the lid on, which had been right next to it.

The man stood and stretched his neck. "Over there, see those jars? Those were full of food. Those ones are fruit stored with sugar, and those are meats stored with salt. None of it is edible anymore. I think some of those look like vegetables. That's a pot of jam, which is fruit made into a paste you can spread on bread. This one looks like it might have been butter, and that ceramic pot used to have milk in it. Which tells me they had a cow. Which probably went in that barn."

"I thought this was my story," said Ignasi, picking up a length of thin rope he found and testing it.

"I'm not telling a story. I'm just pointing things out," said Hèctor. "But here's the point. A lot of people worked hard to make the stuff you see in here. Someone made the cloth on that bed, and carved those chairs and that table, and someone made those iron hinges. Someone else dug up the iron and smelted it. If we lose the guy who digs up the iron, then no one gets hinges anymore. If we lose the guy who grows the sugar, no one makes any jam. Do you see where I'm going with this?"

Dirt considered it. He relied on Socks, of course, but that's because they were friends. But did it really affect the pups if there was one less of them around? Not really. There wasn't a pup who made iron, and another who milked cattle. Every pup had everything he needed—claws and teeth. Same with the trees. Each tree had everything she needed—sunlight, fog for water, and soil to grow in. Did it change anything in the forest if there was one less tree? Not in a way he knew about.

Socks had said once that it didn't matter if there was one less human, because who cared about humans? Or something like that. Dirt couldn't remember it exactly. But that was wrong, wasn't it? It did matter, because every human had something they were responsible for giving to everyone else.

Dirt finally said, "I think so. Maybe? But it's different from anything I know about. I just eat whatever I find, and I don't need any clothes. Or at least I didn't before."

Ignasi said, "This is how things fall apart, dear Dirt. Tiny piece by tiny piece or all at once, but they always do. The wilds gnaw at us, breaking apart our kingdoms. Then they eat our baronies and counties, and then our cities, towns, villages."

Hèctor said, "It's been like this too long for anyone to guess. It's said that the ancients knew how the world was made and when men first appeared. That gods were great and ruled the whole world instead of the small things like a mountain or lake or village. But there's one thing we all know—it's getting close to the end. I won't be here to see it. There are still too many of us around. But it's coming. Maybe a hundred years, maybe two hundred. But it's coming. There will be a final day of man."

"Perhaps all that's left of us will be wild boys running around with wolves, never knowing a thing about their kind," said Ignasi. "As for me, what do I care? I am alive, and there are still things to enjoy. Why get upset?"

"You still came, though," said Hèctor. "Ah ha!" he roared suddenly. He pulled out a long bottle from behind some brown pots. It had a sturdy wax seal around the top and was filled with a dark, sloshing liquid.

"I still came. Because why not? Perhaps we'll make contact with Marina's village and push off the final end for another hundred years. Perhaps we will rebuild this town and reclaim that tower and survive another two hundred instead. It will give me more time to enjoy that wine. Pop it open, Hèctor. Let us teach little Dirt about the finer things in life."

CHAPTER THIRTEEN

The wine was the worst thing Dirt had ever tasted. The flavor was nothing but rot, with the addition of burning. Dirt wasn't sure any even made it down his throat because as soon as it hit the back of his mouth he started coughing, and that sent it up his nose. The burning scent made his eyes water, and from there it was nothing but misery.

Hèctor and Ignasi laughed uproariously, which brought Socks to his feet with a growl forming in his throat. But he paused before biting them in half and turned to Dirt. *-That was a prank. They think you will be fine.-*

"Why would anyone drink that? Is that really wine?" complained Dirt. The smell filled his head, even his skin; everything in his face burned. He coughed again, but it didn't help.

Hèctor, still chuckling, took the bottle away and handed his waterskin over. "Here, wash it out. You'll be fine."

"Okay, but what was it?"

"It was wine. Plum and apple, I'm guessing, and strong," said Hèctor. He lifted the bottle overhead and gulped loudly, taking several big swallows.

Ignasi jumped up and grabbed it away, spilling some on Hèctor's beardless face. A splash got in his eyes, and he hissed in dismay. "Hèctor, dear man, you must be careful. You must be careful to share," said Ignasi. Then he took a drink just as loud and deep as Hèctor's, and both men laughed.

Dirt backed away as the smell got worse. His throat still burned and felt like he needed to cough, but there was nothing to cough up. He drank some water and swished it around, then swallowed. It only helped a little, until the third or fourth swallow.

"This was a bad idea on an empty stomach," said Ignasi, amusement in his voice.

"Your cheeks are already turning red, you lightweight," said Hèctor. He took the bottle back, peeked inside with a look of deep contemplation, and plugged the stopper back in.

Dirt leaned over to look at the bottle again, as if something on the outside would give away the secret. "Okay, but really, what was it? I thought wine was supposed to be rich and smooth and bold. Words like that."

Ignasi asked, "Why did you think so? Did someone tell you?"

Dirt shrugged. "I don't know. I just remembered that from somewhere."

Hèctor said, "If you know how to describe something you've never had, then you must not have been alone your whole life. Feel like telling us anything, boy?"

-Dirt has never seen living humans before you,- said Socks, to everyone. The men glanced at each other and chose not to argue.

The pup had his thoughts hidden, leaving the light of his mind almost perfectly blank. He was thinking about something he didn't want Dirt to know just yet. Dirt looked at his friend carefully and saw his eyes drifting to the bottle, then at the waterskin Dirt was holding. Just a tiny flick of his tail, and Dirt realized what was up. He'd have to smell anything he drank for a while, because Socks was plotting his revenge.

Dirt pushed that thought aside and locked it up so Socks wouldn't know he'd been found out and turned back to the men. "Anyway, if you're not supposed to drink that stuff with an empty stomach, do you want some sap for breakfast?"

"No, dear boy, we have something better in mind. Noble Socks, if I may ask you a question?" said Ignasi, with a charmingly deferential air. He gestured with his hands in a way Dirt made sure to remember, since it was graceful and humble at the same time.

-What?-

"The wind that arose last night. Did it stir up any new smells? Shake the dust from these houses to reveal what's inside?"

-Yes. It is very interesting now. Why?-

"Then look closely, if you wish. These grains are called wheat, and wheat can last for a very long time. We grind it into powder, like so," said Ignasi. He placed it on a ceramic plate and ground it with a rock he pulled from his pocket, crushing it into little crumbles. "That powder is called flour. With flour, we can make fresh bread. Tell me, mightiest of creatures, can you smell any flour or wheat? Save us the trouble looking everywhere?"

Socks reached his big head in through the doorway as far as he could go, getting his nose right up to the plate. He sniffed twice, just to be sure, then pulled himself back outside. He wagged his tail excitedly and disappeared.

Hèctor said, "You're ridiculous, Ignasi."

"Thank you, and you're welcome," said the other man with a little bow.

Dirt went out first. Socks was easy to spot as he bounced from house to house, sniffing in all the doors and windows, even the half-burnt and collapsed ones. Dirt and the men started walking in his direction, but the big pup wasn't moving in a straight line, and they realized they'd never catch him.

"Ignasi, head over that way and check those two houses. Dirt, come with me, and we'll check over here," said Hèctor. He turned and started across the grass-covered street to a row of shorter houses with flat roofs, all built close together. Most of them still had shutters closed over the windows, although every one of them was missing the door.

"Why over there?" asked Dirt.

"Because those people were poor, which means they didn't have much. Which means whatever they had were the most useful things they could get," said Hèctor without turning around. He kept a quick pace, and Dirt had to scramble to keep up.

"Why were some people poor?" asked Dirt.

"Because they had less money and fewer things. Come on," said Hèctor. He peeked into the first doorway but didn't go inside.

"What are we looking for?"

"Anything useful," said Hèctor. "If you're not sure, it's probably not."

"I don't think the wine was useful. If I find any more, I'm not telling you," said Dirt.

Hèctor snorted in amusement but didn't say anything.

Dirt picked a different house and went in. There wasn't much inside, just a big bed made from a wooden box with straw inside, covered with blankets. No real mattress. Rusty pots hung from hooks on a board stuck to the wall, and some shoddy shelves held grimy old plates and cups. There was a wicker basket with a lid, which Dirt opened with the staff just to see if he could, but it just had cloth in it. No dead bodies, at least.

The next two houses were similar except for big holes in the roof. Everything inside was rotting and covered in mildew and even a few mushrooms. He found a shirt that looked like it might be his size, but when he lifted it up, the cloth tore, so he dropped it again.

Useful. What was useful? He had everything he needed. More than he needed, in fact. He didn't need the knife, or the pants. He would be just fine without them.

-Come. I found some flour.-

Dirt hurried out and spotted the pup halfway across town, standing on a roof. He sniffed, then looked around, then sniffed again, tail wagging furiously the whole time. Dirt grinned to himself and wondered what had gotten him so excited, but he supposed it was because wolves liked to hunt, and this counted.

-In here,- said Socks when they got closer. He pawed at the roof of the building he was standing on, which was different from the houses. Its stone walls set it apart, and notably, it was circular instead of square.

"Looks like he found the *molí*," said Hèctor.

-The scent was faint, but I found it anyway.-

"Very well done!" shouted Ignasi, coming up from behind. Dirt glimpsed at the man's mind for traces of mockery but found none. More like amused respect.

Socks hopped down and peeked into the open door with one eye. *-It's in bags. Watch out for the dead human.-*

"Is it moving?" asked Dirt.

-No. -

"What a peculiar thing to ask," said Ignasi. "Please, do not elaborate. My heart can only hold so much horror."

-I think he got injured and crawled inside, then put that bar over the door to keep the goblins out. It worked, but he still died.-

The inside of the building was all one room with a large contraption in the middle, which Dirt recognized as a mill. Wooden poles to rotate the millstone reached almost to the walls, and the basin for catching the flour was empty. A stack of full sacks made of pale cloth rested against the far wall.

Sure enough, a dead human lay in the middle of a wide stain on the dirt floor that was probably old blood. The body was next to a chair against the wall, which it had probably fallen out of when it died. The corpse was face down and all in a lump, so Dirt couldn't tell if it had been male or female.

Ignasi reached back to place his hand on Dirt's chest and said, "Do not make any of your magical fire in here."

"I wasn't going to, but why not? Is there something dangerous?"

Hèctor said, "Grain dust can explode if it catches a flame, but I doubt there's any in the air right now."

"Better safe than on fire," said Ignasi.

All the same, Socks grabbed Dirt with his mind and pulled him out, setting him a safe distance away from the door, and then getting in between. The wolf poked his head in the door and said, *-There, in the back. Those sacks that are stacked up are full of flour. I opened one.-*

"This one?" asked Ignasi from inside.

-Yes. -

Socks backed up and let Ignasi come out, holding an open bag. "How did you untie it?" the man asked.

-With my mind.-

Ignasi looked at the string that used to hold the bag shut, and then at the enormous wolf pup, who was acting pleased with himself.

-I watched Dirt's little fingers.-

"It's one thing for you to throw large things around. You are a large thing," said Ignasi. "But . . . somehow, this bothers me."

"Can I come look?" asked Dirt, stepping as close as he dared, which was about even with Socks's hind leg.

-No.-

"The flour smells fine," said Hèctor.

"It's been sitting there so long it lost the smell. Taste it. Wait. No. Taste it out there, so we can all watch," said Ignasi.

"I'll take your word for it."

-He's right. It's rotten. Why do you drink rotten things, but not eat them?-

"Because eating rotten things doesn't get you drunk," said Ignasi, "and the drinks have to be the right kind of rotten."

Hèctor started making noise inside, tapping on wood and pushing things that creaked and groaned. There wasn't much to check, apparently, because he soon said, "Good as new. Come help me push this, you lush."

Ignasi said, "You found grain in there?"

"Yep, and poured it in. Come on. Also, Socks, that boy is stronger than he looks, right? Let him help. There's no problem if there's no fire," called Hèctor from inside.

-What if there is a problem?-

"There won't be a problem," said Hèctor. "This mill fed everyone in this town the whole time it was here, and it hasn't exploded yet. Ignasi was mostly kidding."

Ignasi said, "It's true. I was mostly kidding."

-Fine. Dirt, you can help. But if there's a problem, then there will be a PROBLEM,- said Socks. He let the last word resound, almost as loud as Mother's voice. Dirt was sure he heard shutters rattle.

Dirt walked in and rubbed his hands on the bare floor to get some dirt on them, clapped them together, and grabbed a push bar. "Okay, I'm ready."

Ignasi said, "Looks like you know how it works."

"Well, sort of. I know I need to push this."

"Yep. Now, don't push too hard. Keep it steady so you don't get tired. It'll take a while," said Hèctor.

"I'll be fine," said Dirt.

With a pop and a creak, the three humans got the wheel turning. It was heavier than Dirt expected, but he had no trouble keeping a steady flow of mana cycling to strengthen his arms and legs. Around and around they went, listening to the muffled grinding sound and making sure to keep it even.

Socks lay down and watched through the doorway, and from how he flitted his ears, he was probably keeping track of the whole area. Both men were panting and sweaty after countless turns, but Dirt was still fine. When the milling stopped sounding so muffled they paused. Hèctor looked around for an empty bag and couldn't find one, so he took a full one and stepped outside to empty it. He began scooping the flour out of the basin under the millstone and started filling the bag.

"It looks like it's exactly enough," said Dirt.

"Almost like someone thought of that, huh?" said Hèctor with a flat tone of voice. A peek at his mind showed he was amused, though, not annoyed.

"Finally, some proper food!" said Ignasi, taking a pinch of the flour and tasting it. "Let's go find a stove to cook on."

The very next house over was larger than average and had a whole room dedicated just to cooking, which was convenient. Most of the goods left there were too old, but Hèctor pointed out some salt and other dried powders that were still usable. The brick stove built into the back wall was close enough to the kind Dirt's people had used for him to recognize it—a space for firewood and baking, a chimney for the smoke, and a flat metal surface to heat up and cook with. The cook-plate wasn't very big, just large enough to set a pot on, but it would do. A handsome stack of evenly-chopped firewood lay ready and waiting.

Poor Socks couldn't fit that far into the house. He tried to peek through the one window but couldn't get an angle to watch what was going on, so Dirt shared his sight, and the pup sat down outside and closed his eyes.

Ignasi showed Dirt how humans were *supposed* to start fires, when they didn't have magic wolves as friends. Take some wood, shave some of it really thin, then get some slightly larger pieces, and make sparks by rubbing iron on flint, which was a special kind of rock that Dirt couldn't tell from any other. The sparks made small flames in the kindling, and then you added bigger and bigger sticks until you had a nice fire.

While Ignasi got the fire going, Hèctor pulled a bowl off a shelf, blew in it to get the dust out, and shook in a couple handfuls of flour. To that he added a few pinches of salt and some dried green flakes and mixed them together with his finger. Then he took a small pot of grease from his backpack and used a spoon to throw a big dollop of it in with the flour. Finally, he dribbled some water from his waterskin and started mixing it all together with one hand.

Even Dirt could smell how it started to come together. That grease was animal fat, and the scent of the flour changed completely when it got mixed in. Hèctor mashed and squeezed and pulled the dough, adding a bit more of this and that until he was satisfied. When the stove was finally hot enough, he set a frying pan on top and added a tiny bit of grease to the pan, pinched off a ball of dough, flattened it, and fried it on the pan.

The rich aroma filled the room before Dirt even had time to count to thirty. It smelled nothing like the bread Hèctor had given him that first day. That had been too boring and unappealing to finish. But *this* was completely different. Hèctor had to keep pushing Dirt away because he couldn't help but get closer and closer to the frying pan, and he was getting in the way.

Hèctor slid the flatbread out onto a cool part of the stove and said, "Let that cool off a bit before you pick it up." Then he started cooking another one.

Dirt waited patiently for about three heartbeats and then grabbed it, burning his fingertips. He hissed and tossed it from hand to hand to keep from burning any further, which made Hèctor chuckle. Before he finally took a bite, he shared his sense of taste with Socks, who was sitting up now and sticking his nose in the window to enjoy the smell.

The fresh bread was the most incredible thing Dirt had ever tasted. Everything tasted so *bold*, so vivid. Far more than anything else—blood and meat, innards of various kinds, baby ferns, grubs, eggs. Lots of things had a good flavor, but they all seemed mild in comparison.

The flavor awoke a deep nostalgia in him, colored by Prisca's memories and the holes left in his own. Memories of doing just this—cooking fresh bread and eating it with friends, gathered around a stove. Or perhaps family. Perhaps both. The taste and scent tugged at his mind so sharply he expected to get some of his own memories back, but they didn't come. Only the feelings did, the warmth and happiness. Comfort and safety from the weather, affection. There was so much rushing in, yet still so little.

"Ah," he muttered. He felt his chest tighten as a tear slid down his cheek and dripped off his chin. That made his nose start running and he sniffled. Another tear slid down. He took another bite.

Hèctor noticed and didn't know how to react, choosing to look away and ignore it while he cooked the next one.

"This is really good," said Dirt, quietly, around a mouthful.

"This is just a start," said Ignasi. "This is only flatbread. Proper bread has leaven to make it large and fluffy. It needs butter and jam on top and currants or sweetmeats baked in. It gets much better than this."

-I like it too,- said Socks, only to Dirt. His voice took on a note of sympathy as he added, *-Strange things make you sad, little Dirt.-*

"I know. I can be silly sometimes. But it's hard to explain, I just . . . well—"

-I know exactly how you feel and why. You don't have to explain, - said Socks.

Of course he did. Dirt smiled a little and sent a puff of affection to his best friend.

Hèctor made enough flatbreads for Dirt to have two, which he appreciated, and for himself and Ignasi to have three. Dirt made them all go sit at the table to eat, each person in a chair. Dirt rested his elbows on the heavy wooden table while he nibbled, but he couldn't see the appeal. Maybe if there were lots of kinds of food, like drinks in cups and plates with different things on them, it made sense to sit up here instead of just on the ground.

Socks hadn't gotten anything to eat, though, so as soon as the humans were done, they went outside and Dirt fed him sap from the Homestaff, lump after lump until he was satisfied.

It seemed like every day it was one more lump than before. The pup really was growing quickly lately. When they'd met, Dirt had to duck slightly to walk under his belly. Now he had to reach his arm up and stretch to touch the fur. Socks's legs were getting long and lean, and his fur was losing some of its poofiness. His face was slowly sharpening, too, growing more predatory to match the big scar over his eye. In the meantime, not a single thing about Dirt had changed at all.

Oh well. His body was already eight years old, and he was only halfway grown. Another eight years, perhaps, and then he'd be an adult. Socks would have been an adult for several years by then, maybe even claimed some territory and taken a mate. Hopefully he'd still want little Dirt around. That thought disquieted him, probably due to the lingering nostalgia.

-You are worrying about silly things again. I don't have to take a mate right away. I will wait until you are grown up, and then we can take mates at the same time,- said Socks. Then, to everyone, he said,- *I want to go*

hunt. I will bring back an animal, and you will cook it for me. I will share if you do.-

Ignasi said, "Wonderful! Bring us a fat cow or deer, noble wolf, and we will give you a feast worthy of you."

-Show Dirt more human things while I am gone. Everything you do is complicated with a lot of steps, so make sure he pays attention. Do not let him get hurt.-

"I'll be fine," said Dirt. This got him thinking, though. Complicated, with a lot of steps. Socks was right. How many things did it take to build a house like that? How many pieces? And all the ingredients for bread. He'd never really thought about it that way, but humans should be complicated, with lots of steps. Plans and tools and little pieces of things. Wolfish excellence was found in strength and speed and cunning, in sharp senses and all kinds of magic. In knowledge of ancient things and the world.

Dirt was learning those things as well as he could, and he wasn't about to stop, but maybe that wasn't natural to humans. Maybe human excellence was in careful consideration, in accurate plans and fine details. He'd have to watch the men and think that over. It made him curious what human magic was like. He used to know, a long time ago.

And more relevantly, what could they do with meat, now that they had salt and spices for it? Plain meat cooked over fire hadn't been that impressive, but now he had to wonder. What did meat become, with a few more steps?

Speaking of plots and plans, another thought crossed his mind. "Hey, Home? Good morning. Sorry I didn't say that earlier. I hope you're having fun with Marina." That was unfortunate phrasing, but oh well. "Is she ready to come back yet?"

The staff twitched, but nothing else happened. Dirt rested the staff in the grass just in case, but Marina didn't appear. "Okay, well, take good care of her, please, and give her back soon." Then, in their language, Dirt said, "So what else is there for me to learn today?"

CHAPTER FOURTEEN

It took Socks what seemed like forever to return with the meat, since the herd was at the far end of the valley. In the meantime, Dirt joined Ignasi and Hèctor as they rummaged around the dead city. One of the first things Hèctor found was a pull-cart designed for a person instead of an animal, which dramatically increased the number of things they decided they needed. Ignasi saw it and went pale and acted tired, making a big show of how eager he wasn't to drag that thing across the landscape. Hèctor had to fix it, so Dirt followed Ignasi for a while instead.

Ignasi was better at looking for things than Dirt was, since he knew what everything was and how people lived, and it didn't take long to find plenty of stuff worth keeping. Dirt had thought to look for child-sized beds to find a house with child-sized things in it, but that wasn't the case—everyone put all their children into one bed, so a house with more than one large bed was the best place to look. A bed for adults, and a separate one for children. A house with just one bed might still have children, but they were poor, which meant a smaller likelihood of useful supplies.

Dirt ended up with a full set of clothing to complement his pants. He got a wide, yellow tunic, a red shirt with black borders, and even gray woolen socks and leather shoes that didn't have any holes in them. Those had belonged to a woman, and they were too big for him, but they'd do on the rare occasion he felt like putting something on. To top it off, Ignasi tossed him a good woolen blanket in case he got cold or wanted to sit on it instead of the ground.

Much of the rest were things Ignasi wanted but Dirt didn't. Dirt didn't need any candles or oil, or a second knife, or a spoon, or anything like that. Some things might have been nice but were rotten, like the scented oil. And he didn't need any dried old medicinal herbs or bandages, since Socks could just lick his cuts. Ignasi took all that stuff. Dirt did, however, take a little pot of salt. And while they didn't come across any backpacks for him, Ignasi did find a hefty twine sack that he wove a couple straps into and converted. The man even put a little cup at the bottom and a loop at the top so Dirt could rest the Home-staff in it and have both hands free if he wanted.

-I am coming back. Get the fire ready. A lot of fire. I have a whole bull,- said Socks, to everyone.

Ignasi laughed and stood up from the bottom-shelf jars he was looking through for more wine, because apparently eleven wasn't enough bottles now that they had a cart to put them on. "A whole bull. How is he carrying an entire bull? In his teeth?"

Even though the man was talking to himself, Dirt answered, "His father can carry eight bulls at once in his teeth. But Socks is probably carrying it on his back. I bet he's going slow because it's heavy, or he'd be back already."

Ignasi said, "You have a habit of saying insane things that I can't help but suspect are true. I hope I never meet his father. Now come. Socks might like *you,* but I am not interested in testing his patience."

When they found Hèctor, he was carrying a big armful of crumbling old firewood into the grass where a narrow street had been, right between two short stone fences. He dropped the chopped logs, and they fell apart into splinters and sawdust, making him cough.

"It looks like you have this handled, Hèctor. Shall we leave you to it?" said Ignasi, his voice subtly jovial.

"I wonder if that wolf pup has ever tasted human flesh. Wanna find out?" said Hèctor.

"Actually, he has," said Dirt.

"I thought you never saw a human before us," said Hèctor.

"Socks has. He saw exactly one, before you," said Dirt, trying not to smile. It was Dirt's flesh he'd tasted, when licking his wounds shut.

"Wait," said Ignasi.

Hèctor said, "Just get some more firewood. Actually, Dirt, you get the firewood. The stuff in the middle of any stack will be in the best shape. I need a lot, so hurry. Ignasi, I saw some rosemary under a window by that house. Go pick it all and look for more. And get some salt."

Dirt hopped over the fence and headed to a stack of firewood taller than he was, against the rear wall of the nearest house. It was all split into triangles and stacked tightly, and when he tried to pull some out of the middle, it wouldn't come. He pulled harder, then harder, and then used a little mana and really gave it a tug.

The whole stack fell over with a crash, and wood went flying everywhere.

Hèctor called, "Dirt, are you still alive?"

"Yes, I'm fine!" He grabbed as much as he could carry and hustled back around to where Hèctor was. The man pointed at a spot, and Dirt dumped it over the wall.

"Good. I need twenty more of those."

"Okay!"

After ten trips, Dirt wondered if there was an easier way to do this, but there probably wasn't. He could only carry four or five pieces without using mana, and his arms weren't big enough to carry more than that anyway. Too bad Socks wasn't here because he could've moved the whole stack at once. Dirt decided he really ought to learn the trick of that. Even though he had arms, moving things with his mind would be useful.

Once Hèctor was satisfied there was enough wood, Dirt watched him stack it in a careful circular pattern that got higher and higher. Inside the circle, he stuffed fibers and shavings and splinters. When the firewood tower was complete, he stepped back and said, "We need a lot of coals, so we're going to get it burning and topple it when it's ready. Now go find me a rake."

"What's a rake?"

"Never mind, then. Sit over there and stay out of the way," said Hèctor. Dirt obliged and took a seat on the fence. The man knelt with a flint and steel and popped off a bunch of sparks until finally one caught, and a thin wisp of smoke appeared. He blew on the tiny flame, and it was only a moment before the entire stack was burning, sending flames five paces into the air and creating a trail of smoke poofs that reached much higher than that.

Ignasi returned with a wicker basket containing an alarming amount of rosemary, which was a plant with thin, needlelike leaves and a sharp scent. "Think this'll be enough, dear Hèctor?"

"It's a start," he said with a flat voice and a twinkle in his black eyes.

"Come help me chop this up, Dirt," said Ignasi. He headed toward the nearest house, and Dirt followed him in. He headed to the cooking area and pulled out a hard, graying panel of wood and set it on the table. "This is a cutting board. That is a knife. I suppose you can guess what I want you to do?"

"I can guess. But I'm going to use my own knife instead of that rusty one."

"Don't. You'll dull it with all the chopping."

"It hasn't gotten dull yet. I didn't know that could happen."

"What do you mean it hasn't gotten dull?" said Ignasi. He gently plucked it from Dirt's hands and tested the edge. Then he held it out in both palms and gave it a good look.

"I cut all sorts of stuff with it. Wood, mostly, but sometimes flesh or bones. And Socks and I used it to fight a couple times. He chops things up with it."

"You've never sharpened it? Have you ever oiled it to keep the rust off?"

"No. Was I supposed to? Where do I get oil?"

"Well, I suppose we're about to find out if it will need sharpening. Start chopping. That rosemary deserves it."

Dirt obliged, hacking away and trying to cut every leaf at least once. He had to lighten the blows, though, because if he struck too hard the cutting board started chipping. Ignasi went next door to get another cutting board for himself, and when he returned the two of them made short work of the rosemary, leaving a giant stack in the middle of the table.

The scent was incredible. It was complex and sharp and curious, unlike anything Dirt had ever smelled before. It didn't smell edible, was the main thing, and when Dirt tasted some, it was bitter. The oils from the plant seeped into his fingers, and they smelled like rosemary long afterward.

Ignasi took Dirt's knife again to give it another examination. He held up a length of cloth and ran the edge against it, and the cloth sliced in two just as expected.

"Hèctor," called Ignasi.

"What?"

"Guess what Dirt has?"

"A boil?"

"Even better. An eternal blade."

To Dirt's surprise, Hèctor stepped away from the fire without complaint and came in to see. "Look at this."

The other man took it and examined it closely, from smooth hilt to tip. Ignasi said, "He says he's never sharpened or oiled it."

"Where did you get this?" asked Hèctor.

"In a tomb. Socks and I found an old city and explored it."

The man regarded him, eyes piercing again, and Dirt peeked at his mind just a little. Hèctor wasn't sure if Dirt was lying, and the boy's face wasn't giving it away.

"Do you mind if I try to dull the blade a little? If I do, I'll sharpen it for you," he asked.

"Sure, go ahead."

Hèctor stepped around to an unused corner of the table and smacked the edge into the wood, at least twenty times. He swung with force but didn't keep his arm rigid to try to cut through. Just enough to flatten the edge, not that it would work. Dirt had tried to cut a rock once, and while it hadn't succeeded, it also didn't hurt the knife.

"What's an eternal blade?"

Ignasi said, "A blade that never needs sharpening. I only know of two, but there are supposedly more. One is a sword held by our king, and if anyone else touches it, they're executed immediately, no matter who it is. The other is just a rumor, but it's a dagger much like this one, I suppose. It's called the Wandering Curse, and anyone who picks it up can never drop it until they kill a loved one. In the days of the old kingdom, a man held it his whole life, never putting it down until he died. They buried it with him, and someone dug up the grave a week later."

"If there's only two, how come you have a word for them?"

Ignasi shrugged. "Because they come from ancient times, so old no one can name the kingdoms that made them. Tradition holds that the king's sword wasn't forged by humans, but I don't believe that. And like I said, there are supposed to be more. I hope this is a third, and not the Wandering Curse."

"Well, I can put it down," said Dirt.

"Good point."

-I am here. Come out.-

Hèctor turned immediately and stepped out, mouth pursed like he was still thinking. Dirt and Ignasi followed him out.

Socks was near the road and stood over a headless bovine, missing all its guts. His face was bloody from ears to whiskers, and judging by how he wagged his tail, he'd been enjoying himself.

-Cook it,- said Socks.

"We're just getting the fire ready. It's going to take a while. I hope you don't mind," said Hèctor, voice unsure, like he was trying to decide how polite he wanted to sound. "Can you pick up things that are burning like you pick up little Dirt, there? Or would that hurt you somehow?"

-It won't hurt me. The fire has to get on me for it to hurt,- said Socks.

"Good. Then can you knock that burning tower over and spread it around right there? Wait, here," said Hèctor. He took a stick and drew two lines, making a square with the stone walls on either side. "Try and push all the wood between these lines and spread it out evenly."

Socks paused, thinking, head tilted as he stared at the tower. The pup's mind spun as he puzzled out the best way to go about it. He glanced at the stone fences to either side and got an idea. The tower crashed forward in a huge shower of sparks. A rush of heat hit Dirt all the way back by the doorway, but instead of going everywhere, the burning logs crashed into an invisible wall and bounced around inside it. They came to rest in a near-even layer on the ground, and Socks spread them just a bit more to make it flat.

"Oh, you did it different!" thought Dirt.

-I never tried it like that. I always only grabbed things, but I can put a barrier. It was a lot easier than grabbing each piece,- said Socks, just to him.

"You could do all sorts of things with that. Can you make it big and block the wind?"

-I bet I could. I'll practice. How are they going to cook it?-

"I don't actually know," replied Dirt. Then, aloud, he said, "So how are we going to cook it? Do we just throw it on the fire?"

Hèctor said, "It has to be above the fire to cook, not in it. It'll just burn if we throw it in. Ignasi, get a pot for the fat."

He stepped over near the fire, more ember than flame now and hot enough he had to squint. He picked up some rusty metal poles that Dirt hadn't noticed before and held them up. "We're going to put the meat on these and hold it over the fire that way. Come here."

Dirt followed Hèctor to the dead bull, where the man knelt and got to work with Dirt's knife. Dirt and Socks watched with great interest as the man took the carcass apart. First, he removed the skin in one large piece and laid it out nearby. Next, using clever spiral cuts, he removed the meat in long chunks no more than a finger's length thick, which he piled up on the skin. He also removed the fat and set it all in a heap on a different section of skin.

Ignasi brought out the chopped rosemary in a bundle of cloth, which he set near the carcass along with a pot of salt. Then he scooped up all the fat into a metal pot and carried it back inside.

Dirt and Hèctor salted the meat and rubbed rosemary all over it, then skewered it on the metal in a wavy pattern that helped them pack as much on as possible. Once as much of the meat was as skewered as would fit, which was most of it, Socks lifted the roasts and set them over the fire, with the metal poles held up by the two stone fences.

Socks sat down close to the fire so he could watch and smell it as it cooked, since the scent changed over time. Dirt sat inside his front paw, arm resting on the pup's foreleg. "It already smells good. How long does it take?" he asked.

Hèctor sat nearby, but still a couple body lengths from the pup. "A while. Big chunks take longer. I've never cooked this much at once, but I can tell you it won't be done at the same time. We'll eat it bit by bit. Or Socks will, I suppose."

-You little humans don't eat very much. I can share.-

"I figured. Thanks. Dirt, I want to hear more about that ruined city where you found this knife," said Hèctor.

Dirt told the whole story, starting with those rolling hills and chasing the deer. How they'd seen the road and followed it up to find a whole city up there. Its name had been Ocriculum, he now knew, and that statue was a famous hero that Prisca's memories recognized but didn't name. Dirt talked about walking into the buildings and wondering what it had been like when people lived there, but didn't mention how he was sure he recognized it and started crying.

He told how they'd found the rusted metal doors to the underground and explored, accidentally letting out the smoke monster and how Father scared it off with a howl. Both Hèctor and Ignasi shifted uncomfortably at that part, and Dirt didn't need to see their minds to know they'd been waiting for something like that, something to justify not doing what Dirt had been up to. Humans didn't seem to do a lot of exploring these days. He left out the twisted statue of the god in that giant burial room, though, since he still wasn't sure himself what to think about it. The story ended with him opening the tomb and taking the knife.

Hèctor had a certain glint in his eye, and his mind spun with possibilities he shied away from instead of embracing. Things he wasn't sure he dared let himself dream. Finally, he asked, "Do you think there are more? More knives, or other treasures in a place like that?"

"Probably. We only opened one tomb. And the lamps still worked, if you wanted to take those. Why? Are you thinking of going on an adventure?"

Hèctor snorted. "No, no, this is more than enough of an adventure for one lifetime. We might save a lot of lives if we succeed. Maybe turn back the end for just a while. I'm content to do one thing that matters. But I can wonder. All that gold, and maybe even an eternal blade. I never thought I'd see one."

Ignasi had been listening from the doorway nearby, close enough he could peek back at the pot of fat every so often, and the men fell silent after that. Dirt only allowed himself a few peeks at their thoughts, and both men were thinking bright and vivid things, grand imaginings about unearthing gold and other treasures and winning fame and comfort.

Just the glimpses Dirt got filled him with that familiar longing for his lost people, that grand and beautiful empire. These men dreamed of winning a few scraps, but they'd never know the truth of it, how glorious it had been.

-You told me not to let you think about that too much,- Socks told him.

Dirt grinned. He'd said that, hadn't he? It always made him sad. To change things up, he held up the Home-staff and said, "Home, I hope you're having fun watching this. It's interesting, isn't it? Will you ask Marina if she wants to come join us for dinner? Are you done with her? Is she ready to come back?"

The staff shook slightly in response and then fell still again. A moment later it vibrated so strongly he almost dropped it, since he wasn't holding it very tightly. It kept trying to jerk toward an open spot of grass, so he stood up and carried it over, set it down, and stepped back.

Marina appeared with a heavy thud and a groan, like she'd fallen from above and landed there. Even expecting it, Dirt still jumped in startlement and took a second to process what he was looking at.

"Oh . . . Oh! Look, she's back!" Dirt yelled. The men had been watching, though, and already knew. They hurried over while Dirt rolled the poor woman onto her back and wiped the hair out of her face. "It's okay, Marina. Just lie there for a moment. You'll feel better soon. Trust me, I know. Can one of you give her a little water?"

"Ow," groaned Marina. Her clothing was all dirty now, especially below the knees, which Dirt only noticed because the dirt was black and stood out. Her straight brown hair stuck to beads of sweat forming on her forehead, and her narrow face was pinched with pain.

"Are you alright?" asked Hèctor, leaning in.

"Ow, I said."

"She'll be fine. The first time the trees did this to me, it made me so sick I thought I was dying. They've gotten gentler, but not by much." Dirt patted her head softly.

"Thank you, Dirt, but that doesn't help. Would all of you back up a little and give me room to breathe?" she said.

Dirt and the men obliged, getting up and moving back a step or two. Socks, however, leaned down and sniffed her thoroughly. *-She smells like ferns and dirt. Dirt's dirt.-*

"I miss that dirt," said Dirt. He leaned in and sniffed as well. "She does. You smell like my dirt, Marina."

"Thank you? Wait, what was that?" Marina said, confused. She sat up and looked around, squinting as her eyes adjusted to the bright sunlight. "That voice?"

-That was me, silly human,- said Socks, wagging his tail.

"Socks?" she said.

-Yes.-

She slumped back into the grass and rubbed her forehead. "Ow."

Ignasi said, "Believe it or not, the giant wolf who speaks in our minds is not the most frightening thing we saw while you were gone."

"Oh, you have no idea what frightening is," said Marina.

"I think we have some idea," said Hèctor.

Marina sat up again, color returning to her face. Dirt peeked at her mind just to be sure, and fortunately the dizziness was wearing off now. She was fine.

"So, dear Marina, what do you have to say for yourself? Where have you been, while we were doing all the work?" said Ignasi.

"Where do I start? I guess with this," she said, holding up one hand to show a bracelet of living green vines wound tightly around her wrist.

CHAPTER FIFTEEN

The dryads—the trees—put this on me. At first, I only talked to one, whose name was *Home*," said Marina, showing the bracelet of twisting vines. She used Dirt's word for *Home*, not her language. "She was a little gray child, a girl, with green hair. But there were others, hundreds more, mostly little girls, but there was at least one boy. None of them were as naked as Dirt, except that one. The rest covered themselves with little leaves or moss. It was—oh, those trees!"

She paused and looked up at the few clouds floating softly in the sky, remembering.

"I told you the trees were big," said Dirt, grinning smugly.

"What were they like?" asked Ignasi.

"If I had to guess, not counting the roots, which were huge themselves, the trunks were maybe forty paces across? At least? I have no idea how tall they were. Too tall to even guess. But the lowest leaves must have been higher than those clouds. It felt like a dream. The whole time, seriously, everything felt like a dream."

"Was the naked one Callius?" asked Dirt.

"I think so. He asked me a few questions about you, but I hardly saw him after that," said Marina.

"He was showing off, then. It's harder to do a whole body," said Dirt.

"Huh. Well, mostly I talked with Home and Ona and Montse."

"Wait, who are Ona and Montse? Were they dryads?"

"They certainly weren't human. But those two were girls the first time I saw them, and right in front of my eyes they grew into women. Young women, perfect and beautiful," said Marina. "I'm sure I screamed. That was one thing that I never got used to—how often they liked to shift their features or shape right in front of me."

"I never met those ones, I guess," said Dirt, unsure how he felt about that. It felt like she'd been treading uninvited on *his* ground and found things he didn't know about.

"Oh, you did. They knew you. They just didn't have names. I named a whole bunch of them," said Marina. "That was quite a day. It was my first day there, after the night they took me. Dawn asked me something, and I told her I knew more names than I could list, and then all day after that, every few minutes another one would just *appear*, standing right over there like she sprang up from the ground, and ask me for a name. At first, they asked me what the names all meant, but I kept saying I didn't know because they're just names, and eventually they gave up. I think to them, every name has a meaning instead of just a sound, I guess."

As she talked, her eyes looked into the distant horizon, or up at the clouds, or into the embers of the fire. Always distant and always moving, as if her memories were all out there somewhere, waiting until she looked at them before they came back to her.

Dirt said, "I like how there's always the leaves up there, never just sky. It makes it feel like you're always inside. I used to get scared of the sky because I had nightmares about falling up into nothing."

"Well, it just made *me* dizzy, and if I kept looking, I'd get nauseous. It's too high up. Too big. Something about them just isn't right."

"Dear Marina, I think you've told us about everything *except* the bracelet," said Ignasi, eyes twinkling.

She looked at him, face blank for an instant. "I'm getting to it," she said, unconvincingly. "Actually, let me just start over. The night they took me, I was sure I was going to die from the bite. I knew how bad it was. But then I got . . . transferred? It hurt, and it was fast, and at the other end I was stunned. It was darker there, the shadows deeper, and all around me are these little girls with glassy eyes. They almost look like dolls, except they move like people. I can see they have gray skin, and their hair is all green, and they're wearing clothing of moss or leaves, but none of it matches. And I'm lying in this damp, wet dirt, blacker than any I've ever seen before, and one of them says something in a language I don't recognize."

Dirt nodded and said, "They were probably speaking my language. I didn't know there was more than one language until I met you."

"Yeah, I'm getting to that. Just listen. So this little girl smiles at me with all the grace of an old lady and babbles something, and I scream. I have no idea what's going on or where I am, and she terrifies me. I try to get up and run, but there's nowhere to go because I don't recognize anything. There's nothing to recognize. Just trees, but I didn't understand that at first. Not until the next morning. I thought there was another earth up there, a whole different world, and the tree trunks were pillars holding the two together," said Marina. She paused again and leaned over the fire to examine the meat and rotate the spits, but Dirt suspected it had more to do with trying to gather her thoughts than minding the fire.

She continued. "They grabbed me and held me down, and the little girl talks again, and I can see her face is sad, full of compassion, and she's trying to explain but I don't understand a word. I'm screaming, and she's trying to calm me down, but there are twenty more of these horrid little monster girls holding me down, and then . . . then nothing. I wake up the next morning in a bed, right out in the open. I think it was the same spot."

"Was it a bed of those little fiber clumps?"

"Yeah, it was."

"I love those things. The only thing better is puppy fur."

"Just let her talk, Dirt," said Hèctor. He didn't look angry, though.

"Sorry."

"He's fine, Hèctor. And yes, it was comfortable, but that's not what I was thinking about at the time. It was cold and foggy, and I couldn't see the trees anymore. It was early, still twilight, and I can't see anything. I'm looking in every direction, and there's nothing. I can't see ten feet in any direction. Just my bed, and ferns. That's it. I'm starting to think I died, honestly. I'm thinking, Marina, this is the underworld. That's why there's a second earth up above. You're in the land of the dead. It's not so bad, really. Comfortable. Restful, maybe, if those horrid children stay away. I'm sure they'll be back, though, so I sit up and that's when I realize my stomach isn't injured anymore. Even my clothing is stitched up, but I can see where it was stitched. I pull up my shirt, and all I find are little lines where the teeth marks should have been. No redness, nothing. No pain."

Ignasi said, "Noble Socks licking my arm had the same effect. By the next morning, I hardly knew I'd been bitten."

"Incredible, right? Well, at this point I'm sure I'm dead. I'm *sure* I'm dead. And then she appears—the one from last night. Except now I can understand her. She says her name is Home, and she's a friend of Dirt's. I ask if I'm dead, and she chuckles like an old woman. Not a little girl giggle.

"I finally take the time to get a good look at her, and I still can't tell what she is. I'm wondering if she's a witch, maybe, or something worse. A living puppet, except she's far too realistic for that. She moves like a living thing. So then I think maybe they're some kind of *fada* I've never heard of, and I'm in the land of Faerie. Either that or dead, and they're spirits from below. My mind is spinning, but I *feel* alive, so I'm not sure.

"She sees how upset I am and gently rests her hand on mine, in a comforting sort of way. She says she healed me, and she wants to learn more about me, with my permission. What I'm made of. How I'm put together. I don't understand her at first, because what on earth could that mean? But she wants to give me something as her part of a bargain, so what do I want? And remember, I'm thinking she's a *fada* or a spirit or something."

Marina paused again, a fingertip rubbing along the braids in the bracelet. She gazed deep into the fire, and Dirt and the others all waited, hardly breathing, to find out what came next. But she was content to let them wait, deep in thought. Finally she said, "I told her I wanted a child."

"You didn't!" hissed Ignasi.

"Did you . . . get one?" asked Hèctor, eyes deeply wary.

"It's not what you think. She wasn't a witch. She's a tree, like Dirt said. But I tell her I want a child, and that's all I want, but I'm barren. She smiles at me and says, 'We have learned much, but there is still more we wish to learn.' And then she says she can *fix* me, fix my womb so I can bear children, and she will do it for free, asking nothing in return. But if I'm willing, then when I get with child, they want me to come back, and they'll make sure it's born healthy and strong."

"She wants to take your child?" asked Hèctor, his eyes a little wider in concern.

Dirt cut in to say, "No, I'm sure they just wanted to see how it grows. They don't know anything about the world. They're trees. They didn't even have eyes until they made dryads. They didn't know what the world *was*."

Hèctor and Ignasi both shot him a short glare for interrupting, but Marina said, "Yes, as the boy says. Home explained what Dirt just said. She says she's curious about the world, how babies are formed and how they grow. She explains that inside me are halves of a seed, and the other half comes from a male, and those grow into a new life. She says if I let them figure out how I'm put together, they'll find out why my part isn't working and why I'm barren, and fix it."

"Well, that's not true," said Ignasi. "Women do not have seed."

"I know. But still, she was pretty convincing. And certain. She was absolutely certain."

"So what's the bracelet for?" asked Hèctor.

"I'm getting to that. She looks at me with those glassy eyes, and her face is full of wisdom and concern, like an old lady's, like I said. Except she's a child, and not human. So I say I don't know, and she promises it won't hurt, because they've had a lot of practice. Well, that doesn't help either, because so does the butcher. But then she says she practiced on Dirt, and he's fine, isn't he? She says all I have to do is lie down and hold still. No pain.

"Well, obviously, they have my attention. If they can make me fertile again, any price would be worth it. So I do it. I lie down on the bed and tell them to go ahead. I'm scared, and I have no idea what's about to happen, but Home smiles and rests her hand on my forehead, and I fall asleep. Then I wake up a short time later, and it's already over. That was it," said Marina.

"Wait, they put you to sleep first? Lucky," said Dirt.

Marina shrugged, having hardly noticed he spoke, too engrossed in her story. "Yep. Home tells me there was a problem with a passage in my womb, and my seed-half couldn't get to the right place, and now it's fixed. I'm fertile again. Just like that. A short nap, and I'm fertile. She also said there was something wrong with my heart, and she fixed that too. I say it was Home, but it wasn't just her. There were others around.

Always. Usually just a few close by, but always dozens out there in the ferns, watching.

"She helps me get up, but I feel fine. I thank her and ask where we are. She says she doesn't know, but would I like to see her tree? Then she points at the biggest tree I've ever seen, and I finally realize it's a tree, because the fog has lifted, and I can get a good look at it. This is when I realize I'm in the place Dirt told us about—that giant forest. These are the dryads, his friends. I guess that means they *were* puppets after all, just very good ones.

"They show me around, and there's all sorts of things going on. Lots of work. They're preparing something, so I ask them what, and they tell me, except it's a secret. It's a gift for Dirt, and you'll find out next time you visit. That's what they told me. I guess I shouldn't say any more about that. But they show me all sorts of things, like Dirt's little house under Home's branches, and some old ruins. They asked me if I knew what they were, but I had no idea. It was old, though. Very, very old."

"So, the bracelet?" asked Ignasi again, a twinkle in his eye.

"Oh, fine. The bracelet. It'll bring me back to her when I'm pregnant again. And in the meantime, it'll help me keep healthy and make sure I don't run out of seed halves before that happens. I told her it takes nine months for a child to grow, so she wants me to stay there during the whole pregnancy," said Marina. She rubbed the bracelet again, and Dirt could see something healthy in her face, like a happy sort of hunger. Yearning, about to be fulfilled.

"Was that all, or was there more to the deal?" asked Hèctor.

Marina looked at him, her brown eyes sparking at first and then withdrawing. Dirt could tell she didn't want to say the rest, but it was too late. She'd have to. "No, there was more."

"Do you have to give the evil fae your child?" asked Ignasi, humor in his voice. His eyes, however, looked more serious now.

"Sort of."

"Marina!" shouted Hèctor and Ignasi at the same time.

"It's not like that! Listen to the rest first," said Marina. She crossed her arms over her knees and looked back into the fire. "Home told me if I agreed to give birth there and let them watch the child's first few months, then I'll never get sick. Any wounds I get will close and never take a rot. If I agree, then I'm certain to die of old age.

"So I'm thinking to myself, if I have a baby, or even several, I want to watch them grow up. I have to be alive for that to happen, but so do they. So many die, you know? So I say, 'Then you have to promise to keep them healthy as well,' and she agrees," said Marina. "I think that's what she was hoping for in the first place. But I've heard worse agreements, right?"

She shrugged and looked at her companions for affirmation, but they had their brows furrowed and didn't even nod. She continued, "So that's the deal. My children will be born there, but I'm free to leave after a time, with my child. It's not so bad there, I don't think. I wasn't there long enough for everything to stop feeling creepy, but I could get used to it. They don't know how unnerving they are. And a child wouldn't know any better."

"There are worse places to live," said Dirt, quietly.

The other humans looked at him, then looked away before meeting his gaze.

"I'm sorry, Dirt, I know you're from there, but . . ." said Marina, trailing off.

Dirt found he had nothing to say. Hearing her talk about his beloved trees in a way anything other than glowing affection bothered him. He understood, of course; he knew better than anyone how scary they could be at first. But they were still his friends, and he still loved them.

"Dear Dirt, if you don't mind me asking, did you make any bargains with them as well?" said Ignasi.

"Oh, no, nothing like that. They're my friends. For example, I agreed to carry this everywhere, which is part of Home," said Dirt, gesturing with the staff. "But it's because I want her to see the world with me. She can't really travel on her own because she's a tree. She makes me sap and water if I need it, and she's also a really good weapon when I need one. But it's not because we have a deal. It's because we're friends."

Marina went pale and said, "Oh, I forgot about that. She's watching through that staff right now, isn't she? I'm sorry, I didn't mean to call them creepy. I just—"

Dirt grinned and interrupted. "Oh, don't worry about that. Home is way, way, too old and way too powerful to get offended by a little tiny human. If anything, she's going to fret that you didn't say anything about it when you were there so she could figure out what you meant. Although she's so smart I'm sure she already did."

Hèctor said, "So will you live out your days in that forest, once you get pregnant?"

"Oh, no, just for a while. But maybe. If the dryads aren't going to hurt me, then I can't picture anything else there being any threat whatsoever," said Marina.

"Well, mostly there aren't any threats. Not anymore," said Dirt.

"What do you mean?" she asked.

"Goblins, although the dryads kill them now. And there was a gryphon once. There might be other things. The really bad one was the living skeleton named Prisca. She was—"

"Stop! Stop right there, Dirt. I don't want to hear about any walking skeletons when I'm sitting within arm's reach of so many non-living ones," said Ignasi.

"Stop being so cowardly about skeletons," said Hèctor. "They're just bones."

"Yes, and boats are just floaty wood, but you still won't get on one, will you, Hèctor?"

"That's not the same."

Marina said, "That was one thing they showed me. The building where . . . Prisca was. It was incredible. I've never seen a building so grand."

"It looked better when it was new," said Dirt, sighing.

Marina just gave him a curious look, and Dirt realized what he'd just said. "Not that I would know. Just from how it looks now," he hastily added.

"What do you mean?" she asked.

"Well, it's all collapsing now. The pillars are cracked and fallen, part of the roof caved in, the whole garden is so overgrown there's nothing left, the roof lost most of its arch. Stuff like that."

"Oh. Pardon me. I've said too much," said Marina.

"What? What did you say? I'm confused," said Dirt.

"Never mind. I think some of the meat is done. Don't you, Hèctor?"

Dirt recognized she was hiding something, but before he could peek at her mind and see what it was, Socks said, just to him, *-Don't look.*

And don't ask why. I know what she is thinking about, and you will be happier if you find out later.-

"Well, that's hardly fair."

-It's perfectly fair. Just trust me. And don't think too hard about it. I am trying not to pry and learn more either.-

"Fine."

Dirt scowled, and since shifting his mind away from a good puzzle was near impossible, he stood up and stepped over to the fire to watch Hèctor cutting and testing different sections of meat.

The man poked at a spit on the edge whose meat was sliced thinner and wrapper tighter than most of the rest. After peeling a length of it away from the iron bar, he nodded and sliced off quite a bit, which he deposited on a serving platter. It would scarcely make a bite for Socks, but it was enough for the four humans to eat their fill with plenty left over. Even so, Hèctor decided it would be more prudent to share with the giant hungry wolf first than make him wait. He put a few decent slices onto some plates that Ignasi had brought out and took the rest over to Socks.

"How do you want to do this? Do you want to lick it off, or open up and have me throw it in?"

Socks eagerly rose to his feet and got his nose close to the platter. *-I will do it. I am worried you will miss.-*

The sliced meat lifted from the platter in a bundle, and Socks snapped his jaws to bite it right out of the air. He let it linger on his tongue, enjoying the flavor, then chewed a little to try to spread it out before finally swallowing.

"Well? Worth all the wait and effort?" asked Hèctor.

-Yes. I like it.- The pup sniffed the fire, already ready for more. He'd have to wait, though. *-Humans are silly, but this is clever.-*

Dirt's mouth watered as he took his plate from Ignasi. The aroma, now that it was right in front of his face, was incredible. The rosemary turned the meat into something else, giving it a pleasant richness. He waved his hand over the plate to cool it off a bit, then picked it up and took a bite.

He'd thought the bread was the best thing he'd ever had in his life, and maybe it had been up to that point. But *this* was far, far beyond that. The meat had layers—a bit of ash and char, a gray well-cooked section, and some paler red in the middle. It dripped juices that Dirt slurped up. The spices complemented the meat perfectly, and the salt brought out the flavor in a way he never would have guessed. It was incredible.

"Do you like it?" asked Ignasi, amused. "Look, his mouth is too full to answer. I guess he does."

Dirt nodded vigorously and took another bite, exactly as much as he could possibly fit and still chew. He did so slowly, letting the juices mingle and run down his throat on their own.

The rest of the day passed much like that—Marina shared her experiences with the dryads while the meat cooked, and as more sections were ready, everyone ate their fill. Ignasi and Hèctor told her what had happened while she was gone, although they were a bit vague about precisely *where* Dirt had gotten the lights he'd used to chase off the angry ghosts.

By the time night fell, the embers were low and quiet, and Socks had eaten almost the entire bull. He rested his head on the ground near Dirt, who idly petted and scratched the areas he could reach. The two of them silently sent puffs of affection and enjoyment back and forth as they began to nod off.

But it wasn't time to end the day just yet. The humans' conversation turned to their plans for tomorrow, which were mostly just more rummaging around for things, and maybe checking out the upper floors of the tower.

Socks had other ideas, however, and told everyone, *-That is not the plan for tomorrow. It is time for me and Dirt to leave. We have been here too long already. You can come with us if you promise to hurry.-*

"Where are you going?" asked Marina.

-It doesn't matter, but somewhere new.-

"Then how about we go to the city together and find out if it's still there?"

"Do you know the way from here?" asked Ignasi.

"I'm certain," said Marina. "That way. We follow those mountains until they flatten out onto the plain, and cross from there. When we get to the hills, we should start finding farms, and it should be obvious the rest of the way."

-Then we will go look at all the humans in the city. Climb up so we can go to sleep now, Dirt.-

CHAPTER SIXTEEN

Dirt woke several times during the night, sure he heard ghostly whispers. But each time, all was silent except for the wind, which blew in long, steady gusts. Sometimes someone shifted in their blankets, or Marina breathed loudly. At one point, Hèctor started making a terrible sound that took Dirt a moment to recognize as snoring, since he'd never heard it before. After only a moment, though, Dirt heard a smack, and Hèctor rolled over and quit. One of the other two must have hit him.

Socks didn't let him stay awake for long, though, and quickly dragged him back into their shared dreams. They walked on the clouds in an upside-down world, with the ground and buildings and hills and everything high above them; they had to hop from place to place to keep from falling into the blue abyss. They chased birds and peculiar little balls of colored light that danced and laughed any time one of them got close, and explored caves and castles of white that couldn't be seen from the ground.

He woke with a wistful sort of weariness, regretting the dream was over and remembering the majesty of that inverted landscape, and feeling like he hadn't gotten enough sleep. He lay there for a while waiting for Socks to wake up and wondered if it *had* been whispers that woke him up once or twice.

Did ghosts have anywhere else to go? He suspected these ones' ability to affect the world had been greatly diminished and might still be around. So what happened to them in general? Did the dead just hang around, waiting for a new body to be born in? The dryads said everyone only ever gets the same one and has to wait for it to reappear.

He thought about the purple smoke monster that had been waiting in the mausoleum for so long, the one Father had scared off. And the god, fallen from his pedestal and lying on the floor, twisted and tortured. Maybe the god was supposed to be helping the dead and couldn't anymore, leaving them to wander. Thousands of years like that, possibly, with no shepherd to guide them to their next destination.

There was darkness in that thought. Guilt. Maybe Dirt had caused all this when he broke the world. Not only had he thrown down the entire empire, but also the gods and everything that depended on them. It left him melancholy, his mood bitter and gray like the low and roiling clouds that had rolled in overnight.

Until Socks woke up, that is. The pup woke with such a start that Dirt tumbled roughly to the ground when he leaped up to stand. *-Sorry.-*

"It's okay. Good morning, Socks."

The pup leaned down to sniff Dirt a couple times, then gave him one quick little lick and raised his head back up to look around warily. The pup seemed restless, and when Dirt looked at his mind, he found fear and the memory of pain. Jaws from the earth. Terror.

-I sense the Devourer. We have been here too long. He is not here yet, but he will find us if we wait,- said Socks timidly. Gone were the bravado and reckless curiosity. For once, the pup sounded like the soft little child he still was, when measured against his own kind.

Ignasi was nearby, just over by the fire, poking around to see if there were still any warm coals. Hèctor and Marina were in the house by the table in the front room, where they'd pulled everything out of her pack to check it all.

"Good morning, you two," said Ignasi, rising and spinning the stick he held. He had an open bottle of wine and took a little sip. He pointed the stick upward and said, "It looks like we'll have to stay a while longer, noble Socks. The rain will be nasty, I am sure."

Socks said, to everyone, *-Dirt and I are leaving right now. If you want to come with us, then you have to come right now, and you have to promise to hurry, or we will leave you. I am only bringing you because Dirt wants to find the humans, and we don't know where they are.-*

That was a surprise, but not much of one. Socks didn't scare easily, and those scars on his stomach hadn't come from anything they'd done together.

It didn't seem like much of a surprise for Hèctor, somehow. To Dirt's amazement, he stepped out of the house and said, "Understood. How long have we got to prepare?"

-Put those things in the bag, and we will leave right now.-

"You got it," said Hèctor. He stepped inside and started throwing Marina's things back into her backpack while she watched in confusion.

Ignasi said, "What's the rush, exactly?" He moved slowly toward his pack and wistfully stoppered the wine.

Socks didn't answer, instead raising his nose to smell the wind. His head turned every direction, and he stepped from side to side, unable to keep still. Dirt put his little backpack on and sent Socks a mental puff of encouragement.

Marina finally asked, "Hèctor, what's going on?"

"We're leaving. You heard the wolf," said Hèctor. He quickly made his way to his own pack, where he rolled his blanket back up and tied it on.

-You are good at hurrying,- said Socks appreciatively.

"No, I feel it too," said Hèctor. "We need to leave. There's something on the wind I don't like."

Marina stepped out, wearing her pack. "You and your feelings," she said, sighing.

Ignasi unstoppered the wine, took a quick swig, stoppered it again, and shoved it in his pack. "Hèctor is, after all, a man known for his many feelings," he sighed. "Just look at him. An emotional, feelings-driven man, our Hèctor."

"Stay here, then," muttered Hèctor.

"See? That is annoyance, which is a feeling," said Ignasi. He tossed his pack on his back and adjusted the shoulder straps. Then he took out a small comb and began straightening his hair and beard. When Hèctor shot him a look, he said, "What? I'm ready to go. Why are you dawdling?"

The others were right behind, though. Marina was ready, and as soon as Hèctor got his pack straightened away, he was ready as well.

Dirt used a little mana to jump up onto Socks's back before the pup could pick him up and asked with his mind, *"Are you going to carry them, too?"*

-No. I am not a pack animal. And they don't want me to, anyway. All three of them are thinking about it and hoping I don't.-

"Oh."

Leaving town was a strange experience. Dirt had started getting used to having buildings everywhere he looked, even though at first they'd been novel and unfamiliar. Perhaps he was merely adopting the atmosphere of it, but it was a human place, and it made him feel more human. But now, the path before them held nothing but the wilds. Two rows of steadily shrinking mountains and empty plains beyond that. It felt meaningful to return to the wilderness somehow, like he was a different person out here. Maybe civilization was like the pants he had on—something he wore, but not really part of himself. He suddenly felt like taking them off, but didn't.

No, he realized, the civilized person had been Avitus, when he'd lived in the Sunset Empire and been an old man. Dirt was the wild boy. The Sunset Empire was gone, and so was Avitus. Maybe Dirt would stay Dirt forever, and Avitus would never crawl out of the ruins he'd collapsed under.

Socks struggled the whole way. The terrain was flat and dry and would be until the rain came, but the pup strained to keep from going faster. The poor pup's hackles wanted to rise, and no amount of soothing from Dirt did any good.

The three humans kept up only with significant difficulty. Hèctor was the only of the three with the energy to keep looking back to see if his ominous feelings had presented a source yet, but all three of them panted and strained to walk at the quick speed Socks set. Just under the speed where they'd have to start jogging, since that would tire them out even faster. Frankly, Dirt was glad he wasn't down there, because walking that fast for so long had to be hard. The wind kept changing direction, too, and when it blew against them, they all slowed down.

After a hard-fought morning that left the poor humans enervated and hungry, and left Socks increasingly nervous and skittish, the clouds burst open, and the rain hit them like a crashing wave. Gusts of wind blew so hard the rain almost fell sideways, freezing cold and sharp, and it only took Dirt until about the count of ten to decide he hated it. He'd been wondering what rain was like ever since Socks told him about it, but now that he saw it for himself, rain was no fun.

The ground turned muddy, and it got much harder to walk. Marina was the first to give up—after falling for the second time, she slid out of the shoulder straps of her backpack and rolled onto her back, where she lay panting in a puddle.

Hèctor said, "We have to stop, Socks. Give us a few minutes." He was careful to drop his pack on the grass instead of the mud, but after that he sat so hard it looked like falling.

-A few minutes,- said Socks, recognizing the impossibility of going any farther.

Even Ignasi was too winded to make any jokes, which showed it was serious. His face looked haggard and red, and the rainwater dripping out of his beard made him look colder than the others.

Dirt hopped down, landing with a splash in the mud, and was immediately annoyed at how the wet cloth stuck to his legs and restricted his movement. He looked at his pants in frustration, wondering if he really should just take them off. They wouldn't just slide down, though—he'd have to peel them. And now that he thought about it, would that make him warmer, or colder? Either way, he was feeling somewhat miserable.

When he felt resentment start to build, however, he pushed it away. Socks wasn't in a pleasant frame of mind either, and if both of them were in a bad mood at the same time, it might lead to conflict. That was unimaginable.

"Oh, Socks, can you try something?" Dirt said aloud, for everyone to hear. "Can you make a wall with your mind to keep the rain off while we rest? And maybe block the wind? I know you're fine, but us humans don't have any fur to keep the rain off."

Socks was not, in fact, fine. He was as soaked as everyone else and being cold wasn't helping his mood. His thoughts kept returning to his nice warm den, which was always dry, and had other pups to play with in it, and Mother and Father to feed him.

Dirt snapped his fingers and summoned his little ball of light, then another and another, until he had three like the other night. He inhaled more mana to feed them, making them grow bright, and smooshed them into each other to make one big one.

Then he closed his eyes and tried something new. He felt how the mana cycled inside him, always on the edges of his perception but no less real. Making the light had been instinctual for him, something so practiced for Avitus that Dirt could do it without knowing how. And now that he tried, the understanding didn't come easily. There were no mental words like with wood shaping, no speaking to tell something to change. Just power, manifesting itself in an almost pure form.

Well, what he needed right now was heat, not light. If the lights got bright enough, they also got warm—he'd discovered that with the ghosts. He kept his eyes closed and pictured the magical blaze above him growing dim, like the soft red embers of yesterday's fire. In a normal fire, flames were bright and yellow, but the dull, quiet red embers were much hotter.

He felt the heat on his skin, subtle as it was, and let that perception shape the magic instead of his eyesight. Dirt didn't need eyes to use magic, since the trees didn't either. He tried adding mana, and that made it a bit warmer, but so bright he could see it through his eyelids. So then he withdrew mana instead, imagining only the brightness losing its power, while the heat kept going.

That seemed to work. The mana slowed to a trickle, but the faint heat remained. Dirt placed his mind into his mana body as far as it would go, straining to sense the world the trees understood effortlessly, and drew more mana from it. It took a shocking amount of concentration to try to separate the magical perceptions of heat and light, but they were indeed different. They had different characteristics, different signatures, which wanted to blend together and become one unless he forced them apart.

He carefully fed a trickle of mana into his work, filtering out everything except heat. Pure mana was uncountable things all at once, all of creation melded into pure white, but Dirt filtered it by concentrating with every inch of his body. The trickle of mana accumulated and gathered, and Dirt felt heat growing on his skin, radiating at him like the sun on a warm day. He made it a little hotter, then a little hotter than that, until if he wasn't soaking wet, he'd be sweating.

Then, with a tired sigh, he stretched out his arms and stood with his legs apart and let himself start drying out. Only then did he open his eyes. A red ember, dim and hot, floated nearby, radiating all the heat he could want. It rained all around, but not on them; an arc-shaped soft wall of force stopped most of the wind and rain, which gathered in small pools and dripped off to the sides. Dirt had imagined Socks's mental walls to be perfectly smooth, but apparently they weren't.

Ignasi seemed relaxed and relieved, but Hèctor and Marina stared appreciatively, both at the shield above them and the hot little ember over Dirt's head that was quickly warming up the area. Dirt summoned another one, almost losing his concentration in the process, and sent it hovering close to Socks. The look of relief on the pup's face was all the thanks Dirt was offered, and it was all he needed.

Marina said, "One of the first things Home told me, I think you'll find this funny. She said that Dirt was a human. She looked me right in the eyes, got all serious, and said, 'Dirt is a human child, and not anything else. Do you understand?' I guess she was watching through the staff the whole time, and it upset her that we weren't sure."

Dirt grinned slyly and said, "I am just a human . . . like Home is just a tree."

Marina snorted in amusement and said, "You're kinda short to make that comparison."

"But he does produce sap, so that's one similarity. Speaking of which, dear Dirt, do you mind? I am terrified to see the state of our travel rations right now," said Ignasi.

"Oh. Yeah. I guess I'm hungry too. Home, would you mind making some sap for everyone?" said Dirt. He held the staff up. But instead of sap leaking out of the bark, a twig grew off the side, sprouting a couple small leaves and then the buds of small flowers. The buds grew into fist-sized globes of green and dropped their petals, then darkened to red and then to purplish black.

"What's this?" he asked the staff, but Home couldn't reply.

"Berries," said Marina. "The dryads asked me a lot about what humans ate."

"I think I've seen these, but I didn't know you could eat them," said Dirt.

"And to think, you had almost convinced us you were human," said Ignasi. He plucked a fist-sized berry from the twig and took a shallow bite. "Am I still human? Or did I turn into a cat? Or turn purple like the berry?"

Dirt tossed one to Hèctor, who hadn't moved, and Marina, then plucked one and almost took a bite. Instead, he turned and threw it to Socks, who snapped it out of the air and stood up, wagging his tail.

-I want some more. I want enough to taste them,- he said, sniffing eagerly.

"Sure. Home, can you make a bunch for Socks?" asked Dirt. The tree obliged and produced about thirty, in groups of eight or ten. Dirt threw them all in at once, and that was enough for Socks to mash them with his tongue and chew them and get a good taste. He could tell the pup liked it from how some of the tension in his muscles faded. Dirt reached up and patted his friend's snout, right above the nose, and gave it a good scratch.

When it was Dirt's turn to finally eat one, he found that a single berry filled him up and reenergized him in a way he hadn't expected. He felt it from his wet, chilly toes to his slowly drying hair. "Oh. Oh! She put mana in them! Home, next time I visit, you have to teach me how to make these."

Marina held up her hands, which were red from the cold rain, and flexed her fingers. "I can't believe it," she said.

Hèctor stood and said, "Let's go. I still feel it."

A flash of light blinded them for an instant, followed in the same breath by an earsplitting crack that hit them like a slap. Dirt screamed and ducked down, too shocked to react any other way. Socks and the humans jumped in startlement, but he quickly recognized they weren't as scared as he was. He stood back up and shouted, "What was that?"

Hèctor started answering, but was interrupted by another flash of light, farther away, and another loud crack that was more of a rumble. "Just lightning."

"Lightning?"

"Just lightning, boy. Haven't you seen lightning before?" said Hèctor, trying not to act too impatient.

"No, never. Or rain. This is my first time," said Dirt. "Is it dangerous?"

"Yes. Don't go under any trees. It'll kill you if it hits you."

Dirt sighed, trying to calm his racing heart. Another flash, followed by another peal of thunder, kept that from working.

"We really need to get moving," said Hèctor. "Right now."

-Yes. It is him. He has found me. He is trying to slow me down while he comes.-

CHAPTER SEVENTEEN

"What do we do?" asked Dirt in a panic.

-We run. The closer he gets, the more accurately he can detect us. We might still get away.-

"Who is 'he'? What's coming?" asked Marina.

Dirt said, "It's complicated. But it's something that scares Socks. Come on!"

"Do you two need to leave us?" asked Ignasi, his face calmly serious.

-Not yet, but we will if we have to.-

Ignasi dropped his pack, letting it fall gracelessly into the mud. He tugged off his long jacket and dumped it on the ground, then stretched in an exaggerated way, as if basking in warm sunlight instead of drenched in heavy rain. "Hèctor, Marina, you should start moving before I have time to strip completely."

Hèctor nodded and dropped his pack as well, then with a wistful expression, his sword and jacket. Marina did the same and started running before the men did. Socks followed at a nervous trot, ushering the humans forward at what they probably thought was a fast jog.

Dirt shifted his weight to slide off and run alongside them, but Socks caught hold and told him, *-You stay on me in case we have to run fast.-*

"Okay. If we leave the others behind, will the Devourer kill them, too?"

-No. And probably not you, either. Just me. But I am not telling them that, or they will not hurry as much.-

Dirt grinned and lay down to hug the pup's fur more tightly. He discovered that if he really pressed down, Socks was warm enough to offset the cold from the rain. It failed to comfort his nervousness much, however. The wetness of Socks's fur brought out the faint, tangy scent of fear and anxiety, which Dirt only recognized after spending so much time sharing senses. In fact, he might be imagining it, just from knowing how Socks felt right now.

The humans ran in the widest-open areas they could find, despite the wind and heavy rain, as lightning crashed all across the valley. Dirt only flinched some of the time, but after each booming wave of sound shook them, he patted Socks gently and sent him another useless puff of reassurance. It was all he could do.

Dirt took a moment to watch the minds of the humans, just out of curiosity. They were not as used to this as he was, so what did they think? It turned out to be very different things. None of the three were particularly scared of the Devourer, although they all had a nervous tinge to their emotions. Hèctor was pleased at how energized he felt after eating that berry and was enjoying the feeling of easy athletic motion. Marina's thoughts were largely concerned with fear for her unborn baby, yet to be conceived. She already had a little knot of eager love growing for it, even though it didn't exist yet. It seemed she'd already ruled out Hèctor and Ignasi as sires and was wondering how long it would take her to find a mate once they reached the city.

Ignasi's thoughts were the most surprising, though, since they didn't seem to match his outward demeanor. He was frustrated and upset that nothing went how he pictured, and his dismay seemed to be symbolized in his mind by that nearly full bottle of wine in his abandoned pack. Dirt supposed that Ignasi being the most decisive didn't make him the happiest with the results.

A deep rumble shook the earth and built into a roar—something like thunder, but from underground. It was followed by a series of shuddering groans and cracks, each ear-splittingly loud despite sounding distant and muffled by the rain. Tremors passed like waves through the ground, and although Socks had no trouble with them, the jogging humans stumbled each time and struggled to regain their feet in the mud.

But those sounds faded, leaving no explanation for what they had been. Perhaps the very earth was being torn open to find them, but in all the wrong places. Dirt wasn't eager to find out.

They ran on, long enough for the terror of the unseen sounds to fade, and to go back to being regular miserable in the cold rain. Surprisingly, the humans never slowed, which Dirt attributed to the berries and the small amount of mana they had provided. Dirt could still feel it working inside him, keeping him sated and energized. Indeed, Dirt began to wonder if they'd escaped already.

Until a wave of mana washed over them from behind. It contained a shocking amount of power, so much that it seemed the skin between worlds shuddered and threatened to tear. The mana contained a command, an unspeakable word of magic that Dirt nonetheless recognized, being very close to something the dryads had taught him: *GROW.*

The ground rumbled in every direction, punctuated by cracks and creaks. Green sprouts popped from the ground and grew to become stunted, twisted trees; sickly and weak, but nonetheless solid. Their trunks refused to go straight up and down, each one bent at precarious angles to make as much of an obstacle as possible. From one moment to the next, the run was brought to a complete standstill.

Dirt stepped up onto Socks's head, and the pup straightened to give him a slightly better view. It was hard to see very far through the rain, but it thinned in places if he watched carefully and revealed that this wet plain of grass had become a forested swamp in an instant. No paths cut through the knotted mess of trees and bushes and vines, and everything was just tall enough that Socks couldn't step over it without jumping. There would be nowhere to land if he did.

They weren't truly trapped, but they might as well be. Socks didn't have anything to say, nor was he even thinking in words. It was quickly sinking in that the situation had gone from serious to deadly, and Socks was starting to panic. He whined as he stepped left and right in the tiny space that remained to him, mind spinning to find a way through.

"I'll handle this," said Dirt, sending the biggest mental puff of reassurance he could. He jumped all the way down, staff in hand.

His mind-sight showed him countless new trees, young and excited. They slowly explored the world with their alien senses and discovered there were others, with whom they began to speak in their way. Their minds were nothing like *his* trees, nowhere near as grand and complicated, but they were every bit as alien and incomprehensible. The only thing he could make out was a concept that seemed related to air or wind. And their greetings, simple and affectionate—those he could recognize, if not quite understand.

Dirt inhaled as much mana as he could, then let his staff wave loosely in an arc in front of him. It brushed against vines and spindly bushes and tapped a tree trunk, and all of them he commanded: *Bend.* Just as the dryads had taught him, he used their words and ideas to communicate his intent, and his own mana to actualize it. He stepped forward and raised his staff to brush the branches of the next tree, which were too short for Socks to pass under. *Bend.*

Another, and another, and the path began to open. Where he found two trees talking to each other, he commanded them both at once. Where the bushes or ivy could be stepped through, he ignored it. The plants all wondered at him, unable to understand what was happening or where the magic was coming from, but only briefly before moving on. The world was all too new to dwell on one experience.

Thank Grace, it got easier the farther they got. The trees began to establish their web of communication, allowing Dirt to direct increasing numbers of them out of the way at once. Even so, it took the utmost focus to discern that judging by *this* connection, that mind-light belonged to *that* particular tree, and so on. He had to bend them in the right direction to make a path, after all.

Dirt never managed to do it fast enough for a jog, but they kept up a decent walk. At least it was fast enough to keep Socks from panicking and whimpering and trying to get away by jumping over the treetops, which Dirt was sure would result in getting his lanky wolf legs tangled up and possibly broken.

Behind them, some of the trees bent back to their previous shape, and others didn't. The magic faded, leaving them stuck however they'd chosen to end up. It wouldn't matter much, since they didn't know what a shape was, let alone that they had one, but it still made Dirt wonder why they did that.

Dirt's anxiety faded completely before long, discarded beneath intense focus on his task and seeing so many happy new trees. Surprisingly, lack of anxiety made it easier, not harder, even though the task was urgent.

He felt like a great master for a time, unstoppable and unshakable in his own right, and the faithful certainty that gave him empowered his magic.

Despite making good progress, the wind and rain got worse, whipping the green branches of the trees and even breaking some that caught a gust at the wrong angle. The lightning never quite found them, always at a distance as it struck random trees in every direction, but neither did they leave it behind.

However, the farther they got, the more the trees spread out, and eventually Socks could pass through them unaided. Dirt finally relaxed his mind, which felt weary in a strange way that affected the rest of his body. When Socks picked him up and returned him to his usual perch, Dirt was flooded with so much relief that he almost fell asleep. If nothing else, lying down kept him out of the worst of the wind.

Now Socks felt it was safe to run, and this time he had no patience for stubby little human legs. He picked up the three humans and held them in the air while he darted this way and that through the trees, anywhere he could find a path. The rain went from unpleasant to stinging as Socks went fast enough for the water droplets to become sling missiles. Dirt tried to lift his head to watch where they were going, but the rain blinded him.

Which made him wonder how Socks was going so fast. Dirt looked at his mind, and it turned out ghost sight had almost no perception of rain, and Socks was using that. The pup didn't even have his eyes open since the pelting rain stung too much. Despite the storm he saw the landscape in the same stark, colorless grays that he would at any other time, with only a faint wispiness to indicate the presence of the brutal storm. The clouds were visible here, but they were unusual, like a blur from seeing them all roll by at once. Lightning, interestingly, had the same bright flash there as it did here.

Socks saw a landing spot in the distance and leaped, accelerating at even greater speed. Countless trees sped by underneath them while the three humans screamed for their lives, which Socks found mildly amusing. *-Dirt laughed the first time I jumped while carrying him,-* he told them. It did little to comfort them. And to be fair, Dirt had also screamed. It had been a mixed experience.

The pup ran and ran, and the three humans became increasingly miserable as time went on, while Socks and Dirt got happier, knowing they would escape. The poor humans weren't used to being carried, for one, and didn't enjoy it. It was cold up there, too, whipping through the wind and rain with no way to shield themselves. One by one, they curled into balls, which Socks facilitated.

Socks didn't have it easy, though. The rain kept getting up his nostrils, where it burned and made him want to sneeze. The rain had soaked so far into his fur that his body heat was sapped away like everyone else's, exertion notwithstanding. And to make it worse, his paws were getting sore from running so fast with the added weight.

The trees ended before the rain did. The farther they grew from the epicenter of the Devourer's spell, the sparser they became until finally there were no more. Nothing but storm-flattened grasses and streams of rainwater washing away the dirt to leave rocks and gravel behind.

"Socks, where do you think all the little animals go when it gets like this? Do a bunch of them just die, or do they have somewhere to hide?" Dirt asked Socks. *"The really little ones. Mice and snakes and stuff."*

The pup slowed, suddenly curious. He sniffed around a bit as he trotted, but the rain was dampening even his superior senses too much to get a good answer. Dirt considered asking the humans, but they were fairly certain they were going to freeze to death and didn't seem in the mood.

That little detour was just enough to lift Socks's spirits enough to press on with a bit more energy, but fortunately the hard part was over. The storm finally broke. Dirt had expected it to fade out slowly, with the rain slacking into mist and the low and gloomy clouds rolling away over time, but that wasn't what happened at all. The whole storm just fell apart in an instant, with the rain stopping suddenly and the clouds quickly breaking up. That was a relief. Dirt hadn't been looking forward to having it linger.

The sun was now high in the sky, bright and hot. Despite feeling like they'd just been chased from one end of the world to the other, the day was only half over. Socks slowed and stopped, then gently set the freezing, bewildered humans on a grassy spot of ground. Dirt slid off Socks's back to stretch and get some life back in his limbs, and Socks found a good spot to lie down and rest.

Dirt dropped his dripping-wet backpack and lay down near Socks's head, close enough to pat his muzzle, which he did. He only had to lie there for a count of five before discovering that his top half was warming up while his bottom half stayed cold, and decided he'd had enough. He peeled his wet pants off and set them aside, then lay back down with a contented grin as the hot sun enveloped him. He idly scratched the fur above Sock's nose and let all the stresses of the morning melt away.

"Are you drying those out?" asked Marina, face pale, wet hair dripping everywhere. She stood a few steps away, shivering.

"Yeah," said Dirt, even though it hadn't been true until she asked. Now he was, though. Now he was drying out his pants, and that was what he was doing.

Socks huffed his amusement, and the pup's hot breath stirred the grass all around him. Dirt grinned.

"I take it we're stopping for a rest?" asked Hèctor, sounding harried.

-Yes. We are far enough away that he will not find me again soon. He wasn't that close yet anyway. It is worse when he is.-

Ignasi said, "Strangely, noble wolf, I don't find that very reassuring. But no matter. If we're resting, then I'm copying the boy." He started tugging his wet shirt, which only came off with difficulty. His hairy chest now bare, he wrung out his shirt and squeezed an alarming amount of water out of it.

Hèctor considered doing the same, but after glancing up at the hot sun, decided he'd be fine. He said, "So what was that?"

When Socks didn't immediately reply, Dirt said, "There's a thing called the Devourer that hunts wolf pups. We're trying to stay away from it until Socks is big enough that it's not a threat anymore."

Hèctor said, "Fine, but what *is* it?"

"I don't know, and I'm not allowed to find out. You shouldn't try either."

"What do you mean you're not allowed?"

"I mean that Mother, Socks's mother, said if I ever find out she'll kill me. She could probably do it from here," said Dirt.

I COULD.

The humans all startled and ducked down, peering around wide-eyed for the new threat. Dirt giggled, and Socks started wagging his tail as evidenced by the thumping sound it made on the ground.

Hèctor pieced it together quickly and asked, "Where . . . is she?"

-Far away,- said Socks. *-Too far to come quickly.-*

Dirt said, "She doesn't have to be close by to speak to us. If you saw her, you'd understand. But don't worry about it, since you probably never will. And you wouldn't want to. But still, I'm glad she's watching us."

Ignasi must've only meant stripping off his shirt, since he kept his pants on. Or maybe he'd changed his mind after Hèctor and Marina didn't join him. He said, "I also find it reassuring to know an even bigger wolf is watching us at all times."

"Is there anything we need to know?" asked Hèctor.

-No, except that Dirt and I will keep moving until I grow up. We can't stay in one place for long, or he will find me again.-

"Should we get going now, then? Is it safe here?"

-My paws hurt. I carried a bull yesterday and you today. I want to rest, at least until I start drying out.-

Dirt sat up and asked, "Is anyone hungry?"

"No," said Marina. The men shook their heads.

"Me neither," said Dirt. "Socks, do you want some sap?" He patted the pup above the nose again and scratched his fur a little.

-In a little bit.-

They relaxed for a while, the humans milling around or sitting restlessly since they weren't tired. Dirt stayed right near Socks's nose, keeping him company. He wished he could do more for the pup. Socks needed other pups to wrestle with, for one. No matter how much Socks loved him, Dirt wasn't a giant wolf who could play fight and communicate by scent. Dirt almost regretted running into humans so soon, since it made him feel lonely on Socks's behalf.

At least it wouldn't be long until it was time to go back. Socks was supposed to come back once each season, and while Dirt wasn't sure how long a season was, it couldn't be that much longer until this one was over. Then came autumn, and winter, and spring.

Socks eventually decided he was hungry after all, so Dirt had Home make a bunch of sap for him, tossing in clump after clump until the pup had his fill.

After that, Socks gingerly rose to his feet and gently stepped around a bit. He decided his paws were not that sore anymore and asked, *-Marina, do you still know where we're going?-*

"I'm pretty sure we're getting close. We should start seeing farmland soon," she said. She seemed eager to get moving, full of restless energy.

Her hair had mostly dried, and her clothing had gone from soaking to mildly damp. No doubt they'd all be sweating before long, and Ignasi would regret drying out his shirt.

"Well, let me know if anyone gets hungry," said Dirt, rising to his feet. He picked up his backpack and pants, and nonchalantly didn't put them back on, hoping no one would notice. "Let's go. Socks, do you want me to walk or ride?"

-I don't care. Walk for now, and ride later.-

Dirt nodded and put his backpack on, then slung his pants over one shoulder.

"Are you going to put those back on, Dirt?" asked Marina.

"Oh, I guess, if they're dry," he said, feigning ignorance. They were, and he grudgingly pulled them back on and tied the drawstring.

Ignasi grinned and said, "I think he just doesn't want to wear them, Marina."

"Well, he has to learn if he wants to be let into the city," she replied sternly.

"Even in summer, the kids run around clothed all the time?"

"That's beside the point. That's *their* kids. Dirt's a stranger, and he needs to look civilized," said Marina. Dirt suspected that was an excuse, and she simply didn't like having him naked for some reason, but he didn't peek at her mind to find out.

Hèctor smirked and said, "I think the wolf will be a bigger problem than the pants."

Ignasi said, "Oh, I don't know. I think if we comb his fur, Socks could look like a civilized wolf. I mean that in a dignified sense, of course, not a tamed one."

"Dignified enough to keep them from filling us with arrows?"

-If they try to hurt me or Dirt they will regret it.-

Hèctor sighed. "That's what I'm worried about." He started walking.

CHAPTER EIGHTEEN

Socks walked in front for the rest of the day and kept a pace quick enough that the humans had to press to keep up. Not so fast it wore them out, but fast enough they didn't feel like talking much, which was fine with him. Dirt and Socks spent the day filling their minds with pure and childish imagination, which they hadn't been able to do much lately.

They played the game where Dirt would imagine something like a boring rock, and then Socks would change it somehow, like putting a bug on it, or making it green, and then Dirt had to do something to it, and back and forth until it got too silly. This resulted in a lot of laughter from Dirt, which the other humans thought was coming out of nowhere, making it even funnier.

When they got tired of that, they played the game where one of them would try to imagine a monster, and the other one had to figure out how to kill it. It had to be a fun way, though. Not a single stab or just twisting its head off. Nothing like that. The first one that Socks came up with was a big toothy lizard that had wheels instead of feet and rolled everywhere with shocking speed. Dirt killed it by sharpening a straight log into a spear shape, and then lifting it at the last second to skewer it when it tried to run him down.

The first monster Dirt came up with was a beast like those diggers, except that instead of claws, it had big grabby fingers. Socks killed it by handing it something to hold and then tossing it in the water to drown.

If they had a disagreement about how the fight would turn out, then they had to imagine their interpretation for the other person to watch, and then the other person had to redo it differently. Socks had a hundred natural advantages—speed, size, strength, magic, senses—but imagination was one arena where Dirt was his equal in every way, and that kept the game interesting long into the evening.

The effect of the berries Home had given them that morning wore off at nearly the same time for everyone. First Ignasi stumbled and gasped as the strength left his limbs, and before Hèctor and Marina could figure out what was wrong with him, it hit them too. Dirt didn't get it quite so bad, but he still felt a wave of weariness that a trickle of mana couldn't quite wash away. That was it, and from one instant to the next, the day's travels were at an end.

The place they'd stopped was exactly like everywhere else in the grassy plain—flat and boring. It was strange looking in any direction and seeing nothing at all, except the mountains retreating behind them.

"Is anyone ready for some water?" said Dirt, plopping down on the ground to relax, as if he hadn't been lying on Socks's back half the day.

"No waterskins to fill," said Hèctor.

"Make a cup with your hands, silly," said Dirt.

The beardless man scowled but didn't hesitate to hold his hands out. Dirt raised the staff and said, "Home, would you mind?"

Water poured gently from the end of the staff. Hèctor slurped it down the instant his hands were full, then held them out for more. Marina was right there when he was done, only because she outmaneuvered Ignasi. Once everyone had gotten their fill of water, Home gave them a bit of sap, which Dirt and the other humans weren't hungry enough to swallow more than a couple bites of.

Ignasi was the first to fall asleep, simply shimmying into a comfortable spot in the grass and nodding off before the stars even came out.

Despite clearly being exhausted, Hèctor was too restless to do the same and Dirt got the sense that the man *really* missed his pack. He fussed around helplessly for a while, then got up and poked around looking for firewood. Unfortunately, he found nothing, not even a bush with thick enough branches to burn, and finally gave up. He didn't say a word as he lay down near Ignasi and closed his eyes.

While Hèctor was doing all that, Marina stayed up to brush her hair with a comb she had in a pocket, humming a song Dirt didn't recognize. She hummed a little louder when she noticed he was listening, and he sat quietly and tried to memorize it. When she was done combing her own hair, she quietly said, "Come on over here, Dirt. I bet your hair's never been combed, has it?"

He scooted over and sat with his back toward her. She got up on her knees and gently started combing, resting one hand on his shoulder. It was a strange feeling, having human hands on him. It wasn't like the dryads at all. Marina's hands were warm, for one. The dryads were always the cool ambient temperature of the forest.

She kept humming, which he found pleasant, and combed his hair for longer than he felt was necessary. When she was done, she said, "All right, turn around and let me get a good look at you."

He spun around, staying seated, and faced her. She pinched his chin to turn his head for an examination under her critical eye, then combed the front again a couple times. She used her sleeve to rub off a bit of grime near his eyebrow and another under at the edge of his mouth. She nodded and quietly said, "Much better. Very handsome."

Socks got up and leaned in, head tilted slightly sideways to get a better look. He huffed and pulled away, unimpressed. *-Why bother?-* he asked.

Marina said, "There's no harm in looking neat and tidy. When we get to town, maybe we'll grab a few rakes and comb your fur. I bet you'll like it."

-I am neat and tidy enough already.-

"You'll enjoy it. You'll see. Dirt, you have a shirt in that little pack of yours, don't you? Can we get it out?"

Dirt obliged, grabbing the pack from where he'd dropped it and handing it to her. She pulled everything out—the tunic, the shirt, the shoes and socks. And underneath, the blanket. "Oh, I forgot that was in there. If someone gets cold, they can use it. Let's leave it out," he said.

Marina spread out Dirt's new clothing, biting a frown at the corners of her mouth. He saw why, and said, "They're still wet from the rain, huh? Let's spread them out, and maybe they'll be dry in the morning."

"I was hoping to see you try them on," she said.

"Yeah, but they're wet. And I'm fine right now. I'll even keep my pants on when I go to sleep," he replied. Something about her wanting to get him all dressed up made him *not* want to, even though he'd been planning on it when they got to the city, just to see how it went.

"Oh, that's fine. Whenever. I just wanna see you with them on. I bet you'll be charming," she said, trying and failing to act nonchalant. Her eyes glanced at the Home-staff, and Dirt wondered if the dryads were conspiring with her. He almost peeked at her mind to find out, then decided it would be more fun to try to figure it out like a normal human by watching for clues.

"Yeah. Maybe. I should probably find another river to wash off in first, though. Don't you think so? Wouldn't I just get them all dirty on the inside?" he asked, testing.

"You're not that dirty right now. Not like when we first met," she replied.

"I guess that's true," said Dirt. He realized that for him to keep up the charade and act like an innocent child to get more information out of her, he needed to know how an innocent child actually acted, and he had no idea. So that wouldn't work. He'd have to think of something else.

There was a lull in the conversation in which Dirt couldn't think of what to say. Marina was the one who broke it, asking, "There's one thing I'm not clear on. The dryads told me you woke them up, but you said they raised you, right? So you learned to speak from them?"

"Oh, no, I knew before. I just woke up one day in the forest, and I don't remember anything before that. But they noticed me and then figured out how to make dryads," said Dirt, leaving out some important steps.

"So who taught you how to speak? Who fed you when you were a babe?" Marina asked. "You have to have a mother somewhere, don't you?"

"No, I'm sure I had one, but I don't remember anything about her. I didn't just appear in the dirt in a pile of goo," said Dirt. He shifted uncomfortably, realizing that he was telling the truth and lying at the same time. He'd have to be careful if he wanted to stay honest. "At least not at first. I had to have been born at some point. But I'm sure she's gone, because that was a long time ago."

"What happened to you? How did you get there?"

Dirt knew how he'd gotten there, roughly, but explaining would give away a lot of things he didn't want her to know. Maybe someday he'd explain that he was from the ancient past and that he'd broken the world, but not now.

"One day I just woke up there, lying on the ground. I really don't have a single memory of my own from before that." He hoped she didn't catch the "of my own."

Marina plucked the teeth of her comb with her thumbnail, wondering. It made musical little plinking sounds, and Dirt almost reached for it to try himself. She asked, "So the trees noticed you, made dryads, and then you taught them how to speak?"

Dirt thought about that. Had he? "No, actually, I don't think I did. I wonder where they learned my language. And yours. From what you said, I don't think they would have heard enough words to figure it out themselves."

She frowned, fretting over something he was sorely tempted to peek at her mind and learn. He didn't, though. Finally she said, "Seems kind of sad to me, Dirt. No parents, no friends. Just you and the wilds. Every child deserves better than that."

"Socks is a better friend than you can imagine," said Dirt, anger creeping into his voice. "I love him, and I love the dryads. They're incredible."

"I meant human friends. You need someone to talk to—"

"We talk all day! In our minds!"

"Dirt, listen. You're a charming little man, sweet as you please and clever. You can do some terrifying things. But if you can't learn to be a little less wild, you'll never fit in anywhere. That's all. I don't want to take anything away from you. I just want you to have a little more, so you have options when you're old enough to decide what you want."

Dirt started angrily at that but calmed the more he thought about it. She hadn't really meant to insult Socks; she just didn't understand. She couldn't know. But she was probably right about learning to be less wild. Nothing in Prisca's memories accounted for how Dirt was living his life.

He wasn't about to make any major changes; there'd be time for that someday, and he couldn't be happier than he was now. But would it really hurt to let her tame him a little, just to learn? Dirt pondered that and let the moment stretch into an uncomfortable silence, and soon it was clear neither of them had anything else to add. Dirt finally just said, "Thanks. I'll think about that."

"Good. Good night, little Dirt," said Marina. She ruffled his hair, ruining her efforts to comb it. She grinned, and he smiled back at her to share the joke. He could still sense her frustration, mild though it was. After that, she curled up in the grass to sleep.

Dirt crawled over to snuggle in with Socks. He shared his sight with the pup and watched the sky as the stars came out, since Socks couldn't see them very well.

-She is right and wrong at the same time,- said the pup.

"I know. I guess if I want to be the best human, I'll have to learn a lot more things," he thought. Socks sent him a puff of affection, which he returned. That was all the discussing they needed for the "not friends" aspect of the conversation.

"We're not staying up, are we?" he thought.

-No,- replied Socks, just to him. *-The Devourer is too near to be out after dark. I should not have stayed up so late the last few nights.-*

As usual, all the questions Dirt couldn't ask came to the fore, and Socks had to wall off part of his mind where Dirt couldn't see it. Questions like, how come only pups were in danger? And if only pups were in danger, how come Mother and Father couldn't kill the Devourer? And more than anything else, what *was* he? If only Dirt knew more, perhaps he could find a solution or help in some way, and Socks wouldn't have to spend his puppy years in constant danger.

He reached up and patted Socks on the side of the snout, fully aware how tiny his human hand was and how little good it did. Socks deserved another big puppy to play with, and it pained Dirt he didn't have one. But the mental affection they sent back and forth was sincere, and knowing Dirt would drown in pity kept Socks from feeling too sorry for himself or spending too much time being afraid. Together they watched the stars come out, and then the moon rise, and then they went to sleep.

The next morning Dirt awoke with a huge sneeze, then another. Something tickled his nose, and he sneezed a third time before he even opened his eyes. When he did, he found Ignasi standing over him with a long piece of grass, tickling his face with the fluffy tuft on the end. "Hey!" he shouted, trying to decide if he was mad.

The men laughed, and Socks leaned down to give him a little lick. *-I have learned a new trick,-* he said with a mischievous air.

"You have a nose, too!" said Dirt.

-You can't reach it,- said Socks. He picked up a stalk of grass with his mind and waved it in Dirt's direction, snout raised high.

Dirt giggled and rolled to his feet, then snatched a stalk of grass of his own and used mana to leap all the way up. Socks dodged, of course, but the game was on. The two of them rolled and ducked and jumped to get away from the other, and in a small play area, Dirt had the advantage of speed. His body was simply more flexible, and he could change direction faster. No matter how Socks tried to escape, unless he decided to *really* run, the pup couldn't get away from him.

Socks, however, had the advantage of being able to hold ten stalks of grass at once and attack from different angles, which he used to great effect. Dirt could only look in one direction at a time. Neither of them managed to make the other sneeze, but each scored plenty of hits on the other's nose.

Dirt was losing until Socks leaped sideways, nose forward, in that way he did when he found something fun enough to leap in excitement about but wanted to keep his eyes on. Dirt anticipated where he'd land and got there in only a few lightning-quick steps.

Too late, the pup realized his mistake and tried to twist in the air. It wasn't going to work, so he tried something Dirt wasn't expecting. He made a shield of force with his mind and hit that instead, just before he landed where Dirt was waiting.

They were both so startled it worked that they stopped dead and stared at each other. They had the same thought, and without Dirt sending a single word, Socks made a flat shield parallel to the ground and lightly stepped onto it. He stood a full human pace in the air as if hovering there, wagging his tail.

The pup's weight quickly multiplied, though, doubling and doubling again until the shield collapsed. He dropped into the dirt and landed heavier than he should have. His legs crumbled, and his torso hit the ground hard enough to knock the air out of him.

Dirt ran forward and stopped short of hugging Socks, in case he was actually hurt. "Are you okay?" he asked aloud.

-I'll be fine.- The pup rose gingerly to his feet and held his head down for Dirt to hug. Dirt squeezed him and scratched between his ears.

The humans stood at a distance where they'd retreated for their safety. Seeing the game was over, they came back over. Ignasi sighed and said, "It's all fun and games until someone gets hurt," but he sounded more amused than upset.

Hèctor said, "Someone getting hurt is how you know it was fun and games." The man had a twinkle in his eye and cracked a rare grin.

-Yes,- said Socks. *-Usually it's Dirt, though. That is a good trick, but the weight has nowhere to go, so I'll have to be careful.-*

"Yeah, if Socks gets hurt, I can't carry him the rest of the day," said Dirt. He made room for the others to come scratch poor Socks around the ears, and it wasn't long until the pup was feeling better.

Home provided everyone a nice breakfast of sap, which Marina asked for in place of the all-day berries without explanation. After that, since no one had a pack except Dirt and his had nothing but clothes in it, there was nothing else to do. No camp to pack up, no fire to put out. They were on their way quickly, and with no trail to follow, they ended up walking side by side.

Dirt chose to walk, too, and for the first time, he found himself appreciating wearing pants. Although most of the grasses were shorter than his waist, a lot of them were scratchy and would have scraped up his legs. Since he didn't have fur, he supposed this was the next best thing.

Once, later in the morning, Socks caught a scent on the wind and raced away without explanation. Hèctor asked, "Should we be worried?"

Dirt said, "No, if the thing we should be worried about was here, he'd be here. But I bet he comes back with his face all bloody. Probably a deer or something."

Marina asked, "Shouldn't you go with him?"

Dirt said, "No, I can't smell well enough to help him circle the prey. Sometimes we go together, and sometimes he likes to go by himself. He'll be back soon."

Sure enough, Socks came padding back a short time later, muzzle and front paws bloody. He kept his nose low to sniff the ground as he walked, wagging his tail in a self-satisfied manner. A mysterious bundle the size of Dirt's leg hung from a strap Socks held with a front tooth.

First thing he did was lick Dirt's face to tease him, leaving a scent of blood behind that even Dirt could smell. Marina looked sick, which amused Socks so much that Dirt suspected that's why he'd done it.

Socks licked him again, and Dirt giggled and said, "Stop that! Okay, so what did you find?"

-Goblins. And look what they had.- The pup dropped the bundle, and it fell open to reveal three swords resting on a filthy cloth.

Hèctor got there first and hastily picked one up, then unsheathed it and examined the blade. It was rusty from hilt to point, but still straight and sharp. He looked up, disturbed, and said, "Goblins don't make swords. They don't make anything at all. Where'd they get these?"

-How should I know? From whatever makes them. Are those from humans?-

"Yes, humans made these. What I meant was, why do goblins have them?" asked Hèctor. He checked the blades of the other two, and they were rusted as well. Tossing one to Ignasi and Marina, he wiped the blood off the sheath of the third on the grass, then looped it over his own shoulder. Then he added, "I hope your city's still there."

"With all the people in it, unlike the last one," said Ignasi.

"It had walls. No goblins are getting through that," said Marina, but there was a note of uncertainty in her voice that everyone else picked up on. "We'll find out soon enough, though. Today, even, maybe. We should be close."

Socks sniffed the air again, and they resumed their walk.

CHAPTER NINETEEN

-I see a fence,- said Socks, well into the heat of the afternoon. Since he was the tallest, everyone else had to keep walking to see it, but sure enough, there it was. All wood, with thin posts and smaller branches woven between them to make a mat. It looked weatherworn and forlorn, with no difference in the scenery on one side or the other.

"Where'd they get the wood?" Dirt asked, since he hadn't seen a tree all day.

Marina said, "Trees don't grow well here. The soil is loose, and strong winds tend to push them over, if they grow much at all. The city keeps a bunch of groves, though. You'll see them when we get closer. Back in the One Kingdom days, wood and charcoal were brought from elsewhere and traded for grain, but that's been a long time now. Lots of cold people in the winter."

"Have you seen winter?" Dirt asked.

"Of course," said Marina. "Happens every year."

"Oh. Well, how cold is it? Is it as cold as water, or colder than that?"

"As cold as which water?" asked Ignasi, cracking a smile.

"You know, like when you jump in, and it's cold," said Dirt. "And it takes you a moment to get used to it. Like that."

-The water in the pond wasn't very cold,- said Socks.

"Oh. Yeah. I guess you're right. I was thinking of that basin."

"It's probably colder than that," said Ignasi.

"Is there anywhere you can go in winter where it's warm instead?" asked Dirt.

"Yes. You can go inside. Marina, shouldn't there be a road somewhere by now?"

She walked the rest of the way to the fence and pulled away one of the branches, which crumbled in her hand. "This fence is about to collapse. We're still too far from town. Whoever's field this was isn't tending it anymore. Socks, do you smell any sheep or goats? Any cattle?"

-No. Should I?- he replied. Curious, he raised his nose high to sniff the wind. *-No animals.-*

"Yeah, this one's abandoned. So we're probably on the far end of the field, and it's a field no one owns. The roads'll be farther in," said Marina, with an ease in her voice that didn't sound quite natural.

Hèctor didn't say anything. He kicked straight through the fence, shattering it into splinters and dust, and kept walking. It seemed he was pretty clear on what he thought had happened and had no interest in pretending otherwise. His footfalls were heavy with dismay, and that killed the conversation for everyone else.

They trudged on in silence, their steps heavy, despite having no packs on their backs. Dirt looked around for minds, wondering if he'd find something interesting, but he could see nothing except his companions, all the little things that lived in the grass, and the grass itself, which looked almost like a smooth carpet of fog, with so many tiny minds so close together.

It seemed like it should have been obvious, now that Dirt thought about it. Why would a whole city be safe and alive, only a couple days' travel from a big town where everyone was dead? And which hadn't been touched for years? There was still plenty of stuff there, so if any people remained to go get it, they would have. Maybe they wouldn't have stayed there, with all the ghosts, but surely it was easier than making new stuff.

No, it seemed increasingly likely that Marina's city was all going to be dead too, which made him wonder what they were going to do with the three humans. They couldn't walk fast enough to travel with him and Socks everywhere, so bringing them along wasn't an option. Could he and Socks just leave them, though? He supposed they could make it back to the tower, get new packs, and go home after that. It wasn't that far, even for slow humans.

Still, thinking about it made him uneasy. He'd been hoping to see where they settled in so he could come back someday when Socks was big enough to be safe from the Devourer. Marina would probably go live with the dryads when she got close to bearing her young, so Dirt could visit her there, but what about Hèctor and Ignasi?

-I smell more goblins,- said Socks, to everyone.

"I wanna come this time," said Dirt. He tossed his little pack to Ignasi to hold and jumped onto Socks's back. "We'll be right back. You can keep walking if you want. We'll find you."

Hèctor just nodded, then scowled again, his face betraying something deeper than his angry exterior. Regret, possibly. He kept walking without slowing down much, and the other two followed.

Socks left at a run, following the scent on the wind. He hopped over a fence, crossed the large field, and hopped the next fence at the far side. Nearby, Dirt saw a mound all grown over with grass, which might have been a house once. It had something poking up that might have been a wooden plank. There was another one a short distance away, right outside another fence.

"Hey, jump really high for a second. Let's see if we're close enough to see the city from up there," thought Dirt. He held a little more tightly, and Socks leaped from the ground with all his strength, burning a great deal of mana at once. The sensation of speed gripped him from hair to toes, and Dirt squealed as soon as he could catch his breath. The air slowed. Their momentum slowed.

For an instant, they hovered in the air. Dirt looked as hard as he could in every direction, and sure enough, in the distance was a ring of gray stone located across a sparkling river. Only a few hours' journey on foot, or a few minutes for Socks, and they'd be there. *"We're close! It's right over there,"* said Dirt, sending a mental picture.

Then the fall began, and Dirt held on for dear life again. They hit the ground hard, but Socks was moving forward fast enough to absorb the worst of it and keep running.

The goblins weren't much farther, a pack of at least ten. Socks threw Dirt right into the middle of them, which was perfect. They were so surprised they hardly had time to scream with their high, raspy voices before Dirt started swinging the staff with both hands and bashing their heads in. With mana in his arms, it almost didn't matter where he hit them. The staff wouldn't break, but the goblins sure did.

Socks grabbed one with his teeth and front paw and tore it in two, flinging the top half at the next one. The thick, heavy corpse slammed into it with a resounding thud, and Socks pinned it down and tore that one apart, too.

Mindful of his clean pants, Dirt danced away from the spray of blood and bashed another sideways in the knees, then straight down on its head. The skull shattered, but fortunately it burst backward, not forward.

A few heartbeats later it was over, and the goblins were all dead. One of them had a rusty axe that looked human, and another had a broken sword. Socks took the axe, then turned over two more goblin corpses until he found a second axe. He spun them dramatically through the air with his mind, looking pleased with himself. Then on a whim, he picked up one of the more intact goblin corpses and tried hacking at it with the axes. They held up a lot better than a sword would, swiping right through the body with a splash of gore while remaining unharmed.

-I want a big weapon. One big enough for me. I wonder if we can find one somewhere,- said the pup, excitedly imagining how much fun that would be.

"That would be the scariest thing ever! Can you imagine? Just swoosh, and kill that tentacle monster with one swing! What kind would you want?"

-I don't know. One that wouldn't break. But it doesn't need a handle. It could be all blade.-

"How about a big ring, a great big circle, that's only sharp on the outside? You could wear it around your neck if you get tired of carrying it with your mind," said Dirt.

Socks thought about that and decided he loved it. *-The inside could be soft. Then it would be nice to wear. I bet no wolf has ever had something like that before. Now I want to make one.-*

"Well, we'll keep our eyes out for enough metal. And maybe Hèctor knows how to make metal stick together or go into the right shape."

-He might know,- said Socks. He leaned down and sniffed the ground, then the air. Then he started wagging his tail and said, *-There are more goblins around. I smell another group somewhere.-*

Dirt looked around for minds but didn't see anything close enough to recognize as goblins. *"How far away?"*

-It's hard to tell. The scents carry a longer distance on the wind here because there's nothing but grass.-

Dirt and Socks looked at each other for a moment, then in the direction of the wind. Dirt rubbed his toe on the grass to get a bit of blood off. *"Let's go back to the others, and then go to the city. We should warn the people there not to go out because there are too many goblins around."*

They both knew that was a degree of optimism bordering on insanity, but Socks didn't argue. He didn't have to. He just gave Dirt a bloody little lick and tossed him up onto his back.

After a short race through the fields, they found the humans hadn't waited, but neither had they gotten far. Marina scanned Dirt for blood before even welcoming them back, and seemed relieved when he wasn't covered in it, except some on his face where Socks licked him. He wiped it off with his hand, then onto the grass.

Dirt said, "I saw the city. It's still there. It's over a river, right, Marina?"

"Yes, that's it! Did you . . ." She trailed off.

"We didn't get close enough to see the people, but there are more goblins around, so we're going to go warn the humans before we hunt any more. Just in case," said Dirt.

"The tower was still there, too," grumbled Hèctor.

"Where's your sense of joyous optimism?" said Ignasi trying to sound mirthful, but his dead-looking eyes gave it away.

"Good point. Maybe they left all their wine behind!" said Hèctor, trying to mimic Ignasi's tone of voice, which he did very poorly.

Their failed attempt at banter made the mood worse, not better, and no one had anything to say after that. Socks walked behind, only directing them to turn a little this way or that to keep on the most direct path. They passed through field after field, and the closer they got, the more cultivated the area looked. Still no houses; at least, no standing ones. Some had been burned, but most of the others looked like they'd simply been knocked over and hadn't been sturdy to begin with.

By the time they got their first glimpse of the gray city walls, many of the fields showed signs of more recent work. Furrows had been dug, now just long rows of weeds and bare dirt. Irrigation ditches wandered everywhere, some full of mud and silent, reeking water.

Marina looked like she was about to cry, but she stoically kept her head up and faced forward. Hèctor and Ignasi were in equally black spirits, their feet dragging with a weariness that had nothing to do with tired legs.

Only Dirt held out any hope at all, because those walls had to be good for *something.* He didn't dare let himself accept that humans were almost gone from the world, and perhaps only four remained at all. It was certainly starting to look that way.

The full city came into view, or at least the walls did. They were taller than Socks and made of flat gray stone, carved almost as well as Dirt's people used to do. They made an impressive unbroken circle around such a huge area they almost looked straight.

Socks suddenly got an eager lightness in his step that only Dirt detected, and when he looked at the pup's mind, Socks shut out his thoughts just to tease him. But Dirt could guess what he'd seen. He looked with his mind-sight and sure enough, at the barest edges of his perception, a number of bright minds appeared. They were too distant to see exactly what they were, but Dirt already knew.

"There are people!" he shouted. His heart filled with such relief and happiness that it almost turned into tears, and only focus and willpower kept him from cracking.

Hèctor said, "What? How do you know?" He was the first to answer, but Ignasi and Marina had been about to, and now awaited his reply.

But Dirt gave no explanation, choosing instead to sprint the rest of the way to the walls. It was a longer distance than he'd estimated, since the walls were huge, but Socks happily raced him, and an instant later, Dirt was standing close enough to throw something and hit the stones.

"Hello!" he shouted. His voice hit the flat wall and echoed back to him.

They waited. No answer came. "Hello! Hello, humans!" he shouted again.

Dirt used his mind-sight again. There was no direction, since he and Socks weren't melding their thoughts, but he could guess the distance. There were hundreds in there, too many to count quickly. The town was alive! Most of them were farther in, with only a few who'd been close enough to hear. Those ones looked at each other in confusion—a group of four women with dark hair like Marina.

"We're outside! Hello! How do we get in?" he shouted, as loud as he could.

The women reacted in horror and whispered to each other. There could be no children outside the walls. Not living ones, or human. This was some new, terrifying threat.

"It's okay! We're not dangerous! Hello?"

The women ran, thinking they had to find and tell someone. Danger. Dirt realized he should have been just focusing on one instead of trying to watch them all at once, because he might've gotten more information that way.

Socks stepped up to the wall and stood on his hind legs. He stretched out as far as he could, and it was just barely enough for him to peek over the wall into the city.

Hèctor reached them first, running without enthusiasm. Marina and Ignasi weren't far behind. "There's no one on the walls. The town's dead," said Hèctor, his black eyes betraying a flicker of hope.

-Dirt was not lying. There are humans in there. Plenty of them. But not as many as I expected. They are afraid of us, even though they haven't seen me yet,- said Socks, to everyone.

"How do we get in?" Dirt asked. "I can just jump over, but that can't be it, right?"

"There's a gate, Dirt," said Marina, with such an air of exasperation that Ignasi started cheering up.

"Oh. Of course. Are you going in that way?"

Marina said, "It was closed. If you hadn't run off so fast I would've told you. It's over that way. Come on. If there's still anyone in there, they'll be watching the gate."

Dirt said, "I already said there are people in there."

Marina turned to walk in the direction of the gate, but Dirt opened his backpack and took his fresh red shirt and pulled it on for the first time. It was itchy and smelled old, but it was soft and flexible, and he'd get used to it. He looked down to see how it went with his green pants, and decided he liked it. Then he plopped down to put his shoes and socks on for the first time, too. The socks felt weird and were probably a little too tight, but they'd be fine. The thin leather shoes were loose on his feet, making an odd contrast. The socks squeezed his toes, but slid around inside the shoes.

He rose to his feet. "How do I look? Can you comb my hair again?"

"You almost look like you came from a womb, not a seed," said Ignasi.

Marina gave him a half-hearted smile and quickly combed Dirt's hair. "I'm pretty eager to get moving now, if you don't mind?" she said.

"Nope. Thank you. Go ahead. Socks, can you wait for a little bit so I can warn them about you, so they don't all scream and run away?" said Dirt.

In answer, Socks leaned down and gave him an encouraging lick. *-I will wait unless you get into trouble,-* he told Dirt. *-But not for long. I smell food in there, and many other things.-*

"I know, but you're big and scary. Just try not to kill anyone until I get a chance to make friends. It worked with Marina and Hèctor and Ignasi."

"What are you doing?" said Hèctor. "Come on, get moving."

"Okay," said Dirt. "I'll see you soon."

He turned and ran to the wall. With each step he inhaled a bit more mana until he was full, his body protected and muscles strengthened. He gripped the staff tighter and held his knife with the other hand so it wouldn't come out.

Then he jumped right over the wall, soaring over the wide area atop it where people could walk, and coming down on the other side right into a tile roof that shattered under his feet. The hard tiles flew into tiny bits and exploded everywhere, but he didn't go all the way through. He caught on a crossbeam and had to carefully extricate himself without ripping his pants. It took him a moment, but there was no one in the immediate vicinity to mock him.

When he slid off the roof and finally landed on the stone walkway leading to the building he'd damaged, he closed his mind-sight. The city inside the walls was dense—that was the most interesting thing. All the houses were built so close together they made one long building that ran up either side of the road. Ahead, he could see some open areas, and a small alley to his left led to a fenced area that might be a little pasture.

This was something new. A completely new place, with humans inside to meet. He dusted himself off, let a sincere and eager smile break out on his face, and started walking up the road in what he assumed was the direction the women had gone.

CHAPTER TWENTY

The roads weren't as straight as Dirt's people used to make, nor the angles of construction anywhere near as exacting, but there was a certain similarity that felt familiar. The city inside the walls had houses that went right up to the edge with doors that opened right onto the street, and most were at least two stories, even the narrow ones. Covered alleyways led between them to other streets, or small gardens, or the gods only knew what else.

Many of the houses had shops on the bottom floor, with colorful signs that Dirt still couldn't quite read, since most of the letters looked different and the words weren't his original language. The shops seemed untended, with closed shutters or dusty cobwebs in windows that opened into darkness.

Still, it wasn't abandoned. This part of town looked like it was dying, but not dead, and there were still plenty of humans. Too many to count, the farther he got, but none that looked close enough to be in any of the buildings on this street. What had those four women been doing, then?

The street ended at an intersection, and Dirt turned left, since it looked like it would lead him closer to the center of town. An old woman stared at him out a second-story window, gray hair peeking out from under a shawl. She reminded Dirt of a pale, wrinkly goblin, and Dirt couldn't help glancing at her mind.

Her thoughts about him were complicated, but informative. He shouldn't be out running around alone like this. Loners were trouble. And where did he get the new clothes? He must be stealing, but everything was already picked over. When she closed her shutters and withdrew into her home, he decided to stop looking at all their minds unless he felt threatened. He was already going to stand out; humans had a very small set of things they found acceptable, and it'd be best if he wasn't too far outside it.

Near the end of that street, it intersected with a bigger one that went straight to a building at the center of town, which was nicer than all the rest, with towers at each of the four corners and stylistic stonework all the way up and down. Humans milled about in the area surrounding it, marking that as the city's forum. That house might be a temple, perhaps, or some sort of civic building he wasn't familiar with. People often gathered there for the city's business, it appeared, some standing under tents or awnings and others carrying baskets or sacks.

A group of children all smaller than him ran out from one alley, across the street, and into another alley, before he could stop and say hello. A dog barked from inside a nearby house, sounding surprisingly unlike a wolf. Dirt was almost tempted to go find it and see what a dog looked like. Later, perhaps.

This was it. Dirt was in a truly human place, one still occupied. New scents and sounds surrounded him—baking bread and laughter, rotting garbage and slamming doors. It seemed everywhere he looked was something new. That shop sold meat, even though it looked like they didn't have much; that one sold clothing but it wasn't open right now. Up ahead, a man pulled a cart whose contents were under a blanket, and two women fell in behind him and chatted loudly about running out of salt.

He walked down the center of the street, tapping the staff with each step and listening to how the sound vanished in the growing turbulence of life. A man younger than Hèctor gave him a long look, then nodded. Dirt nodded back and the man turned away. In fact, it seemed everyone noticed him, looking him over without coming to say hello, and he wasn't sure if that was normal.

Was he already standing out? He had all the same clothing as they did. Pants, shirt, shoes. He was holding a staff, and they weren't, but did that matter? He opened his mind-sight again to see if he could learn anything, but it overwhelmed him, and he closed it again. It'd take a little more practice to learn to tell them apart with so many, and now was not the time to just stand there with a blank look on his face.

Commotion seemed to be growing in the forum, so Dirt hurried along in that direction. All along the street, people stopped what they were doing and looked to see what was going on, even though there wasn't much to see. Or hear. Dirt supposed they were stopping to look because everyone else was.

He kept walking, but before he made it to the forum two men with bows came walking boldly from the crowd. Everyone scrambled to get out of their way, except for four women who followed close behind, who pulled up their skirts a little so they could walk fast enough to keep up.

"Make way!" one of the archers shouted, his voice echoing off the buildings all the way up and down the street. He didn't need to, though—there was plenty of room to get through. People got out of the way anyway, moving toward the edge of the street. Dirt was too slow to react and found himself standing alone in the middle of the road.

The two archers and four women reached him and slowed slightly, giving him curious looks, or disapproval.

Dirt made a quick decision and said, "Hey, are you looking for me?"

"Get out of the way!" scolded one of the women. They passed him and kept going.

"From outside the wall?" Dirt called after them.

That got them to stop. The men slyly drew arrows and turned around, not quite nocking them, but ready to in an instant. Seeing that, the crowd quickly went silent, then began whispering to each other to figure out what was going on.

"Were you playing a trick, boy? What were you doing near the wall?" said an archer. He wore a round metal helmet and had a long, bushy mustache that covered his mouth but not his chin.

"I wasn't playing a trick at all. I just said hello, but no one answered," said Dirt. He loosened his grip on the staff a little and relaxed his posture, hoping it made him look friendlier.

"What did you say, exactly?" said the other archer, with the less impressive mustache. He looked a lot younger.

"I yelled hello and asked how you get in. I'm sorry, I didn't mean to scare anybody. I didn't know there was a gate until right after that."

"That's what we heard," said one of the women. They were older than Marina, but not all crinkly like the woman in the window, and not wearing anything to make them stand out. If anything, their clothing looked a lot more worn than he would have expected.

The men angrily put their arrows back and slung their bows over one shoulder. "I knew this was a waste of time," said the first one. He turned to walk back toward the forum.

"If you can find his parents, tell them to whip him red and purple. Don't come running to us with stupid stories again," said the second.

One of the women, who had a pudgy face, said, "There was no mistaking it! It obviously wasn't him!"

The first archer gestured at Dirt and said, "Then how did he know what you heard? Boy, was it you who shouted?"

"Yes, it was me," said Dirt. "Was I not supposed to do that? Sorry, I didn't know."

"Pranks about the walls are serious trouble!" yelled the first archer, leaning forward to make himself more intimidating. He pointed a finger in Dirt's face, and Dirt felt himself instinctively wanting to shy away from it. This must be how humans raised their young, like when Mother growled at her pups.

"It wasn't a prank," said Dirt. Actually, was it a good idea to tell them he was from outside? There were so many people here that they weren't sure if he belonged or not, which had never occurred to him. "I'm sorry. I won't do it again."

"See that you do not!" yelled the man, a speck of spittle somehow making it past his giant mustache to land on Dirt's shirt. "Or I'll throw you over it! Understand?"

"I understand," said Dirt. He shied away from the looming man and peered around for a path to escape. He should just go to a different street and meet some other people, or maybe find children his size first and talk to them.

"Do you? Or do you need some bruises to help you remember?"

"I'll remember!" He looked in the man's dark brown eyes while he said it, to look more sincere. The archer nodded and stood back up straight. He peered down side-eyed at Dirt, nodded, and stepped to leave.

"Where'd he get the shirt?" asked the fat-faced woman.

Dirt looked down at his nice red shirt, with black embroidery all around the hem. "What's wrong with it?" he asked.

"Where'd you get it, boy?" she asked, stepping forward.

The men looked exasperated and ready to be done with this, but they didn't stop the woman from getting close and pinching the hemline around Dirt's neck.

"Are you going to pretend like you recognize it now?" asked the younger archer. "Turn him from a prankster to a thief?"

"Of course I recognize it," she snapped back. "This pattern is from Llovella, and it's too clean for a fifteen-year-old shirt."

Dirt squirmed, trying not to look too guilty. He glanced around with fresh eyes at the clothes everyone else had on, and most of it was ragged and repaired with patches, not just these women's. He might have the only complete, unmarred shirt on the entire street.

"Sixteen years, now," said one of the other women, with graying hair. "Looks like he stepped right out of a painting, doesn't he?"

They all started giving Dirt long, appraising looks, considering his attire from head to toe. At least his hair was combed. Still, he hadn't expected this. Looking *too nice*?

-Do you want me to come?- asked Socks.

"Not yet. I'm not sure how to tell everyone," said Dirt.

-Just tell them, and if they get mad, then I'll come,- said Socks.

"Okay. Here goes," replied Dirt. He took a deep breath and stood up straight. Aloud, he said, "I got the shirt in . . . How did you say the name? Llovella? Is that a town with a big tower in the middle? Is that what it's called?"

No one answered, and the atmosphere grew tense. Dirt swallowed and said, "I guess that's what it's called. Marina never actually said, now that I think about it. Anyway, I'm not scary or anything. I just wanted to come meet some humans."

The first archer snorted and said, "I suppose you simply walked up and jumped over the wall?"

Dirt felt fear creeping in, nervousness that he was about to ruin everything. Why was this so hard? He was a human just like them. At least they weren't pointing a sword at him like Hèctor had done.

"Okay, well, if I show you something, can you promise to listen and not attack me or anything? Or scream and run away?"

"He's a goblin in disguise," muttered one of the women.

Another woman snorted at the obvious joke, but the good humor died immediately as everyone started wondering if that was possible.

"I'm not a goblin. I'm human. Obviously. I'm not even green!"

The younger archer said, "And he's not walking around shouting *Boy! Meat! Good boy!*" However, he didn't use his own language for the "boy, meat" part. He used Dirt's.

Dirt felt the blood leave his face. It'd never occurred to him until this moment, but goblins spoke *his* language, didn't they? His old one, from the Sunset Empire. At least the few words they knew. How was that possible?

"I promise I'm just a normal human. And I have friends coming to the gate. If you take me there, we can meet them, and they'll explain," said Dirt. He could tell by the way they stood that he was becoming less convincing with every word he said.

"What's your name, boy?" asked the older archer.

"Dirt," said Dirt. "It means *Dirt*."

"And your father's name?"

"I don't remember."

"Mother's?"

"Her either."

"Do you have a family name at all? Any names besides Dirt?"

"Avitus," said Dirt, and immediately regretted it.

Fortunately, the older archer thought it was a joke and just laughed. "Good name for an orphan."

"I really do have friends coming to the gate, though. Can you tell me where it is so I can meet them before I do something else stupid?"

The older archer looked at the women, then twitched his entire mustache. He exchanged a knowing nod with the younger man and said, "Fine. Come with me, little Avitus. Genís, you escort the ladies home and check the walls. Just to be safe."

The younger archer said, "Don't get eaten, old man."

The older man snorted again and gave Dirt a little shove on the shoulder to get him moving. Dirt didn't know which direction he was supposed to walk, though, so he just stumbled. Then, just like that, the archer was leading him through the bustling streets. They didn't pass through the forum, turning instead onto a less-populated side road, then another. Each turn led them somewhere emptier and emptier until finally, there was hardly a soul to be seen.

Satisfied they were isolated enough for conversation, the man said, "Where have you been staying, boy?"

"Just kind of all over the place, I guess," said Dirt.

"Who's been feeding you?"

"A friend. A couple friends."

"Who?"

"I doubt you know them. Home, and Socks," said Dirt. He started feeling a little guilty about the misdirection, but it didn't quite count as lying, so he decided it was fine. They were honest answers, after all.

"Did you steal the clothes you have on?" asked the archer, quietly.

Dirt stopped walking, thinking. He furrowed his brow and squeezed the staff. He looked around and found that there were only a handful of people around, and no one was watching. "Remember when I asked if I could show you something?"

The man gave him a knowing look, but there was something of pity in it. He said, "I was an orphan like you, boy. Dirt. Avitus." That name made him grin again. "I know how it is. But you'll have to be smarter from now on because you're not fooling anybody. Wearing stolen clothes that obvious, then causing commotion? You're going to get beaten. If you're lucky. If you're not lucky, whatever baker you're stealing from will kill you and toss your body into the river. So let me ask you, boy. Do you need help?"

Dirt looked at the ground, feeling ashamed, if not for the reasons the man thought. Dirt took only the briefest glimpse at his mind and found troubled sympathy. Pity. That made it worse. He was going to have to explain, and the man would think him a liar who spurned a moment of charity.

"Don't run, Avitus. I won't hurt you. I won't do anything at all, if you don't want. But I know a safe place you can stay. You can even bring a friend or two. Shall we sit down and talk about it?" asked the archer, gesturing at a bench built into a house's façade. "My name is Vidal, by the way."

Dirt sat where Vidal indicated and leaned forward on the staff, his mind spinning as he tried to think how to approach this.

"When I was your age, times were not this bad," said Vidal, looking down the street the other direction. "People still traveled, and boats came on the river, and there was plenty of food. But not for me. Not for little Vidal. Roach, they called me."

The man paused, apparently waiting for Dirt to speak.

"Vidal, can I ask you something? Do your people know any magic?"

"No one in the guard knows any magic. That's women's business, curses and such. Women and noblemen. Why do you ask me that, of all things? Have you been cursed?"

"It's complicated, but not like you're thinking. But I want to show you something, and you have to promise not to scream and run away. Or attack me."

Vidal's kind face hardened a bit, his eyes growing more wary. "Show me what? Something wrong with your knife?"

"No, that's not it. Watch," said Dirt. He gritted his teeth and snapped his fingers, making a light. It hovered lazily above his head, hard to see in the sunlight but still bright enough to add to the shadows nearby.

It took Vidal a moment to realize what he was seeing, and his eyes got wider and wider. He leaned away to get a clearer look and almost fell off the bench.

Dirt said, "I'm not from here. Those ladies were right. I was outside, yelling over the wall, just a little bit ago. I jumped over, but I have no idea where to go from here."

Vidal's mind spun until something clicked. He jumped to his feet and shouted a word Dirt didn't recognize, drawing an arrow and unslinging his bow in one quick motion.

"Wait! I'm not scary! I won't hurt anyone!" yelled Dirt, standing and holding out his hand. He made the light go out, but it was too late.

Vidal fired an arrow at him, but it was a trick and never would have hit. It was meant to scare him. But he only realized that in midair as he jumped up to the nearest roof to get away. Dirt landed on the hard tiles and froze, realizing he'd ruined everything. That was not a typical human jump. He turned and saw Vidal nocking another arrow, and something in the man's eyes told Dirt the next shot wouldn't miss.

Dirt jumped again, and an arrow whistled inches from his head. He landed on the roof across the street, then ran along it and jumped to the next one.

Behind him, Vidal shouted, his stentorian voice roaring up from the road and seemingly filling the whole city. It wasn't a word, but rather just a pattern, three short bursts of sound. A moment later, a bell rang, then another.

Dirt ran from one rooftop to the next until he hit a loose tile and slid all the way down, falling two stories onto the hard cobblestone. Mana saved him from breaking any bones, but people saw him land, then rise, and jump again. A chorus of terrified shouts followed after him.

Bells rang and horns called, echoing through the hard streets. Doors and shutters slammed, and hard-booted feet clacked as soldiers ran. All this just for him? This was so stupid! Why does this happen every time? He should've just walked in like normal with Marina and the others and kept his mouth shut. He should've known. Humans were wary and mistrustful creatures. Weak and small and skittish. The slightest thing could set them all off. And to make it worse, Vidal had turned out to be someone Dirt genuinely wanted to be friends with.

Dirt ran up the street, wondering if he could just stop and hide and let everyone forget about him for a little while. Only Vidal and a few others knew what he looked like, so maybe if he took his shirt off?

No, he should head out and let Hèctor and the others figure out what to do. He inhaled more mana and jumped up to the roof again, then sprang like a bug to the next one, soaring high in the air. High enough to see the wall, and over there, the gate. Socks was standing patiently not too far beyond it. Dirt jumped, ran, and jumped again, and soon he landed in the middle of the widest road in the city and sprinted down it at wolfish speed.

Archers, dozens of them, stood on the walls over and around the gate, all their bows drawn and facing outward. Dirt slid to a stop, wondering why they'd be more concerned about outside when the alarm had been raised in here.

"Loose!" shouted a foreman.

Dirt screamed "No!" as countless bowstrings were plucked, sending a hail of arrows down onto his friends. "Stop! He'll kill you all!"

The men shouted in fear as the arrows all bounced off of nothing in midair, many of them flung away as if by a swiping hand.

"Stop!" Dirt shouted again, screaming as loud as he could. Everyone but the archers ran the opposite direction, away from the gate and into the town, but at least they weren't screaming. They probably hadn't seen Socks yet.

Before Dirt could shout again, the gate vibrated and then shattered inward, the whole thing coming off its rails and flying into the street. The concussive sound was deafening as it echoed on the stone.

Socks calmly walked in, blocking all the arrows with a mental shield. Hèctor and the others crouched beneath him for safety, creeping as he went.

-Hello, Dirt,- said the pup, walking forward until he got to Dirt. Then he licked him. *-Are you all right?-*

CHAPTER TWENTY-ONE

I'm fine," said Dirt, panting. He tried to hide how bothered he was by the last few minutes, but of course Socks knew. The pup could smell it on him and see his thoughts.

An arrow clattered to the ground behind Dirt. Socks's lips pulled back into a snarl, and he growled, low and menacing. It was loud enough to make the roof shingles rattle. He shouted, *-THE NEXT PERSON TO SHOOT AN ARROW IS GETTING RIPPED APART, WHETHER IT MAKES MY HUMAN MAD OR NOT.-*

Ignasi jumped out from his hiding place under the wolf and raised his arms and shouted, "Stand down! He's friendlier than he looks!"

Hèctor followed him out. He didn't shout, but he did mutter, "And a lot more dangerous."

Dirt held his breath, hoping no one else would shoot. If they did, they deserved what happened to them, but he still wanted to make friends with the city if they could sort things out.

Socks shot his gaze to the wall behind him, fixing on one particular archer who had nocked an arrow and drawn it. *-DO IT. I WILL PAINT THAT WALL WITH YOUR INSIDES.-* The archer tossed the bow off the wall and raised his hands.

The pup's mental voice couldn't make the houses rattle, but Dirt was sure it was deafening across the whole city anyway. Socks was being about as loud as Mother or Father, just on the edge of causing physical pain. Dirt was used to it, sort of, but no one else was. A few fleeing humans ducked and uselessly covered their ears. Several archers dropped their bows and tried to flee, which wasn't very effective atop the narrow wall. They had nowhere to go and just crashed into each other.

Socks scanned the wall, eyes stopping on each archer in turn while he growled, making waves of deep rumbling thud in Dirt's chest. Even though they were best friends, Dirt could do nothing to stop the animal fear that rose in him any time he heard it. He told himself he was afraid for all the humans Socks was about to kill, but that wasn't quite true.

Fortunately for them, none of the archers fired another arrow. After Socks was satisfied, he dropped the arrows he was holding with his mind and they fell to the stone with a rushing clatter. He stood up on his hind legs to sniff a couple archers, who froze and tried not to scream. Satisfied that they weren't going to shoot any more arrows, he got back down and came to sniff Dirt again.

"I'm really okay, Socks, I promise," said Dirt, patting his nose.

-Fine. Now that you humans have all calmed down, who is the father human? Come out, wherever you are.-

"The what now?" asked an amused Ignasi, his nonchalant manner making him stand out about as much as Socks did.

-The father human,- said Socks. *-The one whose den this is. The oldest. The father.-*

"That's not how it works," said Ignasi, grinning.

-What do you mean?-

Ignasi said, "The person in charge is not the father of all the people who live here."

-He lets other families live amongst his brood?-

The city's uproar kept growing in the background. Crashing sounds echoed down the street, or bells, or trumpet calls from all over town. Dirt's anxiety grew as well, wondering just how much damage this much panic could cause. Most people wouldn't know whose voice that was in their heads, or what that huge crash had been when Socks smashed the gate open.

-Who is the father of the men on the wall, then? Which one?- asked Socks.

"I'm a father," said one of the archers. He sounded young, even though it was hard to tell beneath their conical metal helmets. The man probably meant to shout, but his voice was too unsteady from terror, and it didn't come out that way.

"He means the captain," yelled Hèctor. "Who's the captain?"

One man raised his hand, who looked just like all the rest. Dirt had expected him to be taller, at least, or have a different color shirt.

Socks plucked the man from the wall, causing several others to scream. One archer raised his bow again but lowered it again when Socks's yellow eyes glanced in his direction. He set the captain neatly on his feet next to Dirt and said, *-This is my human, Dirt. He came from far away and wanted to meet some humans, so be nice to him.-*

The captain was too stunned to speak, eyes wild with fear, mouth hanging open. He couldn't even twitch his fingers. Ignasi stepped over and put his arm around the man's shoulders, leaning on him in a friendly, familiar manner. "Let me help you, friend. That is a giant wolf," he said, grinning widely and pointing at Socks. "Make sense so far?"

The captain hesitated, but nodded.

"Good! Now this, this is a little boy," he said, pointing at Dirt. "Still with me?"

The captain nodded, a hint of clarity returning to his eyes.

"Good! Now for the confusing part. The wolf and the boy are friends. Take a minute. Think about it. Nod when you're ready," said Ignasi, sounding almost ready to laugh. He was having too much fun, and it was infectious. At least to Hèctor and Marina and Dirt, anyway. No one else was amused.

"They're friends," said the captain, after a breath or two. Dirt could tell from his voice that he didn't believe it, or wasn't quite understanding what he was saying. "The boy and the wolf. Are friends."

"Very good! Believe me, you're picking it up faster than I did. Hèctor even threatened the boy with a sword; can you believe that? The stupidity! But we are all foolish sometimes, and such is life. Now, because the wolf and the boy are friends, if you are nice to the boy, then what will the wolf do?"

"I . . ." It took another breath or two for the captain to shove down his animalistic terror sufficient to finally process what was going on. Instead of answering, though, he stared, swallowing hard.

"Come on, now, my good man," said Ignasi. "It's important. Let's try this again. What is that?" Ignasi pointed at Socks, whose tail twitched in growing amusement.

"I get it! Get off me," said the captain, finally regaining the rest of his wits. He turned to Dirt and said, "Why did you attack us? What do you want? Who are you?"

"Maybe answer those in reverse order," said Ignasi.

Dirt paused, then grinned. "I'm Dirt. I want to see a human city with the people still in it. And I didn't attack you—you attacked me."

"No," said the captain. "We did not attack you. The wolf attacked first."

"Yes, you did. A man named Vidal shot an arrow at me, and then raised an alarm so everyone would chase me down," said Dirt, allowing some of his offended peevishness into his voice.

"Vidal from the guard? Big mustache? Why would he shoot an arrow at you?"

"Because I did something wrong, I guess."

"What did you do?" asked the captain, leaning back like he expected Dirt to try to hit him with the staff.

"Well, I'm certainly not going to do it again, am I? Look what happened," said Dirt.

Most of the people around had fled, except the archers. But a few others lingered, having realized they were not about to be eaten and curious about what was going on. They watched from inside windows or huddled behind barrels, or other such places. Another crept nearer and hid, a child. Then an old woman. The alarms ringing across the city only increased.

"This is not how I pictured our arrival," said Hèctor.

That got a chuckle out of Marina, who stood with her hands on her hips, feigning exasperation. It was only momentary, though, and quickly faded into a bright-eyed eagerness she did nothing to hide. "Captain, there's far too much to explain. But I can vouch for the wolf and his pet boy. They won't harm anyone who doesn't try to harm them first."

"And who are you?" asked the captain.

"I'm Marina Sumar, and I was in Oriol's band. I'm a daughter of Ogena. It's been twenty years, but I've returned." She said it triumphantly, like she expected applause. She didn't get it.

He asked, "What is Oriol's band?"

Socks interrupted. *-Those of you coming to the gate better calm down. If you shoot an arrow, I'll kill you,-* he said, adding a sense of predatory menace to his words to make sure they got the idea. He had his ears up and head high.

Dirt hadn't heard the clatter over all the other noise, but now that he looked up the street, a band of armored men were running in tight formation toward the gate. Their metal boots pounded the stone street in near-perfect unison as the few remaining stragglers in the road jumped out of their way.

One soldier shouted, and the rest shouted back in unison, as if making a greater animal out of themselves by adding their voices together. Dirt had no idea humans could be so loud, but the sound struck him with fear, almost as bad as Socks's growls did. It was a dangerous, threatening sound, and those soldiers showed no sign of stopping.

There were so many! Rows and rows of them, ten men across. At another shout, they tightened their formation. The front row readied their shield as the rows behind lowered their spears, pointing them forward with menace.

-All of you stay here,- said Socks, just to the few people standing right there talking with him. The pup stepped over them, moving in the direction of the army. Behind them, the entire gate lifted from the ground and floated forward. Socks's steps grew heavy and slow from the strain of carrying that much weight, solid wood reinforced with bands of metal, but he didn't slow down or let on. Dirt only noticed because he was watching for it.

The army was only a few dozen paces away now, and admirably, they didn't all split up and run away. As Socks stepped calmly forward, he made the gate slam sideways into a house, shattering the whole second story from floor to shingles and sending the pieces flying. Then he smashed a house on the other side of the street, easy as Dirt crushing a bug with his palm. At least, if you didn't notice how the reverse momentum made Socks slide on the street, despite digging his claws in.

The gate rose high in the air and moved forward over the soldiers. Despite all their discipline, they couldn't help but slow their assault and look up.

The gate flew downward, pressed faster than simply falling.

And stopped, inches above their heads. Dirt felt the wind from its fanning all the way back here. The soldiers screamed as one, most falling to the ground or jumping to the side to try to get away. Socks shook it slightly, letting it rattle overhead.

-STOP ATTACKING IF YOU WANT TO LIVE.- Socks's mental voice was loud enough that Dirt was sure every creature heard it from here to the mountains. *-I AM NOT YOUR ENEMY, BUT I DON'T CARE ABOUT YOU ENOUGH TO KEEP TOLERATING THIS. STOP THE HORNS AND BELLS AND SHOUTING.-*

One soldier picked himself up faster than the rest and gave a shout, words Dirt couldn't make out and wasn't sure were even words. Some of the others fell into formation, but most of them tossed their weapons aside and raised their hands.

"Cowards!" shouted the first soldier. "Get up and fight!"

Socks continued his calm forward pace until he stood close enough to sniff the nearest soldiers. One tried to play dead, and two others hastily scrambled away. A fourth man whimpered and clutched his spear, unable to bring himself to stand up and fight. Socks said, *-You cannot hurt me. I am being very patient because of Dirt and because you are harmless. But I will only be patient for so long, and this gate is heavy. Want me to drop it?-*

At least twenty men yelped and ran to get out from under it, and that was the last of the soldiers' formation. Socks let the gate slam onto the street, landing perfectly flat to make it louder. Then he stepped forward, on it and over, and approached the first soldier, the one who'd tried to rally them. He was the only one Dirt could see with a sword instead of a spear, and his helmet had ornamentation that stood out from the rest.

Dirt ran up to join Socks, since it looked like the fight had been avoided. He patted the pup's leg and sent him a puff of affection. *"Thanks for not killing them all. I think they'll see reason if we can just talk a little."*

-I like that they were brave.-

"Me too. Did the gate make your feet sore?"

-No, it wasn't for very long.-

"Good."

The head soldier looked from Dirt to Socks and back again, face distraught. He was a young man as well, clean-shaven, with eyes nearly as dark as Hèctor's that seemed to lurk inside his helmet. "Who are you?" he asked.

"Now this is a man among men!" said Ignasi, suddenly nearby. "See him, the man who keeps his wits the first time he meets Socks! And an angry Socks as well!"

"Which one is Socks?" he asked. "Whose voice was that?"

"We are having to repeat ourselves. If I explain again, will you promise to get word around so we don't have to stop and tell every flower seller and urchin we come across?" said Ignasi, whose good humor continued to be perfectly at odds with the atmosphere of the area.

"Are we under attack?" asked the soldier.

-Not yet. If I felt like attacking, you'd know.-

"That's . . ."

"Yes, friend, that's the wolf. He speaks to your mind and uses a fortified gate like a woman's fan, and a hundred other terrifying things. But a creature this handsome and dignified is only dangerous when he wishes to be. His name is Socks, which has a meaning I'm not going to share because you won't believe me. And this is his little human, Dirt, whom he found somewhere and has been carrying around for company on his adventures."

"That's one way to put it," said Dirt.

"Am I wrong?" asked Ignasi with an exaggerated flourish. The man was truly having a great time.

"No," Dirt said, breaking into a smile.

"Then don't complain. I am Ignasi, and this scowling grump is Hèctor, from the city of Nullor."

"Why is the wolf here, though? And what happened to the gate?" said the soldier, still gripping his sword as if he hadn't completely made up his mind.

Marina edged slightly in front of Ignasi and said, "The boy and wolf helped us find our way. I'm Marina Sumar, and twenty years ago, Oriol led a group of us to Nullor. I've returned. We need to speak with the duke."

"You're from outside? We're not cut off anymore?" asked the young soldier, his dark eyes gaining a glimmer of hope that softened his face considerably.

"We're from outside," said Hèctor. "You're not cut off anymore, and neither are we."

"Get the avitus first!" came a shout from a side alley. Startled, Dirt turned to see Vidal, his face red from exertion, leading a small group of guardsmen with bows. They saw Socks and trembled but kept their wits. "The boy in red!"

Vidal raised his bow in an instant and fired an arrow that took Dirt in the stomach. It felt like getting punched, the force of it knocking him backward. He stumbled and fell over, jarring the arrow further. It had gone straight through him and stuck there.

Vidal rose into the air, floated forward into the street, and screamed in horrified agony as his arms were torn off. Socks flung them around, spreading blood all over a nearby wall, then ripped him in half in a burst of bloody viscera, which dripped to the ground like rain. He dropped the remains right there with a wet, heavy thud, then plucked the guardsmen's bows from their hands and broke them in half.

-I WARNED YOU.-

"Ow, that really, really hurts," said Dirt, rising to his feet and plucking gingerly at his shirt. Tears came to his eyes, and he started choking, trying not to cry. His stomach was in agony, and touching the arrow just made it worse.

"No!" whispered Marina, covering her mouth with her hands.

"Socks, can you just pull it out, please?" Dirt asked, voice tight.

The pup wasted no time and yanked it the rest of the way through. Dirt screamed and started crying in earnest. He awkwardly lifted his shirt and pulled it off.

Socks leaned down and started licking his wound. The pup licked him so much that saliva soaked his pants to the knees, but the blood soon stopped, and the pain diminished.

Dirt turned around, still crying softly. "My back too," he said.

Socks dutifully licked his back while Dirt tried to regain his composure. Even though the worst of the pain had been temporary, it still ached inside like he'd been punched.

When the wound on his back had closed sufficiently as well, Socks tenderly lifted him onto his back and laid him down. Dirt settled into the pup's fur, still sniffling.

Ignasi was the first to speak. "It is always something new with these two," he said, his voice warm and friendly. "They are a charming pair, aren't they? Don't worry about your shirt, Dirt. It can be washed and mended. It'll be good as new."

"Thanks," said Dirt. He could hear everyone else's horror in their silence, and that helped him settle down a little. Let them fret, stupid humans.

-How many more of you will I be killing today?- Socks asked, his voice protective and angry.

After only a short pause, the leading soldier shouted, "Cancel the alarms! Stand down!"

CHAPTER TWENTY-TWO

A soldier raised a small horn to his lips and blew a different pattern than the others blaring across the city, and it was picked up and repeated. One by one, the bells stopped ringing, and the horn calls ceased. The city fell to silence, merely bustling now with a sense of nervous activity.

The lead soldier said, “I am Greater Marc Torrent. You wish to speak with the duke?” He sounded relieved, and Dirt guessed it was because he realized they were going to be someone else’s problem soon.

Hèctor said, “We do. What’s the protocol?”

“Given the circumstances, I think we can dispense with protocol.”

That got a chuckle out of Ignasi and a grudging smile from Dirt.

“Greater,” said Hèctor, “How are we going to reach the duke without any more unfortunate arrows? Got any ideas?”

“I do. Honor guard. Oleguer, blow ‘Honored Visitor.’”

“Been a while since anyone heard that one, Greater. Think they’ll remember it?” asked a raspy-voiced soldier.

“They better. Blow it, and then go find the quartermaster and get a team on putting the gate back. Get a repair time estimate to the palace as soon as possible,” said Greater Marc Torrent.

“Yes sir,” said the soldier. He blew a new sound on his horn, one that made more of a little song than the others. A fanfare, perhaps. An announcement, a welcome and happy one.

One street over, a horn replied with a different call instead, which sounded like the tone of voice for a question. The soldier Oleguer repeated the fanfare, then once more for good measure. Everyone paused to see if the city's forces could handle such a sharp change. They could. First one horn, then several more, and then it was everywhere. Greater Marc Torrent breathed a sigh of relief so loud Dirt was sure it was meant for others to hear.

Dirt decided he'd rather sit up and watch what was going on, despite the lingering ache in his guts. He was glad he did, because no sooner did the new horn call sound than windows everywhere opened with muffled clatters and heads peeked out, wondering what was going on. Dirt waved at a young woman and got a timid wave back.

Greater Marc Torrent said, "Alright, dividing line is right here," making a chopping motion with his hand to divide the dozens of soldiers into halves. "This side in front, this side in back. Honor formation, parade march. You three and the, uh, giant wolf, you walk in the middle. Just walk, don't try to march."

Hèctor said, "I know how it works."

-I don't know how it works. What are we doing?- asked Socks.

Greater Marc Torrent made eye contact with Socks for only the briefest instant before looking down and trying to hide his fear. "How do I explain this?" he asked.

Ignasi said, "Come now, Greater, just because he is a vicious predator from wilds unknown does not mean he is slow to understand. Quite the opposite, you will find. It is a simple thing, noble Socks. If they march for us, then everyone will know we are important and not to be shot at."

-Then they should have done that as soon as they saw me,- said Socks. *-Who decides if we are important?-*

"I can, as a Greater," said Greater Marc Torrent. "I officially decide you are important."

Peeking heads in windows tilted, confused, and looked to other people inside their homes. Dirt smiled slightly, amused at the confusion. They were hearing Socks and didn't know where it was coming from. No doubt they'd all still be trying to get the story straight long after he and Socks had left.

Dirt asked, "Is your name really Greater?"

The others gave him a blank stare until Hèctor figured out what Dirt meant. He said, "No, *major* is a title in the military. It means he commands other soldiers."

"Oh. I thought he had three names like my people used to," said Dirt.

"I thought you had two names," said Marina.

"Well, it's complicated. I only remember part of mine," said Dirt, climbing forward on Socks's head so he could look down at her. "The first name usually has a meaning, so I thought Greater was his."

"Dirt means *dirt*, so what does . . . the other one mean?" she asked.

"Grandfatherly," said Dirt. "Or elder, or ancient."

Ignasi and Hèctor grinned and met each other's gazes.

"That makes sense," said Hèctor, dryly.

"Indeed. Running naked in the wilderness, romping with vicious beasts? Exactly how one expects a grandfather to act," said Ignasi.

"The pure embodiment of grandfatherliness," said Hèctor.

Marina rolled her eyes, but there was a bit of humor in the edges of her lips.

Ignasi said, "Although, to be fair, none of his stories are believable or even make sense."

Hèctor nodded sagely. "That's true. I suppose the name is apt after all."

Dirt wished he had a joke to toss in, but he didn't know anything about grandfathers.

Socks had one, though. He said, *-Well, he does walk with a staff.-* The pup must be reading their minds, which Dirt now regretted not doing.

"And he is fond of socks," said Hèctor. "Nice, warm, fluffy socks."

That was the joke that finally got a laugh out of Ignasi and Marina. Even Socks wagged his tail furiously with amusement. Dirt didn't get the joke, but he grinned anyway, since they were making it funny.

The major shifted his weight impatiently and shouted, "Get in formation!" The soldiers' boots clacked on the paving stones as the men got into position, all in perfect rows, holding their shields and weapons in the same way to make themselves completely uniform. Since they lined up in front of and behind Socks, it was clear where the pup was meant to walk. He stood a little straighter, though, raising his head as if to strut a bit. Or maybe just give Dirt a better view.

"Are we ready?" asked the major.

-Go,- said Socks.

The major turned around and gave another shout that Dirt didn't think was a word. The soldiers' boots all pounded in unison to begin the march. Socks kept pace, head high as he peeked into windows and sniffed the air, and while it was fun at first being flung this way or that every time the pup turned his head, Dirt quickly decided it hurt his stomach too much and slid back down to his usual spot just behind Socks's front shoulders.

-There are a lot more humans than I thought,- said Socks, just to Dirt.

"Yeah. There used to be a lot more, but it's nice there are still this many," said Dirt. He waved at a woman in a window holding a toddler. She waved back, and so did the little one. He tried to find the child's mind, but it was impossible to locate in the blaze of so many others, all so close.

-Is this the kind of place you want to live when you grow up and take a mate?- asked Socks.

"I don't know. I could. I don't want to live too far from your territory, though. Maybe I can find an old city from my people and live there. Rebuild it how it was."

-What's wrong with here?-

Dirt thought about it, looking up and down the street at the interlinking two- and three-story buildings. Most of them were painted yellow or green with dark wood frames, and the farther into the city the marching soldiers took them, the fresher the construction got and the nicer the buildings appeared. Overall, it looked less and less like a city of *his* people the more time he spent here. The narrower, twisting streets, the buildings smooshed against each other. Few trees and no sculpture. Almost no decoration on the façades. The roofs were all at different angles and orientations, making the whole place feel even more jumbled. Honestly, the city was a confusing mess, but aside from where he'd first landed, at least it felt lived in.

Marina had been right about wearing clothes. Dirt hadn't been convinced because from what he saw in Prisca's memories, children or laborers often went naked and no one noticed or cared. But here, the only people without pants on were very small children, and most of those still had a shirt. A few shirtless men and boys in multicolored pants stepped out to watch the parade, but not very many, and they often had a sheen of sweat and grime that made Dirt think they must have been working in the sun. And aside from men doing manual labor, the people were clean. Marina's revulsion at how dirty Dirt had been that first time seemed more justified now. Dirt had to admit that if everyone was as naked and filthy as he usually was, he might not view them the same way.

"Sorry, what did you ask me, again?" Dirt asked, realizing he'd gotten distracted.

-I asked you what's wrong with this place. It has plenty of humans in it, so it must be a good place for your kind.-

"Oh, nothing, really. But it's the only inhabited place we've been. Maybe there's better. After all, these people are afraid of goblins, and that just seems embarrassing to me," said Dirt. He waved at a man with long hair and a fine white shirt, decorated with ruffles. The man didn't reply, probably because he was so focused on the giant wolf he didn't notice the little boy on his back.

-I don't like that they shot you with an arrow just for making a little light,- said Socks.

"Yeah. I'm going to have to be even more careful from now on, but at least now I can watch enough humans to get a better idea of what's normal. Why do you ask, anyway?"

-No reason.-

"I hope it's not because you're thinking about finding somewhere to leave me. I won't let you, no matter how scary the Devourer is, so get that thought out of your head right now. I'll chase you," said Dirt.

The pup turned his head to look at him, tongue wagging. *-You would never catch me.-*

"Nope. But I would chase you. And get lost."

Socks sent him a puff of amusement, trying to play it off as if he'd been joking, but Dirt knew better. No matter how much fun they had, the Devourer was always in the back of Socks's mind. In fact, that might be why he hadn't killed more humans on his way in—he thought this might be a safe place to leave Dirt for a couple years while he grew up.

Dirt added, *"We're never splitting up until it's for happy reasons. I might not be very strong, but I'm still not letting you face the Devourer alone."*

-I know.-

Ahead of them, a small child ran toward the marching soldiers and had to be yanked back by its mother before it got trampled. From here, Dirt couldn't tell if it was a boy or girl, but the little creature pointed from its mother's arms and said, "Puppy!"

Socks noticed as well and plucked the child from its mother's arms with his mind, then brought it in to inspect it closer. It had dark, curly hair that looked more tangled than elegant and a round face with charming baby proportions. The child screamed fitfully at the sudden treatment and reached for its mother, but Socks gave it a sniff and a little lick first, then said, *-It's a girl.-*

He delicately returned the toddler to her mother. Dirt tried to wave and smile to reassure her, but the woman never even looked before fleeing, screaming child clutched tightly in both arms.

Ignasi turned back and said, "Now Socks, how would your mother feel if someone picked up one of her pups without permission?"

-Nothing would dare. But I see your point. Sorry,- said Socks, looking uncharacteristically abashed, if only slightly. Then he said, very loudly, *-I AM NOT HERE TO HURT ANYONE, SO DON'T BE SCARED.-*

Several marching men slipped and nearly lost the rhythm. All up and down the street, people reacted with surprise or confusion or dread. From somewhere a few streets over, one of the little horns even blew the question sound again, which Dirt found humorous.

"That isn't helping," said Marina.

Dirt peeked down at her. "Why not? That's the thing I'd most want to hear, if it was me."

"Yes, but . . . it's . . ."

"Oh, I know. I'm just kidding. But how else is he supposed to talk?" said Dirt.

The major had no idea what to think of any of this and very pointedly didn't look back or say anything. From the set of his shoulders, though, Dirt knew his full attention was on the wolf and people behind him. He shouted a few commands and helped the marching soldiers get back into rhythm, and onward they continued.

The road curved until they could see the palace in the center, and as they got closer, it turned into a bridge that crossed over the river, so wide it didn't feel like a bridge at all. The riverbanks on both sides teemed with people. Women washed clothing, children swam and splashed, and so on. The river was slow-moving and seemed shallow, from how far out some people were wading.

Or at least, that's what they did until they noticed Socks. Word couldn't spread faster than they were walking, so each new person who saw them had no idea what was going on. Even with the soldiers marching and Dirt sitting up there waving at everyone who met his gaze, most people stood dumbfounded or backed up until they fell down and screamed.

The buildings nearer the city center grew not only more ornate, but taller, too. Some were as many as four stories tall, towering over Socks. If the outsides were decorated, it was intricate carvings in wood with details too fine for Dirt to make out from the middle of the road. Street merchants hastily withdrew their carts and wagons to make room, and more than once, a soldier near the front had to rush ahead to help someone get out of the way, like the skinny man with one leg or the very old woman who couldn't stand up straight.

The plaza around the palace was packed so full of people that Dirt was glad for the soldiers splitting the crowd apart. Each person wore a different color and cut of cloth, it seemed, and the tumult and variety made the field of shifting humans almost impossible to take in. Their terrified reactions lessened, thankfully, by the presence of the soldiers giving the wolf a bit of legitimacy. Dirt suspected they weren't sure if Socks was a guest or a captured foe, but at least they stopped to watch instead of stepping on each other trying to run away.

The buildings around the plaza had stately façades that wouldn't have been out of place in one of Dirt's old cities, built in a neat, even circle around the center as was proper.

The road stones here were a different sort than the earlier parts of the city. Those had been bouncy and uneven, like a bunch of river rocks laid out to make temporary paving. But all through the circular plaza, the ground was slabs of cut stone the same color as the walls.

Even with all the color and chaos of the plaza, Dirt's eyes were drawn beyond the crowds to the palace in the center, which was much finer than he realized before. It had an unusual number of spaces for windows, which were curiously covered by a colorful, reflective material in handsome patterns. It took him a minute to realize what he was looking at, but when he did, his jaw dropped. Those windows were full of *glass*. It was a strange experience—he knew what glass was, now that he saw it. But that wasn't enough to explain his reaction, which must have come from a part of himself that hadn't burned away in the void. This was a completely new thing, never seen in Prisca's memory or his own instincts.

The front of the palace was dominated by a large doorway inside a perfect, symmetrical pointed arch. The door itself was larger than any other except the gate itself, and when they got close, it took two men to open, revealing a well-lit interior. The walkway to the palace's door was lined with soldiers in impressive armor that looked to be one complete suit of interlinked pieces, instead of separate parts like Dirt's people made. It covered the men inside from toes to hair, even hiding their eyes in the shadows behind the face plate.

-Look, Dirt, it's the humans wearing metal like Mother told me about,- said Socks, wagging his tail again. *-She said they are pests, and now I wonder if she meant only those ones, or all humans.-*

Dirt noticed a few heads turning and realized Socks had said that for others to hear. He replied aloud, "Probably all of them, but she mentioned those ones because they're hard to chew."

Ignasi barked a laugh, then said, "You can cook them in the armor, but then you have to peel them before eating, and it's a whole process. Best to just leave them alone."

The armored men remained perfectly still, but Dirt grinned to imagine their glares. He wished there weren't so many people around so he could find their minds and see their thoughts.

A man in fine clothing, more intricate and decorated than any Dirt had ever seen or even imagined, sauntered easily from the palace door and into the sunlight. He stood with an easy grace, showing no hint of fear or even trepidation as he regarded the approaching party.

The soldiers leading them forward parted ways, ushering Socks and the rest forward along the walkway, between the armored men.

Marina knelt a few paces away from the well-dressed man and bowed her head. "Your Grace," she said. Ignasi and Hèctor did the same. The man held his hands forward in welcome.

Socks stepped over them and leaned down to give the man a sniff, and to his credit, he simply tucked his hands behind his back, stood straight with head tall, and allowed it, never letting his easy smile drift from his face. *-You are the father human,-* said Socks.

"Indeed. I am Pere Çaburgada, duke by right of my birth and the grace of King Alfonso," said the man, his oiled hair and jeweled clothing shining in the sunlight as brightly as his dignified smile. "Welcome to my capitol, Ogena, although I must admit we have lately lost contact with the rest of my territory."

-You are very brave. Every other human was afraid of me at first,- said Socks, his mental voice curious.

"I am the duke," he replied, as if that was sufficient. And somehow, it was.

Dirt was amazed at his dignity. Socks knew the man was afraid, since he could smell it clearly, but Dirt could only tell by looking in the pup's mind. The duke's mind was lost in the jumble of the crowd, and nothing in his bearing gave the slightest hint.

Socks looked back at Dirt, and the glance said it all. Dirt nodded. This was the man he needed to emulate if he wanted to be the best human.

Marina said, "May it please you, I am Marina Sumar, and this is Hèctor de Alces and Ignasi Cervera. We've come from Nullor to reestablish ties and save our people."

"That is quite a distance," said the duke, raising his eyebrows just a hint. "I welcome you and am eager to see what aid we can offer. It has been too long since those roads were traveled. And who is this?"

-I am Socks,- said Socks. *-I am from Father's territory.-*

Dirt jumped down and matched the man's posture, folding the Home-staff in the crook of one arm. "I am Dirt. I'm from . . . a forest in a place that was once called Turicum. Now it has no name."

-We are here to help these other humans, since they were lost and we wanted to see the city,- said Socks. He turned his head to sniff one of the armored men.

The duke nodded and asked Dirt, "Does everyone in the place once called Turicum have such a noble pet?"

"He's my friend, but if one of us is the pet, it's me," said Dirt with a slight grin.

"Of course. And a very handsome boy you are, and well-mannered. He must be proud of you. I see you have a cut on your stomach. Do you need treatment?"

"No, Socks already licked me," said Dirt.

"Very well," said the duke. He smiled again, radiating nobility and effortless grace. "One moment." He turned to a quiet, shorter man standing right next to him and said, “Clear out the main hall, and bring every cushion in the palace so our big guest has somewhere to rest.”

“Yes, milord,” said the man, who darted off.

“Now, please, Marina, Ignasio, and Hèctor; Socks and Dirt. Come in and rest. The palace will see to all your needs. Simply speak to any servant for whatever you require. When all has been tended, we can discuss at length,” said the duke. “I fear you may have to duck to get in the door, Socks, but there is room inside.”

He turned and led them in.

CHAPTER TWENTY-THREE

The palace interior was extravagant in a way Dirt wasn't prepared for. Every surface sported bold decoration, from polished tilework floors to frescoes painted into the arched ceilings. Walls of lacquered wood gleamed with light from windows. Golden lamps, lit even during the daytime, illuminated any shadowy corner. Intricately carved molding shining with gold leaf raced from floor to ceiling, carrying images of people and beasts and flowers.

Dirt stopped a few paces in, having simply forgotten to keep walking, but Socks pushed him forward with his nose and followed in. The big pup had to duck down and bend his spine quite a bit to get through the doorway, but as promised, the ceilings inside were tall enough for his ears.

The duke led the opulence-dazed party through the entry hall and turned down a hallway to the left, so quickly it felt like Dirt had hardly had time to even understand the beauty unfolding before him. The only sound was Socks's nails clicking lightly on the hard floor as he walked. It seemed no one but Socks and the duke even dared breathe in the presence of such extravagance.

-It all looks very complicated. Humans build interesting things,- said Socks, the first to speak. He sniffed a painting hanging on the wall, showing two men in armor atop horses jabbing a bull with long spears. *-Look at this, Dirt. Why did they make this?-*

"To look nice, I suppose," said Dirt quietly. He almost felt a fool to think humans were dying out, if they were still capable of *this*.

The duke stepped over to the painting and said, "This is my great-grandfather in red, and this is my grandfather in white. The painting was made to commemorate their first hunt together, when my grandfather was only fourteen. This bull had wandered into the hunting grounds and was not happy to see the hunting party. It charged, and in the foolishness of youth, my grandfather lowered his lance and charged it right back. That's why he's in front here. He didn't even lose the horse; he caught the bull in just the right part of the shoulder to turn its horns aside. It made him quite popular with everyone, except the farmer who owned the bull."

Dirt's people had had paintings, of course, although not in this style. Prisca had taken an academic interest in them at one point in her career, although she herself had moved on and forgotten much even before Dirt found her. He wished he had one of her paintings to compare this to, to see if the craft had gotten better or worse since his people's time.

-It smells like many things, but looks like something else. Very clever,- said Socks, a bit of excited appreciation showing in his voice.

The duke paused and raised an eyebrow. "Ah, yes, that'll be the paint. Each color is made from different materials."

-You carve wood and stone to look like people, and mix minerals and eggs and oil and wax to look like horses and bulls. Even Dirt likes to shape wood, except he uses magic he learned from the dryads,- said Socks, sniffing the next painting, then a tapestry, as he sauntered down the hall.

"I would very much like to see that," said the duke in a friendly, avuncular tone of voice, walking just ahead.

-I will not let him show you,- said Socks.

"Why is that?" asked the duke.

-Because the last human he showed magic to shot him with an arrow.-

The duke showed not even the slightest dismay or offense. "A perfectly reasonable caution, then. I will not ask again, until you decide to show me on your own. Now, please let me know if I can tell you about anything else. I worry that if we arrive too quickly, the servants won't have enough cushions for Socks, and I will not have a guest resting on bare floor."

As if to make the point, two older youths in tight green clothing dodged through the party carrying too many cushions, even using their teeth to carry an extra one.

"They're gonna trip," said Marina quietly.

"If so, they'll have a soft landing," replied Ignasi, much less quietly.

They didn't trip, so no one saw how well they'd land. But a few steps past the group, one cushion slipped out of a boy's grip. The youth turned around with a pained look on his face, toeing it like he wanted to kick it back up. Socks picked it up for him with his mind, setting it neatly atop the others. The youth went a little pale, but otherwise kept his wits. He nodded, turned around, and ran to catch up with his friend.

"Who did that?" asked the duke politely.

-Me.-

"Ah, of course. Thank you for helping. He was going to drop the rest of them trying to pick that one up," said the duke. That got a chuckle out of Ignasi.

Dirt might have asked about every painting, but he could sense the others' anxiety and eagerness, so he kept his mouth shut. Marina could hardly keep still, always shifting her weight or shuffling her feet. Her eyes passed over the glories of the palace's interior without truly seeing any of them, her mind elsewhere.

The duke, of course, seemed to have noticed before Dirt did, but wanted to make sure Socks and the others didn't feel rushed. He kept a careful eye on each of them, his gaze flickering at any movement to catch their body language. The man noticed Dirt watching him as well, and something in his demeanor made it feel like they were sharing a secret. Or perhaps like they were teaming up to watch the others, good-natured co-conspirators.

A wolf could show dominance by where he stood, how he turned, and many other subtle clues. Dirt had never realized humans were the same way, but now that he saw a human leader in action, it was as undeniable as a full moon in a clear night sky.

When Socks had nothing else he cared to inspect, the duke led them into the great hall, servants still rushing around them to bring in cushions. Sunlight refracted through the colored glass windows and lit the entire cavernous space with not only beams of white, but multicolor rainbows and shadows of every hue. The room itself was far smaller than Mother's den, but that was hardly a fair comparison. It might be the size of the main room in Prisca's schola, where'd she'd kept him in the dark after catching him.

On the right side of the room, against a long wall decorated with drapes and tapestries, a pile of cushions grew, one armful at a time. It was already big enough to accommodate Socks, but the servants kept finding more somewhere, leaving Dirt to wonder what else was in the palace. Just lots of bedrooms for all the visitors?

A long table of dark wood sat under the windows on the other side of the room, clattering as servants brought plates and knives and other dishes to fill it for a meal.

Socks wagged his tail and pushed past the others to make his way over to the cushions. A servant boy yelped and jumped out of the way, missing the pile with his thrown cushions, then scrambled out a small nearby door. Socks sniffed at the pile, whole body exuding eagerness. After pacing right and left a bit to consider his angles, he put up a mental wall of force to hold them all in place, then stepped over it and settled in, shimmying his long torso to even out his bed. Once everything was in place, he released the mental wall. Most of the cushions stayed put.

Dirt had never seen him look so comfortable and ran over to pet him on the snout. Socks raised his nose and gave Dirt a little lick, then rested again with plain contentment.

The duke rested his hand on Dirt's shoulder and said, "Help me, little Dirt. What do I offer such a guest? Would he like a basin of water to sip, or does he drink wine or beer? We have some pigs roasting since this morning, but I am sure it will not be enough."

"Oh, that's a good idea. Just the water. He, um . . ." Dirt gripped the Home-staff, debating making the water himself. "If it's not too heavy."

"Of course it's not too heavy. It will simply take several trips. Water will be brought," said the duke, not to anyone in particular. Dirt noticed, however, that more than one of the servants in earshot nodded slightly and left.

-There is a man over there touching his sword and looking at Dirt. He'd better stop doing that,- said Socks.

"There is nothing to fear, good wolf. The soldiers mean only to guard me, just as you guard your own. Think nothing of it," said the duke.

-He was thinking about whether he would want to cut down Dirt before Hèctor or Ignasi.-

"Yes, and that is well. He must plan for danger if he is to protect me. Just as you do, watching carefully for any threat and considering how you might react. But if you watch him a little more, you will see he has no desire for violence and prays it will not happen," said the duke, not backing down in the slightest. There was no challenge in his voice, however; just explanation.

Socks huffed and peered around the room again, then gave the duke a short, surprised glance. Then he was satisfied, relaxing more fully.

"Come, Hèctor, Ignasi, Marina. Have a seat at my table and wet your throats. The meal will be a while yet, but a bit of fruit and wine will ease our conversation. My wife and children will be here shortly, and we want to hear everything. And come, Dirt. You can sit right next to me where Socks can keep an eye on you," said the duke.

"You have children?" asked Dirt, following. The nervousness he'd felt when he first tried to meet Marina and the others suddenly came back.

"I do. I have a son who just turned nine and a daughter who is twelve. My two-year-old is napping, so we won't see her for a while. She slept right through all the excitement, and I hope she keeps doing it," said the duke. A servant pulled out a chair near the head of the table, and Dirt took a seat. The duke then stood in front of the larger of the two chairs at the head of the table, and a servant pushed the chair in under him. The duke sat with impressive grace, making something that should have been awkward look effortless.

Ignasi wasted no time pouring himself a glass of wine, then sipping it with a contented sigh. "You are right, Your Grace. This will certainly loosen our tongues. I'd better occupy mine, lest I start talking before the lady duchess and your children get here." He grabbed a piece of something Dirt felt he should recognize and took a bite.

Dirt sniffed the containers of drink on the table and settled on the water, since everything else smelled rotten. He poured himself a glass, then followed Ignasi's lead in taking a piece of fruit. It had yellowing, white flesh with a red peel and smelled impossibly sweet. He bit it in half and chewed twice before exclaiming, "Apple! It's an apple!"

He looked around excitedly. Marina, Ignasi, and Hèctor all gave him knowing smiles, but the duke looked like he was missing the joke. Dirt said, "I've never had one. I've never even seen one before. I forgot all about them!"

Socks reached out, and Dirt shared his sense of taste, finishing off the other bite of apple slowly, letting the juices squeeze out with gentle bites and linger in his mouth.

"What is this one? Is that a plum?"

"No," said Marina. "That's a cherry. Where did you get the apples so early in the season?"

"I have one tree that produces early apples, and the cherries have been storing nicely in the cellar," said the duke, watching Dirt with increasing curiosity.

Dirt picked up the cherry and bit it in half. Or tried, anyway. It had a hard stone in the middle he wasn't expecting, and it made his jaw pop open by reflex. That resulted in dripping bright red juice all down his bare chest, but he caught the drop that would have landed on his pants. Good thing he hadn't had a nice clean shirt to put on, or he might have ruined two in one day. "I forgot that was in there," he said, licking his palm. He wiped some of the juice off his chest, and licked that too. "Are you supposed to eat the hard thing? No, right? You're not supposed to. It's a cherry."

"Have you never had a cherry?" asked the duke.

"Nope, no fruit at all," said Dirt. "I've never even seen any before today. But I think I remember it now."

"You say the strangest things, lad," said the duke.

Hèctor said, "You have no idea, Your Grace. He has not even begun to say strange things."

Dirt smiled and reached for another slice of apple. "I'm normal. I don't know what you're talking about."

Ignasi snorted, and Marina smiled down at the table.

They waited for only a short time before the duke's mate arrived. A man opened a door at the back of the room and said, "The Duchess Teresa."

Everyone stood, which surprised Dirt, but he slid out of the chair to his feet in a hurry to match them. The duke looked over to Socks and said, "Stay resting, friend. You look too comfortable to bother."

-I will. I am,- replied Socks, sounding happy.

A woman walked into the room dressed even more finely than the duke, in a dress that spread out around her legs like a circular tent. The cloth she wore had a reflective sheen and countless precious stones sewn along the seams with decorative embroidery. Her hair bounced inside a gentle net of silver threads, and a necklace with a red stone in a golden setting rested between her breasts.

She strode with the same easy grace as the duke, at once powerful and relaxed, except that her movements were unmistakably feminine in a way his weren't. She walked with head high and shoulders back, just like he did; but when she walked, she glided, arms light around her waist like drifting feathers. Dirt was almost startled to see such a contrast, which was hardly noticeable between Hèctor and Marina. Maybe Marina just needed some time back in civilization.

Behind her came two children, both with the same dark hair and eyes that most people in the city had. First was a girl shorter than her mother wearing a dress of similar color who edged farther and farther from Socks as she followed, her face stony instead of smiling. She held the hand of the second child, a boy just a bit taller than Dirt who was all but hiding behind her. They walked like their parents did, if less convincingly, imitating the style but not the substance. For one, it didn't help that the boy couldn't keep the trepidation off his face as he made sure his sister was between him and the wolf at all times.

"Duchess," said Marina, Ignasi, and Hèctor, each bowing. Seeing how it was done, Dirt did the same.

She had a pleasant voice, if not loud or particularly musical like the duke's. She said, "Welcome to our home. Please do not hide behind manners if there is anything we can do to make you more comfortable. Speak."

"Thank you, Your Grace, we will," said Marina, trying to return the same charming, noble smile she'd been given.

-Hello, Duchess,- said Socks. He kept his head resting on the pillows, but his eyes were lively as they darted around the room. *-Do humans always show strangers their brood?-*

The poor woman paled, her smile faltering but not vanishing.

The duke said, "Just speak aloud, as with anyone else."

She nodded, regaining her perfect composure. She didn't step an inch closer to the pup, though. "It is good manners to show the family to guests in one's home. And why should I not, when I am so proud of them? Everyone, this beauty is our daughter Èlia, and the timid little man here is Màxim. He's usually a bit bolder, but, well, I'm sure you understand."

-I understand,- said Socks, even though the duchess had been speaking to everyone. *-When I first met Dirt, I didn't know what he was, so I snuck up to sniff him. When he saw me, I was already right there, and he was too scared to even scream. He was so scared he peed. I thought he was going to die of being too scared, like a mouse. But he had just been chased around by a goblin, so he was already in a scared mood. He didn't run, though. He stayed and talked to me. Ignasi and Marina and Hèctor all ran away screaming.-*

Ignasi grinning. "To be fair, friend, you did growl. Anyone who hears that and doesn't run is a fool."

-You wanted to run before I growled, though.-

"Yes, I did. And the next time I saw you, and the third. Anyone who sees cute little Socks here and does not run away screaming and pissing himself is already doing better than average," said Ignasi. "Although his wisdom may still be a topic for debate."

The duke smiled like they were old friends. "Cute and little are not words I would use for him."

Dirt said, "You would if you saw his parents. Mother and Father are way, way bigger than he is. He's still just a puppy."

"How much bigger?"

"It's hard to say exactly. But they could step over the wall without touching it, easy," said Dirt. He looked at the two children, who shot him glances every so often but kept their eyes focused on the wolf, and said, "Do you want to come pet him?"

Both children froze, even holding their breath. The boy slid a little further behind his sister. All the joy went out of the parents' faces, even though they kept their smiles plastered on.

Ignasi said, "Maybe move a little slower there, Dirt. They're still debating running away pissing themselves like sane and reasonable people."

"Oh. Sorry," said Dirt.

"Nothing to be sorry for, lad," said the duke. "I'm sure my dear Màxim will be happy to play with you once he's had a moment to settle in first. He and Èlia just arrived, after all. Please, everyone have a seat. Now that my wife is here, I'd like to hear what brought you all the way from Nullor to Ogena."

At that cue, everyone took their seats again. The duke and duchess sat at the head of the table, and the children sat farther down, separated from the others by two empty chairs. Màxim met Dirt's gaze and gave him a little wave, which Dirt returned. Dirt decided children weren't typically seated by the adults, but he probably shouldn't move from the spot the duke had placed him. He and Màxim would have a chance to talk soon.

"Where do we start?" said Marina.

"With the famine," said Ignasi.

"Right," she said. She took a deep breath and shifted her wine cup a bit on the table, then picked up a piece of apple and put it back down. "Sorry, just, I've been thinking about this for a long time."

The duchess reached over and put her hand atop Marina's and said, "Don't fret, dear. It might be your first time meeting royalty, but we see commoners every day. I know it's difficult, and I know you'll do just fine."

"Thanks, Your Grace," said Marina. After one more deep breath she began. "Two years ago, a hailstorm took out half the grain in Nullor's fields. The year before that, during the night, something crashed through some of our best orchards and broke nine trees. The year before that, something stole a chicken every night for a good portion of the summer. We think it was a gnome. Each year, it's something. A storm, or the wilds encroach, or a farmer breaks a leg, or something. And each year, our stores of food get just a bit smaller, each spring just a little hungrier. Well, each thing that happens, you can fix, right? You can get new fruit trees and laying hens. But it adds up. When Pol broke his leg, his wife and children could only farm about two-thirds as much that year, and instead of a surplus to sell, they had to borrow. It's a hundred little things, and they add up."

She paused and took a sip of wine. "Sorry, I'm not getting to the point, am I? Nullor wasn't supposed to be a frontier city. Our band made it all the way there with no trouble, twenty years ago. But shortly after we got there, they lost contact with Alpica, and we didn't hear from Seramenat for five straight years. Fifteen years ago, we stopped hearing from Llovella entirely, even though it was too big and prosperous to just disappear. You probably know all about this, since I bet it's not just happening to us. All this is your territory, after all. Sorry, I'm wasting your time."

"You are not wasting our time, Marina. You have hardly even begun," said the duke, gently. "Please continue."

"I'm just really nervous. Pardon me," said Marina.

"Really puts the duke's boldness in front of Socks in perspective, doesn't it, Marina? He hardly seems affected," said Ignasi. "Or the duchess, for that matter."

"Don't tease her, Ignasi," said Hèctor.

"But I have nothing else to contribute!" said Ignasi.

She glared at Ignasi before cracking a smile. "You ass," she said. "My apologies, Duchess, don't let my coarse speech offend Your Grace. I'll continue or Ignasi won't stop. I told the major that I'm from Ogena, one of your own people from your capitol. And it's true, I was born here. I left with Oriol's band when I was just a girl, hardly older than Èlia. My parents were dreamers until the day they died, always thinking of adventure and new glories. Nullor wasn't supposed to be frontier then, like I said, but when we got there, it was. We settled in and became like everyone else, but I still remember the milk I was raised on. I know it's naïve, but I still think there are good things on the frontier. There are, at least, a few good people left."

"I have never doubted the goodness of my people, or their courage," said the duke. "I have seen enough for them to earn my respect and service."

"Thank you, Your Grace," said Marina. "You see, I think we have a deeper problem than just dwindling food. When I think about the old stories, about King Raimon who founded the First Kingdom of the Camayans, it's not a story about being careful and prudent. He was bold and used whatever force it took to get the job done. But that's not how we act anymore. We're too scared and too beaten down to make a lasting fix. Nobody cuts back the forests and starts a new field on the edge of the territory, not anymore. But everyone will abandon the far fields if they become too unsafe. Short-term fixes. We'll try to chase out the gnome, but no one's going into the mountains to look for the rest to eradicate them."

She paused and took another deep breath. Dirt had thought she was easing up the more she spoke, but apparently not. "The famine. Back to the famine. We lost ten adults to starvation that winter. Not so many the town is about to disappear. It's still there, doing fine. Losing children is one thing, but losing ten adults? That's a lot of work no longer getting done.

"And here's the point. This is what I thought about all winter, and all spring, and every day until I convinced these two fools to come with me. So what if no one's come on those roads for years? If anyone had been brave enough to take a wagon and reopen the road, they might have come back with grain, and those people might have survived. But they didn't. They were willing to lose some rather than risk losing more to preserve it. And that's the problem with us, my lord and lady. It's the whole people. It's the entire Three Kingdoms. We've been hit so many times we're too afraid to fight back.

"And that's why we're here. Like I said, I never forgot the milk I was raised on. We started out with a cart and two horses, and each mile we ran into new trouble. But when we set out, we did so to get here or die, and we made it. We walked into this city with nothing but our clothing, but we made it. All three of us know the entire road now, and we know what to expect. We can get back," said Marina. At this she paused again, letting silence rule the room.

Everyone could feel that she had more to share, just a bit more, and she seemed to be struggling to put it into words. She sat rigid, hands folded in front of her as she anxiously ground her fingers against each other to help her mind work. Finally she said, "The wilds were hard. Worse than we imagined. We almost died more than once. But I just had that hope, and we kept going. And we made it. And along the way . . . well, I don't know how to explain it, and I don't know what it means. But not everything in the wilds wanted to kill us. We found Dirt."

CHAPTER TWENTY-FOUR

Everyone turned to look at Dirt, who wasn't sure what he was supposed to do. Look at all of them in turn? Look away?

Marina said, "Dirt is . . . Where do I even start? Do I skip to the trees?"

Ignasi said, "No, Marina, you will make it too complicated. Let me put it this way: See him sitting there, handsome and mild? He is an honest, friendly little boy, deserving of all affection. And yet, all the most terrifying moments in my life have involved him in some way."

Hèctor snickered. "That's a good way to put it."

"What are some of these terrifying moments?" asked the duke, leaning forward very slightly.

"Well," said Hèctor, "there's the giant wolf. But you knew that already. So how about the time he talked the gryphon into not eating us?"

"I will never forget the ghosts, personally, no matter how hard I try," said Ignasi, taking another drink of his wine.

Hèctor said, "Or the time he killed goblins with that stick and the thing he was worried about was getting blood on his pants."

-He is a human, though,- said Socks, sounding a bit protective. *-And not anything else. You are making it sound like he isn't one again. He is human.-*

"And you'll never catch me saying otherwise," said Hèctor with a hint of a grin.

"He's quite a child," said Marina. "Dirt can talk your ears off telling you his stories, and you should let him. But what we came to ask you for, my lord, was for your help reopening the roads. And believe me, we know better than anyone what that means. Not just patrols. It means workmen to keep them in good repair. It means reclaiming Llovella. Now, I know you have a good reason for not doing it yet, after all this time. But we're here to tell you it's possible. Me and Hèctor and Ignasi were willing to die to prove it. The frontier might be at your doorstep, Your Grace, but we're here to tell you it's time to push it back."

Hèctor said, "We thought we'd be sitting here with a wagon full of goods to make a better case. After we lost the wagon, we thought we'd be showing you packs full of goods. Then we lost the packs. But we made it. It's possible. I'm going to be honest, though. It's not a safe road. We almost got killed more times than I can count. I can't promise everyone you send is going to survive. But what I can promise you, is that if we don't do it, if we don't take the risk, then we're going to die. All of us. Every last human. I can feel it, Your Grace. We all can. Marina's upset everyone's being cautious, but that's not quite it. I think everyone knows the end is coming, and we're trying to hide from it."

An uncomfortable silence followed. The children shifted in their chairs, and the duchess's folded hands tightened subconsciously. The duke furrowed his brow and scratched his cheek, unable to give a quick response.

A servant stepped in quietly and set a large cooked bird, plucked and still steaming, in front of the duke. Shortly after, another brought out a bowl of steaming vegetables, and another brought two loaves of bread. They didn't stop there, and soon the table was covered in more food than Dirt had seen in his life, all of it steaming and aromatic, with too many smells for him to tell apart. In the center of it all were two fat pigs, all carved up and ready to eat except the faces. They were enormous, possibly weighing as much as Dirt did, and had to be carried by two people.

The duke flicked a finger to summon a servant and said, "How many pigs do we still have cooking? Any more, or just these two?"

"Two more, my lord," whispered the servant. They all wore the same clothing, which was making it hard for Dirt to tell them apart.

"Are they done cooking?"

"Yes, my lord."

"Good. Take these two over to our largest guest, and bring out the other two for him as well. Socks, I apologize if this is not enough to fill your stomach, but we were not expecting you," said the duke.

-It is fine. I want to taste the pigs,- said Socks, lifting his head. A bit of drool dripped from his lips and darkened a pillow. *-Four of those will be a very good meal, but I will need Dirt to help me get the meat off the bones. Mother will not let me eat cooked bones yet.-*

"Don't worry about that. The meat will come right off the bones all its own. You will see," said the duke.

Before the servants had a chance to carry the pigs from the table over to Socks, the pup lifted the platters with his mind and carefully brought them over by himself, taking great care not to spill anything off the sides.

Seeing the pigs floating across the room was enough to get everyone but the duke to stare in shock. Even the duchess's jaw dropped, and Màxim stood up on his chair to get a better look, unable to believe what he was seeing.

Socks shifted around on his pillows so he could sit up. Most of the bones had been removed, it turned out, and just as described, the remaining bones slid right out of the meat on their own. Socks deposited them in a little pile just beyond his cushions, then tilted the first platter right into his mouth, shaking it to get it all.

The duke nodded, then cut a slice of roast bird and set it on his mate's plate. "My lady," he said politely. Then he cut a piece for himself and set the knife and fork back on the platter, gesturing for Dirt to cut himself some.

Marina, the two men, and Dirt wasted no time filling their plates, but the others couldn't stop staring at Socks. The pup ate the second pig in sections to draw out his enjoyment of it, and when it was gone, he watched the door eagerly for the next two.

"Tell me, Dirt," said the duke, raising a bite of bird with his fork, "How are you involved in this? What is your place with them?"

"Oh, they're . . . some friends," said Dirt, trying not to be too obvious about peeking at them from the corner of his eye to see if they objected. They didn't. "I haven't traveled with them for very long, but it looked like they could use some help, and I wanted to meet some humans. They taught me their language and lots of other things."

"I knew I heard an accent in your voice. What language do you speak, aside from ours?" asked the duke.

"I don't know what it's called, but it sounds like this. *Hello, my name is Dirt, and I am talking in my own language right now*," he said.

The duke sat up in his chair. "No!" he exclaimed.

"What?" asked Dirt, shrinking back in his seat.

"The language of records. That was the tongue of the ancients! To think there are still some who speak it, out there somewhere beyond my borders," said the duke. His eyes took on an excited gleam that replaced his carefully dignified demeanor.

"Well, just me, probably. But you can still find old ruins with our writing on them," said Dirt.

"Say something else, so I can be sure. I want to hear more," said the duke.

"In a sea of delightful wine, a mouse may only die," said Dirt, sharing a popular tongue twister. Then another. *"Although they are under the water, they try to curse under the water."*

"See if you can translate this. If you can, then I will know for sure. *Boy, meat, you want, good boy!*" said the duke, more excited each moment.

"That means, 'boy, meat, you want, good boy,'" said Dirt. He sank further in his chair, knowing why the duke asked. "They also know 'come out,' I think."

The duke had no blame to lay on him, however; instead, the man grew more excited than ever. "Your name means 'dirt,' doesn't it? What does the wolf's name mean?"

"Yep, it means dirt. And his name means socks, like you wear on your feet," said Dirt.

"Marvelous!" cried the duke. "This is a day of days. Tell me, Dirt, please—you must know, why do the goblins speak the ancient tongue?"

"I have no idea. When I first met one, I didn't know there were other languages in the first place. It took me a while to realize," said Dirt.

"Ah, a shame, a shame. Do you know much of the ancient people? Does any of their lore survive among your kin?"

"I think I said already, but I don't have any kin. These are the first humans I ever saw. But I know a little about the Sunset Empire. What sort of thing?"

The duke had yet to take a single bite. He still held the chunk of meat on his fork and waved it around to gesture with. "Anything! Wait. Tell me this, first. How were you raised without any parents?"

"I just woke up in the forest one day. I met Socks, and then . . . I learned how to talk to the trees and made friends with them too," said Dirt. He took another bite and only then realized that it was even better than the cow meat from the other night. The bird was tender and bursting with flavor, herbs, and salt and a hint of sweetness. He'd been so distracted by the conversation he hadn't tasted his previous bites.

"And the forest was in a place once called Turicum? I thought I recognized that name. Can you answer this? Did the Sunset Empire ever truly exist?"

Dirt said, "I'm certain it did."

The duke clapped his hands and said, "This is incredible, truly. Scholars have been arguing for centuries whether the empire was a fanciful legend or the truth. We have so little from those days, and the things those writings tell us! I was one of those who never believed. I only learned the language to read the old records. Have you ever seen any of their writing?"

"Yes, I've seen some," said Dirt. "Not a whole lot, but I read the sign on a tomb once. It was in an old ruined city called Ocriculum."

"Do you remember what it said?"

"Sort of. Do you want me to say it as written, or translate it?"

"Both," said the duke.

"I think it was something like, 'O Shepherd of the Dead, Here lies Callius Something Something. He was a magistrate, and he was sixty-six years old when he died. His heir closed this door,'" said Dirt in their language. Then he said it again in his.

"Marvelous! We only have the names of a few of their gods, and that is one. Now it is certain," said the duke.

The rear door opened again, and four servants entered carrying two more pigs. Amusingly, they only dared get close enough to Socks to set them just out of his reach before they scampered away, and the pup had to slide them into range with his mind.

After watching to make sure the pup got the rest of his dinner, the duke said, "If I bring you some texts, would you read them?"

"My lord," said the duchess, "let the poor boy eat. How often do you think he'll see a duke's table, and here you are interrogating him."

The duke paused, then visibly schooled himself into calming down. His countenance smoothed from uninhibited eagerness into convincingly sincere affection. “Of course you’re right, my lady. Later, I will insist he tell me everything. But I am being an ungracious host. After our meal, we can speak more about these plans to reopen the roads. I fear it will be harder than you all realize, but I will not refuse you so quickly, when you’ve brought me such a treasure. Shall we have some music?”

“Yes!” said Dirt immediately. “Please? Who will sing? I can, but I only know one song.”

“No one, darling boy,” said the duchess. She gestured to a servant, who knew what she wanted because he’d been listening. He hurried out of the room, leaving everyone munching on their meal and watching the door in anticipation. When he returned, he led a group of four musicians with different instruments to a corner of the room. One had a flute, but the other three had stringed instruments Dirt didn’t recognize. They weren’t lyres.

The music they played was lively and complicated, allowing each musician to demonstrate their skill. Dirt gave up trying to follow the melodies and simply let the music carry him into a happy reverie, eating food that was more delicious than he’d imagined possible. The others talked, but their words passed over him without leaving much effect. He smiled when he heard laughter, but his thoughts were elsewhere.

Until he saw Socks sit up and peer around, having noticed something odd. -*What do you think that is?* - said Socks. No one else reacted, though, so the pup was only speaking to him. Socks sent him an image of mind-sight, showing a dim and misshapen mind through which passed periodic images of roofs and buildings and not much else.

“I don’t know. Do you want to see where it is?” replied Dirt.

-*Let’s,*- said Socks, and their minds slid together. Socks and Dirt looked at the minds nearby, pleased they could tell them apart much easier now. Well, the boy’s mind could, anyway; the wolf hadn’t had any trouble in the first place. But now there was no doubt which mind belonged to whom, since they could place them. That was the duke, and behind him, a servant, and another, and then the musicians over there, and behind the door, two more servants hurrying down a corridor.

The minds of the city came into clarity and were no longer a field of indistinguishable lights, but instead, a sky full of stars, each one fixed in space. And far above them, surprisingly, the misshapen-half mind hovered on the drifting currents of high breezes, gazing downward.

"-What is that?-"

"-We still can't tell. Does it look like something only half-alive, like the tentacle beast?-"

"-It does, but it is not the same.-"

"-Is it a threat? Do we need to go catch it?-"

"-Maybe. How are we to know?-"

"-We should go look at it.-"

"-Let us send the boy, then. The wolf doesn't fit through the doors.-"

Socks and Dirt had the boy stand up, pushing his chair back, and say, "We'll be right back. We need to check something."

They hoped the boy didn't sound too odd, since they'd never tried interacting during a mind meld before. The wolf closed his eyes while the boy sprinted from the room, leaving a chorus of surprised comments behind him.

The boy raced down the ornate hall and turned down the entryway. They pushed the door open, careful not to slam it, and stepped outside. The soldiers in metal remained, still standing guard, and now Socks and Dirt could see each of their minds distinctly enough to know they wondered what he was doing out here alone, even though they didn't speak or even turn to face him.

"We're just checking something," Socks and Dirt had the boy say.

The wolf lifted another bite of pig into his mouth, letting its savory richness linger on the wolf's tongue so they could enjoy it. Dirt and Socks said, *"-That really is good. We think it's better than the bird.-"*

Meanwhile, the boy gazed up into the sky, shielding his eyes from the sun with his hand. There was nothing there, at least nothing close enough to see.

Dirt and Socks had the boy turn to a soldier and say, "Do you see anything up there? In the sky? Can you help us look?"

The soldier didn't reply, nor did he look up into the sky. He kept his eyes on the road ahead, keeping vigilant watch for any approaching danger.

Socks and Dirt sighed and kept watching. They might be imagining it, but there was a shimmer in the blue, a flaw like ripples of heat in the distance. As they watched, it circled in gentle arcs, but no form appeared, and it might have been nothing, or the result of staring into the sky with the boy's human eyes. No birds or other flying creatures to see, just the ripple in the sky. Whatever it was, its mind took note of buildings and people, but only in a flashing, disjointed way, as if the greater part of its thinking was happening elsewhere.

"-We don't know what it is, but we don't like it.-"

"-No, we don't. It seems wrong.-"

"Dirt?" said a timid Èlia, the duke's daughter. She'd come out to get the boy, and the wolf hadn't noticed.

"Oh, yes, we're fine," they had the boy say. "Do you see that up there? That shimmer? The ripple in the sky?"

Èlia stepped the rest of the way out the door, and Màxim followed close behind her. She asked, "Are you sure you're okay? Do you want to come sit back down?"

"We're fine, we promise. But please, can you look? Do you see that? Either of you?" said the boy, pointing up at the sky. The two children stepped into the sunlight and gazed upward.

"That wave?" asked Màxim.

"Yes. Good, you do see it. We are wondering what it is. Do you know?"

The misshapen mind spotted them down there, three children staring up at it from the ground. An instant later, it vanished completely. No mind in Dirt and Socks's mental sight, no tiny ripple to see in the sky.

"I don't see it anymore," said Màxim.

"I still don't see it," said Èlia.

"It's gone now," said Socks and Dirt, using the boy.

Ignasi stepped out the doorway. "Dirt?" he said.

Socks and Dirt sighed to themselves, then severed the mind meld since their prey was gone anyway.

"Sorry, did I make you worry?" asked Dirt sheepishly. "I'm coming back in now. I just had to check something."

"You didn't seem yourself for a moment there. Are you well?" asked Ignasi.

"I'm fine. Let's head back in so I only have to explain once," said Dirt.

Màxim and Èlia gave him looks of mild concern, then beckoned him to follow. Dirt wished he could still see their minds, but his mind-sight revealed only a glowing haze of white with almost no distinction, just like before. He resolved to get some serious practice at that, because losing his mind-sight any time he was in a city would be a serious handicap.

The children led him and Ignasi back down the entryway, along the hallway, and back into the large, glass-lit room. The duke stood when they entered, but it seemed more to get a good look than because he was supposed to. "Is he alright?" he asked.

"It wasn't that weird, was it?" asked Dirt.

"You were a completely different person. I can't explain it," said Marina.

"It was that weird," said Hèctor.

"Sorry. I had to check because there was something in the sky. Màxim saw it too, but it's gone now," said Dirt, timidly making his way back to his seat.

"What was in the sky?" asked the duke. "And how did you know it was there, if you're inside?"

Before Dirt could answer, a note rang out in the distance. A horn, blowing an alarm.

CHAPTER TWENTY-FIVE

The room went silent, the duke's family growing pale and fearful and the man himself biting back annoyance to maintain his dignified demeanor. A moment later, a second alarm sounded from outside, only faintly audible through the sunlit windows.

"An army," muttered the duke. "My guests, I regret that my company will shortly be required elsewhere. For the second time in one day, I may be called out to oversee a battle. You don't happen to know anything about that, do you?"

-We do not have any armies. What is it an army of?- asked Socks.

"Goblins, I would say; I might be more certain had our first little invasion not been a harmless boy and a giant wolf. They have been an unreasonable nuisance the last few years."

-Will the men in metal armor fight them?- asked Socks, perking up. *-Will they ride horses like in the painting?-*

"Socks," said Ignasi, "I bet if you go put the gate back up where you found it, we can talk him into sending some men with horses and armor."

Socks looked over at the duke, ears perked up in eagerness.

"We'll help fight them, too," said Dirt, in case this was something the duke needed to be convinced about.

-No, Dirt will not help fight unless he is needed. He will scare the other humans. But I'll help kill the goblins if the men in armor come along,- said Socks.

The duke needed very little time to think and soon turned to one of his servants, a fidgety man who seemed anxious for everyone to get moving, and said, "Go tell the quartermaster to get enough workmen to reattach the gate. I want them there immediately with tools and supplies. And you, Miquel, go tell Ramon that the Palace Guard will be attending me in person, in full strength. I want my horse and armor. Run, before my city is plundered."

The two men left at full sprints, leaving through different doors and not even closing them behind themselves.

Socks stood, wagging his tail eagerly. *-Will you fight too, since you are the father human?-*

The duke said, "If a hundred men are sent, the hundred-and-first will add very little. Whether I fight will depend on how badly I am needed."

-My father would be worth more than a hundred of me,- said Socks.

"My lord," said the duchess, resting her fingers on his arm, then rising from her chair gracefully and sweeping herself into his arms for a hug. "Take no risks. Come back in one piece."

He kissed her hair and said, "As you command, my lady." Dirt felt a puff of affection between them despite the interference of too many local minds.

The duke's two children approached on timid feet. He grinned and gripped them both on the shoulder and gave them a quick hug at the same time. "No need to fret just yet. It is surely not that serious."

Dirt suspected that the reason the duke mentioned the severity of the threat at all was because he suspected otherwise. "I'll go with him. Socks probably won't let me charge in by myself anyway while he's holding the gate up. He'll be safe."

The duke smiled in a way that Dirt found somewhat condescending. "I appreciate that, little Dirt, but a battle is no place for children. I will want a stronger guard around me."

Hèctor said, "I wouldn't underestimate the boy, Your Grace. You may be glad to have him. He's plenty capable."

-As far as I can tell, he is the only strong human at all,- said Socks. *-If he is not with you, then he will be with me.-*

"I cannot have an unarmored boy at my side in the middle of a battle," said the duke with finality.

"Dirt, why don't you jump up there and touch the ceiling?" said Ignasi with a sparkle in his eye.

The room went silent, with even the unnoticed servants freezing in their tracks and slyly turning to watch. Dirt remained still, though, unsure if he should do it. Humans didn't seem to like that sort of thing, and Socks had told him not to.

Into the silence, Ignasi said, "What, you thought a boy with a friend like Socks would be otherwise ordinary? Is there anything about those two that strikes you as ordinary? Anything at all?"

"Thanks, Ignasi, but it's okay. I'll just go with Socks. Nothing will get past us anyway. But my lord the duke, Your Grace, please don't have anyone shoot me with an arrow if I do something surprising. Once is enough for one day," said Dirt.

"You only need to say one title at a time," muttered Marina.

He took his little backpack off and set it on his chair. "Oh, you don't have to put any of that food away yet. We'll be right back," he told a servant.

"How long do you think this will take?" asked the duke, showing a bit of indignation for the first time. "We are under attack!"

"How long do *you* think this will take?" replied Dirt coolly. "Come on, Socks. Let's hurry."

-We will meet you there. They are getting in already. Remember to come with your armored men so I can watch them fight,- Socks told the duke.

Dirt started walking across the room to go back out, but the duke said, "Wait!"

He and Socks stopped and looked back.

"I must come with you so my men know not to attack," said the man, striding forward. "If they are already breaching our walls, then there is no time to waste. Gonçal, tell the others to meet me there. I will be armored on the field. Bring my horse. Socks, will you give me a ride?"

Dirt grinned, proud to see the man's daring, and looked at Socks.

The pup said, *-I like this human. Come. They should make a painting about us.-* He bent under the doorway and led Dirt and the duke down the hall, around the entranceway, and back out the building.

The armored soldiers outside were already moving into lines, with more and more of them running across the plaza from different places to get into formation. The sound of their metal boots pounding on the stone clattered loudly, even over the chaos of the crowd clamoring for news from behind the short fencing surrounding the palace.

"My lord!" shouted one of them, whose extra decorations marked him as a leader of some kind.

"Come when you are ready. I'll be going on ahead," said the duke, standing regal and calm. He raised a hand, gently beckoning Socks. "How shall I get up?"

The pup lifted the duke with his mind and set him down on Dirt's spot. The crowd of soldiers and men reacted in shock and horror, many screaming. Some stepped forward to help, and others stepped backward to flee. But the man raised his hand again, smiling freely and without fear. He waved at his people until they got the idea and calmed down somewhat.

Dirt jumped up as well, sat down in the duke's lap, and said, "Don't worry about falling off. Socks won't drop us. But if you get nervous you can hold on to me."

"I have never felt more secure," said the duke. "This is quite comfortable."

"Good," said Dirt. "Okay, Socks, we're ready."

The pup left at full speed, leaping over countless people to land in a small open space, then jumping again. The duke held back a scream at great difficulty, clutching Dirt with surprising strength and making a long whimpering sound instead.

Dirt laughed and shouted, "Faster!"

The duke hissed in fear, but stopped when Socks hit the ground and sprinted with all his might, moving so fast they couldn't hear anything over the wind. The duke hugged Dirt so tightly he could tell the man was holding his breath, so he patted his arm, not that it would do any good.

Only a moment later, and they were back at the gate. Socks slowed and stopped, and the duke let out a loud gasp, then took a deep breath and did his best to regain his composure. The man's heart was beating at triple speed, but he smoothed out his fine clothing and hair and regained most of his dignity.

"It's fun, isn't it?" said Dirt, teasing the poor man.

It was the wrong time for a joke, though, because the area was a mess. A surprising horde of goblins were assaulting the few dozen soldiers pressed together in the gateway, blocking with their shields while the second row thrust swords and spears through to fight back. The line held, but it wobbled and bent under the press of wretched green flesh.

At least fifty of the horrible creatures had gotten through. Some had rushed into houses and were making it hard to get them back out, while others moved through the street in clusters, daring anyone to come charge them, snarling and gnashing their crooked yellow teeth. Screams and alarms rang out from everywhere, and the nice gray paving stones were already slick with blood and corpses, not all of them green.

Socks grabbed the nearest clump of goblins with his mind, all six of them, and tossed them back over the wall, high enough they'd crunch when they came back down. He yanked two more through a house window and ripped them in half, then tossed the remains over the wall as well. Then another group, and another, to the horrified awe of the men who'd been struggling with their lives to bring them down.

The men fought desperately, boldness giving way to despair. The acrid, unmistakable scent of fear mixed with the reek of blood and injuries as women and children screamed from inside houses they'd been too slow to flee, helplessly watching the carnage in the streets.

The duke sat through it all, riding regally with one hand resting on Dirt's shoulder, but he gripped ever tighter with each new horror. Dirt was content to keep sitting there for a bit, because it looked like the humans were doing fine for the moment, and if he jumped down, he'd get his shoes bloody.

A goblin from inside tried rushing the rear of the soldiers holding the line, and Socks jumped forward and ripped it in half between his teeth and right paw. He stepped right up to the line of soldiers, sniffing around and looking to get a good idea what was going on, then filled the air outside the gate with sparks.

A wall of fire erupted and burst forward, filling the air with searing heat and the scent of burning flesh. Socks drew deeply on his mana and made the fire hot, so hot that most of the goblins caught right inside it died before they could do much screaming. Then he made a second wave of sparks a bit farther out and erupted that into a much wider fire. Now that he had some room, he stepped right over rows of soldiers who cowered and hid their faces from the heat, and out onto the sizzling ground outside the gate.

-That is a lot of goblins,- Socks said. And he was right. Too many to count, well into the hundreds, and possibly thousands. More goblins than there had been digger-beasts, for certain.

"I wonder if it's the same army that killed everyone in Llovella," said Dirt mentally, since there was too much screaming going on to talk with his voice. *"This could be really bad. I'm not sure we can chase this many off."*

-They won't be able to get through the gate, no matter how many there are,- said Socks. *-That's why the city is still here.-*

The roaring shriek of the screaming goblin army sickened him as much as its appearance did. They made a roiling sea of green flesh, paler than his ferns but just as dense, with too many twisted, stretched faces and gnarled teeth. Ears curled or straight and pointy, many of them damaged or sliced. They stood so close together that they hardly had room to raise their fists, many of which held clubs or rusty swords. Dirt had hated them *before* he'd seen a crowd of humans, and now that he had something to compare goblins to, he hated them twice over.

"The gate!" the duke shouted. "Go back in!"

"Wait, let's try something first real quick!" shouted Dirt. Then with his mind he told Socks, *"Make one more fire. I'm going to try blowing it with wind and see what happens."*

Socks obliged and cast a field of sparks over the next goblins, who were already gathering their courage to rush forward over their suffering, dying kin. The flames erupted with a roar and a wave of force that seared lungs and melted flesh, causing eyes to burst and killing broad swathes at once.

Dirt raised the Home-staff and drew on his mana to call a wind into being, blowing down from the sky to spread the flames farther across the horde. It spread the flames with ease but did little to make them stronger, since there wasn't any proper fuel to ignite. Socks's fires died out, killing fewer goblins than before, but singeing others enough to make them angry.

-Well, it was a good idea,- said Socks. He looked out anxiously over the army of goblins, stiffening his hackles slightly with growing trepidation. He padded back in through the gate, stepping over the soldiers and letting them cut down the goblins who had been too close to burn.

The gate wasn't where Socks had left it. Someone had attached ropes and dragged it most of the way back to the wall, where it still lay flat on the ground. Perhaps the humans could have gotten it up and into place by themselves if they'd had enough time, but they had none. Socks hefted it upright with his mind and moved it over to its place, where he held it overhead, waiting for room.

"Back three! Back three!" shouted the duke, hands around his mouth to make a horn. They heard him over the chaos and repeated the call, then the major, Marc, shouted, "One! Two! Three!"

With each count, the whole line moved back as one, all stepping at the same time and keeping the line intact. A man who'd been dawdling at the periphery dove forward to pull a fallen soldier out of the gateway, just in time.

The gate slammed down into place, turning a whole row of goblins into severed bits and paste that splattered a surprising distance. After such a shock, the ones who'd made it inside were easy work for the soldiers and soon after, the work of killing ceased inside the city.

It didn't get quiet, exactly, but it did get quieter. The gate blocked most of the noise from the goblins, but could not silence their screams. Those blurred into an unpleasant roar that rolled over the gates and made everyone's heart tremble.

"Please let me down, Socks," said the duke, releasing the tight grip he'd had on Dirt's shoulder this whole time. "I must see to my men."

-You will get blood on your shoes,- said Socks.

"I have other shoes," said the duke.

Socks lifted him with his mind and set him down gently, feet first, in an open spot a few feet away, one of the few patches near the gate where the stones were still clean.

He strode directly up to the major and said, "Report."

"My lord!" said Marc. "They rushed us out of nowhere, already massed. We were so focused on helping move the gate we didn't see them until they'd entered the plain. They came right for us, and it's my opinion they knew about the gap. We got a line up in time, but they broke through around the left side once, and a third of your men are going house by house to hunt them down."

"Tell the archers to hold their arrows for now and send the footmen to make sure none remain inside my walls. This gate will hold. Get me a count of the killed and injured," said the duke, hands behind his back as he listened with a calmness that spread to everyone who saw him. "Offer anyone who was bitten their final mercy and send those who refuse to their families for their last hours."

"Yes, my lord," said the major. He turned and barked orders at the men behind him, and the soldiery sprang back into action, spreading out to check every shadow and corner for hiding goblins.

Socks kept holding the gate, which pounded with goblin fists and clubs of bone or wood as the men tried not to stare at it in dread. But then the sounds changed, becoming sharper, and Dirt realized along with everyone else that the goblins were hacking at the wood with weapons of metal now—the rusty swords and axes he'd seen before. A worried murmur passed through the men.

The injured were deposited along the street to rest their heads on whatever cloth could be found for a pillow. Mostly nothing, just the hard ground. One by one they were brought, some with minor wounds and others holding their guts in. The goblins were short, resulting in more injuries to the lower parts of the body; but the wounds were no less gruesome and deadly for it.

Dirt watched one man bleed out from a deceptively deep gash on his inner thigh and breathe his last. The sight affected him more than any other death, and he'd seen plenty. It struck a whole chord of emotions inside him—fear, heartbreak, and a nameless sense of wrongness. He wished he could have seen what happened to the man's mind for clues about where his soul had gone and at least draw some comfort from that. He couldn't.

He began to appreciate the desperation of the men around him. Even the duke felt it, showing it only in the slightest ways, a tightness around his eyes and lips that his commanding dignity couldn't completely erase. Death hung over everything. Socks and Dirt would make it out regardless, but if this place fell, no one else would. All those people, ripped apart.

"Oh, hey, Socks, would you mind licking some of their wounds? The ones who are going to die soon?" asked Dirt mentally.

-If they bring them to me. I am going to sit down before my feet get sore. The gate is heavy, and the goblins hitting it makes it worse. I don't know how long I have to hold it, because the men to fix it still aren't here

yet.- And sure enough, Socks lay down to rest, paws forward and head up to remain wary.

Dirt slid down and hopped between clear spots on the stone road as he made his way over to the injured. They'd begun field medicine where possible, doing clever things like sewing wounds shut with needle and thread or applying salves and bandages. As tempted as he was to watch and learn how they did everything, it wasn't the most efficient just now.

"Excuse me," said Dirt to the nearest uninjured soldier, a man holding a fat roll of bandages that others kept cutting lengths from. "If you want to take the people with the worst injuries over by Socks, he'll lick their wounds, and they'll get better. People with goblin bites, too."

The man stared down at him with a blank expression, unable to make sense of what he was being asked. "That won't help. Just stay out of the way."

"Yes it will. He does it all the time."

"Go talk to the major or the duke, son. I can't deal with this right now."

"Just watch, then," said Dirt. He stepped through the crowd of soldiers performing desperate medicine until he found a likely candidate, a young beardless man with no hint of a mustache, who was busy applying pressure to a stab wound just under his rib cage. He looked pale and the skin around where he was holding looked bruised and unwell from bleeding on the inside.

"My friend Socks is going to save you. Don't be scared," said Dirt.

The young man could hardly focus, turning his head and saying, "What?"

"Just a moment while I carry you over," said Dirt. He inhaled a good amount of mana and used it to strengthen his muscles, then awkwardly lifted the man in a cradling position and carried him over to Socks. Some of the medics came over and tried to stop Dirt, and the man himself squirmed and moaned in pain and begged to be put down.

Socks looked at the ones approaching and gave a low growl, and that was enough to get them to back off.

Dirt put the man down and held his arms away, pinning him down. He was strong, despite his injuries, but not compared to Dirt using mana. Socks licked the man's wound, lapping up all the blood and digging in with his huge tongue as deeply as he could. A moment later, the soldier's breathing relaxed, and a bit of life came back into him. Socks lifted his head away and the man sat up, drawing surprised gasps from those watching.

"I'm healed!"

"Mostly," said Dirt. "It'll hurt for a day or so. So, anyone else? Just the people who are going to die. How about that guy? Hold his intestines in and bring him over."

CHAPTER TWENTY-SIX

Only eight men had been wounded to the point of death, and Socks made quick work of those. Another six had been bitten by goblins, and they seemed more serious and ashen-faced than the man holding his guts in, or the two who had passed out from blood loss and awoke expecting to see the afterlife. Once all those were taken care of, Socks made an exception to Dirt's "only the dying" policy and had a man hold a severed hand in place while he licked it, just to see if it'd work. It did, it turned out; the bone remained severed, but all the flesh sealed back together.

During the last few treatments, Dirt heard a loud clattering sound but was too distracted to pay attention. When Socks was done, however, he saw that the duke's armored horsemen had arrived, riding up the street five abreast in tight formation. They carried tall spears on one side and shields on the other, and Dirt had never seen fighters so grand, not even in Prisca's memories.

Some wore richly embroidered tabards over their chests, and others carried flags, or had ribbons tied to their lances or around their arms. Even the horses themselves were dressed and armored, so well-covered that Dirt still wasn't sure what a horse was supposed to look like. The armored men matched the palace, Dirt decided, as prime examples of human accomplishment—skillfully ornamented and redoubtable.

They couldn't get the horses too close, though. The animals could see Socks in the middle of the road and probably smell him, and no amount of training or encouragement was going to get them any closer.

-So much for those things being good at fighting,- said Socks, just to Dirt. *-Do you think those men would have to get off if they wanted to poke me with their lances?-*

"That just proves the horses are smart," replied Dirt. *"What should they do, come up and lick you? Do horses lick?"*

-They have tongues, and everything with a tongue can lick.-

"Humans don't lick each other to say hello. In fact, I don't think they lick each other at all."

-You have not met enough humans to say so,- said Socks. *-You should try licking the next humans you meet, so we can see what happens.-*

Dirt grinned at that, finding the picture amusing. But then he thought about it and wondered why it was funny and why it seemed so strange. Maybe he *should* try it one of these days. Although . . . *"Maybe I will if I see the duke do it."*

He and Socks both looked at the duke, who was patting his own horse, its brown and white spots only scarcely visible under a barding of silk and gold thread. Two youths stood nearby holding armor far more ornate than any of the rest, probably waiting for the duke's command to put it on him.

The duke noticed their gazes and left his entourage to walk over at a brisk pace. Two attendants with swords followed hurriedly behind, taking deliberate effort not to look like they might be trying to threaten the giant wolf, which Dirt and Socks both found droll.

"Socks, a question," said the man, standing straight and fearless, only a few steps away from the pup's nose. "Would you be able to lift the gate away to allow my men a charge, then close it again? And open it again when they return?"

-Yes.- The pup stood and wagged his tail, mouth hanging open. *-Are they ready now? Wait, I want to watch.-*

Socks radiated excitement as he hopped up onto a nearby house, walking to the edge where he could peek over the wall. The building creaked beneath him, and some of the tiles cracked and slid off with a loud clatter, but it held him. He wagged his tail ever harder as he looked out into the field, then back at the men, and back out again.

-I am ready. You men, go, and I will open it just in time, so the goblins don't all get in.-

Dirt decided he wanted to see the moment when they first crashed into the goblins and hustled over to the gate, slipping easily between the handful of defenders waiting behind it. He stood right up against the stone wall, only a step or two away from the opening, where he'd get the best view of their charge.

Surely the duke hadn't meant they were going to go *right now,* and surely Socks knew that, but he was too excited and couldn't help himself. And besides, the duke wasn't put off-balance by the pup's haste in the slightest; at least, if he was, he didn't show it. He raised his hand and spoke with a voice that echoed off the stones. "The gate will open for your charge, and open again for your return. In my name, and for the glory of our king, charge! Charge now!"

Socks eagerly lifted the gate a few inches just so they'd get the idea, and to their credit, the men lowered their lances and spears and spurred the horses forward. Dirt watched in surprised respect at how fast the horses allowed themselves to be driven right into a closed gate; they must be plenty smart after all and knew what was happening. He wished for the hundredth time that the city wasn't so crowded it blinded his mind-sight.

At just the last moment, when the lead horse was turning its nose and about to stop, the gate flew upward, to the surprise of the dozens of goblins hacking away at it with rusty swords and axes.

The horsemen smashed into the crowd of squirming green bodies with a resounding percussive force. And they kept coming, row after row of them, charging forward and shredding the fallen goblins with their hooves. They didn't even need those long lances—with the goblins only as tall as a human child, the armored horses barely even slowed, running them over despite their thick musculature.

Dirt watched, entranced, his ears filled with their thunder, until the last rank of horsemen had passed the gate. Right on cue, the heavy wooden door slid back down and shoved itself forward a few feet to rest in its frame.

-Look at them go! They are just stomping all over the goblins. They don't even need the armor,- said Socks loud enough for everyone to hear and still wagging his tail hard enough to knock people over. Good thing he was on a roof.

Since there wasn't much to see until they came back, Dirt made his way over to the ladder and climbed up onto the wall so he could watch. The walkway atop the wall was wide enough for two men to walk side by side, but that was all. Its height made it feel much narrower, even though the stone fencing to either side made it impossible to fall off.

"You shouldn't be up here, boy," said one of the archers, a long-faced man with stubble instead of a beard whom Dirt had never noticed before. Despite his words, he made no effort to usher Dirt back down.

"I just want to see the horses," said Dirt, making no effort to move if they weren't going to force it. "Say, has this ever happened before?"

"Never so many," said the archer. "And they've never been smart enough to hack at the gate. That's new. My turn for a question. Did they chase you all the way here? Is that why your, uh, friends were in such a hurry to get in?"

"No, not even a goblin is stupid enough to chase Socks," said Dirt. He was glad he'd come up here—the view was fantastic, plenty high enough to see the armored horsemen cutting through the army like so much waving grain. They'd spread out into more of a wedge than a mallet and left a trail of muddy carnage behind them, making their passing unmistakable.

"Okay, I have another question," said Dirt. "With those armored men and horses, how come the goblins are still a problem?"

"Couple reasons. One is they don't form into armies very often. Usually just little groups, sneaking around hunting for whatever meat they can find. Hasn't been safe to farm out there for years, and there's no way to get them all. Two, that's a lot more dangerous than it looks," said the archer.

"Why's that?"

"That's every horse the duke has out there. All sixty or so. A few go down, and the best case is they don't have enough horsemen for a second charge. Worst case, the formation falls apart, and we lose everyone who can't make it back on foot."

"The armor should keep them alive, though. There's nowhere for a goblin to stab," said Dirt.

"Sure, but if they pull you down, you're not getting back up, and they'll get that armor off you eventually. Just takes one bite to kill, after all," said the man. He lowered his voice and looked around a bit guiltily, even though the man to the right and left of him would hear it regardless.

He asked, "My turn for a question. I've heard whispers they saw an avitus, around the time your, uh, friend came in. Did you see one? Do you know anything about that?"

Dirt kept his face blank while he thought about how to answer. "What does an avitus look like?" he asked.

The man's neighbor answered for him. "An old man wearing a white gown, or maybe it's supposed to be a robe. He walks through town, and any child he touches gets palsy. It's a stupid story."

"No, the way my parents tell it, is it only looks like an old man until you get close. It's a monster in human disguise, and it kidnaps children and burns them alive."

"Yeah, I've heard that version, too. And the one where he goes around pointing at things, and everything he points at will collapse or die before the next full moon," said the neighbor. "And the version where it's a shapechanger."

"Well," said Dirt truthfully, "I didn't see anything like that."

The horsemen in the field turned to make an arc through the rear of the goblin army, where the bodies were much less dense. Dirt expected them to cut right across to the other side, then angle back inward. They left a trail that was easy to follow, and Dirt kept glancing along it to see if anyone had fallen or been separated, but so far, so good.

-COME BACK NOW. RIGHT NOW,- said Socks, loud enough to give Dirt a brief, mild headache. All around, people ducked or reacted in some other way to the wolf's voice thundering in their minds. Way out in the field, a ripple of recognition passed through the horsemen's formation, and one man raised his banner and waved it. The horsemen turned an impressively sharp corner and made directly for the gate. The distance they now had to cross, and the horde of raving creatures covering it, looked much more sinister now.

"What is it?" asked Dirt aloud, since Socks would hear him regardless.

-Something half-dead is coming. More than one, I think.-

"Where?"

-I don't know.-

Dirt looked up, and there it was—the same ripple overhead, circling slowly as it watched them.

-Not that. FASTER. HURRY.-

The horsemen could only go so fast, but it looked like they tried, spurring their horses and crushing everything in their path. Two hundred paces. A hundred and eighty.

Between the horsemen and the gate, a thin, green arm as long as four horses together rose from the midst of the goblins, followed by another, and another. A monstrosity vaguely shaped like a spider arose, all made of writhing, sickly flesh the same color as the goblins. It had no teeth or even a face, just arms and legs and limbs that were a wretched combination of the two jutting out from a flat, round body.

Every man on the wall gave a cry of terror or alarm, and Socks kept jutting forward, as if wanting to run out there and fight it. The problem was the gate. He didn't want to let it fall over to let them all in, and he couldn't fight while holding it in place.

"Report! Report!" shouted the duke from below, but he didn't get one; what were they supposed to tell him? A few men glanced back toward him, faces pained, but couldn't sum it up in a return shout.

"Socks, lift the duke up to the wall. I'll make room," Dirt said, directly to the pup's mind. He wrapped both arms around the waist of the man he'd been talking to and carried him out of the way rather than waste time trying to explain. And sure enough, just as the man began a confused splutter of protest, the duke floated up and landed in that spot, as gracefully as if he'd done it by himself.

"My lord!" said the men close enough to notice, but the duke gave them no more than a nod as he gazed out into the field of battle. His hand shot to Dirt's shoulder and grabbed it tightly once he saw the spindly green monstrosity, and Dirt felt tremors of fear in the man's fingers that didn't reach his face.

"We shall have to trust them. They are the finest among us," said the duke, his voice quiet despite the noise around him.

The horsemen didn't turn aside and try to go around like Dirt expected. They slowed, horses rearing to stomp on any goblins who approached as they readjusted their formation. Those who still had lances moved to the front, and the edges of the wedge tightened, narrowing the focus of their attack.

They spurred their horses forward again, giving a great shout that cut through the screams of goblins and the cries of the men on the wall and gripped Dirt's heart, electrifying him.

The goblins between the monstrosity and the horsemen realized the danger they were in and gave up trying to fight. They clawed and bit each other instead, pushing down their fellows and climbing over them as they fought to get out of the way.

Every man on the wall held his breath to watch the charge. The monstrosity turned to face the riders, even though it had no discernible front or back, and raised three of its limbs. Hands the size of barrels curled into fists and waited.

The first lances stabbed its contorting limbs just as it swung down, hammering into the front of the armored formation. The lancers left their weapons in its body and rode onward, but not everyone followed. Four horses had been killed instantly, their riders crushed as well or thrown to the side, and the creature raised its fists again, four of them this time, and hammered down at an angle instead to sweep the next rank of riders to the side.

But the men on the ends hunkered under their shields and deflected the blows upward, even while its monstrous strength threw them to the ground. The formation was secure, and the next rank of riders crashed into the beast. Some stabbed with lances, and others struck it with their shields. The effect was immediate.

It shuddered and flailed, injured and dangerous. It jumped to the side, landing in the crowd of struggling goblins, and changed its tactics, grabbing riders off their horses instead. Two it tossed away, and Socks caught those right out of the air and brought them back over the wall. But the others weren't so lucky, getting dropped on the ground and then hammered with its barrel-sized fists.

The right side of the formation curved away to charge directly at it, their lances aimed straight at the monster's core. It tried to swat them away like the others, but too many of its limbs were injured, and it failed to protect itself fully. It crushed one more horse's head and cracked the legs of another, but that wasn't enough. A lance punched into its body, and the man rode right under it to get back into formation. Then the next, stabbing it a second time and leaving the lance in place.

The monstrosity curled up into a ball and simply waited for the rest to pass. The goblins screamed in anger and rushed for the horsemen again, but it was too late to stop their charge, and they rode at full speed toward the closed gate.

"See how they trust me," said the duke, his face unable to hide the pure emotion that held him.

At the last moment, Socks flung the gate upward again, with such sudden strength that the return force on his body pressed him right through the house he was on, collapsing it with a loud crash.

The riders charged inside an instant later, and everyone raised their fists and voices in a shout of triumph. Socks flailed to extricate himself from the ruined house, throwing planks and stones every direction until he could crawl out and stand back up. When the last horseman passed through, he brought the gate down and slid it back into place.

The duke hastily climbed down the ladder to greet his men and get their status, but Dirt kept his eyes on the field for a moment longer. And it was a good thing he did, because the monstrosity rose again and pulled the lances out of itself, one by one. Most it threw away, but two it gripped for its own use.

Socks hefted a long beam from the fallen ruin of the house and placed it against the gate. *-Hold this for a moment,-* he said. *-You, you men standing there. Put your hands on it. Hold it. Right now.-*

Once a few defenders braced the beam, the gate loosened in its place to indicate Socks had let go of it.

-I'll be right back,- said the pup. Socks effortlessly leaped over the wall, landing lightly on the field of battle. He ran out toward the fallen horsemen, ignoring the goblins' useless attempts to swat or bite him as he passed. He found one, and lifted him out of danger with his mind, then another. And another.

The monstrosity hesitated, its many wounds oozing a thick, dark brown fluid that swallowed the sunlight, and Socks was content to ignore it until he found them all. Then he raced back over the wall and gently set the recovered horsemen alongside the other injured soldiers.

Dirt jumped clear off the wall and ran right over to the gate, resting his hand on its planed wood surface. It was smooth beneath his fingers, the old polish still holding strong, at least on this side.

Working with dead wood was much, much harder, but not impossible. Dirt inhaled mana and told it to *grow. Grow, grow,* he commanded, and it grew, slowly, resisting, taking far more mana than living wood. This door had been dead for ages, possibly centuries, but the word of magic the dryads taught him commanded it nonetheless. He drew more and more mana, inhaling it as fast as he could to fuel the process of growth and expansion.

The brace holding the gate up fell aside with a heavy thump as the door put out tendrils that grew into thick branches and grasped the stone gateway tightly, both front and back. It expanded in every direction, thickening and pressing the arch above its frame upward until gaps appeared between the stone. Dirt breathed more power into the process until its bumpy surface filled the entire gateway, flush with the wall and held in place by branches thicker than a man's leg that stretched three paces in every direction.

Dirt turned to see a sea of stunned faces. Everyone had been watching him do it. They all knew, now. He hesitated, almost hiding behind the Home-staff.

But before anyone shot him with an arrow, the duke raised his fist and gave another shout of triumph. An instant later, so did everyone else, and Dirt was so relieved he almost cried.

Men stepped over to pat him on the head or shoulder, smiling widely, leaving Dirt to grin back and nod awkwardly. First a few, but then twenty and more. So many rough hands on him should have been uncomfortable, but instead, he found they made it feel warm inside his chest.

The archers gave a cry of their own and started firing their arrows. The duke shouted, "Report!"

"My lord, it's still alive, but it's too injured to climb up!"

-Then save your arrows. I smell others on the wind coming down from the hills,- said Socks. And with that, the temporary moment of jubilation ended.

CHAPTER TWENTY-SEVEN

I really thought this wouldn't take very long," said Dirt, sighing and thinking about their meal getting cold, sitting there on the table. He wondered if Ignasi and the others had resumed eating, since they weren't here. "How many are coming? Is it the same kind?"

-Enough are coming for me to smell them from too far away to see, but I don't know how many that is,- replied Socks. He shook from tail to nose, flinging the last of the dust from the collapsed house away. The crowd of guardsmen parted to allow him through, not that it mattered; he could step right over them. Reaching Dirt and the gate, he sniffed both, then gave Dirt a little lick. *-You really stuck the gate in there tight.-*

"It doesn't do any good if it falls off or the goblins chop their way through," said Dirt.

-It depends on which direction it falls off,- said Socks.

Dirt grinned and looked around to see if anyone else thought that was funny. Mostly, they looked unsure whether wolves could tell jokes.

The duke waved for Dirt to come over, then stood expectantly with his hands behind his back. Dirt nodded and slipped through to go meet him with Socks following right behind.

"I am impressed, little Dirt. There is much I will ask, once we have time for a long conversation under more pleasant circumstances," said the duke. He furrowed his brow and looked at the ground, thinking. "I . . . hmm."

-Dirt can shape wood, speak to plants and animals, call wind down from the sky, create lights, and several other things. He can also fight. He learned

some of it from the trees and some of it from me. There. Now you don't have to think of a way to ask,- said Socks, his voice tinged with amusement. *-And before you ask, he really is a human. I already said that.-*

"You did indeed, friend. You did indeed, and you are the expert on the matter," said the duke. "Our confusion is simply that humans do not do what Dirt has done."

-That is probably why you are dying out,- said Socks.

"Well answered. But we are not dying out today," said the duke. He turned and gestured at the now-permanent gate. "Or anytime soon. With the only remaining entry closed, the city is secure. We will watch until the goblins leave, but they will disperse once they start getting hungry. They never come with provisions. In the meantime, we must consider what is to be done about the other things you smelled on the wind."

-They will climb over the walls when they get here.-

"First, have you smelled them before? At any point on your travel down from Llovella?"

-No, never. I don't know what they are.-

"Neither do I. Second, could you be mistaken? Perhaps you smelled them because that is where they live," said the duke.

"Loose!" shouted an archer. Dirt and the rest turned to see the archers atop the wall shoot their arrows at something on the other side.

"Report!" shouted the duke.

Before anyone answered, a monstrous hand reached up, bloody and pierced with at least four arrows, and tried to grab one of the archers. The man dove off inside the wall at the last moment, saving his life at risk of breaking his ankles. He had the good fortune to be caught by Socks and set down safely.

The creature's hand reached for another archer but got only a vicious sword wound for its efforts. It grabbed the lip of the wall with its long, green fingers, and pulled an entire rectangular stone down, leaving a section of walkway bare of exterior railing. The rock was so heavy that Dirt felt the thump of it hitting the ground all the way from here.

Socks raised his hackles and drew his lips back into a snarl. *-I want to growl, but I will scare the horses. Come, Dirt, we will fight.-*

"Surely you don't mean to take the boy out there?" asked the duke, reaching forward to place his hand protectively between Socks and Dirt.

-Dirt is like me. We are very nice until it is time to be ferocious. I want to scare off all the goblins before those other things come, or they will get in the way, and it will be complicated.-

"How long do you think we have?" asked Dirt. He sat down and untied a shoe, then pulled it off and put it in his pack.

-There are a lot of goblins,- said Socks.

"Wait," said the duke. "What are you doing?"

"I don't want to get blood all over my clothes, so I'm taking them off. Don't tell Marina," said Dirt. He pulled his other shoe off, then his socks, and put them in his pack, followed by his shirt. Then he stood back up and hopped out of his pants. He rolled those up before putting them away. "Can you hold this for me?" he asked, handing the backpack out for the duke.

"You can't be serious," said the duke, his perfectly disciplined demeanor slipping. A tinge of worry appeared at the edge of his eyes, a tightness in his lips under his finely oiled mustache. "You can't go out there like that."

"I'm not naked. I have this sheath for my dagger. That counts," said Dirt, hoping to elicit a smile. It didn't.

"Boy," said the duke sternly.

"Please just hold this?" said Dirt. He turned to the armored man next to the duke and pressed the backpack into his stomach. "Or maybe you can? I don't know your name. But can you hold this for me until I come back? I don't want to lose it."

"I never agreed to carry bags for children," said the man, taking the backpack from Dirt and handing it to the duke.

"Sir Vidal?" asked the duke, eyes widening as surprise removed another layer of his discipline.

Dirt glanced at Sir Vidal, hearing the same name as the archer who'd shot him, but it was a different man. A different Vidal. Apparently, more than one person could have the same name.

The man said, "My oaths are about fighting, not carrying. Let us join them, my lord. If the wolf is willing to lift us over the wall, we will take the field. We'll leave the horses and fight on foot. I'll keep the boy safe if I can."

"How will you get back in if you have to flee?" asked the duke, his worry no longer concealed in the slightest.

"We'll stack the bodies and walk over, my lord. We had but a taste of blood today and wish ourselves another portion," said the man, radiating resolve.

The duke looked him in the eyes, clear respect showing through his worry.

"Please, my lord."

"I forbid it," said the duke. He handed Dirt's backpack to an unarmored servant.

"My lord!" begged the armored man.

"I forbid it! I'm not leaving the fate of my duchy and the king's people to a puppy, a naked boy, and a band of knights with an absent lord! Armor! Armor, now!" shouted the duke. He pulled his thick, multicolored shirt off by himself, leaving a much thinner undershirt, and tossed it to the same servant who held Dirt's backpack. The man barely caught it before it hit the ground.

From there it was one of the most elegant dances Dirt had ever seen. Four young men dressed the duke, first in padded clothing, and then layer after layer of armor. The duke moved with perfect accuracy to assist them, holding out an arm or leg at just the right time and angle. Even with so many practiced hands, it took a surprisingly long time to get the duke into his armor. There were straps to pull, then test, then pull again. Bits and pieces to adjust, more than Dirt could keep track of. He and Socks had the same thought, which was to be impressed at the incredible artistry that went into crafting it, now that they could see enough to appreciate it.

And it truly was something to appreciate. To Dirt, armor was simple. The most complicated armor his people had used was rows of metal plates fastened to a shirt. Most of the armor in the Sunset Empire had been solid metal, not an intricate work of thousands of perfectly-shaped bits of metal. At least, if his people had had anything like this, Prisca's memories didn't contain it. And judging from his gut reaction to what he was seeing, he was sure such armor was a new thing in the world, fashioned long after his era.

A few minutes later, the duke was encased in solid, gleaming metal, and snapped his visor down with a loud clack. He stood turned to face his armored men, and said, "We will fight in formation. Defend your neighbors, and do not allow yourselves to be killed. Tonight our children shall sleep to lullabies, not lamentations and dirges. Socks, if you would be so kind as to lift us over the wall, it would be our honor to join you on the field of battle."

-You never asked me. What if I say no, after you spent all that time putting your armor on?- said Socks. His voice was serious, but his tongue was out, and he was wagging his tail, giving him away.

Dirt grinned as the band of armored men swallowed the cheer they'd been about to erupt into. "Be nice, Socks," he said.

-I am only teasing. It is good for the father human to fight with his brood,- said Socks. *-You little humans are very brave. Almost as brave as Dirt. Come. I can't lift you all up at once. Dirt, go clear a spot for them to land.-*

"Finally!" shouted Dirt. He ran back through the growing crowd of onlookers as he inhaled a full measure of mana, then jumped right over the wall. At the height of his jump, he raised the staff and gave an excited shout, which he intended for a battle cry but didn't sound like one.

To his left, the big misshapen creature was unmoving and trampled by goblins, finally killed for good. It had about fifty arrows in its round little body and at least that many more in its malformed limbs. Dirt swung his staff down with both hands to crush the skull of the goblin he was about to land on, then expended a surge of mana to spin and fling them all away to start making room.

The Home-staff swung with inexorable weight, the massive tree's momentum crushing so far into goblin flesh that it ripped arms apart and burst chests open in a spray of gore. And just like that, Dirt proved he'd been right to undress first. Not even long enough in the field to blink twice, and his front was coated in red.

Dirt swung the staff in wide arcs, holding it on the bare end, crushing screaming goblins and flinging their mangled bodies left and right in heaps. Being so close to them again reminded him anew how much he hated them. The scent of their breath and skin, their exaggerated features. Their eyes, so close to human but lacking any intelligence at all. Dirt hated even the taste of their blood, which got past his closed lips and flavored his teeth, but his disgust was offset by the satisfying cracks of their bones, their screams of fury whimpering out into death rattles.

They rushed him from behind, their claws sliding uselessly off his mana-protected skin, and he spun, letting Home do her work and throwing their dying bodies into their crowding fellows.

The first group of armored men landed around him, eight of them with swords already drawn. They tightened into a circular formation that Dirt jumped right over.

The goblins were starting to realize the threat Dirt posed and shied away, but the size of the army meant there was nowhere for them to go. Dirt charged the next clump, swatting and striking to erase their hateful faces from his sight, just as the next group of armored men landed and folded seamlessly into the formation.

Glancing back, the duke wasn't here yet, so Dirt kept focusing on making room. He snarled in his most wolfish way and leaped on another goblin, spitting the blood of its siblings into its face before crushing its knees with a single stroke. Dirt turned to kill the next ones, and the next, swinging the staff in great arcs. But the one whose knees he'd destroyed grabbed his ankle from the ground and pulled him back, locking its teeth around his calf. Dirt felt the mana there sizzle and spark as it burned away to protect his flesh, and before he could yank his leg away and get back up, another fell atop him, clawing his face and going for his neck with its teeth. Dirt rolled hard and freed his ankle then crushed the staff through the goblin's hissing mouth, shattering its teeth and breaking its jaw. Another shove downward broke its neck at the base of the skull.

The next group of men landed with the ones after that following close behind, and the armored men quickly started to look like quite the formidable force. They had no need of shields, and most had left them in favor of using two weapons. Their armor was sturdy enough to turn aside the rusty weapons and gnarled clubs the goblins wielded, and the soldiers' swords and axes swung with such fury that a haze of red blood-fog formed in the air around them.

The duke landed with the last group and pushed his way forward to take a position in the front line. He joined in the work of death with the same vigor as his men, showing himself no less of a killer than they.

Finally Socks arrived, tearing in every direction with teeth and claws and mind. To his left he destroyed the goblins with bursts of roaring flames, and to his right he lifted them with his mind five at a time and tore them in half. Dirt ran toward him and jumped, letting Socks grab him from the air with his mind and swing him through the goblin ranks, crushing dozens at a time with the Home-staff.

Over a hundred goblins must have been killed already, but it was so few compared to the rest of the swarming army that it may as well have been none. Socks fought with glee, leaping from place to place and leaving craters in the field of bodies. The pup's enthusiasm was so infectious that Dirt found himself laughing as he was yanked from place to place and thrown into groups of goblins to mow them down with his staff.

The army was little more than a chaotic swarm of feral beasts, despite looking like they should have at least *some* intelligence. It turned out that moving unpredictably throughout the entire army instead of giving them a stationary target to focus on brought them nearly to a standstill. Instead of pushing forward at the gate so tightly that some of them suffocated and fell, they began to wait, unsteady and unsure, for Socks to come to them.

"Split them up! They're—"

-I see it!- replied Socks exultantly. Now that the goblins lost their reliable targets, they stopped refilling the areas where Socks had landed and killed another pocket. Those areas were starting to form threads, dividing the army roughly into four parts. The armored humans were doing very well for themselves, considering their limitations, in the quarter closest to the gate. The duke was on the second row now, and Dirt supposed they were swapping out frequently to keep from getting tired.

Socks carried Dirt low to the ground and had him hold the Home-staff forward with both hands. Then they charged right through the goblins, killing a few but mostly trampling over them without doing much damage. They moved from dead zone to dead zone, opening up gaps and pathways between them.

The first little isolated group of goblins at the periphery started backing away from the rest of the army, and Socks turned toward them and barked loudly, a low sound that started as a growl and erupted into a percussive, angry noise. The group faltered and backed up faster.

"It's working! This is gonna be easy!"

Socks jumped at the group, landing on the edge instead of in the middle, and nipped and clawed and bit to harry them into fleeing. The goblins tried to go around Socks to rejoin the army, hoping for safety in numbers, but Socks cut off their path with a row of sparks that erupted into flame. That was all it took for that segment of the army, perhaps as many as two hundred of them, to retreat with increasing haste.

The pup chased them only briefly, just enough to convince them to keep running, then turned back toward the rest of the army.

Just as he did, the entire army of goblins fell silent. Socks skidded to a halt and pulled Dirt onto his back. As one, every goblin, thousands of them, turned to face them. The wretched things ceased their screaming and wild movements and stepped with purpose into something resembling a formation, closing all the gaps.

Dirt glanced everywhere in confusion and growing anxiety and caught a hint of motion above them. He looked up and saw the ripple in the sky, which had been hovering overhead for some time now, growing and descending.

Socks turned his head to look at Dirt. They had no words. Something new was coming.

CHAPTER TWENTY-EIGHT

Break ranks and cut them down!" shouted the duke, his voice carrying through the eerie silence despite being muffled by his helmet. The band of armored men split up like a disturbed ants' nest and slaughtered with reckless ferocity. The goblins gave no resistance, not even cries of pain as they were hacked apart.

The ripple in the air widened and grew denser, taking on a white fog-like quality. Socks stepped back, his body lowered and fearful, hackles raising. With so many goblins, Dirt found he could differentiate them from the minds of the men across the way, and Socks's mind glowed like the sun. Their minds were silent, as if asleep, even though they were standing and looked alert. The mind in the ripple in the air was the same as before, simply watching, incomplete or damaged in a way that caused a deep sense of wrongness. Its thoughtless gaze was fixed on Dirt and Socks just as the goblins' were, but neither of them could see anything in it that might be controlling the army.

"Should we hit it?" asked Dirt.

-I don't want to get close enough for that until we know what it is.-

Dirt stepped closer to Socks and stood just inside his front leg, since there was nowhere safer for him to stand. The duke's men were killing goblins as fast as they could swing their weapons, but there were so many still remaining, it was hard to tell if they had made much difference yet.

The duke caught Socks's gaze and reconsidered, calling out, "Don't split up too far! Be ready to resume formation! Be ready, men!" It seemed he, Socks, and Dirt all had the same thought at the same time. There was a trick here, and splitting everyone up might be part of it.

Overhead, the pale, translucent blur grew increasingly solid until it became a line, solidifying until it cast a shadow on the bloody mud below. It moved forward in the air until it hovered right above them, perhaps only twice the height of the wall. Dirt could have jumped up and hit it if he wanted, easy. Too close. Socks kept flinching as he debated running away.

The line lengthened until it was twice as long as the pup, at which point it stopped moving at all. Its thoughts remained static, just observing, but there were such obvious gaps that Dirt was sure it was thinking *somewhere,* just like the tentacle monster had. It simply wasn't using its mind to do its thinking.

A crack appeared in the blurry white that ran from end to end and widened like an opening eye. It *was* an opening eye, appearing in midair like something peering in from the void beyond all things. Its colors were inverted, with black where the white part should have been and a blood-red iris that moved only slowly as it regarded them below.

Socks and Dirt stood in open horror. That eye looked bigger than even Father's, if it belonged on a creature proportionate to it in size. Surely it couldn't.

A single tear of watery, black fluid pooled on the lens, the lowest point, and dripped down. Socks jumped away, pulling Dirt with him.

A high-pitched screech erupted from the ground where the liquid splashed, sounding almost—but not quite—like screaming voices. Shimmering threads of blackness in the shape of flames swirled over the spot, causing neither heat nor light, but instead radiating a sickly feeling of wrongness that made Dirt squirm deep in his soul.

The eye turned to find them again, and once it did, it moved in their direction, gliding silently.

Dirt pulled his knife from its sheath and tossed it out in front of Socks's face. The pup grabbed it with his mind and threw it faster than vision could follow. It made a faint thumping sound as it pierced the eye right in the lens, and clear, watery liquid gushed from the hole it made.

But instead of splashing, the liquid clumped together and heaped up into a pile. The liquid poured out faster as the puncture tore further open until the eye hung empty in the air, sagging like an empty sack.

Dirt and Socks looked at each other, wondering if that was it. The incomplete mind of the watcher was gone now, but Dirt wasn't exactly sure when that had happened, distracted as he was. Glancing over at the goblins, they remained as they had been—perfectly still, minds blank.

The duke's men had stopped cold to stare aghast at the black, deflated eye above the battlefield and the heap of clear muck below it. They shrank toward each other, backing up until they were almost in formation again.

"Now what?" thought Dirt.

-I don't know. The other things are still coming from the hills. They will be here soon. I can see them with ghost sight.-

"Can you see the eye thing with ghost sight?"

-Yes, but not very well.- Socks sent an image of the eye above in stark black and white, but the details were strangely obscured, like something incompletely painted.

"Well, I guess we should kill goblins until those other things get here," said Dirt, trying to push away the nagging sense of dread.

Socks crept over to the pile of liquid and sniffed it from half a body-length away. He looked up into the deflated eye, and Dirt stepped out from under him to look up into it as well. The opening was only about as wide as his shoulders, and Dirt had expected it to be all dark inside, but it wasn't. There was faint light in there, multicolored as if from several sources, and something moved inside it.

The knife dropped from the hole and landed on the goo with a loud splat and slowly sank into it.

Socks startled, hopping off his front paws a little in surprise.

"What?" asked Dirt, sneaking back under him.

-I can't grab the knife. I can't reach into that stuff with my mind.-

"What? Really?"

-Don't touch it. And don't stick the Home-staff in there either. It isn't normal.-

"Has that ever happened before?"

-Never.-

An arm thrust out of the hole in the deflated eye, as long as Dirt's whole body, white and gray like the clouds. Socks leaped back, bringing Dirt with him.

A head followed, hairless and featureless, then the other arm and shoulders. The whole thing slid out like it was being birthed, and fell into the pile of liquid. Once its fall was halted, it righted itself and rose to its feet.

Dirt thought it was a particularly tall human at first until he noticed it had no face. It turned its featureless white head to look at them, then stepped forward. Shaped mostly like a human male, the more Dirt saw of it, the more disturbingly wrong it was, from its three-toed feet and hands to the smooth flesh where its sex should have been. A long tail, thick as its thigh, slapped the pile of thick fluid behind it.

The goo evaporated, disappearing with surprising speed. Dirt paled when he recognized it—the same stuff he'd been coated in when he woke up. It had to be. He hadn't thought about that stuff one single time until now, but how could he forget?

The creature stepped toward them, its steps slow but not unsure. It had a presence so undeniable that Dirt thought he could feel it thickening the air. It reminded him of being near Socks's parents, even if it felt nothing like theirs. Their presence was the very essence of predation, ferocious and unstoppable. This, on the other hand, was like being in front of the motion that pulled the moon across the sky.

"Hello?" Dirt squeaked out somehow. It didn't reply, or really do much of anything except take another step. Socks matched it with a step back, hackles raised and a warning growl forming in his huge throat.

Its mind glowed with hardly any color at all, as if with light his mind's eye couldn't completely make out, but Dirt could see its thoughts, such as they were. They were not thoughts that had any reasoning behind them. Instead, it reminded him of the trees, of their senses and processes his mind couldn't understand. This mind wasn't completely inhuman, however, and some of it made sense—a heartbeat, muscles moving in regular motion, nerves carrying sensations. If it had any vision, Dirt couldn't find it.

It was like a mind inside out. All the unconscious things where its thinking should happen and its thinking hidden elsewhere. It did not appear half-dead like the other monstrosities, but neither could Dirt confidently say it was alive. To him, it felt like something that was neither alive nor dead, nor anything in between the two. It was a third thing.

Socks sent a mental image of violence and death, blood and claws and destruction as only a wolf in a frenzy could cause. He practically screamed it, and the armored men quavered, all the way across the battlefield.

The white-cloud-colored creature paused at the threat, inclining its featureless head slightly. Dirt watched its mind for any reaction, but there was no thought there. Tightening of muscles, nerves delivering sensations in a way that robbed them of all meaning. Not earth beneath its feet or air moving against its hairless skin, but mere pressure.

It turned and bent down to pick up a dead goblin with one hand, hefting it by the head while its guts dangled all the way to the ground. It seemed to regard it for a moment, then grabbed another one by curling its long, thick tail around the torso, and carried them both.

Walking over to the ranks of silent goblins, the monstrosity picked up a living one with its free hand. Its cloud-white body contorted, losing definition in its form as it pressed all three little bodies together, living and dead. Dirt felt an expenditure of mana, but accompanying it was a totally new sensation, one that twisted a tiny part of himself he couldn't name at first. But the trees had told him the shape of his being, and he quickly decided this was the final part, the Law, which they had also called Divinity. The monstrosity was reshaping the world on a deeper level than magic, right in front of their eyes.

Socks and Dirt attacked at the same time. Socks leaped to land on it with his front claws, but somehow Dirt got there first and struck it in the knee with the staff. Instead of cracking the bone like he'd expected, the flesh simply gave way, folding in on itself. The creature's tail whipped down and struck Dirt across the chest and arms, throwing him backward.

He lay stunned. The mana should have protected him, but inside him, everything was fuzzy. He flexed his arms, and sore as they were, they didn't seem broken. Nor his collarbone. The mana must have helped, but now it was all disrupted and wouldn't obey him.

Dirt missed whatever Socks had done right after, but the pup quickly stood over him, snarling protectively. Dirt sat up and watched the white monstrosity rising from the ground, reforming twisted and bent limbs as it did. Socks must have crushed it, to no lasting effect.

The monstrosity resumed its work, forming the living and dead goblins together into something new. Dirt's tiny sense of Law stung. Unclarity crept in at the edges of his thoughts and he struggled to understand it. Perhaps the Dream was leaking over, or perhaps it was the void seeping in while the creature did its work.

The goblin bodies fused together into a solid, lumpy mass, all sickly green with bits poking out like ears and noses and yellow-clawed fingers. From there the monstrosity pulled and twisted, shaping it like Dirt did with wood. First one leg, then another, but bent like a wolf's, not a goblin's. It took only a moment before the thing was done and dropped its creation, a green humanoid with long, misshapen legs. Its head was three times the size of normal, and when it stood and opened its mouth to scream, its mouth was so wide the entire head tilted back, revealing thick rows of sharp, yellow fangs.

The creation rushed forward to attack, moving with startling speed. Not faster than Socks could react, though, and the pup took the creation's entire head in his jaws, dug his front paws into its chest, and ripped it apart.

Dirt flushed all the mana he had in him, pushing it outside himself to go nowhere at all. For a brief moment, he was keenly aware of his naked vulnerability, like a soldier whose armor had all just fallen off, but fortunately when he inhaled to draw more in, the mana was clean and pure again.

-It's time to kill this thing,- said Socks. He reached out mentally for Dirt, who responded in kind. Their minds slid together into one. They split up, readying themselves, and darted forward from different angles.

A line appeared on the creature's face where the eyes should be, which opened into a toothless mouth with no tongue. Just an opening. A moment before Dirt and Socks landed their pincer attack, a burst of pressure erupted from the monstrosity's open mouth that stunned their two bodies so thoroughly the mind meld fell apart.

Then it turned and slapped Socks across the face with his tail, right along the scar from the tentacle beast that'd torn him open. The pup stumbled and fell, knocked nearly unconscious. Dirt used the opportunity to smash the staff into its hips, hoping to crush the bones so thoroughly it would never get back up. The strike connected and with punishing strength, but Dirt could feel through the staff that nothing had broken. He'd only changed its shape again, temporarily.

He ducked under the tail swipe he knew was coming, then rolled away from its attempt to grab him with one hand. It strode toward him quickly as Dirt turned and ran, forcing his mind to think instead of succumbing to panic. Crushing it wouldn't work.

Spotting his dagger, he sprinted toward it with mana-infused steps. The clear goo had completely dissipated, leaving not even a stain on the ground where it had been. The blade sat there calmly, waiting for him. He grabbed it with one hand, staff in the other, and turned.

Socks was trying to get up but was having a hard time of it, stumbling and dizzy. His eyes were wild and desperate, unable to quite focus.

Dirt mentally shouted, *"I'm still fine! Don't panic!"* But Socks didn't react, and Dirt wasn't sure he'd heard it.

"Charge through, men! Run with all haste!" shouted the duke, sword raised. At his command, the armored men began running between the goblins instead of killing them.

Dirt struggled with that, wondering if he should tell them to keep away. Better to just kill it before they got here. He sprinted forward, low to the ground, then jumped high at the last second, right over a kick aimed at his face. He struck with the dagger, slicing the only flesh that came within his reach—the shoulder.

The blade slipped right through so effortlessly that Dirt wasn't sure he'd actually connected, until he turned and saw the gash. Bright red blood poured from the wound and ran down its arm in stark contrast to the unearthly white of its skin. The wound tightened and the blood ceased, then evaporated completely to leave the skin bare again.

In its mind, the monstrosity registered pain, but it was the sharpness of nerves sparking in response and muscles failing. Those sensations decreased as it healed itself.

Dirt sprinted forward again, blade ready, and this time the creature was hesitant to let him get close. But the boy was faster and it couldn't back away fast enough. The second slash caught it deeply along the thigh. Dirt hopped over its tail and stabbed upward into its kidneys, twice, then darted away from its grasp.

As before, the creature bled bright red from its wounds, blood that evaporated as quickly as the wounds closed. Well, there could only be so much blood in there. Dirt would have to just let it all out.

Socks had his feet now and hung his head, trying to breathe out the effects of being whacked. He stepped forward, desperate to get back in the fight, but Dirt said, *"Not yet! Don't get back in until you're ready! I'm fine!"*

The armored men were making good progress across the field, which was starting to feel awfully small now that it was turning into a time limit.

Dirt gritted his teeth and stepped toward the wary creature, who was now giving him its full attention, and planned his next attack. It came for him first, flying forward through the air arms-first to grab him.

He slashed one hand right through the middle of the wrist and halfway up the forearm, but its other arm shot down for his leg as he was stepping back, and he couldn't react in time. Its three thick fingers closed around his calf and flung him up into the air, leaving him helpless. It spun and swatted him with its tail.

Dirt blocked with both arms, but the tail drove them into his chest hard enough to knock the air out of him. Despite surging mana to protect himself, he felt a bone crack, and the force flung him spinning end over end until he crashed into a goblin. Their heads collided, and Dirt saw a flash of white and found himself lying on the ground.

When Dirt could see again, the creature stood over him and was reaching down for his head. Dirt had a vision of himself being fused with a goblin and panicked, rolling away limply.

A goblin crashed into the creature, knocking it off its feet. The pup picked up another one with his mind, lifted it high in the air, and slammed it down onto the monstrosity before it could get up. Bones cracked, but Dirt couldn't tell whose. He wasn't sure the monstrosity had any.

The pain from cracking his head kept Dirt from concentrating well enough to gather mana efficiently, but he stumbled to his feet anyway. It hurt to think, so he used his mouth to say, "You have to cut it. Get some goblin swords."

Socks tried fire first, though. He surrounded it with sparks, which glowed yellow and orange against its skin before erupting into flame, creating a pillar that roared high above the battlefield and was so hot Dirt had to shield his face.

When the flames vanished, the creature's scorch-blackened skin sloughed away to reveal muscle, some red and some gray. Its outer layers had been cooked, but it seemed unfazed and jumped toward Socks with its arm drawn for a punch. It was only two-thirds the pup's height, but that was enough to reach the dangerous parts. Socks dodged and ducked away from each of its strikes, his reactions faster than it could move. It followed a punch with a tail swipe, and this time, it didn't even get close.

Dirt leaned on the staff to try to let the pain subside. His headache decreased, but his broken arm got worse the more he thought about it. It was only cracked, not split in two like Home had done to him, but it still made it hard to close his fingers around the knife.

The Home-staff quivered. Dirt looked at it and said, "Are you okay, Home? Is everything all right?" He suspected the tree was worried about him, not harmed in some way, but he had no way of knowing that. To his surprise, the staff's shape changed in his hands, refitting itself to cover first his forearm, then his arm and shoulder. She was protecting him.

Dirt hoped she wasn't about to encase him in solid wood where nothing could touch him. He was smart enough not to resist, though, and held his arms out and spread his legs a bit to let her do whatever it was she had in mind.

The wood closed over his torso, then down his hips and legs all the way to his feet. He leaned to the side to lift one foot slightly, and the wood closed under it, granting him a shoe. It closed around his head, leaving holes to see and breathe through but covering his face otherwise. When it reached his other forearm, it tightened to hold his broken bone in place, which relieved the pain somewhat.

He could still move, just as well as before. He looked down. Armor. Home had turned the staff into armor made of plates of solid wood that fit perfectly around his frame. The joints were flexible material instead of cleverly interlinked metal, but he suspected they'd be nearly as durable.

The armor felt fused to him, holding every inch of skin tightly, even while it hindered him in no way.

Dirt laughed, which made his head sting, but he couldn't help it. It was simply too delightful to do anything else. Boy-sized wooden armor! Time to find out how tough it was. He gripped the dagger and charged.

CHAPTER TWENTY-NINE

Running was easier than he expected, with the armor fitting his form so well he may as well have been wearing cloth. It was heavier than anything he was used to, but not enough to slow him down. Especially not with a little mana burning in his legs to speed him forward.

The monstrosity and Socks danced around each other, seeking blood. The pup snapped and snarled and twisted, his huge body a furry blur. His efforts never got him close enough for a good bite, though, because the creature floated like a leaf on the wind. Each step sent it gliding over the ground, landing only where and when it wished.

Dirt's footsteps thumped heavily in the bloody soil. He ran right for it, dagger ready, and jumped in with a scream when he got close enough. It spun and caught his head in its long, white fingers. It lifted and squeezed while Dirt kicked his feet in the air to wriggle loose. The wood helm groaned beneath its grasp as it tried to burst his skull, but it held. He stabbed its forearm over and over, puncturing it about twenty times. He butchered it so well blood spurted into his helmet, giving him a taste of dusty sourness before it evaporated. It was quickly forced to drop him.

-I can't touch it with my mind,- said the pup. *-Try and get it to stay put so I can hit it with a goblin.-*

"Got it!" replied Dirt. He and Socks circled it from different sides. First Socks darted in for a bite, then Dirt, then Socks again, keeping it off-balance. Dirt finally saw his chance when it planted its feet to counterstrike at Socks with its tail. He snuck in and stabbed right through its foot, pinning it to the ground.

The monstrosity struggled for only a moment before it spun with his dagger as a pivot and kicked him with its heel, right under the ribs. The blow knocked him five paces before he hit the ground and bounced. The blow hadn't done any damage, though, and to Dirt it felt like the force had been distributed through his whole body instead of just his side. The armor stayed perfectly rigid, protecting him until he came to a stop.

It ignored the bloody injury in its foot, which was already healing, and evaded as Socks grabbed living goblins one after the other and slammed them down, trying to crush it.

The duke and his men burst from the goblin army and into the littered field, immediately taking up position to encircle the creature in a wide arc, which they slowly tightened. They did so silently, now that they were so close, with a somberness that evinced their horror. They communicated with subtle waves and nods, understanding each other almost as well as Dirt and Socks did.

Dirt gritted his teeth, wondering if they'd do any good at all or just get slaughtered, but to his relief, they handled themselves admirably. Although it was half again their size, towering over them and raining down blows with its fists, they blocked or redirected with practiced skill. It occurred to Dirt that it was about as tall as a man on horseback, and they must have trained for that.

Socks snarled and jumped in at the same time he threw three more goblins. The creature had nowhere to go but into the human lines where it was met with four blades at once. It kicked upward at a man near the duke, but he braced his sword with his metal gauntlet and drove the blade's edge into its shin. It bit deep, nearly severing the foot.

The creature stumbled back, walking unevenly on the stump while its foot dragged behind on a thin flap of flesh. Even then, its mind held no emotion, no thoughts that demonstrated real consciousness. Just biological activity and motion, devoid of reason.

Dirt gathered up as much fear and revulsion as he could muster, filling his own mind with it, feeling it so strongly it made him nauseous. Once he was ready, he redirected it all into the monstrosity's mind. He could see the mental attack work and watched the intrusive emotions swirl inside it, but they vanished as quickly as they appeared, leaving him feeling as empty as what he was seeing. So where did it go? All that fear had to go *somewhere.*

The armored men stepped forward, keeping their formation steady. It struck down with hammer fists and crushed right through a man's defense, breaking one arm severely. The armor held the shattered arm in the wrong shape, and his agonized scream was ignored by his fellows, who simply stepped around him.

Socks picked up another of the inert living goblins and swiped at the creature sideways, first from one direction and then back again. Dirt took the opportunity to retrieve his dagger while the circle of armored men closed tighter and tighter.

Finally, Socks hammered it across the head and shoulders with a goblin just as a soldier gave it a deep slash in the thigh. The force drove it front-first into the ground, and Socks immediately grabbed another one and slammed it down from above so hard the goblin's bones cracked loudly.

For one breath, it lay unmoving. Two breaths. Longer. All the humans looked at each other, eyes wide through the slots on their faceguards. Socks crept up and sniffed it. Dirt would have suspected it was dead as well, but its mind hadn't winked out. It was still as alive as it ever had been.

The enormous deflated eye hanging in the air, forgotten for a short time, drifted until it came overhead, stopping directly over the monstrosity. The eye skin wriggled, flapping loosely, then suddenly tightened. Its shape morphed and fluctuated. The injured gash in the lens lengthened, and the colors of the iris and sclera blended together.

After only a few heartbeats, the deflated eye had become a mouth with thin, tight lips. The shape was almost human but not quite, and Dirt decided it was because there was no chin. The lips parted and a stream of clear, reddish liquid poured out onto the unmoving monstrosity below. The liquid emptied, and its mouth opened wider, revealing a space full of multicolored lights against a white background. The space inside it was not the void—Dirt could feel that—but it wasn't just another place, either. Something about it felt off to him, like so much else about the monstrosity.

Socks decided he'd had enough and filled the open mouth with sparks. Dirt hastily created a glowing ember and pressed it into the midst of them. He and Socks surged their mana at the same time, and Socks's flames burst into being with a roar and burned hotter than ever before, fueled by the extra heat from Dirt's ember and all the mana they both could channel.

Dirt felt the heat scorching lines on his face through the faceguard. Socks whimpered as it singed his whiskers and the fur around his nose. It worked—the flesh of the mouth burned clear away, into black ash that quickly turned gray. It fell apart and drifted on the air, leaving behind a hole in the sky that was now full of thick smoke.

The monstrosity pushed itself up and rose to its feet, refitting its twisted limbs with popping sounds. Even its nearly severed foot slid back into place and reattached.

Frustration filled Dirt, and he stomped forward until he was right in front of the creature. He swung his arm and shouted, "Just go away!" Then for emphasis, he screamed it into the thing's mind. Over and over, with both mind and voice, growing desperate. "Go away!"

Behind him, Socks stood ready to grab him out of harm's way at the slightest hint of danger, but it didn't attack. It didn't even turn its faceless head in his direction. Above, the hole in the sky trembled and gave a low rumbling sound. It shrank, just a little, and coughed out some of the smoke.

A hole opened in the monstrosity's head, and the entire creature deflated like it'd been hollow the entire time. Its skin collapsed in a heap, turned brittle, and began flaking apart.

Overhead, an eyelid closed over the hole in the sky, the same unnatural white as the creature. Once closed, it gained new features, growing eyelashes and wrinkles. It slowly shrank—no, that wasn't it. It was withdrawing, revealing more of the face. And a face it was, an old man's face, wrinkled and weary. More of it appeared—a sharp nose, the other eye, a forehead and short hair, a mouth and clean-shaven chin.

Dirt gasped and nearly fell over when he recognized the face. It was himself, as he used to be. He was gazing up into the sky at his own face, the one he lost, sculpted in flesh of sickly white.

The duke and his men gave a fearful murmur, tight formation lines rustling. Socks saw what Dirt was thinking and looked up and down at the two of them in confusion.

The giant face's eyes shot open, showing them to be all black and red. It fixed its gaze on Dirt below, its stare penetrating. Its mind showed flickers of awareness now, beyond just the mere senses, which gave Dirt the impression of some great attention drawing near which had been previously distant.

"Please go away," he said, his voice soft. Then he said again in his mind, *"Please go away."*

The face remained unmoving, its expression blank, and Dirt wondered if maybe it was just going to stay there forever, or follow him around from now on watching everything he did. He looked back at Socks, pleading for an idea. The pup had none.

Dirt's old man face opened its mouth and spoke, its voice sounding like a grinding moan. "Avitus Numitorius Urbanus," it said. "Avitus Numitorius Urbanus." Dirt recognized his name. That was the rest of it, the entire thing.

Was he looking at himself? Did he split off and become multiple things? Was this an echo of what he'd done so long ago? Something else entirely? It was himself up there, his own lost face, speaking his own lost name, and it might have broken his heart if it wasn't so terrifying. It saw him, little Dirt standing there in his wooden armor, and knew him. It recognized him.

No, it wasn't himself. It wasn't a part of him. There was something alien in its mind, something inhuman. Not just natural processes, muscles and sight and so on. Whatever mind drove it was out there somewhere, lurking and knowing as if from behind a veil.

"You found me," said Dirt, at a loss.

"Avitus Numitorius Urbanus," it said again, its groaning voice so great the earth trembled beneath him. But what it meant, or what it understood about him, Dirt couldn't tell.

The face froze again, losing all animation and staring blankly, its eyes still fixed on him. A crack appeared from chin to forehead, then another and another, and the whole thing shattered like glass. Dirt crouched down instinctively, but no pieces of it hit the ground.

The mind behind it withdrew, its light fading as it departed. The last thing Dirt beheld was a word imbued with magical significance. A word of command that manifested into the world. A sage's word. "Disperse."

The goblins snapped out of their collective coma, and the field erupted in a wild tumult as they scrambled over each other to flee. The duke and his startled men seemed relieved to have a more reasonable enemy to fight and they roared with valor and resumed killing as many as possible.

-Did you see that at the end?- asked Socks, standing plainly while he thought.

"Yeah. The word 'disperse,' you mean?"

-Yes.-

"That's the thing you're curious about? Not my old face appearing in the sky and saying my old name?"

-That word was in your language.-

Dirt reconsidered and realized Socks was right. It wasn't a word of pure thought and magic, like the dryads had taught him to shape wood or call wind. It was a word like a person might say aloud, like a human mind might have in it, but given magical significance. That might have been a more interesting thing to ponder if his mind didn't keep returning to his own old face, appearing in all his thoughts like a waking nightmare.

Socks leaned down with his tongue out in a licking posture, and Home saw it and got the idea. She withdrew the armor, leaving only a brace around his cracked forearm instead of a staff. The pup licked him furiously, sending him puffs of affection. *-It'll be okay, little Dirt.-*

Dirt found himself hard to comfort. That thing had created a new horror right in front of their eyes, fusing living and dead into a murderous abomination. Was that him, somehow? Or was he responsible for it, at least? And the tentacle monster. That frightful thing in the sky that wore his face and knew his name, had it created them all?

It occurred to him that not only had he broken the world, but he might have created or unleashed or allowed in something that was slowly erasing humanity in general, wearing them down bit by bit. Maybe sometimes it used goblins and monsters, and other times, who knew? Bad weather? The guilt grew in him, mixed with the horror and weariness and revulsion still running thick in his blood, and overcame him. His child's body couldn't contain it, and he wept, hanging his head. His tears mixed with the coating of slaver Socks was giving him.

Socks picked him up with his mind, gently folded him into a fetal position, and held him close against the front of his chest, just under his neck where he could bend his head down to envelop Dirt in fur.

-Whatever happened, you didn't do it on purpose. Don't feel bad, little Dirt. Don't be sad. It was a long time ago.-

"How many humans did I kill, Socks? And how many are still dying because of me? All the humans think they're about to die out, and they're probably right, and it's my fault."

-Good thing you came back just in time to save them, then.-

"But I'm just . . ." thought Dirt, starting to argue. But what stopped him was the honest recognition that he might already be the strongest human alive. If anyone could, he'd have to. And Socks would help, and he was worth an entire kingdom of humans all by himself. Or more. He tried to comfort himself with that thought, cementing it with resolve. *"You're right. I have to figure it out, and then I have to fix it."*

-Good. That's the right thing to think. It'll be okay in the end.-

Despite this, Dirt felt only slightly better, and it took him a bit longer to get all the tears out. When they were finally drained, Socks put him down and gave him one last lick for good measure. *-You're almost clean again.-*

"I guess we'll have to do something about that. Are those other things still coming from the hills? The big ones?" said Dirt, feigning a total recovery that hadn't happened yet.

-No, they dispersed too.-

"Okay. Good. I bet I can kill more goblins than you."

Socks huffed, as close to laughing as he ever got. *-You will need more than a dagger for that.-*

Together they sprinted into the fleeing goblins and laid waste to them alongside the duke and his men. Dirt fought with vigor sufficient to sweat out all the evil he'd taken in, and even through a fresh coating of blood, he felt cleaner somehow. The duke's men felt it too, their weariness and fear and hesitation fading as they lost themselves in a task they could understand.

The goblins made little attempt to protect themselves except to scramble over each other in their haste to flee, but they were such a tangled mess that only the ones on the far edge had any hope of escaping. Sometimes they'd turn around at the last second and lash out in desperation, but to no avail.

The work of slaughter continued long after that, until the armored men were being outrun by individual goblins and finally sat to enjoy a well-earned rest. Socks and Dirt considered chasing down more of them, but they were too spread out. They went to sit by the armored men instead.

Dirt had Home make him water and held his forearm brace over his head to let it pour in. Seeing that, the duke removed his helmet, signaling the true end of the battle. His men followed his lead and looked thirsty, so Dirt went around giving them water to drink, starting with the duke himself.

They laughed and patted his bottom with their gauntleted hands, or gave exaggerated sighs of refreshment, or some such thing, and Dirt enjoyed himself tremendously and laughed right along with them. Socks followed along close beside him, and the men patted his legs as he passed, which he allowed.

The duke watched slyly until Dirt had made it to every last man, ensuring no one was left out, then stood again and announced, "We'd better get out of this armor so our pages can clean it, before the smiths band together to have me beheaded."

The men laughed and stood. They walked across the wide field, strewn with hundreds of reeking goblin corpses, and made their way back home. Socks and Dirt led the group, happy and tired. Socks picked up the man whose arm was twisted in his armor and straightened it back out with his mind. Despite being careful, the poor soldier passed out from pain. He'd get better, though, and so would all the injured from before.

For now, the town was safe. The battle might be over for the duke and his men, at least the big one, but it was not over for Dirt. Many things were just now taking hold in his mind and forming into the task of a lifetime.

CHAPTER THIRTY

"Okay, Socks, go dunk again!" yelled Dirt, grinning. The crowd of children screamed and laughed as Socks rose and jumped back in the river, sending a huge wave crashing up over the riverbank to soak them again. The big pup submerged himself out in the middle where it was deepest, then climbed back out, water pouring off him in sheets. He stood next to the eager crowd and shook, flinging so much water around it may as well have been a thunderstorm.

The children all laughed and danced away as if they didn't really want to get wet, but it was a ruse. Dirt screamed and evaded right along with them. Socks finally squatted down on the paved landing, and his new friends got to work, loud and boisterous all the while. They scrubbed and wiped with dozens of brushes and rags, while others splashed more water on with little buckets, but not in an amount that could do any good. It didn't matter, though, because it was fun.

Dirt hadn't had to do a lot of convincing after the duke asked for volunteers. The man simply had to declare that the children should do it, since Socks was a child himself, and the town's brood had rushed forward to volunteer like mice scared out of the bushes.

Now a horde of them scrambled up Socks's back or snuggled against the side of his belly to reach as high as they could. Some ran along his tail, getting the whole length with one scrub. When they got too much grime or fur stuck to themselves, they dunked in the river and ran right back as fast as they could. A cadre of girls had claimed all the open spots around Socks's face; they were the gentlest of the bunch, and the most doting. For his part, Socks closed his eyes and looked as content as Dirt had ever seen him.

It seemed everyone in town had wanted to come watch the blood get cleaned out of Socks's fur. The half-circle area the adults left them had started a lot narrower at first, until Socks shook the water out the first time. They'd been too close, and it showed in all the red and pink spots on their clothing. But no risk of clothing stain would keep them away, even those who had no offspring in the tumult. It was a novelty they'd likely never see again, and anyone who could squeeze in to watch did so.

None of the children knew who Dirt was other than Èlia and Màxim. And while Màxim stayed close, Èlia preferred girls her own age and all but ignored him. To everyone else, he was just another face in the crowd. He could fit into any cluster just by smiling and joining in with whatever the others were doing. There was no waiting for them to get used to him, or trying to act the right way, or any of that.

A boy his size even leaned in close to tell him, "The wolf has a human with him. I think I know who it is!" He was wrong, of course, and Màxim had laughed and given Dirt a conspiratorial grin. The other boy hadn't caught on.

Dirt didn't stand out, either, since he had a good tan from riding on Socks's back for the last few weeks. Most of them had dark brown hair like Marina's, and his was only a shade paler than average. There were some exceptions to the norm, too—even a few blond-haired children with lots of freckles. If anyone noticed Home in the shape of a cast on his arm, they didn't mention it.

All in all, it meant Dirt could relax completely. No careful speech or thinking, no fear he was doing something wrong. No, he could be himself in a way that had previously only been possible when he and Socks were alone. All this laughter made him feel as clean inside as he was outside.

After Socks looked as clean as he was going to get, the crowd of children dried him off, fluffing his fur with an absurd quantity of towels that had appeared from somewhere, in every size and color. Socks rolled, carefully, to one side or the other to make sure they got all of him, from paws to whiskers. Dirt suspected the sunlight dried him out more than all the towels did, but who cared?

Once that was done, the adults presented about twenty rakes and distributed them to the taller children. Dirt didn't get one, which amused him and Màxim terribly, but Èlia did. They commenced combing him, and Socks enjoyed that the most since it felt like getting scratched all over.

Socks finally stood, thoroughly pampered and unsure what was next. He towered over the children and remembered not to wag his tail too hard this time. Dirt yelled, "Can I have a ride? And him?"

The pup caught on instantly and said, *-You want a ride? Who else wants to come?-*

"Maybe some will want to go slow, and some fast," said Dirt. "But I want to go fast, and so does he." Màxim looked less eager than Dirt did, but he didn't argue.

An older boy stepped forward, then a girl about their age, and Socks decided that was enough for the first go and lifted them onto his back with his mind. Dirt loudly squealed his excitement to put the others at ease, then helped them all squeeze together and hunker down.

-Hold tight anyway, and keep your heads down,- said Socks, and with that, he was off. A great leap carried him across the river where the crowd was small enough for him to land, and from there, he raced down the nearest street. The children screamed in wild terror and held on as hard as they could, which made Dirt squeal with laughter. He knew that feeling.

Socks ran all the way out to the wall, jumped over it, and then back again. Then back up the street and across the river, and then it was over, as quickly as it began. He squatted down to let his passengers slide off, which they did with wide eyes and unsure expressions.

Poor Màxim was unsteady on his feet and leaned against Dirt's shoulder for support. "You do that all the time? That fast?" he whispered.

"Yeah. You get used to it," whispered Dirt back.

The ashen faces of the first set of wolf-riders did nothing to dissuade the next bunch, and Socks picked up five more and gave them the same path. They screamed as soon as Socks leaped, and Dirt listened with increasing amusement at how their voices faded against the city. Finally, someone else knew what that was like!

After a few more groups of those, Socks picked up about fifteen of the littlest ones and gave them a much slower ride around the plaza. He performed gentle leaps across the river and back and set them all down, where they started cheering and hopping and begging for another ride. But it was time for the next group, and the next, and then a few more rides for the braver children who wanted to go again. Both Màxim and Èlia were among those, although Dirt stayed behind to leave a spot open for someone else.

Socks was enjoying himself tremendously, as anyone could plainly tell without even looking at his mind. But Dirt did look, and Socks was as lost in the reverie of play as everyone else. The children collectively produced a great deal of mental happiness which infused the pup and washed away every external concern. It might not be as good as playing with a few dozen of his own kind, but it was close.

The duke waved and said something to one of his servants, and a moment later parents came to collect their children, getting them all dressed again, or if they were already dressed, replacing the wet clothing with dry. Màxim took Dirt by the hand and pulled him through the crowd to a spot near his father where two servants were waiting.

The two boys were then dressed in finery, cloth so soft it almost felt like fur, with a bold red color that caught the sunlight and seemed to glow. It was made of strips of fabric and the seams made decorative lines from top to bottom. The pants were tight, and the shirt poofed out around the waist under a handsome sash that served as a belt. Dirt was given shoes with pointed toes and even a little lace scarf to tie around his neck. If he and Màxim weren't exactly the same size, it seemed they were close enough.

Finally they were presented to the duke and duchess, and the pair smiled their approval. The duke said, "Today we have seen you attired in two very different types of red."

The duchess smirked slyly and added, "And this type will do less damage to the carpets and furniture."

Ignasi told Socks, "They would have loved nothing more than to present you with something charming to wear, but they had nothing in your size."

-They could have given me a little hat,- he replied, wagging his tail in amusement.

"Then a hat you shall have," said the duchess. She plucked the feathered cap from her mate's head and beckoned Socks to lean down. The pup complied, lying all the way down, and the duchess reached up to set it between his ears. She fastened it to his fur with a wooden clip she pulled from her own hair, releasing one lock to tumble onto her shoulder, and stood back.

Socks knew how silly he looked with that tiny little hat on his enormous head, but he thought it was as funny as Dirt did and pranced around a bit to show off. The humans weren't quite sure whether he was serious, though, so when Marina clapped instead of laughing, the others followed suit.

Dirt slipped over to the duke and suggested, "He might like something to hold bags on, like a harness with pockets, maybe."

The duke nodded and leaned over to the nearest servant, an older man with pale hair. "Go tell my saddler to find a couple harness-makers and see what they can come up with. Tell them not to be shy about coming to take measurements."

The servant nodded and slipped away toward the palace.

-Okay, I am done with the hat. If I keep wearing it, they will put it in the painting,- said Socks. He leaned down, and the duchess collected the hat again, plucked a couple hairs from it, then set it back on the duke's head.

From there, they made a grand procession back into the palace. There were no armored guards this time, since most of them had done all the fighting they needed to for the day, but a new set of city soldiers had taken their place. Which was fortunate, because it took all of them to hold the crowds back from getting any closer and coming to peep in all the windows.

The duke's company returned to the large hall, with Socks sliding under the doorways as before. This time, someone clever had taken long ropes and made rings around all the cushions, gathering them together into a tighter-packed bed. Socks sped right to it, sniffed twice, walked around it in a circle, then lay down and snuggled in.

-This is better,- he said. *-The cushions aren't sliding away anymore.-*

Instead of food, the table held some neatly arranged scrolls, which Dirt hadn't expected, as well as some rectangular objects he didn't recognize. He stepped over and picked one up and discovered that it was two hard plates full of sheets of paper, all full of writing.

"These are all the texts I own that contain the ancient tongue. Those scrolls are ageless and, if the scholars are to be believed, may date back to the days of the lost empire itself," said the duke. "I thought you might like to see them, and perhaps answer a few questions about how they should be read."

"Sure, but what's this?" asked Dirt, holding up the object.

"That's . . . let me see." The duke took it from Dirt's hands and looked at the thin edge where all the papers were fastened together. "*The Acts of the Emperors from Justinian the First to Claudius the Seventh,*" he read. "It's a history from, as far as we can tell, some of the final emperors. All their reigns were short. Very interesting."

"No, I mean, what is it? What do you call this thing?" said Dirt, taking it back and waving it.

"The book?" asked the duke. "Do you mean the book?"

"Is that what this is? What's it for?"

The duke took it and opened it, showing the words. He said, "Scrolls are more difficult to read, if you wish to read from different sections one after the other. You must roll and unroll to find your spot and it can take time. A book is slices of a scroll, arranged in order. I can read from here," he said, showing an early page, "and then skip right to here if I want. You . . . can read, right?"

"Yes, I can read it. Especially if it's in my language. What do you want me to read?" asked Dirt. He took the book back, marveling at what a clever concept it was and wondered why his people had never come up with it.

"Anything to start. I'd like to hear the sound of the ancient tongue."

Dirt flipped to a random page and read, in his language, ". . . *which came in those days. The peoples of the southern tribes of that island have red hair and wear tunics of wool, which they dye with local plants in delightful patterns, some of which have been copied in our own embroidery. They herd cattle and sheep but not pigs, owing to the harshness of the winters. Even the land around the beaches is frigid during the darker seasons. They do not have chickens, since they must eat all the grain they grow themselves, and do not like the taste when offered any. Their farms are unimpressive, as is their architecture. They are given to dancing at every opportunity and will drink heavily if they can find any alcohol. Their wine is made of whatever is on hand and never tastes the same twice, unless they acquired some of ours through barter. Indeed, if not for the hardiness of their men, caused surely by the climate, they should never have been a threat to Emperor Astimus' new colonies in the slightest, nor required the three thousand pikes and four hundred cavalry, which he sent . . ."*

Dirt stopped when he reached the end of the page. The room had gone silent, even the servants, as everyone strained to listen. He shyly said, "Should I keep going?"

"Remarkable," said the duke. "He reads as fluently in his tongue as I do in mine."

-Dirt is very clever,- said Socks. *-You should not be surprised.-*

"I say so only because my Màxim can't read so sweetly, and he is taught by learned men every day. Dirt grew up alone in a forest. I cannot fathom it," said the duke. "And did you understand every word of that, Dirt?"

"Of course. It's my own language. How about you?"

"It says they are given to *tripudium.* What is that?" asked the duke.

"In your tongue it's dancing."

"I see," said the duke. His eyes sparkled with undeniable eagerness. "How about *plumarius*?"

"Embroidery," answered Dirt.

The duke turned to Hèctor and said, "And he couldn't speak our tongue at all when you met him? Are you certain?"

"Just a few words is all, Your Grace. He learned more every hour we were with him," said Hèctor.

"Do you remember the first thing he said that you understood?" asked the duke.

"Of course," said Hèctor. "Still gives me nightmares. He told a gryphon 'nice bird' and calmed it down."

The duke nodded, but his mind wasn't on the gryphon. That didn't seem to have registered. "So quickly he learns. If I wake tomorrow and this entire day has been a dream inspired by bad bread, I will be less surprised than if I wake up and it truly happened."

He poked at a few scrolls, then found the one he was looking for. He unrolled the opening, nodded, and handed it to Dirt.

Dirt recognized it immediately from the art at the top—it depicted a two-headed snake with wings, curled around a sphere that represented the sky. "Oh, wow!"

"What is it?" asked the duke.

"I don't know! But I know what it is!"

"Can you read it? No one has been able to. Not a single scholar of any age since the time that produced it."

"Yes, it's just a simple cipher. Everyone who . . . we could all read this. Everyone that . . ." Dirt looked up, eyes losing focus while his mind spun trying to fill in the gaps in his memory. He was so *close*!

No one said anything, so he read aloud. *"I, Pacritus, do write and bless this scroll to preserve it. I write it in the hidden way of the order, which none shall read who are not initiated. Guard well its wisdom, reader, if a reader there be. I fear that I create a paradox—I preserve that which is being forgotten, that it may endure. But perhaps none shall read it in all the ages to come, and its knowledge be reduced to mere ink and paper, devoid of reason. An object, like a chair or ball, which signifies nothing beyond its form. It has been eighty-eight years since the failure of Avitus Numitorius Urbanus, may his cursed name be blighted into eternities even as they forget who he was, by which he ruined the Sunset Empire and invited the calamity that has destroyed so much, and my last apprentice is now . . ."*

Dirt glanced up in surprise, but no one other than Socks and the duke had understood the words, and only Socks knew their true significance. Dirt coughed politely and rolled through the scroll. His disquiet quickly turned to excitement as he recognized what he was holding.

He stopped at a diagram about a quarter of the way in and grinned so widely he almost laughed. He turned the scroll and showed it to everyone. "See, it's a basic primer on magic. This is a method for purifying water, in case a well or river runs unclean. They wrote it with a cipher so no one could learn their secret who wasn't supposed to."

The duke nodded sagely, even as his twitching eyebrows betrayed his roiling thoughts. "I see," he said. "And that must be why it survived so long. There are sixty-eight known undecaying scrolls, and only two that we can't read. The other is in the possession of the king. I don't suppose . . ."

Dirt said, "You want me to show you how it works?"

"I do. Please."

"Sure. I want to try it anyway. Can I have some chalk? And a glass of something that isn't water?"

Marina took a half-bottle of wine from Ignasi's back pocket and presented it with a smirk. It was only a moment until a servant returned with a block of chalk about the size of Dirt's fist.

Dirt copied the pattern onto the table, pleased with how easily it came to him. He could've drawn it in his sleep with his toes if he wanted to, now that he'd seen it. He knew right where to put everything, and the diagram explained well enough that he knew *why* it was drawn that way. This part signified "to purify" and this other part indicated a particular kind of change, while that part meant "to move," and so on. Satisfied, he placed the wine in the symbol that indicated the target and let some mana trickle from his fingertip into the shape on the table.

The effect was immediate. The wine swirled as the room held their breath and watched through the pale glass of the bottle. The liquid lost its dark color, first in strands and then completely. Then it was over. Dirt picked up the bottle and took a little swallow, then handed it to the duke. "See? Water."

It was such a simple display, but Dirt was only maintaining his composure through sincere force of will. He wanted to scream and cheer and run around in a circle because he'd found *human magic*! This was his art, his real art, from when he was an old man. Knowing it was real and that it was *his* again felt as glorious as sunlight, as soothing as spring water. He'd forgotten it existed, but here it was, one of the things he loved most in the world.

"Do you mind if I take some time and read this?" asked Dirt, not really waiting for an answer. He walked over to Socks, where he curled up and started the scroll over from the beginning.

Two days later, Dirt placed his hand on the gate-door and looked back one last time at the huge crowd that had come to bid him and Socks farewell. For one brief moment they had fallen quiet, but after all the clamor they'd been causing up to now, his ears were ringing faintly.

He shrugged and turned back to the gate. No reason to put it off any longer. *Shrink,* he told the gate-door, causing it to withdraw the tendrils bracing it against the stone and shrink back down to normal size, or at least, as close as Dirt could estimate. It just had to fit the frame, and all he had to do was watch the little gaps between the stones disappear, then make the door just a little smaller than that.

Workmen stepped beside him, some bringing ladders, all of them with hammers and awls and other tools. Fresh hinges had been made, nice big sturdy ones, and a new set of lock-bars had been planed and reinforced.

Dirt moved back to give them room, smiling slightly to himself that the crowd wasn't sure when to start cheering again. The workmen hadn't given them the chance, but that was at the duke's order. It wouldn't do to have everyone standing around like empty chairs waiting for the door to work again.

Quicker than expected, the hinges were replaced, and the door swung open. A bit too hard—the balance was off. Oh well. They could fix that later.

Socks stepped through, ducking his head only slightly to keep from brushing his ears. He turned around and sniffed Dirt, then looked at the crowd.

Dirt waved, and the crowd lining the streets erupted back into riotous cheering. Some played horns or harps, others banged pots, and everyone else clapped and shouted. It really was a lot of noise, Dirt decided. It was loud to begin with, but after it all echoed off the buildings and walls and added together, it was making his ears hurt.

The duke stepped in close, making a little circle with the duchess, the two children, and Hèctor, Marina, and Ignasi. None of them could come, and Dirt knew he'd miss them. For now. They'd meet again.

"Thanks for letting us stay in your city, my lord," said Dirt. He had to get so close to the duke's ear to be heard that he may as well have been kissing his cheek.

"Thank you for saving it. I look forward to your return. I know Màxim will be crying tonight, having made a little friend who is leaving too soon," said the duke, right into his ear as well. The man's mustache tickled Dirt's cheek. As if on cue, poor Màxim wiped a tear from his eye before it could drip down. Or maybe just some dust, to be fair. Only a few days, and they already felt as close as brothers. Dirt squeezed past the duke to give the boy another quick hug.

Then turning back to the duke, he said, "Well, I'll be back in two years or so, and I'll teach him like I promised."

"I believe you, or I would not have let you take my scroll, giant wolf notwithstanding," said the duke, his eyes sparkling.

Dirt gave the man a hug, then the duchess, Marina, Ignasi, Hèctor, and Èlia. That was about everybody. Dirt stepped back and waved one last time. Hundreds waved back.

That was it, then. Time to leave, and hopefully the town could survive until Dirt made it back. He'd only been here a few days, but it'd still break his heart to come back and find it deserted.

The duke had promised to send raids on goblins and hunt them out instead of just waiting and hiding, so that was something. Waiting and hiding hadn't worked, and now it was a close thing whether they'd be able to farm enough to feed themselves before the food stores ran out. Socks had said to just eat the goblins they hunted, and the duke was so disgusted by that he turned faintly green. Well, if they got hungry enough, they'd get over it. But maybe Dirt could meet the king and have more food sent down the river before that happened.

He'd done everything he could for them for now. Or had he? Just as he was about to hop on Socks's back to leave, he spun on his heels and beckoned the duke to lean in again. "I just thought of something. Can you come meet me at those grain fields? The ones over that way, around the wall a bit? Get a horse, and we'll meet you there. You can bring the others, but not too many people. You'll see why."

The duke nodded, and Dirt waved a final farewell to the town. He hopped on Socks and sent a quick mental image of where he had in mind, a large fallow field with only a few stalks of grain, which they'd passed just before reaching the city.

Socks didn't particularly hurry to get there, and the duke and his company arrived just after Dirt and Socks did, with the duchess, the children, Marina, Ignasi, Hèctor, two servants, and three soldiers. For him, that was a small entourage.

Dirt slid off Socks and said, "I'm going to feel pretty silly if this doesn't work. Okay, just watch."

He calmed his breathing and mind, quieting down everything in his internal world. He knelt and touched the ground, his fingers brushing against one of the lonely stalks of wheat. He filled his mind with the Devourer's command, whose impossible vastness he could never hope to match. But he'd seen how it made the forest grow, and the idea was the same. Ideas were just ideas. Magic was magic. The world was the world.

He filled himself to bursting with mana, more than he could hold without it leaking out on its own.

GROW.

He let his direct memory of the Devourer and his own intuition fill in the parts of the magic he might be missing, willing the effect into existence rather than carefully planning and diagramming it like proper human magic. Thank Grace, it worked.

His command poured forth through the soil and into the stalks of grain, and they began to spread and multiply. New growth sprouted from the earth—first as tiny green buds, then full stalks of wheat that matured and turned yellow. The growth spread across the field, slowly at first and then with more purpose and force as Dirt's bodies grew into greater harmony. His mana vessel became a gateway through which the world of magic entered. His spirit reshaped that power into physical being. It burned him raw, stinging and aching in every part of himself. Even the dream body made itself known, and Dirt suspected he'd have unquiet rest until it recovered.

But it was enough. Soon he stood on unsteady feet and opened his eyes. Golden wheat, all of it ripe and ready for harvest, filled not just the field he'd planned but the neighboring ones as well. Even the road was now hidden, leaving the small group of stunned humans standing with nowhere to go.

Dirt smiled, trying not to look too pleased with himself. Dignified like the duke, he said, "Alright. Now you don't have to worry about food as much. I don't know if you have time to grow any more before winter, but that should help." He leaned back and almost lost his balance, still dizzy, and Socks propped him up with his mind.

"This is a miracle," said the duke, breathless.

"I wish it was. Maybe the gods will be back someday," said Dirt. "I guess this will—"

His arm twitched. The brace on his forearm, Home, was trying to get his attention. He looked down and saw a thin pole which grew until it was about the length of his leg, so long he had to hold it with his other hand. But then its top sprouted into a tuft of little branches that filled with tiny green leaves. The bottom separated from the brace as twisty roots grew out of the wood, and finally it came away in his hand.

Dirt looked at its mind and saw the pure light of new birth. "A baby tree!" he shouted aloud in pure amazement. "Socks, help me dig a little hole! Hurry, before it dries out! Where should we put it? Closer to the wall. Hurry!"

The duke saw his panic and stepped forward to see what was the matter. He put his hand on the baby tree as if to take it away, thinking it a gift, but Dirt pulled it back. They ran together past the grain and out into an untended area somewhat closer to town, looking for a nice spot to plant it. Somewhere with good soil, not too close or too far from the river, somewhere it would be safe. The area around the walls was all plains, though, and no spot was better than any other to Dirt's eyes. The duke's group followed, still amazed.

-Here,- said Socks. *-The dirt here smells a little damper than the rest.-* With one claw, he dug a hole big enough to plant the tree.

With trembling fingers, Dirt placed the precious infant in its little cradle, standing her as straight as he could measure and filling the hole back in to cover the roots. He sent her tiny, awakening mind happy thoughts, words expressed in pure feeling. *Hello. Welcome. I love you.*

Then, aloud, he said, "Home, can you find her? Is she connected?" Only a moment later, Home made the brace vibrate on his arm, and looking at the little tree's mind, he saw they'd found her. She was part of the forest now, connected to her own kind.

"That is a lovely tree, Dirt. Thank you, but why?" asked the duchess, hardly sure of what to even ask.

Marina knelt and gently traced her fingers along the little trunk and tiny branches, her dark eyes wide with awe. She looked at Dirt, questioning, and said, "This is an even greater gift than the grain, Your Grace. Even greater than that."

Dirt turned and addressed the duchess. "This isn't from me. This is . . . this is one of *my* trees. From the forest I lived in. You have to take good care of her! Even put a guard here, until she's strong enough. Someday, when she's big and strong, she'll be a blessing like you wouldn't believe. But only if she loves you, and you love her," said Dirt. His mind was split between trying to explain and watching in awe as the darling little thing began exploring its mysterious tree world. "And she'll know. The trees are smart. Aren't they, Marina?"

"I suppose they are," the woman muttered.

"So the city has a tree now, like in your stories?" asked the duchess.

"No." said Dirt. He stood and grinned. He checked Socks's fancy new shoulder harness and made sure all the bags were closed. Everything was fine. Of course it was. He was quickly starting to feel rather poorly, and not just from magical exertion. He wanted to stay instead. A baby tree, his new friend Màxim, and so much else to be leaving behind. Sleeping in a bed, eating human food. But it was time to go because Socks had to keep moving.

"No, it's better to say the tree has a city now. Alright, Socks, let's go," said Dirt. He hopped onto the pup's back, and together they sped across the wide fields into the welcome unknown.

About the Author

Ryan English is the author of the Land of Broken Roads series, originally released on Royal Road. He was first introduced to fantasy when he read The Hobbit at the age of seven and has been reading and writing in the genre ever since. English currently lives in Utah and works in cybersecurity.